Why

Why

Born to Please

Georgina Laurier

This is a work of fiction. Names, characters, places, and incidents
either are the product of the author's imagination or are used
fictitiously. Any resemblance to actual persons, living or dead,
events, or locales is entirely coincidental.

Book design by Publishing Push

ISBNs
Paperback: 978-1-80227-236-9
eBook: 978-1-80227-237-6

This Book was written as a personal project to occupy time spent in isolation during the Covid-19 pandemic. The names, characters, and incidents portrayed in it are fictional and are the product of the author's imagination. Any resemblance to actual persons living or dead, places, events, or localities are entirely coincidental. The reader is therefore asked to accept them as such.

A message of gratitude goes to my long-suffering husband. I would never have achieved all that I have without him.

Throughout this journey, Rita found herself fighting a constant battle with herself as to why she always strived to please the people who came into her life.

Why had she found it so unbearably hard to say the word NO, which would inevitably lead her into the darkest and most dire situations beyond her control? Her inability to refuse the demands placed upon her would ultimately have serious consequences on her life.

Chapter 1

Wednesday's Child is Full of Woe; captures the very essence of the life of this newborn baby girl.

It was Wednesday the 21st of April 1944. A woman standing at the bus stop pulled back the cuff of her tweed jacket and glanced at her watch for the third time in the last ten minutes. She looked along the road and watched as a boy on a bicycle appeared in the distance. She glanced up at the sky, watching the clouds skimming across a watery sun. It was going to be a beautiful day she told herself; there was a bit of a breeze but that would dry the washing she had hung out earlier. Her attention was drawn to a man who seemed to be hurriedly making his way to the phone box on the opposite side of the road. She continued to watch as he yanked open the door and flung a heap of loose change on the shelf beside the phone. He dialled a number from a crumpled scrap of paper that he had taken from his right-hand trouser pocket.

Seconds later, she observed him pushing at all sides of the glass panels trying to get out. She watched him as he stood on the pavement opposite her and threw both arms in the air, his face alight with excitement and euphoria.

"It's a girl!" he called out.

"Congratulations!" she called back across to him, realising the reason for his jubilation.

Turning on his heels, he began running. In the time it took him to make it back to the front gate of number 7 Park Road, where he lived with his wife and son, he had made the decision that if he was to give his precious new daughter everything in life that he wished for her, he could no longer afford to smoke.

And so began an inescapably complex and somewhat crazy life.

I was born in Lavender Cottage, a private nursing home, on the day of the Queens official birthday. Despite the attending nurses suggesting the most appropriate and fitting name for me would be Elizabeth, I was given the name of Rita, which I later came to hate due to the frequency of its use, and the fact that it seemed always to be attached to a negative comment.

I was a painfully shy and insecure child. I adored my father, and our ginger cat called Sandy. However, it was not until I reached the tender age of around five that I became aware that the close bond that I shared with my father was beginning to create a division within the family.

I was a constant source of annoyance to my older brother Edward, who was 6 years older than me. He had been born before the war and had been the complete focus of my mother's attention while Dad was away fighting for his country in those long months that stretched into years.

Mother spent all her spare time each day teaching Edward to read and write, and by the time he started school, he had also mastered the art of basic math. Edward had resented Dad's

intrusion back into the family, so when Dad finally returned from the war, Edward no longer had Mother to himself, resulting in him telling his father in no uncertain terms to go back from whence he came.

This story was told with frequency and great hilarity at most family gatherings.

Resentment increased further when I came along, and the fact that Dad seemed totally absorbed with his new daughter only contributed to the formation of two separate camps within the household.

I was not lucky enough to be afforded the same pre-school attention from Mother as Edward had been fortunate to receive, as there were many more demands upon her time.

So, when I started school at the age of five, the difference between my brother's abilities and mine at the equivalent age was stark.

Edward was a sickly child; you dared not say the word spots to him or out they popped, giving rise to extended periods of time away from school. However, on returning, he would fly streaks ahead of everyone else, and, in no time, was better than excellent.

He also boasted a photographic memory, which was indeed a rare gift, and one that I greatly envied. I, on the other hand, who never caught so much as a cold, and never missed a day from school, struggled from the get-go. I managed to perfect the art of making myself invisible by sitting at the very back of the class. Each day, my main objective was to avoid having to answer any questions. I was terrified of being shown up by looking stupid. Being at the very back of the class had even more serious implications for me, as I could not see the blackboard - yet another reason for my slow development. Keeping my head down was my only focus each day, a technique that worked well for me for some considerable time but was finally picked up upon and reported back to Mother.

I was whisked off to see an optician who discovered that I was very short-sighted and had pronounced astigmatism in the right eye. I was prescribed a lovely pair of pink, metal-framed glasses, with one of the lenses completely blacked out to encourage the lazy eye to strengthen.

Returning to school the following day after receiving this amazing solution to all my problems, I discovered that my new seating position was to be right at the front of the class thus making it impossible to avoid attention. I had to now come up with a new plan. The new strategy of pretending not to hear also proved a futile exercise, as the teacher simply strolled over and repeated the question directly at me. There was nothing else for it - I had to come clean and admit I was just plain stupid.

I think that it would have been at this point that most children would have become really naughty and disruptive, in an attempt to distract attention away from the fact they were unable to grasp the content of the lesson, but I was too painfully shy to even achieve that. I'm not quite sure if the teacher just got bone-weary from the sheer effort involved in trying to get through to such a complex child, or that she simply felt bitterly sorry for the daily agony that she was subjecting me to. Whatever the reason, her focus gradually shifted away from me, and I was again able to duck below the radar.

My new look became a source of great amusement to my classmates, who seemed to glean a huge amount of pleasure in thinking up new names for the now one-eyed person within their midst, which did nothing for my shyness, my confidence, or, in fact, my self-esteem. Being singled out in this way made it impossible to face each day with any degree of optimism.

I loathed those glasses; I was convinced that they were the reason I was being subjected to all this misery. I tried several times to leave them on the school bus, but the regular driver knew that they belonged to me. After all, who else was walking around with one eye blacked out? So, every morning, he handed those wretched things back to me.

Dad was also struggling to cope with Mother as both he and I tried to navigate around her moods and tantrums. If things did not go her way, she would take to her bed and remain there until Dad reached the appropriate level of grovelling.

If anyone said the slightest thing out of turn, off she would fly to her bed and Dad would come to me and say,

"Please, Rita, go in there and say you're sorry or she will be in there for days." One day. I refused to apologize as I firmly believed I was not at fault; then the big guns came out. Dad was told to call the doctor, who, after a thorough examination, finally diagnosed that it was I who was the cause of mother's current condition brought about by stress.

I was told in no uncertain terms that it was my behaviour that was making my mother ill. I needed to go at once, tell her how very sorry I was, and assure her that this situation would never arise again. He also informed me angrily that I was guilty of wasting his valuable time. Hence, I never dared try that again.

When mother pulled the same stunt again by taking to her bed on Christmas morning of all days, I was straight in there, no messing, with a sincere apology. Mother, however, was not for relenting so quickly, making Christmas lunch very late getting to the table and the meal was consumed in strained silence. Dad's valiant attempts at making positive comments about the tenderness of the meat, the crispness of the potatoes and the deliciousness of the gravy fell on deaf ears.

He finally conceded defeat and we all resigned ourselves to the fact that Christmas Day had been a complete disaster with the fault being laid squarely at my door. I spent what remained of the day on my own in my room.

I was not a bad kid, I decided in this time of serious reflection, as I studied the yellow roses on the wallpaper. I just seemed to keep saying the wrong thing.

Dad and I continued to tip-toe through life, desperately trying to keep things on an even keel.

We had just moved into our new home in a small village at the top of a hill opposite the local village school. The village boasted a general store, a hardware shop, a chemist, and a butcher.

Dad was a master builder by trade and had spent all his free weekends building us a brand new three-bedroom bungalow. It was absolutely beautiful. It had fitted wardrobes in all the bedrooms, a concept that was considered very new in those days.

My new bedroom was huge compared to my old one and I loved it. The garden was like a football pitch, with lots of trees to climb. I couldn't wait to bring my friends around to play. Also, to my shame, I couldn't wait to show off our new home.

We had only been moved in for a few weeks when my whole life was turned upside down. The day began much like any other. I only had to go over the road to my new school, which was brilliant, as I could make a dash for it when I heard the bell ringing.

This day began badly; it was raining hard, and I could not find my raincoat. I must have left it at school the last time I had worn it. This did not please Mother, so I received the usual lecture about the cost of a coat and my total disregard for its safekeeping. She then happened to turn towards me just at the very moment I was poking my tongue out at her, and wiggling my hands, with two thumbs stuck in my ears. She made a dash toward me, but I was too fast. I bolted out through the back door and into the rain. I made it into school without getting too wet.

I knew that I would be in trouble when I returned home that afternoon but was reassured by the fact that I had spotted my Mac still hanging safely on my peg in the locker room. Great, I thought, problem half-solved anyway. But when I arrived home that afternoon, I was surprised to see Dad there. He was never home at this time of day. He had a strange, distracted, worried look on his face which frightened me. I peered around him to see what he was doing; he was grabbing things off the clothes horse and throwing them into an old green battered suitcase. When I stepped around him, I could see that all the clothes in the case were mine. I glanced quickly around the room.

"Where's Mum?" I asked, with a sense of urgency.

"There has been an accident, Rita, your mother has had a bad fall; she has damaged her back and has been taken to hospital." This did not explain why my father was packing my clothes, but I was soon to find out.

"You are going to live with your aunt and uncle for a while." He continued without even glancing in my direction.

No way was I going to do that, I thought, the panic starting to well up inside of me. That meant living with my cousin Helen, an only child who was the apple of her parent's eyes, and someone with whom I had absolutely nothing in common. That is, except for the fact that for some reason, she liked to always copy me by wearing exactly the same dresses, shoes and even hairstyle as me.

I could never understand why she even wanted to look like me. More to the point, I had made the decision I was not going.

"No, Dad, I want to stay here," I protested.

"That is not possible, Rita," he said sadly. "I have to go to work."

"What about Edward? Where is he going, then?" I asked in a defiant tone.

"Edward is a lot older than you, Rita. He can cope with being left to his own devices; you can't. Please, Rita, don't be difficult. Take that bag and pack some of your toys out of the cupboard. I will bring more of your things over at the weekend." He then gave me a look that told me there was to be no further discussion on the matter.

So it was that I climbed into the back seat of the car, with one final protestation of

"It's not fair." I protested but we were on our way.

On that journey, I considered all options. I considered the possibility that none of this was true about the fall. It must be because of the issue over the Mac that morning that had brought about the terrible situation I now found myself in. Sticking out my tongue and pulling silly faces at her only confirmed to me that she had been so angry that she had contacted Dad and told him to move me out. She was no longer prepared to put up with the stupid girl I had become. Yes, that had to be the reason, I had now convinced myself. After all, they were letting Edward stay, so that was confirmation that I was the problem. I was absolutely heartbroken that Dad had to lie about it and make up such an unbelievable tale about some stupid accident. I explained it away in my head that Dad was probably only trying to protect me by giving me some shred of hope that this situation was only going to be temporary, thus making it easier for him to carry out such a terrible task. Maybe he was hoping that Mum would calm down, given the time and space, and would relent.

By the time we had reached our destination, I had resigned myself to my fate. Just maybe, if I was very good for long enough, I just might be allowed to come back home.

It began even more miserably than I had expected when, on the very first night, the terry-towelling cloth that I had affectionately named as Num-num, which Dad had made sure that he had packed for me and which was my only remaining little bit of comfort, was confiscated.

"You don't need that silly thing, Rita," I was told. "Big girls don't have childish things like that. "Only added to my misery.

My aunt had obviously been informed in advance that I was a bed-wetter and had placed a very thick waterproof sheet underneath a thin cotton top sheet which was like lying on a pair of wellington boots, and made horrible noises when you moved, and smelt strongly of rubber.

I cried bitter tears that first night. Little did I know that this was only to be the beginning.

To be fair, my aunt and uncle tried hard to make my transition into their home seamless.

But as far as my cousin Helen was concerned, I was an unwanted intrusion.

The fact that I was such a well-behaved child, who sat quietly at the dinner table, said please, and thank you, and ate everything on my plate, even asking if I may leave the table, only compounded her resentment of me. My exemplary behaviour was held up as an example of how good children were supposed to behave, sending my cousin into uncontrollable rages that inevitably resulted in her shouting abuse, flying out of the room, and slamming every door she passed through with as much force as she could muster - with the odd expletive thrown in.

This I found particularly shocking, made worse by the fact that it invariably went unchecked.

I was enrolled into my cousin's school part way through a school term. This involved a whole new uniform which was a disgusting shade of purple and grey.

Almost all the children in my new class observed this newcomer with a degree of hostility.

The first lesson was PE which was OK, I thought with a sense of relief, as I had no PE kit. I expected to be sitting the lesson out on the sidelines.

This proved not to be the case. I was told to strip down to vest and knickers and join everyone else out on the playing field. All eyes focused on my old, discoloured knickers as I made my way through the mixed group of boys and girls. Setting aside the humiliation I felt, I was frozen and finding it hard to control the shivering.

"Get moving, girl! You won't get warm standing there like a jelly," shouted the teacher.

There were plenty more of those days to come, I soon discovered, as the decision had been made not to go to the expense of buying a PE kit, as no one seemed sure just how long I would be spending there.

Dad arrived at the weekend as promised, bringing with him more of my belongings. In fact, it looked very much like all my belongings. I wanted to spend the whole of his visit just sitting on his lap, but as usual, I was told that grown-up conversations were private. Not for little ears. I was told to go and play.

This upset me, because I wanted to tell Dad about them hiding Num-num and that they were making me do PE in my knickers in front of the boys at school. I had to have a PE kit, as I just couldn't bear the humiliation. I also wanted him to know that Helen was being mean to me. I wanted to tell him how desperately unhappy I was and beg him to take me home.

I soon realised the opportunity to do so was lost when I was called back into the hall to say my goodbyes. Dad was leaving. With a quick peck on the cheek and a promise to come again next week, he made a very speedy retreat. In fact, Dad did not come the next week, or the week after that. I was told that he had a lot on his plate, whatever that meant, as Mum was supposedly not there to cook his dinner. I did not believe that if he was cooking for himself, he would have very little on his plate. He will come again as soon as he can spare the time, I was told repeatedly.

Many weeks passed before Dad visited again. It was only to be a short visit, he told me, before he had even stepped through the front door. This did not prevent me from wrapping myself around him and hugging him tightly.

Mother, he informed me, was improving. They had her in something they called traction, to help with the pain in her back. This was apparently something to do with heavy weights which sounded highly unlikely to me. I could not ever imagine Mother lifting weights, especially if she had a bad back. This only added even more doubts about the story I had been initially given. I asked if I could go to see her. I needed to try to have this unlikely tale confirmed, but I was told that young children were not allowed to visit in the hospital, which then prompted the question of whether Edward had been allowed to go in to see her.

It was yet again explained that Edward was older than me, so he was allowed to go in for visits. This was clear evidence to me that I was not being told the truth, or, at the very least, confirmation of the very huge differences between what Edward was allowed to do and what I was not. Either way, it was me who seemed to always be on the tough end of things.

Months passed, and my father's visits became less and less frequent. I guessed that he found it all too uncomfortable, that it was all just too painful for him. Either that, or he just got sick of hearing me ask when I was going to be allowed to come home.

I got by the best way I knew how by keeping my head down and being as inconspicuous as I could. I tried to stay out of Helen's way as much as was humanly possible. I amused myself after school by sitting on the bedroom window ledge, watching Helen playing with a group of other kids in the back garden. One day, with faces upturned toward the window, I was spotted by the group in the garden below. They were all pointing up in my direction, peals of laughter ringing out. I don't think I had ever felt so unhappy and so alone as I did at that moment.

I'm not sure just how long I lived with my aunt and uncle, although it seemed like forever. I was told much later that it was about seven months.

The much longed-for day finally came. I stood patiently waiting and watching out of the front room window for a glimpse of Dad's car. He was coming to take me home. My case had been packed for two days. This was truly the best day of my entire life, I decided.

The journey home was agonizingly long, which gave me time to reflect on what should be my best course of action when first seeing Mother again after so long. Leaping out of the car, I dashed inside the house, flung my arms around her neck, and gushed,

"I'm so sorry, Mother, for making stupid faces at you, I will never, ever do it again," I promised sincerely. Huge tears were streaming down my face. This sincere exclamation of these intended changes to my character set a precedent for the future.

With the ever-present fear of being sent away again always in the back of my mind, I made a monumental effort to avoid ever upsetting her.

Today was my mother's birthday. I had nothing to give her, which I found really upsetting. By the time I got to school, I had worked myself up into a complete lather. I so desperately wanted to curry her favour, especially because the previous evening, Edward had shown me a wooden statue of a giraffe that he had been making for her birthday in his woodwork class.

I had to admit he had made an excellent job of it, and I knew Mother was going to be thrilled with his efforts. I also knew that I would be totally eclipsed by his glory.

Yes, that sounds exactly like it was, a big dollop of jealousy.

I knew that Edward would be giving Mother her birthday present when he returned home from school that afternoon, so, my entire morning was spent staring out of the classroom window, dwelling on my best course of action when I got home from school.

I decided that I would go straight to my room, possibly even feign illness, maybe even forgo tea. Although maybe that was taking things a bit too far. At the very least, I could gain some sympathy, if only from Dad.

All this important contemplation inevitably drew the attention of the teacher, who shouted at me to come to the front of the class to explain my daydreaming. Not wishing to be put through the humiliation of standing up at the front of the class to explain to thirty-two other children what it was that had been consuming me, I leapt to my feet, threw back the chair and headed for the door with all eyes following me. Slamming the door behind me, I headed for the girl's toilets, where I curled up inside the furthest cubicle with my knees tucked up beneath me and with heart-wrenching sobs which echoed around the empty room. This racket drew the attention of a passing teacher, who came in to investigate who it was that was being beaten to death inside. After several futile attempts to get me to come out of the cubicle, followed by a lot of cajoling, I finally appeared.

Her name was Mrs Myers, an older lady with greying hair and a very soft, kind voice which quickly encouraged out of me the reason behind this outburst. Mrs Myers wiped my eyes with a red checked handkerchief that she pulled from the sleeve of her cardigan and asked,

"Oh, is that what all this is about?" She could sort the problem out very easily, she assured me. She asked me to meet her in the car park during the lunch break. True to her word, she was waiting as promised in a red Ford Anglia.

"Hop in," she encouraged cheerily.

I had no idea where we were going, or indeed why, but I did as I was told and got in next to her.

I knew that we were heading for town, as I knew that route well. She parked the car in the town centre car park, then took me by the hand as we made our way toward the shops.

We entered the third shop along the main High Street, a gift shop, with every kind of gift for every gender, age, and occasion.

"Go on," she encouraged, "pick something nice for your mother's birthday present."

I just stared back at her in disbelief. I can't do that, I thought, I had no money to pay.

Uncertain of how to handle this extraordinary offer, I was desperately searching for the catch, which could land me into deeper trouble. All these uncertainties must have played out on my face as she quickly added,

"It's alright, it's my treat," she said kindly.

I looked from her to the shelves, and then back at her again. I just couldn't bring myself to do it. This was not something teachers did. Seeing my continued reticence, she reached out across the countertop.

"What about this?" she prompted, holding up a small red velvet-covered jewellery box with a small glistening glass bead on the top. It was beautiful.

"Do you think your mother would like this?" she asked.

Not knowing what to say, I smiled foolishly back at her.

"That's settled then, we will take this one," she said, handing it to the assistant. "Pease can you wrap it in something pretty?" She inquired "It is for a birthday gift."

The whole afternoon was spent in a blurred haze of excitement. I could not believe this had all just happened to little me. I felt as if I had won the top prize in a raffle. I could not wait to get home to give Mother her present.

That evening had to be up there as one of the most memorable of my childhood. Mother loved her gift and kissed and hugged me. She said it was the most beautiful jewellery box that she had ever seen. Of course, she also told Edward that his gift was special too, as he had made his gift with his very own hands, she told him warmly.

I was just elated that mine had been received with an equal measure of motherly love. What a wonderful day to remember.

After the euphoria had died down, I did reflect on the fact that she never once questioned how I came by it. Well, you wouldn't, would you? If someone gave you such a wonderful gift, it would be rude to ask how you came by it, even if it was from a small child who had no access to money.

With that thought dismissed as quickly as it came, I continued to bask in the feeling of wellbeing. It was not such a bad life after all, I decided contentedly. Thank you so much, Mrs Myers. The memory of your act of pure selfless kindness, shown to a small, vulnerable, and distressed little child, will remain with me forever.

By this time, my shyness and my insecurity had moved up to Secondary School. Dad had told me that things would now start to change for me, as older children were much too mature for name-calling, he convinced me.

I tried to start my new school with a fresh and positive attitude.

Within weeks, I had caught the attention of a boy named Terry Parfitt. He was the youngest of two brothers whose parents had a wet fish shop in the town. The pungent smell of fish filled the air whenever either of these boys was close. For reasons that escape me to this day, Terry had become quite besotted with me. He was not in my class but seemed to be outside my lessons each day waiting for me to come out.

This continued for some time. He never spoke a word; he was just there waiting with what I took to be a menacing grin on his face. I could not understand what I had done to attract this unwanted attention, so I just tried my best to ignore him.

This situation soon escalated, however, when suddenly I noticed that he had begun following me home every day, which was becoming extremely unnerving. He wore big black army-type boots, which made a distinctive clump with every step. I thought they must have been too big for him as he seemed to be having difficulty keeping them on. The clumping of these boots following a few steps behind me every afternoon.

On arrival home, I would dash to the window overlooking the lane outside, and peek through the net curtain. There would be his outline on the other side of the hedge, just standing there.

I became quite terrified and did not know what to do to stop it. I did not dare tell anyone for fear that I would be accused of encouraging him in some way. On and on it went, day after day, week after week, month after month. I was living each day in a constant state of fear.

It finally came to a head when he decided to take the fear factor to the next level. He crept into our garden one afternoon and threw a lighted firework into the garden shed that housed my brother's new motorcycle, which very nearly blew the whole thing sky high.

I had to come clean at this point, then copped it in the neck from Mother for not telling her sooner and allowing a serious situation to escalate to such an extreme level. It could have destroyed my brother's motorcycle, I was informed sternly, not to mention the damage to the shed. I should go to my room and reflect on just how serious that outcome could have been. I was a very stupid and thoughtless girl. Not that there was any kind of hint of just exactly how I would be able to resolve the situation in which I now found myself. Mother did not believe in smacking, she proudly told people, so I spent a great deal of time in my room, reflecting on one thing or another, while gazing at the yellow roses on the wallpaper.

It wasn't until many years later that it dawned on me why I had formed a strong dislike of the colour yellow. Regardless of all the forced contemplation, I never seemed able to come to any conclusions as to just how I could improve upon myself.

I had no sleep that night, worrying about it all. Mother seemed unable or unwilling to help to resolve the problem. Telling a teacher was most definitely not the avenue to go down, or one would run the risk of the entire school waiting for you outside the school gates at home time. I reached for the only other option remaining available to me.

The very next day, I told his older brother what had been happening. He seemed genuinely shocked as I imparted the events of the previous months and he promised that he would tell his dad when he got home.

To my utter relief, the very next day the stalking stopped. I guessed he had been given a good hiding. At the very least, I hoped so. It took some time to stop checking that he was not there on the journeys home, purely because of the sheer trauma it had caused me. Yet another piece of baggage to get dumped forever into the dark recesses of my mind, which, I hasten to add, can still muster up a feeling of fear even to this day, making clear that all these experiences and bad emotional bruises that are inflicted on us in our developing years can make a significant impact on who we finally become in the future.

I decided that what I needed now was a bicycle. I tried my father first.

"Ask your mother," came the usual reply. Dad seemed incapable of making any decisions without first getting her approval. However, lots of chores later, and two months of unmissable Sunday school, I was the proud owner of a spanking new pink bicycle with a saddlebag. This, I felt sure, would change my life.

Our school, like many others at that time, had a house point system whereby you could gain or lose points for your house. The winning house at the end of term was afforded a reward or privilege of some sort which was very highly prized and created much competition.

Houses were named after past prime ministers. I was in Gladstone House.

The system had been designed to encourage good behaviour and academic achievement.

Yet, of course, this well thought-out and highly successful system had some very different implications for me. Each house took the acquisition or the loss of these points extremely seriously. Anyone affecting the score negatively could be certain of suffering dire consequences, which always remained at the forefront of my mind as I strived daily to stick to the rules.

Today was the day I had domestic science. I was up early, as I needed to gather all the ingredients. We were making rice pudding. I needed to remember to take a dish to cook it in, and I had underlined it twice in red on my list to ensure I wouldn't forget. Checking the list several times, I finally felt satisfied that I had everything that I needed, including the dish. I packed it all safely into the saddlebag of my bicycle and set off for school. All my double checking had made time extremely short. I was almost at the top of the first hill when the memory of the final remarks made by the teacher the previous afternoon suddenly flashed into my brain like a thunderclap. 'Anyone who arrives tomorrow without their apron will lose a house point.'

I jumped off the bike and flung everything out onto the side of the road praying that the apron would magically appear at the bottom of the saddlebag. But, as first feared, no apron. The colour drained from my face, and I felt physically sick. Our schoolhouse was currently running in first place on the house point leader board, so, there was no way on this earth I could face the humiliation of losing a house point, letting down the whole team. It was not an option. So, I did the only thing I could possibly do in the circumstances. I went back home to get it. Bathed in perspiration, I rushed into my class, which, by this time, was well in progress.

"You are very late, Rita!" the teacher accused. "You have been marked as absent, which is why I am going to deduct a house point from you."

The expected deafening cry went up from the Gladstone team, which happened on every occasion such as this, designed specifically to maximize the level of humiliation and betrayal inflicted on the guilty party.

The complete unfairness of this punishment was overwhelming. I tried desperately to mitigate the damage by explaining the great lengths that I had gone to in order to avoid this very outcome. My voice becoming more and more shrill as I tried to plead my case, shrillness which was now bordering on hysteria. To my complete shock, even horror, I was deducted a second point for so-called arguing the point, (excuse the pun), causing a further outcry even louder and longer than the first. At this point, I conceded defeat and shut my mouth. I don't think I ever recovered from the sheer injustice of that day.

It may be well worth noting that those were the only house points I had ever lost in my entire school experience, resulting in another emotional bruise to my already battered emotional wellbeing.

The day continued much the same as it had started. I was consumed by the earlier events and was preoccupied, reliving in my mind, over and over, the horror of the morning. Due to my total lack of concentration, I added too much milk to the rice pudding, making it too runny when cooked.

Despite riding very slowly home, carefully avoiding any potholes, the pudding had run over the sides of the dish, out of the saddlebag, and was dripping down the back wheel.

By the time I reached home, there was very little remaining in the dish.

"Good God, Rita!" Mother exclaimed when she saw the mess. "Can't you do anything right?" Apparently not, I thought.

"Everyone is good at something," Dad comfortingly told me that evening, as I confided in him the events of the day and my inevitable unhappiness. "You just haven't found it yet, but you will," he said reassuringly, as he wiped away my tears and held me close.

I wanted so much to believe him but, as yet, that one thing that I might be good at had eluded me. Confidence in myself was at its lowest and appeared to be the barrier to succeeding in anything, or even trying to attempt anything new.

The fear of failure had become immense and all-consuming and was the reason I tried to avoid attempting anything at all costs. This personality defect, as I saw it, was never picked up on by any teacher as a justifiable reason for under-achieving. It was not even flagged up as a concern when my school reports came at the end of every year, with the only positive thing teachers could find to comment on being, 'Rita keeps a very neat and tidy desk'.

Neither my school, my teachers, nor my parents ever questioned the outcome of yet another unfulfilled academic year or indeed identified the reasons why I was failing so catastrophically.

However, I continued to try to win my mother's favour and to gain her praises but always missed the mark by a long way. She was so proud of her son and so dismissive of me. My brother had gone up even further in her estimation, from excellent to brilliant. He had reached the lofty heights of the top stream.

This achievement was naturally a great source of pride and praise at home. He apparently took after Mother. He was going to make something of his life that Mother could be proud of. This declaration was imparted to other family members and friends who visited the house.

Rita, on the other hand, they were told by Mother with an expression of great sadness and regret, took after her father. Although why Dad was always used as an example of failure was beyond my comprehension, as in my view, his abilities and achievements were unquestionable and well-proven and far outweighed those of my mother.

I had by now resigned myself to the fact that I was pretty much going to be a complete failure and, therefore, had decided to give up even trying.

Dad did not escape verbal abuse either; he was frequently held up publicly as the person for whom Mother had to do absolutely everything. Everyone who would listen was told that he could not even write out a cheque. The fact he was a master builder and had just completed a wonderful new bungalow for us all to live in always completely escaped her.

This always made me extremely cross, but I dared not utter a word. I would simply make my way toward my dad putting my arms around him, and give him a kiss, in the small hope that I had got the point across that what she was doing was unkind, and that she should stop doing it.

Dad would always ask me,

"Hey, what's all this for then?"

"Because you are the best Dad in the whole wide world," I would reply. However, I could never add, 'and because I feel so sorry for you.'

For this reason alone, I decided that, in future, I would no longer confide in Dad when things were falling apart for me, as he had his own challenges. Life had dealt him a rough deal too, as I saw it, forever trying to mitigate volatile scenarios to keep the peace.

Life did start getting easier as I got older. I was finally finding my place in the scheme of things, starting to form friendships, as everyone drifted into their like-minded groups. I had now made three friends.

My best friend was Louise Langdon. She was a quiet girl, rather plain-looking like me. Her best feature was her hair. God, how I envied her hair. It had a natural wave and curl about it that kind of did its own thing and which gave a softness to her face. Mine, on the other hand, was as straight as a yard of pump water and as fine as a newborn baby's.

'Thanks for that, Dad,' I thought, identifying whose genes were responsible for my less than best feature as I observed him from behind one evening, whilst he was reading his newspaper.

Louise came from a very posh family. Her clothes were always immaculate. The pleats in her skirt were always razor-sharp. Her blouse was always brilliant white, and her T-bar shoes bore no signs of a scuff. You could almost see your reflection in the toes of them.

I would look down at my skirt where only a faint line remained of where the pleats should have been. My scuffed shoes constantly slipped off the back of my heel due to the fact they were purchased with lots of growing space and caused my socks to constantly slide down under the heel.

This philosophy proved ineffective, as the shoes never lasted long enough to realize their full growth potential. Most of the time I slouched about, constantly being told to pick my feet up and pull my socks up. The same philosophy was also applied to my jumpers; the sleeves were always a third too long resulting in me either constantly pulling them up, or alternatively, making thick five-inch cuffs.

I used to alternate this look as my uniform had to last a week until the next wash day.

Louise, however, had a crisp white blouse on every other day, making mine look almost grey as they were invariably washed in the boiler with Dad's work pants, soap powder fighting to compete with builder's dust. I could never understand why it was that Louise chose to befriend me, as I must have been a constant source of embarrassment to be around.

I had now reached the point when I wanted a Saturday job. Most kids at school seemed to have one. I soon noticed that I was the only one who could never afford to go anywhere.

My friend had just got a job at Timothy Whites and had told me of a vacancy coming up at the end of the following week. Someone was leaving to have a baby, she told me confidentially.

I could not wait to impart this news to Mother, feeling quite sure that she would be proud of my new initiative of self-improvement.

With an appointment in the bag for an interview, on Saturday morning, both Mother and I caught the bus into town with me in my best dress, along with high hopes for a successful outcome.

I had practised in my head all the conversational scenarios that I may be faced with and felt faintly optimistic that I was up for the ordeal. Despite all my protestations of going in on my own, Mother informed me on arrival at the store that this was a most unwise plan doomed to failure on account of my chronic shyness. She did have a good point there, I conceded.

I bowed down to her wisdom and followed on behind her as we were shown into the shop's backroom, piled high with cardboard boxes.

The manager introduced himself as Mr Clark. He was a small thin man with close-set eyes and an overly large nose on which a pair of metal-framed spectacles perched precariously. I could not see the point of them, personally, as he peered out over the top of them.

He smiled warmly at Mother as she introduced herself. After casting a cursory glance in my direction, mother launched into conversation in her best telephone voice. I stared at her in disbelief. This was a side of Mother I had never seen before, as she rattled on attempting to impress her listener. I sat patiently waiting for my opportunity to speak. This, however, did not happen as Mother got into the full swing of her charm offensive. It felt to me as if they had both forgotten I was even there.

To this day, I'm not quite sure how it happened, but Mother got the job, starting the following Monday. It took me a while to forgive her for that act of what I perceived as complete betrayal.

She, on the other hand, found it hilarious and seemed to derive great pleasure in constantly reminding me of it over the years. In fact, it was not until I managed to secure a job for myself in Woolworths on the fabric counter some months later that I could come to terms with what had happened that day, and even then, it was bittersweet as I had hoped to be placed on the sweet counter. But hey, beggars can't be choosers.

I finally had a pay packet providing an uplifting sense of independence never before experienced, the entire content of which was spent each week on the same day as receiving it.

Mother stayed at that job at Timothy Whites, which eventually became Boots the chemists, until she retired, so I guess it was one of those meant to be things that you hear people talk about. She took huge pride in her work and recounted innumerable times how she had served many celebrities over the years. General Montgomery was her celebrity of choice with whom she said she had formed a particularly close friendship, and who she affectionately referred to as her friend Monty. He lived in the area and came regularly into Boots to collect his prescription and was her most highly prized encounter.

Life moved on at a boring snail's pace with a mundane air about it, with very little, if anything, achieved. I had finally made it to the last day of school. It was time to go out into the big wide world. We were all elated as we said our goodbyes. We scribbled our names on each other's blouses for posterity. Promises were made to remain best friends forever, to be bridesmaids at each other's weddings, to live near each other so that we could all babysit each other's children, and to share each other's problems.

Not a very high bar to set one's ambitions against, sadly, but these truly seemed to be the general hopes of all those caught up in that final euphoric historical moment in our lives.

We then all walked out through those school gates and went our own separate ways.

Me, not surprisingly, after ten years of dedicated and unbroken attendance, and now at the tender age of fifteen, was about to embark upon an unpredictable and somewhat scary future.

entering the working world, without even one qualification to my name. Well, what did I expect?!

Chapter 2

As expected, the lack of qualifications somewhat limited my options in the world of employment.

My very first job found me stacking shelves at the local village corner shop, but I loved it. It fitted perfectly with what they had discovered about me in the ten years of state education - Rita likes to keep things neat and tidy. Mr Collier, the manager, was a kind and caring individual not far from retirement age, who took me under his very experienced wing.

I soon progressed to serving customers which helped me a great deal to overcome my shyness. I was shown how to slice the cooked meats on the big meat-slicing machine, making me feel very important. I got into the habit of asking every customer, "Do you need any cooked meats today?" just so that I could use the slicer. I also just loved the smell of the fresh-cut meats.

Mr. Collier was quick to compliment my achievements and told me that I had doubled the sales of cooked meats since I had been working there, high praise indeed. I was thrilled to pieces with my achievements and soaked up all the praise levelled at me. I quickly settled into a daily routine.

I was not paid very much in the scheme of things, but I loved my job and was very happy doing it. I faced each day with a new-found enthusiasm, a contentment, and a genuine sense of belonging.

I had been working in the shop for about six months when mother threw a grenade into the harmony. She had been to speak to the owner of a ladies' hairdressers called Snippets in the next village. She had seen an advertisement in the local newspaper for an apprentice hairdresser. She had decided that it would be a good opportunity for me and believed it to be the only opportunity left open to me to achieve any form of career. I could not possibly stay in the dead-end job I was currently in as there was absolutely no future at all for me in that poky little corner shop, she told me. This was an exciting opportunity, and one that I should grasp with both hands if offered, she added.

We had an appointment for an interview on the following Monday morning. I was to speak to Mr Collier to arrange to take the morning off. I was not at all happy about this at all as I loved my job and did not want to let Mr Collier down by asking for time off or to face the upheaval of learning all new skills. But Mother knew what was best for me, or so she thought. Monday arrived, the appointment was kept at Snippets, and despite my best attempts at coming across as morose, I was offered the apprenticeship.

I arrived back to start the afternoon's shift at the shop, with signed apprenticeship documents in my handbag, and strict instructions to give notice that I would be leaving in two weeks.

I'm unable to describe just how unbearably hard I found this task.

Mr Collier had been very kind to me. He had taught me a great deal. He had been incredibly patient and had helped me overcome my shyness. I was being ungrateful, even disloyal.

I even believed he would see this as a serious act of complete betrayal.

The news of me having to leave was delivered through heart-wrenching sobs, and the sincerest and most heart-felt apology that I could convey. I awaited his response in complete trepidation.

However, surprisingly, he appeared to accept it without batting an eyelid, which totally threw me. I had expected him to be as upset about the whole thing as I was, even possibly with an element of anger attached, but he simply handed me a tissue, smiled broadly, and wished me good luck for the future.

My career as a trainee hairdresser had begun. The first six months were spent making coffees, folding towels, and sweeping up hair. My very first pay packet was also a big disappointment when I saw just how little reward there was for undertaking these most menial and boring of tasks. I thought my previous job wasn't well paid, but this measly remuneration had to be a joke. By the time I had deducted the bus fare to get there and housekeeping for Mother, I was left with the paltry sum of £2/10.That evening, I asked Mother how on earth I was supposed to manage on that, hoping desperately that she would consider taking less money for my keep, but pigs might fly, as they say.

I then progressed to shampooing, and then finally onto practising on models.

Mother came every week for her free shampoo and set, and every few months she had her free perm. She for one was more than happy that she had made the right decision for my future.

I knew that I was not cut out to be a hairdresser (excuse another pun). The simple truth was I was just no good at it. I did not have a shred of artistic flare. I tried telling Mother this, but I was told that I had not given it a fair chance and was reminded that a three-year contract had been signed. It appeared that I was in it for the long haul.

"It will all come good in the end, you will be earning good money once you have completed your training," she went on to remind me enthusiastically.

Yeah, I thought, and I would be able to have luxury holidays just on the tips alone. I was beginning to live in the real world and was not so easily persuaded. It seemed to me that Mother was the only one benefitting from my new employment. It was not for the lack of trying, but my boss had also come to realise that to try to make a silk purse out of a sow's ear was simply not achievable. He realised that he too was contractually locked into the three-year arrangement.

A different solution had been found. I was to become the salon's only manicurist.

All the necessary equipment was purchased, which I thought was a bit premature; what if I turned out to be no good at that either?

I was sent to the Revlon College for colour, cutting, and manicurists in London to receive the very best training. I was informed that this was a very expensive course and warned not to blow this most golden of opportunities.

Not too much pressure, then, to place upon someone with such an abysmal record of successful achievements.

My Aunt May and Uncle Harry had kindly offered to let me stay with them in Pinner for three months. This was very scary as it meant that I had to cross London every day on the underground on my own. However, once I had mastered this, I found the whole daily experience exciting. I felt I had finally reached adulthood. Anyone who could cross London in the rush hour had to be considered fully grown, especially a country bumpkin like me.

Despite all expectations, mine included, I went on to complete the course and returned to the salon with a gold-framed certificate, which was hung proudly on the wall behind the reception desk. My very first achievement! I could not have been prouder.

This should have turned out well for all concerned, however, the demand for manicured nails was simply not there. Snippets was a very small salon in a tiny little backwater village that had only seven other shops and a car repair garage.

There were some extremely desirable properties in the surrounding area, but I guessed the occupants of those went into the larger town seven miles up the road when they needed pampering. My days were spent staring out of the window and answering the telephone.

At home, life trundled on as usual except for this one event. It was a warm summer evening, and all the family had been sitting in the garden watching the sun go down, talking about the forthcoming holidays. It was getting late when we all decided to retire to bed. I turned on the bedroom light, drew the curtains, and started undressing. Turning out the bedside light, I climbed into bed, the streetlight outside the school opposite partially lighting up the room. I lay there, my thoughts drifting onto the fast-approaching holidays. Suddenly, the light in the room dimmed right down. That's strange, I thought. Then I heard shuffling noises just outside the window. Kneeling up on my pillow, I pulled back the curtain to investigate, fully expecting to see an animal on the front lawn. To my absolute horror, there, kneeling on the outside window ledge was a man, his arm reaching through the open fanlight window, and his hand was lifting the main window lever to get in. I completely froze; I tried to scream but nothing would come out. On seeing me, he leapt backwards, ran across the lawn and out of the gate. It seemed he was just as terrified of me as I was of him. It was several seconds before any of my limbs would function. Having got everyone out of bed, I related the full horror of the situation. The police were finally called. Detailed statements were taken, and by the following morning, what had happened the previous night was the only topic of conversation on the lips of the entire population of the village.

Several weeks passed and the memory of that terrifying experience was beginning to fade. My focus then began to shift to boys, or the lack of them. The competition was somewhat limited where I spent most of my waking life.

One boy had sparked my interest. His name was Frank. Like me, he too was an apprentice. He worked in the car repair garage. He used to gaze out from under a greasy-looking Beatle haircut as I passed by on my daily errand to the cake shop. I began shyly returning his smile when one day, he strode towards me as I passed by and asked,

"Do you want to go out with me or what?" He spoke in a very direct manner.

Having never been in a situation such as this before, I simply replied dumbly,

"OK." I replied a little too readily.

He then just turned on his heel and strode back inside the garage. I just stood there not entirely sure what should happen next.

That evening, having gone through the usual bedtime routine of light on, curtains drawn, undress, light off. I lay there reflecting on the day's events. All of a sudden, the light in the room dimmed right down, plunging the room into semi-darkness. I looked toward the window making out a dark shape on the other side of the curtains. This time I was ready. I leapt out of bed shouting and screaming. All hell broke loose. Dad and my brother were out of the house in hot pursuit. Dad flew out the gate clutching a wooden pole which he now kept handy beside the bed, while my brother completely jumped the hedge wielding a cricket bat. God help whoever it was if they caught them.

Bedroom lights were coming on up and down the lane. Neighbours, now alerted by all the commotion, were out of their homes, now joining in the chase with similar dangerous implements in hand and were running in all directions. This time they would get their man. There would be no escape. There was no telling what would have been his fate if any of them had caught up with the culprit. It was a complete mystery how he had managed to give so many of them the slip. Apparently, the only person they could find was one innocent-looking young lad, standing at the bus stop at the bottom of the hill supposedly waiting for the last bus home.

The next day, I was eager to relate the previous night's drama to my co-worker, Jean, and was shocked to find out that she already knew all about it. Apparently, Frank from the garage had asked Jean for my home address, which she had gladly given to him.

That evening, he had been with his mates in their car, cruising around like lads do. It was getting late, and they were heading home when Frank asked his mate to do a detour and drop by my house. He wanted to put a note in the letterbox, asking me to go to the cinema with him that Saturday. He had got as far as the gate when he saw a bedroom light come on. He saw me enter the room and close the curtains. He then stupidly decided not to bother with the note; his innocent intention was to tap the window and ask me personally. He'd almost made it to the window when all hell broke loose. The other lads waiting patiently in the car witnessed Frank running like a bat out of hell. They put pedal to the metal and made a hasty getaway, wanting no part of whatever trouble Frank now found himself in and leaving poor Frank to his own devices.

Jean said he had been absolutely terrified at the time, thinking he may well have been killed, but she informed me that now he was just very angry about the whole thing as the last bus had gone and he had to walk home which had taken him over two hours.

That was to be the end of any possible relationship with Frank. He did not mince his words when he told Jean to tell me that that he wanted nothing more to do with either me or my family and added for good measure that he believed us all to be stark staring bloody crazy.

I never got an opportunity to explain about the previous incident, which he had regrettably mirrored so accurately, nor did the original perpetrator ever get caught. So, not a good outcome all the way around.

Still, life moved on. Jean, feeling sorry for my misfortune over Frank, naughtily set me up with her boyfriend's brother Alan, who was a sailor in the Merchant Navy home on leave. She had arranged a foursome. It had been agreed that we were going for a drink at a popular local pub. I was very nervous, but also just a little bit excited. Jean and I were to meet the lads in the pub. I almost backed out at the last minute as the nerves took hold but was literally just pushed from behind through the pub door, so there was no going back.

Following the usual introductions, I sat quietly sipping my port and lemon, taking crafty glimpses at him when I thought he wasn't looking. He was very nice looking, I thought. Much more handsome than Frank. I sat listening to all the back-and-forth conversation, answering the questions that were put to me, but adding very little to the proceedings myself. I just could not think of anything interesting or intelligent to say. By the end of the evening, I had convinced myself that Alan was not blown away with my sparkling personality. I was, therefore, completely taken aback when he asked me out again.

Another two dates followed in quick succession.

One was a trip to an ice rink, where I spent most of the time flat on my back or face down. The evening ended with us sipping milkshakes in the adjoining café, trying not to shiver in my very cold, wet trousers. The second date was a trip to the cinema. He put his arm around me through the whole of the film. At the end of the evening, he bravely kissed me goodnight, which I did not like because he stuck his tongue in my mouth and wiggled it about which I thought was a positively disgusting thing to do. He explained that his leave was coming to an end. I thought, here it comes - it's been nice knowing you.

"I would like it very much if you would come for a meal at my house on my last weekend. My mum and dad are away visiting relatives, so we could get to know each other better."

Oh, how sweet, I thought naively.

"Yes," I said hastily, "I would love that."

He wrote his phone number down on a piece of scrap paper and gave it to me.

"Let me know what time you are coming, and I will meet the bus," he added.

I was already working out the bus times in my mind.

It snowed heavily all day on the Friday and continued throughout the night. I was very worried that the buses would not be running.

Saturday morning came, and I was up very early eager to see what the activity was like on the roads. The snow in our lane was very deep, but cars had compounded a route through to the main road.

I could see from the lounge window that the gritters had been out, and that traffic was moving freely.

Hugely relieved, I set about the task of getting ready. I was out to impress.

A long soak in the bath, lashings of deodorant, copious amounts of Mother's best perfume, and hours spent on my hair and makeup. I was leaving nothing to chance. Suitably satisfied with the result, I set off to catch the bus, taking great care walking down our lane where the snow was thickest not to get my new shoes wet.

It was quite a long journey, passing through several villages, but I spent the time rehearsing what I would say when I met him. The bus turned into the road where I had to get off. I stood up, rang the bell, and made my way to the front. I could see Alan standing a little way on from the bus stop, waiting patiently, all smiles. The bus came to a stop some distance from where Alan was standing. The doors flew open. Thanking the driver, I gingerly made my way down the steps.

I did not like the look of the snowdrift where the bus had stopped, but I had no other choice but to take that last final step down. It was worse than I had feared. There was nothing firm below my feet as I quietly plunged into a blanket of white nothingness, the image of Alan a few yards away disappearing from view.

The next half an hour was spent in a semi-comatose state as I sat on Alan's sofa in his jogging bottoms, sporting his mother's purple cardigan, and with my hands wrapped around a hot cup of tea. Makeup now smudged, and new shoes ruined, I believed that it was at that very moment that I decided there was no God.

The next few hours were spent making awkward small talk while waiting for my clothes to dry on an old wooden clothes horse propped up in front of a log fire.

Well, I could hardly expect him to feel amorous over a girl sitting next to him wearing lad's jogging bottoms, and his mother's purple cardigan, now, could I?

Later that day, I was sitting on the return bus home, wearing my still damp clothes, and with no further arrangements made. On reflection, though, perhaps it was for the best. After all, he was away on his travels again soon, so one less possible heartache was narrowly avoided. Mother was surprised to see me back so early when I walked through the door. She asked,

"Well, how did it go?"

"Oh, great," I lied, refusing to go into detail about what had happened. It was embarrassing enough without getting her view on the matter.

"What happened to your hair?" she asked my back as I disappeared into my bedroom. Not bothering to offer a reply, I shut the door behind me, throwing myself face down on my bed, giving way to silent sobbing.

Back at work on the Monday morning, I recounted all the grisly details of my disastrous weekend to Jean. I was expecting just a modicum of sympathy, but she found the whole debacle hilarious. I had to see the funny side of it too in the end.

Life moved on at a very tedious and boring pace. This can't be it, I thought. There just must be more to life than this. After giving the situation a great deal of thought, I had come up with a plan. I would put pride behind me and contact my cousin Helen, who I had lived with when Mother was in hospital. There was much more going on where she lived. Surprisingly, she seemed pleased to hear from me. She liked the idea of us meeting up and told me about a club called The Cave, which had recently opened and was apparently the in place to go.

We arranged that we would meet up on Saturday evening to go for a couple of drinks, and then finish up at the club. Again, having put my best effort into my appearance, we met up as arranged. By the time we got to the club, I was buzzing. It was the most amazing place I had ever been to. It was so dark you could barely see. There were strobe lights whirling around the room, and the music was so loud it hurt your ears and vibrated through your whole body, almost making your veins thump. I tried to shout how great I thought it was to Helen, but she could not hear me. A few seconds later, she was on the dance floor with a guy with extremely short hair and skintight jeans.

The place was packed. I glanced around me as my eyes slowly became accustomed to the darkness. I noticed that, strangely, nearly all the guys had the same short haircut. How odd, I thought. I remarked on this when Helen returned from the dance floor. She reminded me that this was a garrison town. A lot of soldiers came to the club on a Saturday evening. They seemed to stand around the edge of the dance floor, pint mugs in hand, just staring at all the girls dancing together. This continued all evening, then, about half an hour before the club was due to close, the mood of the music changed from a grinding, pumping, thumping to a much quieter gentle smooching rhythm. The guys then started to make their moves, selecting the girl that they wanted to take home who they had been eyeing up all evening. That was one way of getting out of buying a drink, I thought.

I don't know if I was relieved or disappointed that I had not been chosen for this honour, but I did not dwell on it as I had a fantastic evening. I had decided it would become a regular weekly event.

Every few weeks, a famous singer or group would perform. All the girls would scream the place down, me included. One Saturday, I had heard that Mike Sarne was going to be headlining. I absolutely loved him.

Helen and I had got there very early to ensure a good vantage place in front of the stage. We knew when all the bouncers took up their positions that he was about to make his entrance.

As soon as he ran through the curtains and onto the stage, the screaming started at full volume. It was at this precise second that I did something completely out of character. I lunged forward, grasping my hands tightly around the first thing that I could grab onto, which happened to be the belt of his trousers. A burly bald-headed bouncer who stunk of cigar smoke was quick to react and grabbed me from behind. He pulled hard to get me to release my grip, but I was not letting go. Mike Sarne tried desperately to prise my fingers away from his middle.

Finally, I was forced to release my grip. With the bouncer still holding on, we fell backwards into the crowd of screaming girls who scrambled over us to get to the fast-retreating singer. He was consequently whisked away without even having opened his mouth.

Once calm had been restored, I began to examine the damage. Yep, a fair few nasty-looking bruises appearing, and very little left of my stockings. But it had been an experience worth every minute, and one which I would not have missed for all the tea in China.

Helen told me how utterly disgusted she was with me. I was also not at all popular with everyone else either. Because of me, the evening's entertainment was heading off prematurely to his next venue. I thought this was as good a time as any to head on home.

I never missed a Saturday over the next few months and had several guys asking if they could give me a lift home. I always had the very good excuse that my brother was waiting for me outside in his car. In fact, there he was at turnout time every Saturday night, headlights on full, engine running, making sure I had fastened my safety belt before setting off. I did not mind him doing the big brother thing too much, as it saved me having to stay over at Helen's house. The very next Saturday, however, that was all about to change.

It was early in the evening. I was standing watching the dancing and bobbing about to the music, taking an occasional sip of my drink, when I suddenly became aware of this guy smiling in my direction. I quickly looked around me to see if there was someone behind me that had caught his eye. But no, he appeared to be smiling at me. I shyly returned his smile, then quickly looked away. The next minute, he was beside me, introducing himself as Kevin. He had gorgeous eyes, a deep soft voice, and that very recognizable short haircut, so I knew he was a soldier.

He bought me a drink at the bar and guided me to an empty table in the corner, where we sat and chatted for the rest of the evening. When the music slowed, and everyone hit the dance floor, he took me by the hand and guided me into the middle. He wrapped his arms around me not attempting to grope. It seemed the natural thing to do to put my arms up around his neck as we shuffled around in small circles, our cheeks gently touching. We remained on the dance floor for two more dances, until the lights went up. He walked with me to pick up my coat, then out into the cold night air to the car park where Edward was waiting for me. He bent forwards, gently brushing his lips over mine.

"Are you going to be here next week?" he asked.

"Yes, Oh, yes," however I was a little disappointed that he had not asked to meet me again before then.

"I saw that," said Edward as I climbed into the passenger seat.

"Don't even think about telling Mum," I threatened.

The week dragged by so slowly it was almost too much to bear. Saturday finally arrived.

I arrived at the club early, scanning the faces to see if I could see Kevin. No, he was not among the guys already standing by the bar. I got myself a drink and sat down, watching the door anxiously. The time ticked on by and the club was filling up but still no Kevin. By now, I was getting myself in a state, convincing myself that he was not coming.

But just as I got out of my seat to join Helen on the dance floor, I caught sight of him weaving his way through the throng. My heart did a complete somersault inside my chest, but I tried to appear cool. I said nonchalantly,

"Oh, hi," as he grasped my hand.

"Come on, let's get out of here!" he urged, tugging me toward the door.

Despite Helen's protestations, we escaped the throng and went out into the cold night air, walking hand in hand until we reached the park.

We sat down on the furthest most out of the way bench we could find, wrapped our arms around each other and kissed until our lips went numb. We were so engrossed in each other that we almost forgot the time and had to run all the way back to meet Edward in the car park when the club turned out. We had arranged to meet up again during the week.

Over the next few months, we could not get enough of each other. He occupied my every waking thought. I went with him to London to meet his parents, and his sister, who was married with three children. We stayed at his parent's ground-floor flat in a very scruffy tenement building. His father spent every spare moment in the pub. His mother was a very timid little person, who his father barked orders at in a very slurred voice and addressed her as 'woman'

I could just imagine what my mother would have made of this lifestyle.

But hey-ho, it was none of her business.

This was the weekend when Kevin and I did things. He came and climbed into my bed. I was so scared we would be heard, but I did not tell him to stop. It hurt like hell; it was all I could do not to cry out. But the whole thing was over very quickly.

I can remember thinking, wow, was that it? I had heard so much about it, so expectations were high, and I had to hide my disappointment. I was just recovering from the shock of it when his mother popped her head around the bedroom door.

"Get back in your own bed, Kevin, before your father hears you," she hissed in a whisper. I almost died of embarrassment and was dreading seeing her in the morning. I thought she would ask me to leave but nothing was said. It was as if it had never happened.

Following that weekend, the guilt kicked in. I had stupidly convinced myself that I was pregnant. The way my luck ran, it seemed inevitable, even though I was not even late.

It was a nerve-racking week. I was frantic with worry. But all was well, as my period came as normal. The relief was enormous! I no longer had the fear of facing Mother. However, I had made up my mind that as I had escaped this outcome, I would not let a man do that to me again. Well, at least not before I was married. If he wanted me that badly, he would do the right thing and wait, I told myself. It was not as if it was even enjoyable. God knows what all the fuss was about. It seemed to me that it was obviously something a woman had to endure if she wanted her man to love her.

We were becoming remarkably close as we continued to see each other several times a week. Then, one evening, he did not seem himself. He seemed preoccupied with his own thoughts, as if he were preparing himself to say something. I managed to prize it out of him in the end.

He told me that he was being posted out to The Yemen. This came as a terrible shock, but worse was to come. It was to be a two-year posting. Kevin was worried that I might fall for somebody else over such a long separation. We discussed all possible solutions to this latest development and came to a mutual agreement.

That weekend, Kevin came to my house to talk to my mother and father.

We had discussed beforehand what we were going to say, as neither of us was too sure of what the reaction was going to be. In fact, I was so scared I decided to leave it to Kevin to explain it to them delicately.

"We want to get engaged," he blurted out in a determined and decisive tone.

I think that was the last thing they expected to hear, as a look of complete shock flashed across both of their faces.

They sat in silence for several seconds, staring at us blankly, while they processed what they had been told. I tried quickly to rescue the situation and went on to elaborate further, explaining about the two-year posting to The Yemen. I could physically feel the atmosphere in the room change and the tension falling away from them. Then, and only then did they grant the request.

I guess they did not take the whole thing seriously. I'm pretty sure they both thought that we would both have a change of heart over the next two years and that the whole idea would just fizzle out over time.

"Well, you handled that well, Kevin," I remarked as we left that evening. We, on the other hand, were ecstatic with joy, riding along on a wave of total euphoria. The ring arrived shortly after, adding reality to the excitement which was hard to contain.

The most stunning, large ruby and diamond cluster was officially presented to me at a very, very low-key celebratory occasion. This proved slightly uncomfortable as most family members had not ever met Kevin.

"It must have cost him a small fortune," I proudly announced to everyone as I did my ceremonial walk around the room, holding my hand out for all to admire.

"You are worth it," he whispered lovingly in my ear. I wore it with huge pride.

Two weeks later, the reality of the situation started to dawn as I stood on the platform at the railway station clinging to him like a limpet, tears streaming down my face as we said our goodbyes.

I sobbed all the way home until my eyes were so swollen, I could barely see out of them. Glancing sadly down at my engagement ring, I wondered how on earth I was going to endure the next two years without him. If the truth be told, I didn't. I made everyone's life a complete misery, or that was what I was told.

My brother Edward had left university and had been offered a job in the States and was excitedly making plans for an amazing future. As for me, well, I was still going to be stuck here with

Mother for another two years. It was all so unfair. Resentment bubbled up inside me; things always turned out better for Edward than for me.

How could God keep ruining my life in this way? I swore I would never pray again. His plan for me was obviously going to be an uphill struggle every step of the way. My mood continued to deteriorate as time progressed.

Letters from Kevin started to arrive, one after the other, with declarations of undying love and devotion. The postman's arrival seemed the only real purpose of each day.

We had been apart for nearly two months when one drab and wet Saturday morning, two letters arrived. I read the one first that I knew was from Kevin, which threw everything into a whirlwind of emotion, a mixture of panic and elation, and what can only be described as a sudden and dramatic breakdown of any small shred of sense that I may have possessed.

I could not read the words quick enough, again, and again, and again, to ensure what I was reading was truly there on the page, and that it was not some cruel trick my mind was playing on me. Yes, there it was in black and white.

Kevin had been in to see his commanding officer to ask for permission for me, yes me, his fiancée, to join him to get married in the Yemen. I read on anxiously with heightened excitement.

His CO had agreed. Oh, my God, I thought. Could this really be true? Was this really happening?

I could not contain myself. Without even thinking things through further, I flew into the kitchen where my parents were enjoying breakfast.

"I'm going out to join Kevin," I blurted out. "I'm going to get married out there. Kevin has spoken to his Commanding Officer, and he has said it's OK."

With that, I started to scream and jump up and down flinging the letter up into the air, as I danced around and around the kitchen table.

Mother and Dad just stared at me with open mouths. They looked at each other, then back at me, then back at each other before Dad finally said,

"Now just a minute, Rita, let's not get ahead of ourselves. You can't just go running off to the Yemen just like that, can she, Mother?" he said, looking at my mother for some moral support. Mother, on the other hand, just continued to stare at me.

I stared back at her with equal ferocity with a 'don't you dare try and stop me' expression blazing out of both my eyes.

"You can't stop me,' I shouted at her, and as an extra determination of my intention, I added, "I'm 18 next month; I can do what I want."

"That is very true, Rita, if this is what you really want," came her reply.

This response took me aback and was completely unexpected. I expected a battle. This was not Mother's style at all, encouraging what she must have perceived to be a complete loss of sanity on my part.

With this, I rushed toward her, flinging my arms around her neck, kissing her roughly on the cheek and spilling her tea down the front of her apron.

"Stop being childish, Rita, now, look at this!" she grumbled, removing her apron. "That was clean on this morning."

"Are you sure about all this, Rita?" Dad asked apprehensively, with a worried look on his face. "It's no small thing is this, you know. You do know there is a war going on out there, don't you? People are getting killed. It is an extremely dangerous place to be, which is why the army is out there to sort out the trouble."

But I knew that I was home and dry. I had Mother's blessing. Well, not her blessing as such. To be honest, she would be rather pleased to see the back of me after the way I had been behaving recently.

Dad, quickly realizing the futility of further objections on the matter, had nothing more to add on the subject.

I returned to my room, exciting plans already formulating in my mind. It was then I noticed the other letter that had arrived that day. I was totally unprepared for what it contained.

It appeared to be a default notice taken out for outstanding payments still owed on a 9-carat gold ruby and diamond cluster ring. It stated the HP company had been notified that I was the owner of the ring, residing at this address.

It went on to say that as no payments had been made on the HP agreement, a default notice had been issued. Settlement of the full amount of the debt needed to be paid by the date given or legal action would be taken.

The letter fell to the floor along with my heart. Half an hour passed before I put my head back around the kitchen door.

"Dad," I said slowly. "Can I have a private word with you, please?"

My wonderful Dad paid for that ring himself, I believe, without Mother's knowledge. There was only one caveat attached which was that I would not put the ring back on my finger until I had received the receipt for it. Of course, I readily agreed. Mother never even noticed that I was not wearing it.

The next few weeks were manic, to say the least. Mother came with me to talk to my boss at the hairdressers. There was the not too small matter of negotiating the exit of a three-year apprenticeship contract.

This was going to be a huge hurdle to get over. If he said no, then solicitors would have to be involved because I was leaving, hell or high water.

I had very little sleep the night before; I was trying to work out in my head what I could threaten him with if he was uncooperative. I thought I could perhaps go on a go-slow but quickly disregarded that idea as I did very little as it was.

Another idea that came to mind was that I could keep taking days off, especially on busy days, which seemed a good possibility.

I let Mother do all the talking, as most people found her intimidating.

I could hardly believe what I was hearing when, after hearing mother's proposal, he simply smiled, looked in my direction and said,

"No problem, when do you expect to leave?"

"Next week?" I asked weakly.

"Yep," he replied, "I see no problem with that. I will get the necessary paperwork ready."

"How did it go?" Dad asked that evening, knowing how worried I was that this could well be the one thing that could scupper my plans.

"Very well, actually, Dad," obviously, he was extremely sorry to be losing me, but he was actually very nice about it, considering," I added as an afterthought. I knew deep down, of course, that this had been a heaven-sent opportunity for him to rid himself of a very sore thorn in his side.

This was not good news to Dad's ears though, as he was secretly pinning his last hopes on me not being able to get out of my indentured contract.

The next few weeks flew by in a flash. There were visas to be rushed through, injections to be organised and suitable clothes to be purchased, not to mention the all-important wedding dress.

The army had decided that they were going to use the whole thing as a promotional recruitment exercise.

They had cleverly linked the press coverage to the current film at the time, James Bond, From Russia with Love, which was headed up in our local newspapers as 'From Sussex with Love'

The article was afforded a full-page spread along with a picture of me in my wedding dress, and a detailed article about me travelling thousands of miles on my own, at the tender age of just eighteen, to marry the man I loved, who would be joining a highly respected Royal army regiment which cared about the welfare of their soldiers!

The article went on to explain that the military wedding service with full honours would be held at the local garrison church and I would be given away by the Company Commander with the whole regiment in attendance.

It went on to say that the happy couple would enjoy an expenses paid three-week honeymoon in Kenya, then return to barracks to fully furnished private accommodation until such times as army accommodation could be found.

It was a splendid article. However, I was saddened to read the footnote, which was added almost as an afterthought, that there were to be no family members of the bride attending on the day.

I was the talk of the town; people were stopping me in the street to wish me good luck, and much happiness for the future. It was the very best time of my entire life. I had never received so much positive attention focused on me, and I enjoyed every second of it.

As the big departure day grew closer, I began counting down the hours. I had packed and repacked my cases, and now I was more than ready to start my new life. Mother and Dad drove me to the airport. We arrived in good time, so we went to get some breakfast.

There was a family sitting at the next table with a young man in an army uniform. Dad asked the family where they were going. They told us that they had come to see their son Henry off, as he was joining his regiment. Dad told them that I was also on the same flight and went on to explain the reasons why.

The family seemed quite shocked that I was travelling to such a formidable place so far away on my own and asked if I had flown before. When I replied that I had not, they reassuringly told Dad that their son would look after me and make sure that I was alright.

I know Dad meant well, but I was not at all pleased that he had purposely engineered this arrangement for me. I told them that I was perfectly fine, and not in the least bit scared, and reassured them that I did not need any help but thanked them for their kind offer anyway.

As we made our way to departures, I could see that Dad was welling up, so I pulled away from hugging him, kissed Mother on the cheek and made my way through the barrier. I decided it was best not to prolong their pain by turning around to give them one last wave.

With the excitement now rising, a new adventure was about to begin.

Chapter 3

I found myself a seat close to the departure boards so that I could keep an eye on the information on my flight.

Despite declining the offer of help, the young man from the café plonked himself into the seat next to me. I looked away from him, rummaging around in my handbag, pretending that I was looking for something so that I did not have to look at him.

He seemed hell-bent on fulfilling his duty of the promise his parents had made to Dad.

"Hi," he said pleasantly, "I'm Henry."

"Hi," I replied, "look I don't want to appear rude or anything, but I am perfectly fine. I really don't need any help. But thanks anyway," I added as an afterthought.

"It's no problem, I'm going your way, It is a very long flight, and it will be nice to have someone to talk to," he pointed out.

This was true but I was not really in the mood for chatting. I was far too excited about seeing Kevin again after what felt like forever.

It would not be much longer now before I would be in his arms again, I thought dreamily.

Henry followed me as we boarded the plane, a DC10 aircraft, the captain informed us over the tannoy.

I chose a window seat so that I could see the views as we took off. To my disappointment, Henry lowered himself down into the seat next to me and began chatting about his job. I continued to gaze out of the window, hoping that he would get the hint.

The plane's engines fired up as it began to roll slowly along the runway, turning to line up for take-off. The plane lurched forward to full throttle. I grasped the arms of the seat until my knuckles went white, then, with my whole body pressed back hard against the seat, it finally left the ground.

This was just amazing, I thought, trying to ignore the pressure building in my ears. This was my new beginning. BRING IT ON! I almost screamed.

Henry was right; it was indeed a very long flight. In the end, I was glad of his informal chatter between his dozing. There was no sleep for me, however. I was too excited as I gazed out of the plane window at the glorious sunrise. I thought, if there is a heaven, this must surely be what it would look like to the human eye. We had one fuel stop then continued the journey.

I could feel the plane starting to descend as the pressure started to build again in my ears. I took in the landscape below us which was slowly becoming visible as we descended.

I could see lots of very primitive dwellings dotted here and there. Then, a much larger building came into view alongside the runway. The noise of the engines changed as we made our descent. I could now make out people moving about below.

I glanced round at Henry who was leaning around me, also watching the plane's descent through the window, as we were coming into land. He looked at me and smiled.

"Home sweet home," he said.

I grasped the arms of the seat as before, waiting for the impact. We bumped to the ground with a thud, and I could feel the plane's brakes being applied until we finally taxied to a stop. Everyone began unbuckling their seat belts and gathering their personal belongings. I joined the orderly queue waiting for the door to open, which seemed to take forever.

Finally, with the steps now in place, we slowly made our way along the plane toward the exit.

The very first of two sensations, which will remain with me always, was the heat. It felt just like standing in front of an open oven that had been set to maximum. Good God, I thought, instantly starting to sweat as I made my way down the first few steps.

The second sensation that quickly followed was the smell. It is very hard to describe that smell. It was unlike anything I had ever known before, a mixture between sweaty armpits, sweaty socks.

Before I could protest, Henry had grabbed my hand luggage.

"Here, let me carry that," he insisted as we all started to make our way across the tarmac toward the building, with me following along behind him. We stood together waiting for our luggage to be unloaded. Excitement was now at fever pitch with the prospect of seeing Kevin again. I had almost forgotten what he looked like.

Henry lifted my cases off the carousel, loading them onto a very broken, rusty-looking trolley, but it did the job it was designed for. We exited through a set of double doors into the main waiting area where Arab men in long white dresses and flip flops mingled with men in uniform.

I quickly scanned the faces eagerly. I spotted Kevin some distance away, standing beside a uniformed officer. I hurried towards him, all smiles, fully expecting him to throw his arms around me, smothering me with long-awaited kisses, but his eyes were focused firmly on Henry.

"Hello," I gushed. "I have missed you terribly," I said as I moved closer trying to put my arms around him. Without even shifting his stare away from Henry, he replied stiffly,

"Who's this then?"

"Oh yes, sorry," I said quickly turning round. "This is Henry, Henry this is Kevin."

"Pleased to meet you, mate," said Henry, holding out his hand. Kevin made no attempt to shake it but continued to stare at him icily.

"Dad asked Henry if he would be kind enough to look after me on the journey," I began uncomfortably. "Because I was travelling alone for the first time," then as an afterthought, I added, "Dad was afraid I might get off at the wrong stop," finishing with a nervous laugh. Kevin looked at me and said sarcastically,

"Oh, very funny. By the way," he said turning to the side, "this is my Commanding Officer. You are going to be staying with him and his wife, for now anyway. Come on, let's go." He finished, grabbing my case from Henry without even so much as a thank you.

I said hello to his CO and shook his hand.

"Lovely to meet you; just call me Andrew." We made our way out of the building back out through some sliding doors into the baking heat. I knew we had not seen each other for three months, but this had not at all been the welcome that I had expected. It worried me. I tried to work out the reason for Kevin's strange behaviour and concluded that it must be that he was a little jealous that I had travelled with another guy.

I would explain it all properly when we were on our own, feeling sure that he would understand that it had all been very innocent.

A soldier saluted our jeep as it turned into the army camp gates, coming to a halt beside a grey door with the number two hanging upside down on it. Kevin jumped out and heaved the case down from the back and plonked it down outside the door which suddenly opened. A tall dark-haired woman stepped toward me and put her hands on my shoulders and kissed both my cheeks.

"Hi! I'm Sally Stevens, Andrew's wife," you will be staying with us until your big day. Did you have a good flight?" she asked.

"Yes, thank you, It was long, but I was warned that it would be."

"I will make you a drink, and then you must go for a lie down; you must be exhausted," she said kindly. "I will show you to your room where you can freshen up."

She led me into a plain but comfortable-looking room. I lowered myself down onto the bed as she gently closed the door behind her.

I looked up at the fan on the ceiling, gently rotating to a rhythmic swishing.

I must admit to feeling a little trepidation at this point but brushed it quickly aside. You will be fine, my inner voice told me soothingly. What could possibly go wrong? You have Kevin at your side now, don't you? After changing my dress, I returned to the living room to find that Kevin had gone.

"Kevin had to go back on duty, so he said to tell you he would see you later," Sally informed me.

"Oh," I replied, more than a little disappointed.

Kevin returned that evening and took me out to show me around the camp.

There seemed to be two separate areas. One area, Kevin explained, was the soldiers' married quarters. The second area was the officers' married quarters where I was staying, which seemed much nicer.

There was not much of interest to see really, just a lot of prefabricated buildings containing the mess hall where all the regular soldiers ate.

The officers had a separate mess hall, which again looked very different, with bushes in large containers outside its entrance.

There was a large steamy laundry room where there were lines and lines of washing machines and dryers going flat out to try to keep up with all the regimental frequent bed and uniform changes. There were lots of offices and large kitchens. There was even a gym, which smelt strongly of sweat, where there were several guys working out. Then came a big hut which was called the stores. Also, secure stores that had a soldier posted outside. I was not allowed to go in there, as that was where all the guns and ammunition were housed. Next to this was a huge hangar where there were several army trucks standing idle with their bonnets up undergoing repairs of one kind or another. The last place Kevin took me into was the main mess. Kevin explained that this was where the lads hung out to relax in their off-duty hours. There was a snooker table, a dartboard, many tables and chairs, and a small bar, where most people seemed to want to congregate.

I was introduced to several of Kevin's friends before returning to a table with two drinks. It was so nice to get Kevin on his own at last, but I was somewhat surprised by the first thing that came out of his mouth.

"How come you needed a chaperone, then?" he said, taking a large gulp of his beer.

So, he was still cross about that, I thought. I saw this as a display of jealously and replied,

"I told you, darling, it was just Dad being silly and protective. Please don't be cross with me; it was not what I had wanted to happen. I hardly spoke to the guy. You must know by now it's you I love," I simpered, reaching across the table to clasp his hands, his attitude softening as he took my hands in his.

See, chirped my inner voice, he loves you so much he is frightened of losing you believing this to be a sure indication of how much I meant to him.

I had convinced myself that this was the reassurance I so desperately needed to confirm that travelling to the ends of the earth for this man was indeed the best thing I had ever done.

The days flashed by in a blur. I saw very little of Kevin through the day as he was on duty. So, my time was spent helping Sally with the chores.

I spent most afternoons underneath the fan, on the bed, in my underwear. It was too hot to do anything else. I was told I would get used to the heat, but I was unconvinced.

Most evenings were spent in the mess where I spent much of my time watching Kevin play snooker with his mates.

Kevin seemed extremely quiet in the days leading up to the wedding, but I was busy discussing all the necessary last-minute arrangements, and I did not get a chance to talk to him about what was troubling him. I thought that he was just letting me get on with what I had to do, finalizing all the wedding plans - just woman's stuff.

The big day finally arrived. I was up early; everything was running to plan, bath, hair, nails. I stood looking at myself in my wedding dress in the full-length mirror when it suddenly hit me. Tears started welling up in my eyes.

Oh, poor Dad, I thought regretfully. I had robbed him of this oh so special moment in any dad's life seeing his only daughter in her wedding dress, walking her down the aisle and giving her hand to the man she loved. In that moment, I felt a mixture of huge guilt, great sadness, and just a little bit lonely. Sally and Andrew had been amazing, but it was not the same as having your family there with you on such a special day.

My thoughts were interrupted by a loud knocking on the front door, and the sound of loud and anxious voices, followed by urgent tap-tapping on my bedroom door.

"What's going on?" I asked coming out of the bedroom, looking at the worried faces staring back at me.

"Kevin has called the wedding off," announced the visitor, looking at me with an expression of complete fear on his face, not at all sure what reaction he was about to receive.

I looked at him blankly, while I processed what it was that I had just been told.

"So," I said quietly, "he has sent you to tell me this, has he?" I asked trying to remain calm.

"Um, yes," came the weak reply.

"Well, is that so?" I said with my voice increasing in volume with every word. "Well, you can just go right back and tell him that he was the one who asked me to marry him, and I have travelled halfway around the world to a foreign country to do so, in a church of his choosing, with guests of his choosing, most of whom are total strangers to me.

I have also forgone the opportunity of every girl's dream of having her own father to walk his only daughter down the aisle, or to even have any of my family present on the most important day of my life,"

I continued angrily. "Well, if he thinks for one moment that I am going to quietly get back on that plane, fly all the way back to the UK, only to have to tell everyone that it was called off at the last minute, after all the fuss, all the hype, and all the publicity that there has been surrounding the whole event, then he is sadly mistaken.

I stopped my tirade for one moment and took a deep breath before continuing. "Now you tell him that I will be at the church as arranged, and he had better damned well be there when I arrive."

With that, I turned on my heel and went back into the bedroom, closing the door behind me. I took two very deep breaths, smoothing down the damp creases that I had made in my dress whilst clenching my fists.

With my heart pumping and with my thoughts racing uncontrollably, I tried applying reason to my situation. He was probably just having last-minute nerves, my inner voice whispered soothingly. He will be there, don't worry, I told myself.

But deep, deep down in some very dark little corner of my mind, there was the tiniest little niggle that maybe, just maybe, the right thing to do would have been to get back on that plane.

But as was usual for me, I just could not face the embarrassment. It was definitely the easier option to try to make the whole thing happen at any cost.

With that very intention in mind, I climbed into the jeep which was festooned in ribbons, and we made our way to the church.

A stop was made on the way where we were supposed to pick up some semblance of flowers, but when we got there, its shutters were pulled down. That's that then, I thought. No flowers. Andrew touched my arm sympathetically as we climbed out of the jeep and made our way out of the bright sun into the dusty gloom of the little garrison church.

"Are you sure you want to go through with this?" he questioned.

"Absolutely, I do," I replied determined.

The whole garrison had been ordered to attend the service, so the little church was full to capacity. As I made my way down the aisle on Andrew's arm, I clasped a black prayer book that he had passed to me on the way in so that I had something to hold.

I could feel all eyes on me as I made my way toward the altar, looking straight ahead, my heart pounding with anticipation.

There he was in full uniform facing the small altar to the front. As I came level to him, I quickly glanced at him and smiled.

"I love you," I mouthed silently, just to reassure him.

"I love you too," he mouthed back. All was now well with the world. Or was it?

The following day, we were back in the small airport to take a plane to Nairobi. It was a terrible flight in an old Argosy plane which rattled like hell. The engines were so loud you could not possibly hold a conversation, but I did not care. I was so happy and so excited about the forthcoming trip.

We had a hotel booked in Nairobi. It was a beautiful hotel. I had never stayed anywhere so posh before; the army had certainly done us proud. The first evening, we ate in the hotel. Then Kevin suggested we go out for a look around, and this turned out to be what is commonly known as a pub crawl.

We landed up in a place that was dark and seedy, where a girl gyrated and jiggled to music, while stripping off what little clothes she had on down to her birthday suit.

I tried not to look as she made her way to our side of the stage and started to thrust her hips toward Kevin's face. I felt a conflict of emotions, a cross between sheer embarrassment and uncomfortable arousal. Because of this discomfort, I felt that I needed to get out of there.

"Kevin, I want to go," I pleaded.

"Don't be such a prude; the show has only just started," he whispered, looking straight at the girl's crutch.

"I don't care; I don't like it in here. I want to go now," I demanded, standing up to leave to emphasise the point.

"Oh, good God," Kevin hissed as he followed me back out into the sunshine. "This is going to be one fun holiday," he muttered crossly.

"It's not just a holiday, Kevin, it's our honeymoon," I did not like him wanting to look at naked women. He was supposed to be focused on me. We returned to the hotel where we spent the rest of the evening in the bar.

The next day, with the previous night's debacle put firmly behind us, and after a healthy breakfast, we set off on our travels.

Although still very hot, it was a much more comfortable heat. We were heading to Mombasa, travelling through the Tsavo National Park. Our guide, called Nakuru, knew exactly all the places we would be most likely to see big game, and we were not disappointed.

We were travelling in an open-top jeep so that we could stand up to get a better view. At times, we got a little too close to the larger game for comfort, but Nakuru knew what he was doing and would not have put us in unnecessary danger, he told us reassuringly.

What I found particularly scary was when we had to stop for toilet breaks. Our guide was not very good at finding dense bushes to pee behind, which did not bode well for one's modesty.

But he explained carefully that he needed to be able to see any danger approaching to ensure our safety. This made a lot of sense, but I don't think that I have ever peed as quickly before in my life. It was an amazing journey. We managed to tick off most of the animals that we had hoped to see.

We stopped overnight at a lodge in the middle of the park. We had a lovely room in a small building with a thatched roof. There were mosquito nets hung around the bed and we were warned to always keep the nets around us during the night.

We ate supper on an outside terrace, sipping wine while we watched the elephants and monkeys as they wandered into the grounds to eat the fruits and the left-over salads that the staff had left out for them. We enjoyed the sound of the crickets as we watched the amazing sunset in the cool of the evening. The clarity of the star's constellations was breathtaking. It was so romantic.

I snuggled close to Kevin, nestling my head into his shoulder, gazing up at the myriad of twinkly lights. I had never felt so happy.

The night was a restless one as large insects continuously fell from the thatched ceiling onto the tiled floor below with loud splats. Thank goodness for the nets. It was difficult to know where to tread in the morning to try to avoid all the dead carcasses that were strewn all over the floor. A young lad appeared with a wicker broom and brushed them all outside where several large lizards were waiting patiently for their breakfast.

It was shocking, to say the least, to find tiny frogs floating up to the edge of the toilet rim when I flushed it, and promptly float away again as the water subsided.

I guessed that the plumbing must somehow be connected with the lake we had passed on the way into the grounds. Wow, I thought.

After a delicious breakfast, we set off again for the second half of our journey. It was an amazing experience being able to get so close to animals in their natural habitat. We stopped briefly to watch a rhino and her calf grazing peacefully. However, we had to make a quick getaway when the mother rhino became fearful for the safety of her baby.

I clung on to the seat in front of me whilst watching this huge animal gaining ground behind us. I had no idea they could run so fast. That had been a near-death moment that I did not want to repeat. I was scared witless, convinced that we were all about to die, but our guide was not a bit fazed.

"Happens all the time," he told us. "They can get very aggressive when they have their young in tow," he stated nonchalantly.

I hoped that he would bear that in mind before parking up alongside another one.

Another lodge stopover, much the same as the previous night, then another full day on the trail before arriving tired, hungry, and very dusty, into Mombasa. What a stunningly beautiful place. The sand on the beach was as white as flour. The sea was as blue as the sky. I had never seen such a vivid blue sea before. I couldn't wait to get into it.

The hotel was beautiful too. A young lad showed us to our room. He lifted our cases onto a shelf beside the dressing table, nodded and flashed a smile of the whitest teeth I had ever seen and backed out of the room. I sat down on the bed and kicked off my shoes.

"Have you noticed how bright the colours are?" I asked Kevin.

He looked at me with a confused look on his face. He obviously had no idea what I was talking about. I decided not to try to elaborate.

The next few days were spent eating in the restaurant, swimming in the sea, and making love for hours and hours on end. It was as close to heaven as one could get. Well, not heaven maybe, as his lovemaking was still lacking in respect for me, despite all the practice we were putting in.

I dared not tell him that I was not enjoying his technique, as I knew that he would probably find that very upsetting. I did the only thing I could think of to save his feelings; I faked it.

These were the kind of traits that I had found necessary to adopt to make my relationship work with my mother, again manifesting themselves in my relationship with my new husband - trying desperately hard to please, and actively putting myself second to avoid difficult confrontations.

It was not until many years later that I was able to identify that this was an ever-repeating trait.

On the afternoon of the second day, we returned from the beach to find that the clothes and shoes we had been wearing the previous day had gone missing. I ran around the room looking in drawers and cupboards, but there was no sign of them. I began to panic.

I asked Kevin to go to reception and tell them that someone had got into our room and had stolen our belongings.

He was not happy about doing this, but because I was so upset by it, he agreed to go and report that there had been a serious breach of the hotel's security. I sat on the bed waiting for a visit from the hotel manager. I was therefore most surprised when the door opened and in walked Kevin with the young lad still flashing his dazzling smile, and carrying a pile of freshly laundered clothes, and two pairs of highly polished shoes.

"You no worry, Mamsab," he said, handing me the neatly folded clothes.

Apparently, this was a free and daily service provided to all guests staying in the hotel. I was suitably embarrassed, but not nearly as embarrassed as I would be the very next morning.

We had gone down to breakfast as usual and were just getting seated at our usual table when a very official looking gentleman walked towards our table. He stood in front of me with his hands behind his back, cleared his throat then came straight out with it.

"Mamsab, she put blood on the sheets." He glared at me, waiting for my reply.

I looked straight at Kevin, who simply shrugged his shoulders. No help coming from him then, my inner voice confirmed.

"What?" I said stupidly, looking back at the stern face in front of me. What good I thought it would do to get him to repeat the sentence again, for everyone to hear a second time, I could not imagine, but nevertheless, repeat it he did.

"Mamsab, she put blood on the sheets."

Of course, I knew exactly what he was referring to. I had come on my period and had leaked a little on the sheet. I had tried to sponge it out without success.

"Oh yes, I'm so sorry about that," I spluttered, my face now completely crimson.

He made no further attempt to reply. I continued, "What would you like me to do about it?"

He blew air into both of his cheeks, turned on his heel and marched off.

Still in a state of shock, I exclaimed to Kevin.

"Oh my God, how bloody embarrassing was that?!"

Kevin shrugged his shoulders for a second time in response, while continuing to spread marmalade on his toast. I got up from the table.

My appetite was now completely gone. I returned to my room to try to sponge the sheet again, only to find that the bed had already been stripped. This was a brilliant start to the day, I thought. I found it difficult to get over the embarrassment of it, although Kevin seemed completely unfazed by the whole incident. I was very relieved when it was time to leave.

Our guide informed us that we were returning via a different route that would take us up to as far as Tanzania, passing through the Maasai Mara game reserve, and returning via Mount Kilimanjaro. With the traumatic events of the morning a distant memory, we went on our way.

The days just flew by, as there was so much to see. Our guide was amazing and was extremely well-versed in every aspect of both the local knowledge and the history of all the areas we passed through.

But by far the most exciting event was when we were greeted by the Maasai people who seemed to appear from nowhere. There were several extremely tall, thin men with red ochre colouring on their bodies, and on their closely braided hair. They each had different raised patterned bumps on their chests and had small pieces of material that discreetly covered their manhood.

There were several giggling bare-chested girls standing in small groups. They looked to be in their early teens, and they wore small, beaded necklaces, and brightly coloured bracelets, and other colourful adornments.

But my attention was drawn instantly to the many small children who gathered around us with hands held out, clearly waiting for the gift of money. I began to delve into my bag for coins, which I placed into each of the little held-out palms. I was rewarded with the most amazing smiles and jumps for joy.

One little chap thought he would try his luck for a second time and was quickly knocked off his feet by one sweep of a hand from one of the Maasai men. He had noticed that the little child had already been given coins.

That must be his dad, I perceived, teaching his little son a valuable lesson in life. Although a somewhat harsh lesson learned about greed, still effective, nonetheless. The little chap quickly picked himself up and made off in the direction from whence he had come.

The Maasai men gestured to us to come with them to their village for food. We could just see huts way off in the distance, but sadly, our guide shook his head. We had a strict time schedule to adhere to and needed to press on with our journey.

I was extremely disappointed that we could not accept their generous offer, as it would have been such a rare and most memorable experience. It may have been a little scary as who knows what kind of things we might be asked to eat, but I for one had been most definitely up for the challenge.

So, our journey continued. We packed as much into each day as was humanly possible. In the very last village we passed through, I managed to buy some souvenirs. I chose a spear for Edward, an animal skin bag made from the entire skin of a dik-dik which is a small antelope native to certain parts of Africa. I thought this would be a good gift for Mother when we finally got back to the

UK. For Dad, I got a bow tie and a matching wallet made from zebra skin.

These products made from natural fur were not frowned upon at the time, but of course, in later years, would be hugely controversial and unacceptable, and would quite rightly become banned. I knew it would be a long time before I could give them all their gifts, but at least they would know I had been thinking about them all.

Our last night was spent back at the hotel in Nairobi, reflecting on our amazing travels. It had been a trip of a lifetime with memories to treasure forever.

The following morning, we climbed the steps of what looked to be the same plane as we travelled out in. We made the return journey to Aden to begin our married life; for me to begin the domesticity of being a new wife, and for Kevin to return to duty with his regiment.

We were renting an apartment on the third floor of a building on the main Street. The building opposite was a factory where they milled flour.

Every day around noon, I would stand on the balcony outside our living room and watch the Arab women come out at the end of their working day covered in flour.

They would lift their long gowns, squat down on tin cans and urinate. They then proceeded to wash the flour from their hands before leaving for their respective homes. It was certainly a very different way of life than what I had been accustomed to.

One of my earliest challenges was to provide the daily meal, which was not an easy task as Mother had never allowed me to cook at home, so I found just boiling an egg proved a tricky undertaking. There were many failures before I could honestly say I had cracked it. (These puns come without any thought).

I then progressed on to more complex foods such as meat and veg. However, I had not yet reached the stage of receiving a compliment from Kevin for what was on his plate every evening. Not surprising, as I found it tasteless too.

You could buy most foods on the main street, and of course, I had my favourite shops that I regularly frequented. One general store I liked to use was run by an English woman called Alice, married to the Arab owner.

I was very interested in how they had first met. She informed me that they had met in London where he had been studying English. They had married and had returned to his native country, where they lived with his parents to help run the family business. It was not long before Alice and I became the firmest of friends.

It was one very long street that had lots of alleyways leading off it into the Arab sector, where all the little local shops could be found. The army had barricaded up most of these alleyways, as they had been used as escape routes for terrorists to make their getaway.

Soldiers constantly patrolled the main street and the barricades daily. I had witnessed a woman with a child in a pushchair being blown to pieces when a hand grenade had been lobbed over one of these barriers.

Tragically, it was generally the native population that suffered in these attacks. It was a truly horrifying experience that forever haunts me. We were under very strict instructions never to go up into the Arab quarters in the backstreets as it was extremely dangerous.

Alice and I spent most of our time together in these forbidden areas. Alice was very fair-skinned, with blonde hair like mine, so we stood out like a sore thumb amongst all the black-haired dark faces seen in that part of town. Of course, Alice was very well known, her Arab family by marriage being highly respected. So, if I was with her, my safety was assured.

I had my dresses made for me in the vast array of material shops that could be found in the local shops which Alice and I visited regularly.

My confidence continued to grow as I moved about in these forbidden areas, so much so that I had taken to going on my own on several occasions when Alice was unable to join me, thinking that I too would be afforded the same protection.

One day, on one of these solo trips without Alice, I went to collect a dress that I was having made. This was not one of the usual places that we tended to shop in, but I had liked the material and had decided to go ahead and order a dress to be made.

I entered the store and handed over the order details to a bearded guy who was sitting on a stool in the corner drinking strong coffee. He got up and rummaged about behind a stack of fabric and produced a neatly folded dress, which he handed to me, waving his arm at a curtained-off area to the side of the store.

"Mamsab try, see if OK for size," he said, stepping back as if to reassure me that this was a perfectly normal and safe thing to do.

I took the dress and entered the cubicle, making sure there were no gaps around the curtain for prying eyes. I changed into the dress and was admiring the workmanship and overall effect when the curtain slid back.

The bearded man stepped into the cubicle and stood behind me, putting both hands on my hips. He began pushing himself closer.

A mixture of blind panic and fear was rising inside me. I could smell the strong odour of his sweat, mixed with strong coffee washing over me as he leaned into me. I could feel his erection pushing into the small of my back.

I knew then that I was in a very dangerous situation, which I would be lucky to get out of unscathed. I swung around and pushed as hard as I possibly could, sending him stumbling backwards, knocking over several stacked-up boxes as he fell, ending on his back on the floor.

Before he could get back on his feet, I had grabbed my clothes, scrabbled for some notes from the bottom of my cloth bag and throwing them to the floor in front of him as I made a dash for the door.

It was only when I reached the safety of the main street that my breath returned to normal. This is the outcome of breaking the rules, I told myself sternly. Yet another thing I would never do again, and yet another valuable lesson learned.

Chapter 4

My next period never arrived. This was a complete shock as in my naivety, I thought that the woman had to orgasm for a baby to be conceived.

It was not long before I was spending most of my time with my head down the toilet. I had never felt so ill. The smell of sweat and sick competed daily, leaving me feeling very weak and miserable.

Kevin seemed thrilled about the whole idea of starting a family so soon, which did nothing for my frame of mind. After all, it was not him having to go through this unending misery. He did nothing to help the situation when he arrived home one evening with a feral puppy.

"Thought it might cheer you up," he declared, as he thrust this poor flea-ridden little creature into my arms.

"Good Lord, Kevin, I can't even cope with myself at the moment, never mind an animal," I uttered despairingly. "Plus, the fact that we live in an apartment. Where will he toilet?" I demanded to know. I was quite cross about it. He had not seemed to have considered any of these important issues before taking this impulsive decision. As I looked down at this little scrap, my heart melted. "Ok," I conceded, "I will try to make it work."

I did my very best, but my brain and my body were not in a good place. I was struggling big time not only with the heat, but also with my increasingly swollen legs.

Kevin arrived home the next day with the news that he had organized for a Wasifa to come daily to help with the chores. This was the equivalent of a home help.

I thought this might just be the answer to my problems and was grateful for his thoughtfulness, at least until I could get to the other side of the sickness.

The very next morning, a tall, stern-faced but beautiful Arab girl arrived and stood waiting for her first domestic instruction.

I took her to the balcony where several piles of dog deposits lay baking in the blistering sun. I pointed to the floor, handing her a plastic bag, a mop, and a bucket.

She started shaking her head vigorously as she backed herself into the room. Just my luck, I thought. He chooses the only Wasifa who refuses to pick up dog poo.

"She refuses to clean up after the dog," I complained to Kevin on his arrival home that evening.

"She probably would because I think it's against their religion. Fancy asking her to do that," he scolded.

How the hell was I supposed to know? What good was she if she could not clean up after the dog? No, that was the end. I was past all reason. The ultimate threat was issued. It was me or the dog. The dog had to go, along with the home help. I am a huge animal lover, so this decision continues to haunt me, but at the time, I had almost reached the point of having a complete meltdown.

Pregnancy seemed to be a never-ending, drawn-out, and exhausting process which I vowed would never ever be repeated.

The day finally arrived when I found myself in the military hospital. At long last it was happening.

The whole experience was likened to some form of middle-aged torture. There would be no epidural, no pain relief administered, no gas and air. In fact, one was left very much to one's own devices apart from being made to drink a concoction of castor oil that had been unsuccessfully mixed with orange juice, the two ingredients remaining separated at opposite ends of the glass, proved nearly impossible to swallow without retching. I was assured that it would provide a slippery pathway to assist the baby's successful journey into the world. I had to take their word for this, as it appeared to be the only help on offer in this archaic establishment.

The hours dragged on with me thrashing around in a demonic state progressing to the point where I had quite frankly lost the will to live, begging for someone, anyone, to put me out of my misery.

In the final stages of this truly horrendous ordeal, and with the invaluable assistance of an Arab nurse with hips the size of a hippopotamus, I eventually gave birth at 6.10 in the morning to the most beautiful baby girl I had ever seen. She was perfect in every way.

As soon as some degree of awareness had returned, I was told that Kevin had been absent throughout the whole proceedings. He was finally found, sitting propped up against the wall in the corridor, fast asleep.

Now, I was a mum and found it almost impossible to believe that Kevin and I had made this tiny miracle. In the remaining time that I had to spend in hospital, I passed many hours just gazing down at her beautiful little face, taking in every detail of her from the tip of her toes to the top of her perfect little head.

We decided to call her Lucy. I was finally permitted to take her home. It was quickly decided that living on the top floor of a three-storey building was not conducive to a pushchair, so, the search was on for a ground-floor apartment.

These appeared to be in short supply, and we were therefore forced to accept something that was far from ideal.

It was dark and dingy and had thick rusty bars on all the windows, I guessed for security reasons. It only had the one bedroom and an antiquated kitchen, which had hundreds of deep grooves in the plaster by the door into the hallway. It looked to me as if something had been locked in there for months and had tried desperately to claw its way out. It was a very upsetting and extremely disturbing thing to see.

I could not work out why it was that all the internal doors had locks on the outer side of them. The apartment was obviously harbouring some very dark and hidden secrets which gave me the creeps.

It looked as if this was going to be our home for the duration. We just had to make the best of it.

As the weeks went by, I was delighted to feel my figure settling back to its original shape which was soon attracting the unwanted attention of Kevin.

"No, Kevin, it's too soon," I pleaded, yet another attempt at lovemaking being successfully thwarted. I had yet to have my follow-up appointment to discuss contraception.

Kevin continued to be forcefully persistent. I was slowly being worn down and was made to feel extremely guilty for denying him his marital rights.

My usual desire to please, at whatever the cost to me, took over. I relented.

The discovery that I had missed another period sent me into a complete meltdown. Kevin had promised me that he had taken the utmost care.

Why in God's name hadn't I held firm against his persuasive advances, and constant protestations? I was now castigating myself for my total weakness in giving in to his unwanted advances. As always, this was attributed to me not wishing to upset him. Now, due to my own stupidity, I was facing the unbearable prospect of another nine months of hell. The very thought of two children under the age of two was impossible to even contemplate. The very prospect was utterly overwhelming.

Evenings were spent with me either winging or whining, or in floods of tears until Kevin finally snapped.

We were in the kitchen where I was preparing the evening meal when the enormity of my situation began to overwhelm me.

As the tears began to flow down my cheeks, I turned to Kevin yet again, angrily shouting,

"This is all your fault, you couldn't wait, could you. You are just bloody selfish. Now you are forcing me to go through all of this again," I spat tears streaming down my face.

I did not see the blow coming. I was thrust backwards with such a force that I found myself on my back on the floor at the far end of the kitchen. The pain was excruciating. I lay clasping my stomach, unable to process what had just happened.

I looked up to see Kevin striding out the door without a backwards glance.

"Fuck you," he shouted back at me as the door slammed behind him. I heard the key turn in the lock.

Yes, I thought bitterly, that is about right and exactly why I'm in this mess in the first place.

I sat propped against the wall for what felt like several hours, unable to decided what to do next. It was then I felt a warm trickle running down my inner thigh onto the floor.

Terrified, I staggered to my feet and began hammering on the door, screaming at the top of my lungs.

Kevin appeared within minutes and taking one look at the bright red patch appearing on my skirt, he acted immediately. In no time at all, I was back in the hospital, propped on a cold, hard, steel bedpan, giving birth to a tiny little being which was instantly whisked away.

I spent several more days in hospital reflecting on what had happened to me and why, seesawing between unbearable guilt and utter relief.

I'm ashamed to say that relief was the overriding emotion, but the guilt continued to punish me.

It had been all my fault, I repeatedly told myself. I had selfishly driven Kevin to the point where he felt that this had been the only option available to him to put an end to my incessant nagging and complaining.

It had been me who had brought about this terrible thing. This is exactly what I told an Army officer as he sat beside my hospital bed. My hysterical screaming had subsequently alerted a neighbour who had reported the incident to Kevin's regiment, thus prompting an official visit from the Family Liaison Officer.

"Would you like me to make the necessary arrangements for you and Lucy to fly home?" he asked gently. "You do accept, Rita, that what Kevin did to you was totally unacceptable. He should not have treated you in this way no matter what the circumstances."

But I had convinced myself that the fault lay squarely with me. Although I would never forget what had led up to this terrible event, I had forgiven him. I loved Kevin with all my heart, so I was adamant, therefore, that I was going nowhere.

Of course, as years passed, I came to mourn the loss of that tiny little individual. The sheer selfishness surrounding what had happened that day was unforgivable on both our parts.

Life resumed uneventfully for several months until one evening, Kevin arrived home with an unexpected guest.

When I was told that he would be staying for tea, I was a little concerned that the meal I had prepared would not stretch around the three of us. But, with a little innovative thinking, I managed to produce a reasonable meal.

I left the two of them chatting together as I bathed Lucy, getting her ready for bed. On returning to the living room, I noticed an odd exchange of glances take place between the two of them, and with a nod of the head, Kevin jumped to his feet, reached into his pocket, and threw a small packet onto the sofa. With that, he walked out of the room and shut the door behind him.

The guy smiled at me, picked up the packet and was making his way toward me as he fumbled with his trousers.

I was suddenly aware of what was about to happen. I made a dash for the bathroom, being the only room that locked from the inside, and there I stayed listening to muffled voices and finally the noise of the front door being slammed.

"You can come out now; he's gone," shouted Kevin.

I was given little to no explanation from Kevin as to why he had tried to instigate this event. Only that he thought that I might have enjoyed it, a reason which I stupidly accepted.

"I most certainly would not have," I told him. "It's beyond me how you could have done such a thing," I declared. I was deeply offended that he would even consider that I would have enjoyed it. "Don't ever do that again," I told him in no uncertain terms. I always made excuses for him, wanting desperately to believe him, never questioning further his thinking behind such an unacceptable act.

The final few months of our time drifted by uneventfully.

The main highlight was the day the rains came.

Dust, dirt, urine, and camel droppings added to the indescribably rancid odour that rose from the ground as the long-awaited water ran in rivulets down the main street.

It was a smell the memory of which would never be forgotten. Yet I was glad that I had been there to witness the event, or I would never have believed that such a stench was even possible.

Our regiment was one of the very last to leave. The preparations had been going on for months. I was convinced that something was going to happen at the very last minute that would prevent us from boarding the plane.

It was not until I was safely seated, with Lucy on my lap, that I was able to relax.

Looking back down from the small window as the plane climbed upwards towards the clouds, I was able to appreciate the sheer scale of exactly what was being left behind.

There had been many changes to the infrastructure over time offering a more cohesive way of life for the Arab communities. This was our gift to them to enable them to continue to live in peace and harmony, but only time would tell.

Both sets of parents were there to meet us on arrival back in the UK. I had Lucy in my arms as we made our way through the arrival gates. She was already 14 months old and had never met any of her family before, so I was a little worried she may find the whole thing overwhelming, especially as both mothers were already holding out their arms to take her from me.

I glanced from one to the other, smiling broadly, and gently passed her to my mother. I need not have worried as Lucy giggled as she was being smothered with kisses.

I imagined that Mother must have kissed me in that way when I had been that small, but I could never remember an occasion.

Plans had already been made to go back to Kevin's parents for a welcome home meal.

Oh Lord, I thought, what will my mother make of his parents' home? I knew from past events how judgmental she could be. I just hoped that she could refrain from letting it show in her facial expressions. Anyway, it all passed off well and Lucy seemed to revel in being passed around from one to the other.

After many hours of catch-up conversation, it was decided that we would stay with Kevin's parents for the next few days, then make our way down to my parents.

I felt rather sorry for my parents as they had driven for several hours to meet the plane and were now being told to go home empty-handed, so to speak. But the decision had been made and it was out of my control.

Having finally made it down to Mother and Dad's, we had exactly three weeks before we were to join the regiment in Germany. I was more than ready for this as I was getting increasingly short-tempered with the constant advice, I was receiving on how best to bring up my child.

I was criticised for everything from what I was feeding her, how I was bathing her, to her bedtimes, with everything else in between.

It was starting to get to me. I had come a long way from Mother's control, and I was not exactly sure how much longer I could keep a lid on my temper. But I'm proud to say that I managed it.

I was so looking forward to our posting to Germany and was not disappointed. We were given a first-floor apartment in Monchengladbach, just outside of Düsseldorf. I could not believe how clean everything was.

After our last posting, it was a welcome relief. Unlike our previous accommodation, which had been rented privately, our new army apartment could not have been more different. It was of very generous proportions, large windows, and the most amazing, tiled floors throughout that you could see your reflection in.

Army quarters had to be left in pristine condition by the previous occupants.

Every scratch, mark, or stain has a financial implication. Ovens must look almost unused. Final checks done on the handover day even include the running of fingers along the tops of doors to check for dust. Therefore, when you finally get the keys and take receipt of your new accommodation, you can be assured it comes to you in absolute top condition.

Subsequently, it's important to maintain this extremely high standard.

This, of course, was right up my street as my school reports had rightly identified. Cleaning, polishing, and cleanliness were things I excelled at.

On my request, Kevin's first expense on moving into this impressive abode was to purchase an electric polisher.

Sad as it may sound, I found great therapeutic pleasure in the further improvement of the already dazzling shine to my floor tiles. The gentle hum of the rotating pad from this much-used machine could be heard daily from the flat below, my neighbour informed me.

I was also asked if any of the glaze still remained on the tiles.

Kevin had grown accustomed to removing footwear on the doormat outside before entering. This lapsed, of course, as time went on, but the buffing continued, nonetheless.

We were quite close to some basic shops, and it was not long before I started to get my head around bits and pieces of the language. I was soon able to ask for most things I needed, with a little help from a translation book that had been left behind by the previous tenants.

There was a lot of food that I was not used to, but one adapts, and I soon became more experimental with my cooking.

Once a week, a van selling bread and cakes arrived in the streets below. Everyone rushed to try to get first pick of the cakes, which were something you could only dream about, and the like of which I had never tasted before or indeed since. They were about 6 inches deep and indescribably delicious. I used to count down the days for the van's arrival and nearly always made it to the front of the queue.

People in our immediate area were very friendly, and I quickly made friends with other army wives.

By and large, they were a nice bunch, but I kept my own council on how much personal information I shared with anyone, as all too soon I discovered that the army jungle drums were hugely effective. Before you knew it, your life history could be imparted via many lips and would fly like wildfire around the barracks. Rumours were rife.

At times, it was hard to separate truth from fiction with some of the stuff that you heard.

Living in army accommodation was a whole new learning curve to navigate but I think I had adopted the right strategy.

I found the German locals somewhat reserved, and aloof. Lacking warmth, I would say.

They seemed to find it hard to return a smile in your dealings with them in the local shops.

I was not sure if this was because they had identified us as army personnel, or if it was a culture thing. However, I adapted to this in due course, and stopped trying to be overly pleasant with people.

In the months to come, a few crazy nights out transpired with several of these newfound friends.

These nights out tended to include huge glasses of German beer but always ended in good humour with no one ever getting too much the worse for wear.

It was always best practice to keep in mind the Army rules, which frowned upon soldiers who couldn't handle their alcohol, thus acting as a strong incentive to always apply moderation.

The prospect of time spent in the glasshouse, commonly known as the lock-up, was always the very best of deterrents.

One of these evenings found us all walking around Düsseldorf at the end of a somewhat raucous evening. This was an experience that came as a huge shock to me and one which I personally think the guys in our party had deliberately instigated.

We had turned a corner to find a whole street of big-fronted windows along both sides.

I could not believe my eyes as I stared at the scantily dressed women sitting or standing inside in very suggestive poses.

Some of the women were touching themselves and blowing kisses through the glass, trying to beckon us inside. I looked around at our husbands who were by now cat-calling back in reply to these girls.

I could not understand why young women would so blatantly belittle themselves in this way, but I'm ashamed to admit that I too found the situation somewhat erotic.

I was relieved when one of the other wives, also caught off guard by this display, decided to take control of the situation.

"Come on, you bad lads, party's over; time to head back," she commanded.

My relief was instant. I had been worried as to where this was heading. I knew that Kevin's views on such matters were much more liberal than mine. With their laughter ringing out loudly in the empty streets, they all turned on their heels and we headed for home.

I wanted to ask Kevin if he would have gone inside if the other guys had done so but was a little afraid of what his answer might have been.

In our one-year posting, we managed to fit in one of Germany's famous beer festivals.

These events are staged all over Germany, where people wearing their national costume come together to drink huge tankards of beer, sing German songs, dance to loud music, and eat large, spiced sausage in various forms. These festivals are the highlight of the year and are hugely popular with both Germans and the English alike. These nights inevitably end with everyone standing on the trestle tables, arms linked with other drunken revellers, waving their tankards from side to side to the music whilst spilling copious amounts of beer on everyone around them.

They can get very loud but are a lot of fun and I enjoyed the whole experience immensely.

Whilst we were stationed there, we managed a quick trip to Holland when we had some leave owed to us.

Again, a remarkably clean pristine country. The streets were immaculate. I wondered how they disciplined their citizens to keep such order. My country seemed to have lost the plot on just how to stop people littering.

I would have liked to have asked someone how they had mastered this. It seemed that acquiring such knowledge could be groundbreaking if we could change the mindset of some of the British people.

It was very noticeable that each house hung their duvets out of their windows each morning for the purpose of airing. I thought this to be a lovely custom but that would be one idea that could not be adopted in the UK due to the inclement weather.

It must be lovely getting into bed each night with a freshly blown duvet, I pondered.

My opinion was markedly different when we reached Amsterdam, where we took a canal trip down the river Rhine.

I was struggling to see what was capturing everyone's interest up ahead. As we came closer, we could see a massive mound of rubbish, smack in the middle of which sat a nesting swan with baby cygnets nestled close.

It was a truly surprising sight. The Rhine had seemed, sadly, to have become a dumping ground for unwanted waste.

It was quite a shocking thing to witness, and it changed my initial opinion of the place.

On the return journey, we saw endless acres and acres of fields of tulips as far as the eye could see. The colours were spectacular.

Kevin had now been promoted to lance corporal. We went out for a celebratory meal where I told him just how proud I was of him.

With the year's posting now ending, it was time to pack up again for the move back to what was affectionately termed as Blighty.

In the army way of life, one became accustomed to this nomadic lifestyle. It feels like a constant new adventure beginning. I found it all very exciting.

Handover went smoothly with no costs incurred, which always comes with a huge sense of relief.

With three weeks leave owed, we were able to get round to see all the relatives before heading to our next posting which was to be in Yorkshire.

We were hoping for Cyprus, but it was not to be. I had heard that it was a very nice place and had already started to look forward to going.

I just had to get through the family time. Best not to dwell on that, though.

This time, we were lucky enough to be given a two-bedroom semi-detached house. The army had acquired several properties on a private estate, so we were living alongside civilians.

If it was not for the haircuts, nobody would have guessed that we were army as most personnel tended to live on camp.

Although the rooms were a little on the small side, it was a lovely house that had a small fenced-in garden where Lucy could safely play.

The town had several lovely parks where I whiled away many a happy hour with Lucy feeding the ducks. I was getting a bit bored at home all day, so it was lovely to get out, but I knew that, at some point, I needed to start making a few friends.

Soon I started to get to know some of the immediate neighbours. It was mostly young families with children of similar ages who lived in these new starter homes. To the right of us lived a family of four. They had a three-bed house, and their garden was a lot bigger than ours and accommodated both a trampoline and a swing.

Their children were of school age and seemed a bit of a handful. Both parents worked, and the children seemed to be left to their own devices when they came home from school each day.

I expressed my concerns about this to Kevin one evening as we were sitting down to tea.

"It's not right that those children should be left on their own in that house; isn't it illegal?" I asked him.

"How should I know?" he muttered with a mouth full of food. "Don't get involved in other people's business, Rita," he said, pointing the end of his knife at me.

A few days later, I did make a point of saying to the oldest boy that I was here most of the time, should any of them need help of any kind. Unbeknown to Kevin, of course.

One neighbour, who introduced himself as Tim, lived two doors down and had three girls, one of whom was Lucy's age.

One day, I bumped into him in the corner shop and asked if his youngest child would like to come and play in our garden as I thought it would be nice for Lucy to have a little friend as she was getting older now and needed the company of someone her own age.

I wondered why it was I had never seen his wife about and was shocked to hear that she had walked out on him with his best friend several months before, leaving behind their three girls for their father to raise.

He'd had to give up his job as an electrician to care for them, he told me. I found this news quite upsetting. I could not understand for the life of me how any woman could leave her children behind, and with one so young too.

I imparted this sad news to Kevin that evening.

"There you go again," he accused, "getting involved in other people's problems. Keep your nose out, Rita. How many more times do you need telling?"

"I'm not getting involved, I'm just simply telling you that I could never do that, whatever the circumstances my kids would have to come with me," I told him.

"Yeah, well, you are getting too judgmental for your own good," he replied, getting up from the table and almost throwing his empty plate in the sink.

"You seem to think that you're better than anyone else, but that attitude will get you into trouble if you're not careful."

With that, I heard the front door shutting behind him as he left the house.

Oh great, I thought, off to the pub again. He was getting more like his father with every passing day.

As the months went by, Kevin's mood deteriorated further. I found myself tiptoeing around him rather the same as I had become accustomed to doing with Mother. He was spending more time out of the house than he was in it. I was also regularly catching him out with lies as to where he was and why.

The pub had become his preferred place to hang out in, rather than being at home with his wife and daughter. I, on the other hand, was accused of being selfish and mean-spirited. I was naturally thrilled when he arrived home one day sporting the broadest of smiles. Not wishing to detract from this very special moment, I asked,

"Oh hey, you look like the cat that got the cream." I chanced putting my arms around him, but he pulled away from me.

"I have bought a car," he proudly announced, glancing in the direction of the road where stood a very posh, and very shiny Mercedes.

"What do you mean, you have bought a car? Have we won the lottery?" I asked suspiciously, already aware of the current condition of our bank account.

"No, we have not won the lottery," he replied sarcastically. "This guy at work was selling it at a bargain price for a quick sale. He has been promoted and is being posted abroad, so I got it dirt cheap."

Not wishing to dampen his excitement over this latest acquisition. I asked gingerly,

"Where did the money come from to buy it then, Kevin?"

"I have taken out a small loan," he answered proudly, "It was such an amazing deal it would have been crazy to have let it slip through my fingers." He smiled broadly at me, whilst opening the passenger door so that I could sit inside.

True, it was a lovely car which had obviously been well looked after, but niggling doubts were starting to materialise as to just how small a loan was involved in this latest acquisition.

I did not even try to put this question to Kevin, knowing just how economical he had become with the truth of late.

It was also the case that I was eager to retain this wonderful sudden change that had come about regarding his mood.

Over the next few months, life had returned to something conducive to near-perfect harmony.

This was to be short-lived, however, as one evening, as we were settling down for an evening in front of the television, Kevin blurted out,

"You are going to have to get a job, Rita. You have to start doing your bit to help out financially."

I stared back at him trying to make sense of what he had just said.

"What does that mean exactly?" I asked. "We have a small child the last time I looked, Kevin, or have you failed to notice?" I declared incredulously.

"Don't be glib, Rita. You're sat at home on your backside every day, doing sod all, when you could be helping out financially. Why is it that you expect me to provide for everything?"

He had obviously been gearing himself up for this showdown, and he was now in full flow.

I sat there completely stunned.

After several seconds had passed, I was able to gather my thoughts.

"Do we have a money problem, Kevin?" I asked in the calmest voice that I could muster.

"We have always managed before." I needed to know what had prompted this new development.

"Things are tight, Rita. The loan for the car is now overdue, and if it is not paid next month, I will have to sell it, and I am not prepared to do that."

Oh, well now, here we have it just as predicted, this bloody car was at the root of it all with the ultimatum already delivered that he had no intention of parting with it.

"Well, would you mind explaining to me, then, just how I am expected to get a job when I have Lucy to take care of?"

He had his answer ready.

"You will have to get a job in the evenings, or nights, when I'm at home to have Lucy."

I did not wish to escalate the issue into a full-scale battle, which I knew I would ultimately lose. Neither did I feel that I could face the terrible consequences of going against him over his beloved car which obviously meant so much to him. No, that was an unthinkable option, I decided.

There was no other solution to this. In order to keep Kevin a happy Chappie I had to get a job.

There was only one problem with this as I could see it - the very real dilemma of what kind of job there could possibly be out there that I would be any good at, or that I could do and get paid for. Now, that was indeed the million-dollar question.

The following day found me scouring the news ads for anything at all that might fit my limited level of capabilities. As first feared, some qualifications were required for even the most basic form of employment.

I was becoming increasingly disillusioned when I spotted an advertisement that I believed would suit perfectly. It was for someone to work as a cinema usherette 5 evenings a week from 6 until 10.30 pm. Not wishing to let the grass grow under my feet, I telephoned and secured an interview for the following afternoon.

I could not wait for Kevin to come home that evening to impart the exciting news that I had indeed pulled off the impossible. I was unprepared for his initial reaction.

"What are they paying?" was his first question.

I went back to the advertisement to check, as I had not paid much attention to the hourly rate. I was just pleased to have found something; in fact, anything that I might be able to do, that did not involve a higher national degree was a bonus.

But Kevin was not of the same opinion.

"That's absolute rubbish, Rita, that's not going to even halfway cover the car loan," he complained.

Snatching the newspaper from my hand, he pointed to an advertisement for a bar person in a local nightclub.

"Here, what about this? It's much better pay, plus it's more hours."

"I can't do that, Kevin, I don't know how to mix cocktails; besides, it says here it does not close until 2 am in the morning. I won't get home until 2.30 am by the time I have walked home from the centre of town," I said, shocked, knowing full well that I would have to be up again at 6.30 am with Lucy who had always been an early riser.

"Why is it you always have to find the negatives in everything?!" he said accusingly. "They won't expect you to know everything to begin with. They will teach you how to make cocktails. Don't be stupid," he said, glaring at me. I knew that any further protestations would be futile.

"This will be perfect, Rita; you know we are desperate for the money."

The very next day, two phone calls were made, one to cancel the interview for the usherette position, and one made to secure an interview for a bar person.

The day soon came around for the interview. I had asked Tim if he could watch Lucy for me. I set off dressed to the nines.

Kevin had advised that they would be looking for a bit of glamour to put behind the bar to attract the punters. I did my best to look the part and had even had an expensive professional hairdo that morning and was relatively pleased with the result.

My nerves were getting the better of me as I sat waiting patiently in a very dimly lit area where several people were scurrying back and forth doing various tasks.

I watched as a very attractive girl with large breasts, which bounced about under a thin layer of a silk blouse, came out of a large oak-panelled door.

I know why she got her job, I thought as she passed by me. Judging by her, I stood no chance. Perhaps I should have worn my shorter skirt, I pondered.

Then, breaking my chain of thought, the oak-panelled door re-opened, and a guy who looked to be in his late forties popped his head out. "You can come in now," he said. He smiled warmly and introduced himself as Peter.

Thirty minutes later, I was leaving with the amazing news that I could hardly believe. I had got the job!

Kevin was jubilant that evening, though there were no congratulations, only one question.

"Are you paid weekly, or do we have to wait a month before you get your first pay packet?" The car is due two weeks from now," he reminded me. "If you are paid monthly, I'm going to have to try and stall them again."

This was a disappointing reaction to my news but at least the pressure was off, and we could focus on getting ourselves out of the hole that Kevin had dug for us.

Chapter 5

The training was traumatic as there seemed so much to remember, but someone was assigned to work alongside me for the first week until I got the hang of it.

I liked the atmosphere that I was working in, and the attention I was receiving.

The amount of alcohol consumed seemed to put everyone in a great mood which inadvertently reflected on their generosity.

I was picking up some very healthy tips. On most occasions, I was told to keep the change which I was informed was permissible. This proved to be very lucrative especially if it was a large note given, or if someone had had a big win on the roulette or card tables.

I decided not to tell Kevin about this unforeseen benefit, as I knew it would be commandeered along with my pay packet, which would more than likely end up in the tills of the local pubs at the weekends.

No, this little perk of the job was to be my Christmas kitty, so that I did not have to scrimp when the time came. Forward planning, I liked to call it.

Although I was still struggling with the lack of sleep, I was just about coping, catching a snooze when Lucy took her afternoon nap.

Kevin seemed a lot happier these days which made up for the sacrifices I was having to make.

One afternoon, I had settled down on the sofa to enjoy a quiet break when I noticed something shiny sticking out from the side of the sofa cushions.

I reached across to grasp it and found it to be a lady's hairpin. I slid my hand down further and discovered another two of the same.

Where had these come from, I wondered? It was baffling at first, but I finally concluded that these must have escaped the scrupulous handover regime, pushing it to the back of my mind.

That evening, before getting ready to leave for work, I related the unusual find to Kevin.

"Has it been known before for them not to look down the back of chairs when doing handovers, Kevin?" I enquired, innocently placing the found items onto the table in front of him.

"How do you expect me to have the answer to that?" His expression changing somewhat.

"God, I only wondered," I told him.

But at the back of my mind lurked the knowledge that I had regularly cleaned down the sides of all the cushions and had never come across them before.

It was not until several days later, when I met Tim buying bread in the corner shop, that further worries crossed my mind.

"Is everything alright?" he enquired; concern etched on his face.

"Yes, thanks, Tim, why do you ask?"

"It's probably nothing, but it's just that as I was drawing the lounge curtains around 9.30 last night, I happened to see your Kevin drive off in the car."

"What?!" That's not possible, Tim. It can't have been him; you must have been mistaken. He can't go out; Lucy is in bed at that time."

Seeing the confused expression on my face, he added,

"It was definitely him, Rita, but I'm sure he has a perfectly good explanation," he added trying to sound reassuring.

"I'm sure he has," I replied, hurrying out of the shop.

The afternoon was spent running every possible scenario through my mind as to why Kevin was leaving the house when he was supposed to be babysitting his daughter. This question was put to him most forcibly when he arrived home later that day.

"Where were you last night?" You went out and you left Lucy alone." Before he could respond, I continued, "Don't you dare try to deny it." My anger continuing to rise along with my voice. "You were seen leaving the house in the car around 9.30."

The colour drained from his face and I could see his thought processes trying to cobble something together that he thought might be plausible enough for me to believe.

"I ran out of fags," he said lamely.

"That is a blatant lie, Kevin," I said, pulling open the cupboard door revealing a remaining pack of 200 duty-free cigarettes brought back from Germany.

He knew then that he had blown it; he did what he always did when backed into a corner. He grabbed his coat and flew out the door, leaving me standing there, seething with anger, not knowing what was going on or why he was behaving in this way. I had no idea how I was going to deal with this new situation.

I had an hour to gather my thoughts before I was due to go to work. I could not see Kevin showing his face again in that time after what had just transpired.

I bathed Lucy, got her ready and wrapped her in a blanket and two minutes later I was knocking on Tim's door.

"Tim, I don't suppose you could do me a huge favour,"

"No problem," he said knowingly, standing aside to let me pass.

That evening at work was spent in a daze. I could not focus on anything, which, at some point, had evidently shown on my face. Someone must have complained, as later that evening Peter called me into the office.

"What's up?" he inquired anxiously.

"Does it show that much?" I sighed.

"Yep, come on, spit it out before you lose me any more trade."

I went on to explain what had happened, telling him I no longer trusted Kevin to look after our daughter whilst I was at work. He was very understanding and said if there was anything he could do to help, he would.

I went to collect Lucy when I finished work and talked over my concerns with Tim. I also told him about the hairpins that I had found down the side of the settee.

He was very understanding. He offered to keep an eye out in case it happened again. He also asked for my phone number so that he could get hold of me if he had to.

Although, I didn't think for one minute that Kevin would try anything like that again having been found out, I could not take the risk.

Tim had informed me that Kevin had been away from the house for roughly two hours that evening; anything could have happened in that time. I told Tim that I would put a spare back door key under the leg of the garden seat and gave him permission to gain entry if he felt it necessary to do so. I had to cover every eventuality to prevent my child from being put in any danger.

Kevin was very sheepish when he returned from work that day. He apologized for the worry caused but categorically refused to tell me why he had gone out that evening and had left Lucy alone. All he would say was,

"What is done is done." I was told to shut up making something out of nothing.

It was my belief at the time that he had sneaked off down the pub and thought that nobody would have been any the wiser.

What I found unacceptable was his total disregard for his daughter's safety. This, however, did not explain the small matter of the hairpins, something that was still niggling at the back of my mind.

Three weeks had passed uneventfully, and I was beginning to put the whole incident behind me.

However, this particular evening, I was in the middle of drying the newly washed glasses at the club, when Peter appeared.

"You're wanted on the phone; you can take it in my office."

Oh my God, I thought. What now? I grabbed the phone knowing full well who it must be as nobody else, but Tim had this number.

"Hello," I said anxiously.

"It's Tim," so sorry to have to tell you this, Rita, but thought you needed to know that your Kevin went out in the car 20 minutes ago. When there was no sign of him after 15 minutes, I thought it best to go up and check on things. I could hear Lucy crying; she sounded in a right old state, so I hope you don't mind but I let myself in. I have brought her down to mine and have put her to bed in the girls' room."

"Good God, Tim," I said shocked. "How could he do this to us? I'm on my way." I told Peter that something urgent had cropped up and that I had to get home. I think he suspected what was going on.

As I turned into our road, I was somewhat relieved to see our car parked outside our house. The front room curtains were closed so Kevin would not have been able to see me coming.

I decided to call into Tim's first, to see if he was OK with keeping Lucy overnight.

I could foresee a row brewing, and I did not want Lucy in the house if I could possibly help it.

Two minutes later, I found myself trying to grab onto something in Tim's kitchen to stop myself from falling as my knees began to buckle underneath me. I was struggling to take in what Tim had just told me.

"He has brought a woman home, Rita."

Total silence followed as I tried desperately to process what I was being told

"What? is all I could muster.

"What are you going to do?" he asked.

"I don't know," I stared at him blankly I had absolutely no idea at this point.

"You surely don't intend to go up there and face him tonight, do you? Please, Rita, wait here, at least until he takes her home," he pleaded, "things may turn nasty; I am worried how he might react."

I continued to stare back at him in silence trying desperately to see my way through the fog of numbness that had swept over me, it was at this point that burning anger finally kicked in, forcing me to act.

I flew out of Tim's kitchen and within seconds, I was flinging open the door to my front room to reveal my husband and a slim youngish-looking girl stretched out on the sofa in what could only be described as an intimate act. My anger had now reached an unprecedented level.

As they jumped apart, I was able to register the shock on both of their faces.

I charged toward them, grabbing the girl by her hair. I dragged her half-naked body down onto the carpet.

It was then that Kevin, having quickly taken stock of what was happening, leapt on top of me, pulling me backwards long enough to enable the girl to jump to her feet whilst grabbing a cushion to cover herself.

Now incandescent with rage, I screamed,

"Get her out of here now, you bloody bastard! How dare you bring this slut into our home?"

"Get a grip of yourself, Rita," he shouted into my face as he gripped me hard by both arms. "You will wake up Lucy screaming like a wild banshee. You're hysterical; listen to yourself. You're bloody mental, you are," his eyes now wide with panic.

"See what I have to contend with," he said, addressing the cowering girl, who had by now put as much distance between herself and me as she could in the small room.

"Get her fucking out of here now, Kevin!" I yelled again, before I scratch her bloody eyes out of her head."

Pushing past him, I took some shred of pleasure in informing him that Lucy was not upstairs in her bed but had been taken to a place of safety.

This was the final shot across the bow before I grabbed a duvet from the airing cupboard and headed for the spare bedroom.

It was a sleepless night spent worrying about it all. Wondering what the hell I was going to do. After all, there was a great deal at stake. There was Lucy to consider. I was still churning things repeatedly through my mind when I heard the front door close.

That was him going to work, I thought, peeking out through the curtains, and watching in astonishment as that girl, now dressed in a short skirt and high heels, long hair neatly piled in a heap on the top of her head, calmly walked down our garden path with Kevin toward our car.

In broad daylight. The sheer audacity of it.

Kevin even opened the passenger door for her. I looked on in complete shock, even horror, at the realisation that he had let her stay the night. Oh my God; it also crossed my mind that even worse, more than likely in our bed.

That act of absolute betrayal was what finally prompted the decision that this marriage was over.

I had not worked out what to do next, but one thing was certain. There would be no coming back from this. How Kevin could have been so cruel to do this to us was beyond my comprehension. I had forgiven him for a lot of things that he had done but not this. No, not this.

Later that day, I phoned Peter at work to ask him for a couple of days off work to sort myself out. I had already decided that going back to Mother for help was not an option. After finally getting it out of me what had happened, Peter provided a possible solution.

His sister-in-law, who lived in Blackpool, rented out her spare room. He was sure she would be only too happy to help.

"I will make a phone call. You get packed up with what you need, and I will pick you up at 4 pm before Kevin gets home from work," he promised.

I then went down to Tim's to collect Lucy.

"I've been frantic with worry," he said as he opened the door. "What happened?"

I went on to explain in detail the events of the previous evening. He was aware that the girl had stayed over as he, along with probably everyone else in the street, had seen them both leave together.

"What are you going to do now, Rita? Are you leaving him?" Without even waiting for an answer, he quickly continued, "He doesn't deserve you. You must know that. I have come to care deeply for you, and you and Lucy can move in with us, I would take good care of you both."

I stared back at him in disbelief.

"Oh Tim, you have been such a wonderful friend, you have done so much to help us, but you must know that will not be possible."

I went on to explain carefully that I needed time to heal from all the hurt. Things were very raw and painful. There was no way that I could ever contemplate starting a new relationship. I went on to tell him of Peter's offer to help me escape my situation, and I promised to stay in touch.

I begged him not to disclose any of my plans to Kevin. He promised me that he wouldn't.

As I left his house with Lucy for the final time, he kissed my cheek and wished us luck.

Cases now packed and piled up by the front door, I watched for Peter's arrival from the front window.

I was becoming increasingly nervous as the time grew closer. What if Kevin came home early and caught me leaving him? The last thing I wanted was for Peter to become embroiled in my domestic drama, as I was aware of what conclusions Kevin would immediately jump to in such a scenario.

By the time Peter pulled up outside, I was shaking uncontrollably. We hurriedly piled my belongings into the boot of his Land Rover.

Safely seated inside, I glanced back at the house as it disappeared from view. It was with a huge sense of relief but also with a very heavy heart that we headed for the motorway.

Destination Blackpool.

Fortunately, Lucy slept for the best part of the journey, so we were able to achieve it without a toilet break. The car came to a stop outside a semi-detached house on a busy thoroughfare.

Peter jumped out, grabbed the suitcases and we all made our way to the front door

Moments later, a voluptuous-looking lady welcomed us into a brightly coloured front room.

She introduced herself as Kathleen, before disappearing to make a cup of tea.

Trying to reassure Lucy, I pointed out the ceramic dolls sitting in a glass cabinet in the corner of the room. But I sensed she was still distracted and confused by her unfamiliar surroundings.

I need not have worried, however. Kathleen had reappeared with a tray of tea, and a bag of assorted sweets which she bent down and handed to Lucy. With a soft, patient voice she said,

"There you are sweetheart." Have you been looking at Aunty Kathleen's dollies? I will get some of them out a little later for you to look at; would you like that?" she asked, smiling broadly.

Lucy's head nodded vigorously as she popped a sweet into her mouth.

I knew then that things would be OK.

I expressed my gratitude to Kathleen for taking us in and explained that I would, of course, be paying my way.

Thank the Lord for my Christmas savings which would take the pressure off until I could get things sorted out.

We said our goodbyes and heartfelt thanks to Peter who was heading back home. Then Kathleen took us up to show us our room. It was pleasant enough, with a double bed, which I would be sharing with Lucy. The rest of the furniture consisted of a wardrobe and a dressing table.

Kathleen handed me a pile of towels and pointed out where the bathroom was.

"If you need anything else, just shout," she offered kindly.

With our few belongings put away, I sat down on the bed with my arms around Lucy.

"Everything will be alright, sweetheart," I told her tenderly, as much to convince myself as to reassure her.

A couple of days had gone by before I could bring myself to phone Mum and Dad to let them know what had happened, but when I did, all hell broke loose. Dad was furious with me.

"How could you disappear like that without letting us know your whereabouts, Rita?" he blasted. "That was very selfish of you; we have been frantic with worry. Kevin has been to our house looking for you. He threatened your mother with God knows what if we didn't tell him where you had gone. We tried to tell him we didn't know where you were, but he didn't believe us. I hope you realise that all this worry has made your mother ill."

Whoops, I had not seen that one coming. I had not bargained for Kevin getting to them before I did so all that remained was to try to mitigate the damage.

Without going into any detail, I explained that my marriage to Kevin was irreparable and that I had to find suitable temporary accommodation. I went on to explain that I had not made this decision lightly but had thought things through very carefully. I added that there was absolutely nothing to worry about. I would get in touch again when I had got things sorted.

But Dad would not give up until I had told him where we were staying, and who with. He promised me that he would not impart the information to Kevin.

I was a little uneasy giving him this information but felt I had little choice in the matter.

With an appointment set for the end of the week to get help to find more permanent accommodation, I felt very confident that I was beginning to get our lives back on track.

Two days later, I was getting Lucy dressed when I heard the front doorbell ring. Hearing footsteps on the stairs, I looked up and was shocked to see both my parents standing in the bedroom doorway.

"What are you doing here?" I asked, shocked.

"We have come to take you home with us," said Dad looking concerned.

"No, you have no right to come all this way to tell me how to lead my life."

"Now look here, Rita, there has been a serious development. We had a phone call last night to say that Kevin is in hospital. He tried to commit suicide."

As this information sank in, my jaw dropped open as I stared blankly back at them.

"What has that got to do with me?" I replied defiantly. It was then that Mother intervened.

"Now look here, my girl. You are a married woman now you can't just take your child and run away from your responsibilities, and just give up on your marriage when things get tough. You have to work at it like your father and I have had to."

"I know Mother I don't need a lecture thank you, I am an adult now I can make my own decisions," I pointed out

Mother just ignored what I had just said and continued, her tirade, "You have driven Kevin into doing this terrible thing through sheer desperation at the thought of losing his family, You do realise how serious this could have been, don't you? He nearly died, Rita. You would have had to live with that for the rest of your life," she exclaimed finally.

Now my mind was in complete turmoil. I felt that Kevin had manipulated this situation to get his own way, to get us to go back to him out of sympathy. I believed that if this had indeed been his intention, there would have been no coming back from it. No, he was too much of a coward to do a proper job of it.

As I was unable to fill in the gaps as to why our marriage had ended so abruptly, it left my parents with a less than favourable view of their daughter, and their daughter's actions.

Dad took a more conciliatory tone. He begged me to return home with them. I could still make a new life for Lucy and me, if I still felt strongly on the matter, he told me. But he advised there were ways of dealing with situations and this was most definitely not the right way of doing things.

After another 30 minutes of cajoling, I finally buckled under their persuasive rhetoric and found myself yet again packing suitcases.

Having thanked Kathleen for her kind and generous hospitality, we loaded up the car and began the long journey back.

Who would have ever thought that I would land up back under my parent's roof? I reflected as we made the long and arduous journey back to my childhood home. I consoled myself with the thought that it was better for Lucy to have a more stable environment.

It had, after all, been several years since I had last lived there. Maybe, just maybe, Mother might have improved with age.

Kevin had been informed that I had finally shown up, and at the earliest opportunity, he was banging on the door, begging for an opportunity to 'talk things through, as he put it.'

Although I was absolutely determined not to relent to his pleading, my lack of resolve in this regard was pathetic.

His tactic of choice was that it was all the fault of the army. If he had been in Civvy Street, he would never have done what he did. All squaddies messed about with other women, he confided. If you did not, you were deemed a pussy. His words, not mine.

If he could only get out of the army, he could get a proper job, away from that kind of temptation. He could settle down with his family, who he loved desperately. We could even try for another baby, he offered as a further carrot. It would be a travesty to throw away the love that we once felt for each other, or the possibility of such a perfect life that we could share together going forward. It would be worth every penny that it would cost to buy himself out, he declared excitedly.

He played me well, knowing that I was well-renowned for being a complete pushover. He had successfully worked his magic. The only obstacle to this amazing solution to all our problems remained that neither of us possessed the money to achieve this brilliant plan.

The following week, I found myself sitting next to Dad on the sofa, asking if they could possibly lend us the money to achieve this goal. "We will repay every penny," I promised sincerely.

It took two weeks for the Army to draft the necessary paperwork, by which time I was looking forward to getting back to being a proper family again. I felt confident that, this time, things would be very different.

I think that Mother was also quietly counting down the days as she liked order in her house, with everything in its place.

Poor Lucy had nearly all her toys confined to the bedroom and any deviation from this rule was deemed to be a mess which she frowned upon.

It was agreed that we would live with Kevin's parents in London, where Kevin felt that he had a better chance of getting a job. I was not relishing the idea as it was a tiny flat and seemed cramped at the best of times.

"It will only be short-term, until I get a job, then we can rent somewhere of our own." It all sounded so easy I fell for the dream.

For the first couple of months, Kevin avidly searched the papers and was sending applications out for many positions he thought were suitable. He was experiencing many of the problems that I had when I was looking for a job - lack of qualifications or experience.

Due to Kevin's desire to make a hasty exit from the army, he had left without the benefit of the extensive training courses usually offered when you leave at the end of a contracted term.

These courses are designed to prepare you for civilian life.

Knowledge, you have acquired in the army tends to be very specific and is rarely transferable to the civilian workplace.

I passed the time cleaning the little flat to within an inch of its life. The kitchen was tiled from floor to ceiling in grey tiles, at least I had thought they were grey until I began cleaning. They turned out to be white. Around the cooking area, they were a deep orange.

This proved to be a huge undertaking and by the time I had finished, there was very little left of my fingernails.

Kevin could not understand why I was going to so much trouble and dampened my enthusiasm somewhat by telling me that it would be back to how it was within months of us leaving.

But I was pleased with the result and moved on to the next task - our bedroom.

Lucy had a small bed positioned along one wall, and our double was placed against the other. A chest of drawers fitted into the only remaining space, with our suitcases on top containing most of our clothes.

I had planned to redecorate but, seeing how impossible this would be due to the congested space, I settled for a thorough clean. At the very least, I felt happy that it was clean.

Despite the facelift, it remained a depressing place to be in so much of my time was spent walking around the streets with Lucy, just window shopping. There were no parks nearby to take her to and she was becoming increasingly bored and miserable.

We were now into our third month. Kevin still had not even secured an interview and was becoming increasingly frustrated and angry with the process. He began finding fault with anything that I said. Lucy was also getting the brunt of his frustrations.

I tried everything I could think of to keep us both out of his way so that he could do his daily trawl through the job ads in peace, but his irritation increased when again the search proved fruitless.

Three months on, with still nothing on the horizon, money was tight and living in such cramped conditions with everyone under each other's feet was taking its toll.

Kevin started going to the pub some evenings with his dad. I had not minded at first; I thought it would do him good to get out. It would take his mind off things for a bit.

But when it became a regular nightly occurrence, I began to worry about the money it was costing.

This became an issue when I needed new shoes for Lucy as her feet were now growing so rapidly.

"I need some money for new shoes for Lucy," I told him one evening as he was getting himself ready to go out.

"You will have to wait until the next social security cheque comes," he replied nonchalantly.

"But that's another ten days away."

"So?" you will have to wait ten days then, won't you?"

"No, Kevin, she needs them now; her toes are squashed right up to the top of the ones she has. I don't want to damage her feet."

"We don't have the money she will have to wait," he told me.

"If you were to stay in this evening, perhaps we could afford them," I told him crossly.

He did not comment further. He just applied his aftershave, picked up his house key, and followed his dad out the door.

Kevin was now rolling in every night, stinking of beer, speech raised and slurred, talking absolute rubbish and bumping into furniture. It was becoming increasingly difficult to hold my temper.

This came to a head one night when he stumbled in around three in the morning.

"Where have you been until this hour?" I demanded to know.

"Mind your own bloody business! I don't have to ask you what time I can come home," he slurred.

I could see that there was no point in pursuing this. Lucy was now awake and listening.

So, I just turned over and tried to get back to sleep. Next thing, I smelled the strong smell of beer as the pushing started behind me.

"No, Kevin; Lucy is awake."

"Come on, Rita, you're becoming a right frigid cow, no wonder I'm forced to go elsewhere," he said, turning onto his side beginning to snore loudly.

The shock shot through me like a dart.

The next day, he denied having said any such thing but admitted that he couldn't even remember arriving home.

I refused to speak to him any more on the matter. I was still not speaking to him when he left the flat at lunchtime. He returned three hours later, the worse for wear yet again, taking himself straight to bed.

This routine continued for another two weeks, out to the pub every lunchtime and every evening. He tried to tell me his dad was buying most of the drinks. This may well have been true, but Kevin never had any money left by the end of each week which proved otherwise.

The last straw came when Kevin stumbled through the door late one evening, covered in someone else's blood.

I was in the middle of trying to obtain the reason for this when there was a loud banging on the door. Opening it revealed two uniformed police officers, who promptly handcuffed Kevin and marched him off to a waiting police van.

The following day, Kevin arrived back having been charged with assault. He had apparently just been innocently chatting with a girl. Her husband had got angry and had threatened him and he had been forced into giving the guy a good hiding. He had it coming, he informed me, but I knew the police don't charge the innocent party. The guy was currently in hospital with serious head injuries. Kevin was now facing a court case and possible imprisonment.

It was clear to me that this relationship was never going to work out. Within the hour, I was packed and sitting on the platform in the train station with Lucy on my lap, waiting for the train that would take us, yet again, back to my parent's house.

Four hours later, I was sitting opposite Mother and Dad, relating the full account of what had happened over the last four and a half months.

Mother simply looked at me with disappointment etched on her face. Her old school view always had been to stick it out at all costs, regardless, to simply grin and bear it, whatever is thrown at you.

Dad's usual approach to this issue had a more conciliatory view.

"Well, you gave it your best shot, Rita; no one can say you didn't try."

He didn't even mention the fact that it was he who was now financially out of pocket having provided the money to buy Kevin his freedom, money that he may never possibly recoup.

Kevin only visited his daughter on just one occasion. He arrived one and a half hours late accompanied by a young woman in red plastic-looking knee-length boots, bleached blonde hair, and heavy eye make-up.

She stood leaning against the side of the car, smoking a cigarette, not even giving a cursory glance in the direction of Lucy as Kevin placed her into the back seat. She ground her cigarette out onto the ground with the toe of her boot before getting into the passenger seat. Then they were gone.

It was the first time Lucy had been away from me since she had been born so it was a frightfully anxious weekend. I was terrified that he would not return her. I was unable to focus on any activity, my mind in a constant state of flux, conjuring up all manner of possible horrors.

I had even formulated a plan of action in the event of the worst scenario.

But it all proved unnecessary as Kevin arrived back ahead of time, and it was a huge relief.

I had convinced myself that having gone through the whole ordeal once, it would be easier and less stressful the next time.

It had been arranged that Kevin would have Lucy every other weekend. So, as arranged, we were ready and waiting for his arrival. As the clock ticked on, it became apparent that he was not coming. This made me very cross.

He would have to be told that I would not allow him to upset and disappoint his daughter in this heartless way.

I walked down to the phone box to call his parents to impart this information, and to tell them just how cross his apparent lack of commitment to his daughter had made me.

His mother answered the phone, and before I could embark upon my well-practiced rant, she delivered the news that Kevin had attended his court case, which had not gone well for him.

Due to the severity of the case, he had been given a prison sentence.

This was difficult news which I had not expected. However, as Kevin's victim was still hospitalised with some kind of brain injury, it was an inevitable outcome.

Chapter 6

With the knowledge that Kevin would not be around to provide financial support for his daughter, I had to now begin making plans to secure a new future for Lucy and myself.

I was adamant that I would not be reliant on government assistance. Therefore, the first task in hand was to get a job to allow me to become financially independent.

I could see that this could not be achieved without the support of Mother, at least until I could get on my feet. Mother would have to be on board to help with childcare. Fortunately, she was happy to help.

I did, however, have slight reservations about whether this support could be maintained over the long term.

Sadly, everyone was being made to adapt to the changes brought about by the breakdown of my marriage.

Mother was still working mornings at Timothy Whites, so whatever I did initially, it would have to fit in with her routine.

After trawling through the ads for several weeks, it became clear that finding something to meet my specific needs would be no small task.

Mother came up with a less than welcome solution one evening as we sat around the supper table discussing what I had achieved to date.

"Why don't you give Snippets a call? It's worth an ask, Rita."

I was not overjoyed at the thought of going back there to work, but Mother was trying hard to help, so the very least I could do was to give her suggestion a try. After all, having had to put up with me once, I was fairly confident of the outcome of such an approach.

So, the very next day, I walked down to the village phone box and made the call.

It appeared that fate had stepped in. The timing of my call remarkably coincided with one of their hairdressers leaving on maternity leave in two weeks' time.

There was an opportunity for me to step in for six months on a part-time basis, possibly more if the hairdresser in question did not return after her period of absence had expired.

Well, that suited me fine. Six months would allow me sufficient time to look for something more suitable.

Maybe I could find something entirely different, or even retrain to do something that I can excel at. Now that would be an exciting prospect.

This would certainly take the pressure off for the time being, which was a huge relief.

Mother was pleased as punch that evening when I told her the news that her idea had borne fruit.

We talked through the finer points of how the childcare would work with regards to timings and were satisfied that the agreed arrangements would work perfectly.

Two weeks later, there I was, back travelling on the same bus, going to the same place, to do the same job. It was as if I had dreamt all that had happened in between. I had come full circle back to where it had all begun; how utterly strange life was.

Nobody would believe it possible if I were to tell it, I reflected.

The weeks rumbled on, and everything was running relatively smoothly, apart, of course, from the fact my hairdressing skills had not improved with time. It was my job to take the walk-ins, as they were called, clients who popped in on the off chance without an appointment.

My feelings of inadequacy and lack of confidence came to the forefront yet again.

I was extremely nervous with every client, scared that I would make a mistake, or simply that they would not be happy with my creation.

I could cope if it was just a trim or a shampoo and set. But if it was a colour or a perm, then my coping strategies, similar to those I used at school, came into play.

I would listen from a safe distance to what the client was asking for.

If it fell into the scary category, I would disappear into the toilet, safe in the knowledge that someone else would take the client.

This worked successfully on most occasions as people tended to book appointments for treatments that took longer to do, therefore making it easier for me to get away with my shameful deception. I found it strange that nobody ever caught on to what I was doing. Well, at least, I was never challenged over it.

It never once occurred to me that I would never have been given back my job if they had not been happy with my work.

It's a terrible and painful thing to suffer in this way; a hugely destructive problem that some battle with all their entire lives.

I always left work at the same time every afternoon to catch the return bus home.

One evening, I was waiting as usual, eyes firmly fixed into the distance for the familiar shape of the bottle-green number 53 bus, when I noticed a silver-grey car slowing as it passed by. I took little notice as it picked up speed again and carried on its way.

The same thing happened again the next evening, but this time, it slowed long enough for me to make out a man's head lowered below a sun visor looking across at those of us waiting for the bus.

This is strange, I thought. What's he up to?

The following evening, I was watching with interest as the same car slowed long enough for me to take in the man in more detail. He appeared to be smiling at me. I cautiously returned the smile, and, as in previous afternoons, the car then continued on its way.

This had seriously sparked my interest.

The next day, I found myself actively looking up the road waiting for its arrival, intrigued by this mysterious man. This time, the car came to a halt. The man leaned over and wound down the window.

"Hello, would you like a lift?" he asked.

I was not at all sure what to say as I quickly considered his offer. He seemed nice enough, I decided. I did not think he posed any danger.

"Thank you," I said, climbing into the passenger seat.

He introduced himself as Mark Hanson and made polite small talk on the journey home which was over almost before it began. However, in that time, I was able to form an opinion of him as we chatted.

He was not what I would term handsome but there was something about him that was quite unexplainable.

He was a small-built man with black hair. He had rather a largish nose, with black bushy eyebrows that seemed to almost meet in the centre.

I thanked him for the lift and wondered if it would be repeated, or if it was just a one-off.

Sure enough, the next afternoon, there he was again. This time, I hopped in readily, feeling a little more at ease in his company.

I learned that he was an insurance rep and was working in the area.

He went on to tell me that he was married with a little girl, and that his wife had left him three months ago and taken their daughter. He told me that she had already started divorce proceedings.

Instantly, I felt that we had something in common, a kindred spirit. I did not make the connection that his circumstances were more in tune with Kevin's than with mine.

I went on to tell him about my circumstances, but only touching briefly on how I came to be living back with my parents.

He appeared to be a very caring person by the way he talked and told me how hard the last three months had been for him trying to cope without his wife and beautiful daughter, who, incidentally, turned out to be roughly the same age as Lucy.

"We must meet up with the girls," he suggested. "Access has not yet been agreed but my solicitor is working on it."

He went on to tell me that he was expecting a letter any day and would let me know so that we could coordinate a playdate.

It was not an official date as such as it was purely about the children, but I thought it was a lovely idea and such an arrangement would help to break the ice with the children there.

I could not wait to tell Mother and Dad that I had made a new friend who wanted our children to meet.

"Don't you think that you're jumping in too soon, Rita?"

"No, I don't," I replied defensively. "It's only a playdate for the children, for heaven's sake, not a proper date. Anyway, nothing has been arranged for certain," I said, knowing full well that I hoped it would be very soon and would go on to lead to something more.

"Well, I hope you know what you're doing," Mother went on to say as a final warning.

As it happened, the days rolled on and although I waited anxiously each day at the bus stop, Mark did not arrive. I had, in fact, reached the point where I had given up on the whole idea and convinced myself that he had had a change of heart.

Life continued to trundle on in a mundane routine.

Mother had started to become irritated with Lucy. As she was getting older, she was naturally getting into more mischief.

Each day on return from work, I would be subjected to a barrage of complaints about what terrible things Lucy had inflicted on her throughout the afternoon.

Today was no exception. On my return, I was marched into Mother's bedroom where I witnessed firsthand the reason for her mood.

Drawers had been emptied onto the floor. The jewellery box had been emptied onto the dressing table, and there seemed to be a lipstick drawing on the mirror. There was also a very pungent smell of mother's best perfume hanging cloyingly in the air.

There, in the middle of all this devastation, stood my daughter who appeared to be dressed in one of Mother's best nightgowns with a set of pearls adorning the neckline.

She was perched on a pair of Mother's heeled shoes, and she had jet black eyebrows and bright pink lipstick plastered almost up to her nose.

Taking in the vision in front of me, I could contain myself no longer and just burst into hysterical laughter, collapsing on the bed behind me.

Mother was incensed at my total disregard for the seriousness of the situation as she saw it and proclaimed angrily,

"What the hell do you find funny about this, Rita? This is down to you, that this child is turning out the way she is. You completely spoil her. She is allowed to do exactly as she pleases. You have not the slightest idea about discipline. You need to smarten up your act, Rita, or you will be making a rod for your own back. You would never have done anything like this; I would have simply not allowed it," she added, finally running out of steam.

Trying my best to contain my laughter, I replied,

"She is four years old, for heaven's sake; all children play dress up. There is no harm done. I will clean things up. Anyway, where were you while she was getting into all this?"

There was no reply, she simply turned on her heel and marched out of the room.

"Come on, young lady, let's get you into the bath," I said, scooping Lucy up and kissing her lipstick-plastered face.

Two weeks had elapsed when I saw the familiar car heading towards me at the bus stop. I must confess his absence had only injected more interest for me. In fact, I surprised myself by just how excited I was to see him again. When he pulled up, I hopped in beside him.

"Hi," I said brightly

"Sorry I've not been around; I have been working away."

"Oh, have you?" I tried to sound as if I had not even noticed his absence.

"Well, my solicitor has sorted out the access thing, and I will be picking up Lilley on Saturday afternoon. Do you still want to join us for that playdate? Perhaps we could take a picnic to the park if you like?"

"Oh, yes, that would be lovely," I agreed.

Lucy could hardly contain her excitement and was first out the door when they arrived. She jumped eagerly into the back of the car and smiled at the little girl sitting next to her.

Lilley was the total opposite of Lucy. Where Lucy had straight ash blonde hair and chestnut brown eyes, Lilley's hair was long and wavy and was jet black and matched her beautiful eyes. She was a vivacious-looking child with rosebud lips and a creamy-white porcelain complexion.

"Ready for some fun?" Mark asked, looking at both the girls' little faces.

"Yes!" they both squealed in unison.

So, off we went to the sound of us all singing, The Wheels on the Bus.

It was a delightful day. I was so impressed with Mark's little girl; she was a quiet demure little soul and so well behaved. What a lovely friend for Lucy, I thought. I could envision lots more happy outings ahead of us all.

This sadly proved not to be the case, as, despite my making several attempts to raise the subject of another playdate, Mark was not forthcoming and appeared to be almost reluctant to even discuss the matter.

I was disappointed; I thought that both girls had enjoyed the day and I could see no reason for not wanting to arrange another, but I decided not to push him.

We continued to go out together mostly at the weekends. During the day, Lucy was always included in our plans. Mark was very good with her, and she seemed to have taken to him, happily riding on his shoulders when we were out on walks.

In the evenings, we did the usual things - pub, local restaurants, cinema, and on one occasion, bowling. Things seemed to be progressing well.

I had introduced him to my parents, and, although they said very little, they appeared to like him.

This particular Saturday, he had invited me to his home. He had previously explained that he had a ground-floor apartment in the next village to where I worked. I must admit that I was looking forward to going. I was interested to see how he lived. It also crossed my mind that this might be our first opportunity to be alone together.

I made sure that I chose my underwear carefully for the occasion.

It was nothing like I had imagined; it was bright and spacious, with large windows. The decor was beautiful, with expensive-looking furniture and thick luxurious velvet curtains with tie-backs.

A gorgeous sheepskin rug lay in front of the fireplace, and coloured glass ornaments adorned the shelves. The lighting was low and seductive.

Mark walked over to the stereo and put on some of what he described as mood music.

"Drink?" he asked.

"Oh, yes, please," I replied, still taking in the beautiful surroundings.

He disappeared into the kitchen and came back in clasping two glasses of wine.

"It's a beautiful apartment, Mark," I told him, taking a sip from my glass.

"Thanks," come on, I'll show you round," he said getting up.

I followed him into the kitchen which was very spacious and had marble worktops. I followed him into the bathroom which was a beautiful avocado green and a larger than average size.

The apartment had two bedrooms, the smaller of` which he told me was Lilley's room, a pretty little room designed very much with a little girl in mind.

What I did notice, however, was that everything was still in place, all the child's toys remained as if she still lived there.

I followed him into the main bedroom which had obviously been decorated by a woman; all the colours blended beautifully, with the bedding and curtains all matching. There was a rocking chair in the corner with a matching scatter cushion placed on the seat, and coloured glass ornaments again festooned the window ledge.

Just at that moment, Mark's phone rang, and he excused himself and left the room.

I stood for a few seconds taking in the detail of the room. Curiosity getting the better of me, I reached across and slid open the mirrored wardrobe door.

I was gazing at what appeared to be all of Mark's wife's clothes and, looking down, I could see a line of neatly placed shoes and sandals. I slid the door closed and waited.

I was trying to work out how to confront Mark about what I had seen, so I was trembling when he strode back into the room.

I brushed past him back into the living room where I stood with my back to the fireplace. There was no other way of dealing with this, so I came straight out with it.

"It looks to me that your wife and your daughter are still living here, Mark.

I have been hurt very badly by one man and I have no intentions of making the same mistake again. You have lied to me. Now you need to take me home," I stuttered, fumbling for my coat.

"What the hell are you talking about?" he said, shock written all over his face.

"All their stuff is still here. The wardrobe is still full of her clothes. Your daughter's toys are all still in her room. Don't take me for a fool. Mark,"

"Her stuff is still here because she did not want to take it. And as for the toys, those are all new; I have bought them for when Lilley comes to stay. Here, if you don't believe me, read this," he said, thrusting a Manila-coloured envelope into my hand.

I opened the letter and the heading read Marshall & Ferris, solicitors. I read on; it went on to lay out legal proceedings for the application for a divorce for the above-mentioned parties, clearly giving Mark's full name and that of his wife. It concluded with a date for the hearing three weeks from now.

I looked at him now feeling very guilty that I had not trusted him. I handed back the letter with a sheepish look on my face, thinking that I had totally messed up.

But he simply put his arms around me and told me that I had to learn to trust again and that he completely understood why I had reacted in that way.

He was right, of course, I had to learn to trust again. This night was a good night to start the process.

We made love that evening and fell asleep in each other's arms. I still did not understand why it was his wife had left without taking her clothes and personal items. Nor did I ask the question why he would go out and buy all those toys when he was clearly not intending to have his daughter over to stay.

Every free moment he had, he spent with Lucy and me.

I know I should have asked those questions, but I didn't. I was afraid that he would again think that I did not trust him.

Several weeks went by before I plucked up the courage to ask him when we would get to see Lilley again. He replied that he had come to the decision to make a clean break. His wife had not requested child support, so he thought it would be better for everyone concerned if we all moved on with our lives.

This was not right to me on any level, and I told him so.

"Please, Mark, don't say that. She is your daughter; you can't possibly mean that."

"It is my decision to make, and I have made it and that is the end of the matter," he said stubbornly.

I was saddened by his determination on the matter as I felt very strongly that he would come to regret that decision in the years to come.

But for now, I was pleased that my intervention had not caused further discord between us as our relationship continued to flourish.

In the absence of her real father, Lucy started calling Mark 'daddy' and I just let it happen naturally. He was lovely with her and treated her as his own. She had become very attached to him.

There had been a change in the dynamics at home. My grandmother, who was in her nineties, had fallen in her own home and so the decision had been somewhat forced onto Mother to have her living with us.

This new situation of an elderly lady and a four-year-old living under the same roof very soon began presenting issues.

The problems Mother encountered with Lucy's active personality would be magnified ten-fold.

Not a day passed without some complaint or other about the noise, the untidiness, or the sheer disobedience of my growing child. It was making it impossible to work, as I was beginning to dread going home for fear of what I would face when I walked through the door.

I was particularly tired one afternoon when arriving home. I'd had an awful client who had been extremely rude and had complained about me to my boss. When I walked in the door to a hullabaloo going on in the kitchen, I was in no mood to placate.

The issue was regarding the little coffee table which was set up every teatime for Grandma to have her tea on in front of the television. Lucy had gone into the living room and taken Grandma's knife, fork, and spoon off the table and run off and hid them.

It was completely beyond me why such a drama was being made from such a minor thing.

If I had not been so tired, I would have laughed it off but not this afternoon. In my view, this was a small child just being mischievous. But to the affected parties, Lucy had committed some cardinal inexcusable sin and should be severely punished.

The point of no return was reached when my grandma spat out her venom that the child was out of control, a wicked child who should, in her view, be placed in a children's home.

The red mist descended, I can only say that like a lot of Taurean-born, once angered, look out for the charge. And charge I did! Grandma's expression quickly changed as I bent down and shouted into her shocked face.

"You are a nasty, spiteful, old lady. How could you dare say such a hateful thing about a tiny child?" I hissed. "If anyone should be in a home, it is you." With that, I scooped up Lucy and flew out of the room.

As was usually the case, Mother sided with Grandma. I was declared disrespectful, ungrateful, and inexcusably rude.

To keep the peace, it was yet again me who had to do the apologizing.

In the months that followed, things remained tense as we continued to walk on eggshells.

Mark's divorce had come through. His ex-wife had made no financial claim in the final settlement. She had appeared to have walked away from their apartment, all its contents, her clothes, and all her personal belongings.

She simply took their daughter, and even more odd was that Mark seemed to be perfectly happy with the whole arrangement. He had adopted Lucy and I as his new family and had made the conscious decision to move on.

Although this all seemed very strange, at the time, I stupidly chose not to question the circumstances further. I was just happy that it was all behind us.

My divorce now final, we began making plans for our future together. There was no proposal; in fact, it felt more like a mutual agreement. I don't think either of us mentioned the word love. We just kind of grew together over a period of time; it just seemed the expected thing to do, merely a natural progression of events.

We began looking at houses in the area. There was a new estate being built in the next town. We went and looked at several finished properties and chose a lovely 3-bedroom house overlooking a large green.

I could hardly contain my excitement and could not wait to move. Equally, my parents were more than happy to hear of our plans. They seemed to have taken to Mark and had welcomed him into the family.

We went to meet Mark's parents to tell them the news that we had decided to get married. They lived in a large Victorian house on the coast. It was a strange weekend. His parents seemed very nice but strangely, although sharing the same house, they both lived in different parts of it.

They led separate lives, did their own shopping, and prepared their own meals.

When questioned about this, Mark just said that they had lived like that for as long as he could remember.

We had planned a registry office wedding, a very low-key affair with just parents, two of my work colleagues, and of course, Lucy. The whole thing seemed over in the blink of an eye. There was no celebratory meal. Everyone just disappeared off back to where they had come from with just a final hug and a goodbye.

It had been our choice to keep things simple, as, although we had a sizeable amount of money that had come from the sale of the apartment, we still needed to add to it for a deposit on our new home.

We spent six months getting the house just the way we wanted it. Mark had changed his job. He now worked nightshifts in a factory making fencing panels. It was boring work, but the salary was a lot higher.

Lucy had started at the local school. She had never attended a nursery school, so she found the whole experience traumatic, to say the least. The teacher had to prize her fingers off my clothes every morning as she clung to me, screaming hysterically. She had never been apart from me before, so it was very distressing for both of us. I would return home everyday sobbing, which continued to be a daily dread for several weeks.

The funny thing was, when I picked her up in the afternoon, she was as happy as a skylark. It was about this time I had discovered that I was pregnant. We were absolutely thrilled to bits. There would be a nice age gap between the children, with Lucy now at school, so I could focus more on the baby.

I had made friends with a couple of mums who I had met at the school gates who also had new babies, so I now felt that I was beginning to fit in. I had also made friends with a couple of the neighbours who I got on well with.

One couple were quite posh; their names were Steven and Anita. Steven was in banking, and Anita owned a lady's fashion shop in the town which is where I had first met her. They were a very down-to-earth couple, so I did not feel in any way out of place when I went for coffee.

The other couple were married, and their names were Shirley and Denis. They only had one child; a boy called Antony. Shirley suffered from depression.

I had also formed the opinion that Shirley was a bit of a hypochondriac as she consumed a whole cocktail of medications daily that she carried around in a shoebox.

I felt quite sorry for her husband, who seemed to struggle to cope with Shirley's illness.

But it was nice to form these friendships.

Mark had been working overtime in the last several weeks to buy the nice things that we needed for our new baby. Life was finally coming together.

That was until the unthinkable happened, turning my life into a living hell.

I was busy washing up the tea things in the kitchen and Mark was upstairs getting ready to go to work when there was a knock on the door. Who on earth could that be? I thought as I went to open it.

I was shocked to see a male and a female police officer standing there.

"Is Mark Hanson at home?" asked the male officer in a stern voice.

"Yes," I stuttered, stepping aside to let them in.

"Mark!" I called up the stairs. Looking up, I saw him standing on the top step gazing down at us with a worried look on his face.

The policewoman grabbed me by the elbow and guided me into the kitchen, leaving the male officer talking to Mark in the hallway.

"What's going on, what's happening?" I asked nervously.

"Your husband is being arrested," she replied.

"Arrested," I repeated stupidly, not really taking in what she had just said.

"There has been an allegation made against him."

"Allegation! what allegation?"

"Your husband has been accused of rape."

"Rape! No, that's not possible. You have the wrong person," I stammered.

"There is no mistake," she said gently.

I turned my head to the side and looked out of the window to see Mark being placed in the back of a police car. I looked back at the policewoman, who was now putting the kettle on.

"Let's just have a cup of tea; it will help with the shock," she advised, now guiding me into the living room where I slumped onto the sofa. She sat down next to me and put her arm around my shoulders.

"This is not easy for you, I know," she said, trying to comfort me. She paused to answer her phone then continued. "Your husband has been posing as a professional photographer working for a famous glamour magazine. He has been targeting attractive women with the promise of big earnings. He gained access to their homes and has taken photographs of them scantily clothed, however, on this occasion, he took things to another level, raping the lady in question. She took the number of his car, telephoned her husband, who then telephoned us."

"No, that's not possible; Mark works nights, and sleeps through the day. When is he supposed to have done these things?"

"The incident happened at 9.30 last Tuesday morning."

"Well that's proof it wasn't him then. He wouldn't have had the opportunity to do what he is being accused of, he was working overtime that day and would have still been in his work overalls. "Anyway, I know him, he would not do that to us," I insisted. I began shaking uncontrollably, tears now streaming down my face.

The officer stared at me and continued,

"I have just received the call informing me that a change of clothes and a camera have been found in the boot of his car. If you take my advice, my lovely, you will give him his marching orders as soon as you can."

"I will do no such thing," I blurted out angrily. "Mark has been a good, loving, hard-working husband. This will all be sorted out, I'm sure of it," I said, convinced that this was some huge mistake.

Having established that I did not intend to do something stupid, the policewoman, now reassured, decided that I was safe to be left on my own but handed me a piece of paper with her phone number on, just in case I might change my mind about it.

When on my own, I sat staring into space trying to make sense of the situation in which I now found myself, not knowing what would happen next, or which way to turn.

The night was spent in a mixture of fear, panic, and sheer desperation. I got Lucy ready for school, trying my best to appear normal so as not to cause her concern. I tried to avoid any conversation with any other mums when dropping her off and hurried straight home to sit by the phone waiting for news.

The call came just after eleven o'clock. I snatched up the phone and heard Mark's voice on the other end say,

"Rita, listen carefully. I have not got long. They have charged me; you need to get someone to post bail for me for three thousand pounds to get me out of here," he said anxiously.

"What?" Where am I supposed to find that amount of money from, Mark?"

"I don't care; go to your parents, ask your friends, just get it. I can't stay in here, Rita, it's terrible."

"What have you done, Mark? Is it true what they are accusing you of?"

"Rita, I don't have time to explain all that right now, just get me out of here and I will talk to you when I get home," he said with irritation showing in his voice. "You have to help me, Rita. If you don't, I will be stuck in here until the trial. Please, Rita," he begged.

"I can't ask anyone for that amount of money, Mark. Why would they do that for us?"

"Rita, just tell them as long as I show up for the court date, it won't cost them anything. They don't have to come up with any money, they simply have to sign to stand as guarantor for me. Tell them I can be trusted. I won't let them down."

With that, the phone went dead. He had been cut off.

I had now been placed in the impossible position of begging someone to trust Mark enough to invest the princely sum of three thousand pounds, and that if he absconded, and did not turn up on the date expected, they stood to lose their money. It was a huge risk for someone to take when they have only known you for such a short period of time.

This was a daunting task and one that I dreaded, a task which I needed to summon up a great deal of courage to carry out.

That afternoon, I reluctantly went on my begging mission. Despite not disclosing the full nature of the crime committed, the response was the same in both instances. Sorry, but we don't wish to be involved in anybody else's drama. Well, who could blame them? It was a big ask, and quite frankly, understandable. So, I returned home empty-handed, to try to come up with another solution.

To ask my parents was not an option with the memory still painful of Dad having funded Kevin to begin a new life with a disastrous outcome. I had no intention of imposing this latest debacle on them.

No, I had made my bed; I had to lie on it. I could not, and would not, go to them for help again. It was time to sort out my own mess. Actually, it was Mark's mess, but it was me having to sort it.

By the end of the afternoon and a few phone calls later, I had come up with the solution.

I had borrowed the money using the house as collateral. I knew that I could repay the loan as soon as the court date had passed, with very little interest incurred. I felt quite pleased with myself and could not wait to tell Mark that he would be home very soon.

Chapter 7

Mark had insisted that he did not want me to attend the court hearing. I was, therefore, left completely in the dark regarding the facts of the case. He maintained he was only thinking of me as he could not bear the thought of putting me through such an ordeal.

He had told me that his solicitor felt confident that as it was a first offence, he would most likely get probation, which is exactly what happened. He would be assigned a probation officer who would initially visit weekly to ensure there were no arising issues.

However, very little light was shone on what had happened, or indeed why, as Mark found it all very painful to discuss.

He simply said that he had hoped that this could be a new career for him as a photographer. He wasn't intending to tell me what he had been doing until he had sold his first photos.

He explained that he had a momentary lapse and had gotten carried away. He accused the girl of encouraging him, which she had regretted after the event, panicked, and confessed to her husband. He categorically refused to shed any further light on the subject.

I was therefore forced to stop pressing him on it.

I managed as usual not to listen to the myriad of doubts forming in the back of my mind, one of which was the fact that the policewoman had volunteered the information on the night of his arrest, that the camera found in the boot of his car had no film inside.

If he had indeed been considering a new career in photography, that would have been a bit dumb, to say the least.

Then there was the overtime lie. The hidden change of clothes in the boot of the car. The whole thing was too absurd to be believable.

On and on it went, over and over in my mind, with no possibility of escape from it as he simply would not elaborate further on what he had already said. I was probably never going to get to the truth.

The first problem that I encountered was that the very first Sunday after the case, Dad turned up on the doorstep ashen-faced. He barged into the hallway saying,

"Pack your things, Rita, you're coming back home."

"No, Dad. Why?" I asked nervously.

"You know perfectly well why, Rita. It's all over the front pages of a National newspaper not to mention the local paper," he said agitatedly, thrusting a newspaper into my hand.

"No, I am not going anywhere. Mark has been a good husband, Dad, and whatever he has done, I'm sticking by him. I'm his wife; I'm expecting his baby and we are going to get through this," I told him forcibly.

"Then you have made your bed, Rita, now you must lie in it," with that, he turned and left.

This confrontation was quite shocking as I had naively been unprepared for it to become public knowledge.

This became very apparent at the school gates the next morning as people huddled together whispering and giving me cursive glances from a distance. I found it very upsetting. I chose not to worry Mark with this latest development. However, Mark had also had his share of backlash following the newspaper article, which I discovered when he arrived home not long after he had left for work.

"I've been sacked," he announced, crestfallen.

"Oh, no!" What are we going to do? How will we pay the mortgage?" I asked.

"Something will turn up; I will get another job," he told me reassuringly.

But something did not turn up - his constant rejections were apparently due to his conviction.

Things were beginning to look very bleak. In fact, I was beginning to worry about Mark's mental health. I confided my concerns to his probation officer on his next visit. I had come to trust him over the weeks he had been coming and found him easy to talk to.

He explained that this tended to happen when people had been convicted of a crime. He said employers tended to take it at face value and were not open to looking at extenuating circumstances.

Whatever those might be, I thought; as far as I was aware, there were none.

He went on to say that something would come up; we would just need to be patient. This was all well and good but being patient did not pay the bills. We were slipping further and further into debt, and there seemed no way out.

But Mark had hit on a possible solution.

"We are only currently using two bedrooms, so why don't we let one out? The income will keep the wolves from the door until I can find another job," he said, pleased with this revelation.

Even I thought he had come up with a good plan. There was no time like the present, so the next day, I set the wheels in motion and put an advertisement in the newspaper.

Two days after the advert appeared, we had several phone calls. Two men and three ladies.

After discussing it, we decided to discount the men, as Mark was not happy with me being alone here with them once he was back working.

I agreed with this as I too would not feel comfortable. Two of the girls were not suitable as one was on the social, and the other one seemed too young and had obviously left the care of her family too soon. I called the remaining girl who seemed suitable and arranged for her to view the room.

She seemed a little unkempt on arrival, but I tried not to judge her for that as she said that she was happy to see that the room was clean and well-furnished. I had also agreed to include the washing of her bed linen, which she found an unexpected bonus.

I handed her the key to the bedroom lock that I'd had fitted. She handed me the month's rent in advance and the deal was done and dusted in a matter of ten minutes.

We did not see much of her as she slept most of the day and went out in the evening. I never heard her come in so had no idea what her life involved. It was not my place to pry. As far as I was concerned, if she paid her rent on time, she could come and go as she pleased.

As time went on, it became apparent that we had a problem on our hands.

It seemed odd that I could never seem to catch sight of her with her unusual comings and goings.

Her next rent payment was due, and I had still not gained entry to her room to do her washing.

I had reasoned that perhaps she had been doing her own laundry, so at the beginning, I was not unduly concerned.

However, as the weeks rolled on and I had still not collared her for her now well-overdue rent, things were beginning to cause concern. I had put several notes under her door asking her to make contact, which had been ignored. I began to feel that she was deliberately avoiding me.

We had reached the second missed rent payment when I decided that I had to act.

I was unable to gain entry to the room as she held the only key. This had been an oversight on my part. When a terrible smell started emanating from the room, we were left with no other option but to force open the door.

What confronted us inside was so disgusting that it took several moments to take it all in. It appeared that the room had been deserted for some time.

There were dirty clothes all over the floor and the bedding had been heaped into a pile in the corner of the room. The mattress was completely blood and urine-stained. There were cigarette burns everywhere, on the bedside cabinets, all along the edge of the window ledge, even on the dressing table. Even the carpet, which had been newly fitted, was damaged.

I could not believe that anyone could have such disregard for someone else's property. It was truly heartbreaking. I was utterly speechless.

This first foray into the world of renting had proved an unmitigated disaster. The situation now needed salvaging. I put my best foot forward.

The room was stripped, carpet removed, bedside cabinets and dressing table sanded and revarnished, mattress dumped and replaced, and the door repaired.

We were ready to put this unhappy incident behind us and move on. We had to use the month's rent we had initially received to replace the damaged items, but you live, and you learn.

We were now back on track.

Mark had now acquired another job as a salesman with a small family firm, selling double glazing. Fortunately, there had been no questions asked. He was offered the job the same day as his interview, so things were on the up.

We decided to re-rent the room as the additional money would help us catch up with the debts we had recently accrued.

This time, I was much more cautious. I made sure to ask for references. I had asked for two months' rent upfront to cover any damage incurred. There were only two people who applied. One girl in her mid-twenties seemed by far the best out of the two.

She told me her name was Linda Mayhew and she seemed genuinely honest. She told me that she and her boyfriend had moved down from Sheffield, but they had recently split. She wanted to remain in the area because she had secured a very good job.

She was completely different to the other girl. We sat and chatted together for some time over a coffee.

I found that she had a great sense of humour which I took to instantly. To me, it was a no-brainier. When she left, I handed her one of the two sets of keys I'd had made. I accepted her deposit and was looking forward to having a trustworthy relationship with her.

I got on extremely well with Linda. Every evening, she came in and stuck her head around the kitchen door and, with a broad grin, would say, "Can I smell the teapot?" We would sit down together and chat about the happenings of the day before going she went up to take a bath.

We had formed quite a friendship over the weeks, and I was very glad that she had decided to rent from us.

The extra income was coming in handy, and we had managed to clear our outstanding debts.

Mark had settled into his new job and was doing well with his sales which was good as he worked on a commission-only basis so only got paid on results.

He had formed a good relationship with his boss, who I did not approve of after Mark told me that he was having an affair with his secretary.

I had met his wife when we were invited to their home for Sunday lunch. She was lovely, a naturally stay-at-home type of person, who was the centre anchor of her family of four young children.

She told me that she made all the children's clothes, except their coats. She baked her own bread and made jams and chutneys, which she proudly showed me all the different coloured glass jars, stacked, and dated in her walk-in larder, making me feel most inadequate.

She obviously adored her husband as she fussed over him, ensuring his plate contained every bit of the fare that she had lovingly produced.

I was deeply saddened by the knowledge of her husband's treachery toward her, which left me asking myself the question why.

Surely, he was not in his right mind to put his marriage at risk in this way with the possibility of losing such a dedicated wife, should she ever find out about his unfaithfulness. But then it crossed my mind that it had happened to me. I had been traded in for a more up to date model, so I knew that men often cruelly betrayed their wives. It never occurred to me that it may be something the wife was doing or indeed was not doing that could be the cause of this deceit.

I put this question to Mark on our journey home.

"How could he do that to her?" I asked, concerned.

"He must have a reason, Rita," he replied. "Perhaps there is a problem in the bedroom."

I did not understand this reasoning at all. What reason could there possibly be if a woman was pleasing her man regularly? Why was it that one woman was not enough for a man? After all, sex seemed to be something which had been designed entirely for the benefit of the male species. There certainly seemed to be no pleasure involved for the woman. Well, that had been my experience to date anyway.

Life continued uneventfully for the next few weeks. However, I had noticed that every evening after tea, Mark had been disappearing up into the attic. I had decided not to question him on this, due to an element of mistrust that still existed between us. I also knew I would possibly not receive an honest answer.

Besides, he was in the family home so what was there to worry about? I decided, however, that I would apply a different tactic to uncover the mystery.

One evening, after getting Lucy to bed, I returned to the kitchen to wash up the dishes.

Mark got up from the table, put his dinner plate into the sink and disappeared upstairs for the fourth evening in a row. I had made up my mind to get to the bottom of what he was up to. I gave it ten minutes then went upstairs.

The loft ladder was still in place, but the loft hatch was closed. That's odd, I thought; maybe he's in the bedroom. Not finding him in the bedroom, I knew he was not in the bathroom as Linda would already be taking her usual bath.

I had noticed her bedroom door was open and her clothes were spread out on her bed.

But where was Mark? I was on my way back downstairs when I heard a faint noise above me.

I returned to the loft ladder, climbed up and tried pushing open the hatch, but something was preventing it from lifting. I gave it an almighty shove sending it clattering sideways and took the final two steps up. My upper body was now inside the roof space.

What I witnessed took my breath away.

There was my husband in the corner situated directly above the bathroom, down on all fours with his face to the floor. His bare thighs were showing above his lowered jeans, his arm moving vigorously between his legs. It took only seconds to establish what was going on. He had made a way of seeing through a hole in the ceiling and was getting off watching Linda taking her bath.

I stumbled back down the ladder with Mark hot on my heels, desperately trying to adjust his clothes.

I flew into the living room slamming the door in his face. Undeterred, he burst in, making a grab for me, and trying to put his arms around me. I pushed him away with as much force as I could muster.

"How could you?!" I shrieked.

"Rita, please, I'm so sorry, please, Rita," he pleaded, trying to pull me into his arms.

"Don't touch me!" I bellowed, backing away from him.

I think he took one look at my face and understood the pointlessness of reasoning with me further. Quickly weighing up his options, he retreated.

"I will go out for a while until you calm down, then we will talk later," he said dejectedly.

However, I wouldn't mind betting that it may have crossed his mind that things would not calm down after what he had been caught doing.

My mind was in complete turmoil. I did not know what to do or which way to turn. In the hours that followed, I sat there on my own, staring into space and trying to make sense of it all. My emotions flashed between utter despair and white-hot anger.

What the hell is wrong with men? I asked myself. Why did they behave this way? I tried to evaluate my options.

The thought of leaving was quickly dispelled, as here I was pregnant, and with a five-year-old. I had to seriously consider what effect a further upheaval would have on Lucy.

In the absence of her biological father, she had put all her affections into Mark. He also appeared genuinely fond of her. It was an impossible situation.

The option to return to Mother and Dad was also quickly discounted. I could not face the thought of admitting that I had failed again. It had proved more than problematic sharing a house with them last time. I could not bear a repeat performance of that.

I knew that Dad would welcome me with open arms, but Mother would have a lot to say about it a second time around.

There seemed only one remaining viable option. I had to do my level best to lie in this uncomfortable bed that I had yet again made for myself.

I had to sort this mess out somehow. I was not at all sure how, but those were the cold hard facts.

All these deliberations culminated in the realisation that I was yet again facing similar relationship problems as before, laying bare the possibility that the fault may well lie with me. I began to question my own responsibility for why history was repeating itself.

Maybe this time it was because I was heavily pregnant and no longer looked desirable. I had read somewhere that men could go off the rails during a pregnancy.

Or another possibility was that I was just simply not enough sexually. Maybe I was not doing it right. Maybe there was something that I should be doing that I wasn't doing. Every possible cause was now dissected and carefully considered.

The comment Kevin had made in the early years of our marriage - "You're such a prude, Rita."

Or the recent comment of Mark's when I asked him why it was that his boss was being unfaithful to his lovely wife – "Perhaps there is a problem in the bedroom," he had said.

All these thoughts now adding fuel to my feelings of inadequacy.

After all, it was not happening for me either. I was not, nor had I ever enjoyed the act of intimacy. I had just endured it because I believed that it was my duty, never once denying my husband of his conjugal rights.

Yes, I had pleaded with Kevin to wait until it would be safe after giving birth to Lucy and look what happened when I had finally relented. No, it seemed most certainly a man's world.

It had never occurred to me that I should be achieving a similar level of satisfaction as the man seemed to experience. I knew no difference.

There had to be something wrong somewhere, I decided. After a lot of thought and self-recriminations, there appeared to me to be only really one possible answer to the big question of why.

The problem had to be me. It seemed obvious when you laid out the facts in this way. It was the only way that I could make any sense of any of it.

I had finally reached the conclusion that everything that had happened to me now, or in the past, had been of my own making. I had to therefore accept that I had been lacking. I needed to learn to be less prudish, be more experimental. I had to make more of an effort in the bedroom or I would lose my husband to someone else.

I would have an honest and open talk with Mark when he came home to discover the reasons behind why he felt he needed to resort to such extreme measures to satisfy his desires. I had to find out what it was that I could do to ensure that I could fulfil that need so that something like this would never happen again.

I then made possibly the worst decision I would ever make in my lifetime: I would stay put and I would make it work whatever it took.

I failed to comprehend the familiar pattern that was again reappearing. The cycle of trying to please to my own detriment was beginning all over again, but this time, taken to a whole new level.

Mark could not quite believe his luck that he had come out of such a terrible situation so well.

He seemed positively elated by our heart to heart.

A few days later, on his probation officer's usual visit, he was told that everything was going along very nicely. I had shared the news with him that Mark's company had made the decision to move the business to a new patch as they had exhausted the sales in the area. I went on to explain that they were so pleased with Mark's performance that they had made him head salesman.

He was genuinely pleased to hear this and informed me that as things were obviously working out brilliantly for all concerned. He asked me,

"Is there anything at all that has given you cause for concern, Rita?"

"No, I can't think of one single thing," I lied.

"Have you any worries at all about Mark going forward?" he persisted.

"None whatsoever," I said, trying to sound convincing.

"Well, in that case, if you're completely sure, then I'm satisfied that I can sign Mark off from my care so that you can both make a fresh start," he said, smiling broadly. "Good luck with the new arrival," he added as I showed him out for the final time.

Mark could hardly contain his elation; he felt he had finally thrown off the shackles of supervision.

Me, well, I felt as if I had just lost my safety net. If I fell now, there was no one there to catch me.

Be positive, Rita, I told myself. You can do this. I had a small reprieve, as there was still the small business of giving birth to get through before having to morph into a sex goddess.

Mark was very excited about the prospect of a more liberated wife, but I reminded him that being so heavily pregnant made it almost impossible now to initiate the new me. However, I had promised him that things would change once the baby had arrived.

I had thought it would be along the lines of sexy underwear, nightwear, new positions, etc., and a few dirty words here and there. I could do that, I thought. I might even enjoy it, especially the new positions.

The next two weeks were taken up with the move.

The first thing I found especially hard was to give Linda notice to leave which saddened me. I had grown quite fond of her.

It was, of course, no fault of hers that my husband had seen fit to observe her naked in the bath. Fortunately, she was completely oblivious to what had transpired that evening. I knew she would have been mortified, and more than likely would have given Mark a bloody nose on my behalf.

I was reassured to discover that she had managed to secure alternative accommodation very swiftly which was one worry less.

We had put the house on the market, our furniture in storage, and had made plans to move to a caravan site close to Mark's new place of work.

I had had no say in what we landed up with as it had been down to Mark to find us somewhere temporary until the money from the sale of the house came through. We would then be able to look for something more permanent.

I tried not to show my disappointment on arrival as I got out of the car. This shabby little abode looked for all the world as if it should have been towed to the scrapyard twenty years ago.

Mark picked up on my initial reaction and said hastily,

"It's cheap, Rita, and it's only for a short while." It had better be, I thought, trying to conjure up a weak smile as I unlocked a rusty-looking door. The inside was a good deal worse than the outside.

What the hell had possessed him to get talked into such a pile of junk? I wondered, taking in the threadbare carpets and stained seat cushions.

But make the best of it we did. I worked as much magic as was humanly possible by buying little rugs and covering the seat cushions. I even made new curtains for the windows, with two large pots of flowering shrubs taking pride of place at the bottom of the steps outside the door completing the picture.

Whoever gets this when we move out should afford me a letter of thanks in the local newspaper, I thought, satisfied with what I had achieved.

I had now developed a not very fetching form of a waddling gait and was finding it hard to move about. I was also having trouble sleeping at night as the seat cushions that doubled up as a bed did not seem wide enough to cope with my more ample proportions.

I was frequently clambering over Mark throughout the night to get to the toilet. My bladder was now bent out of shape by the pressure that it was being subjected to, deciding that it must surely be the size of a walnut.

Two days before my due date, Mark drove Lucy to my parents where she would remain until after the baby had been born. I had reached the point where I was constantly shifting positions and clutching my back. Swollen painful legs added to the joys of childbearing.

I had quite forgotten just how desperate you became in the latter stages, just wanting to get it out of you and get it over with, every day praying that any little niggling pain just had to be the start of something.

Three more days on found me in a cottage hospital going through the agonies of childbirth, with my screams adding to the chorus of all the other ladies along the corridors going through the same process.

Mark, unlike Kevin, was by my side throughout, doing what is expected of all new dads. What was even more impressive was when he had to change the gas and air tank when the one, I was using ran out, the duty midwife for the evening now up the corridor dealing with a more demented and louder screamer than I was.

I had done this before with nothing but castor oil, so I was finding the intoxicating substance of the gas and air sheer luxury. If there had been jungle juice on offer, I would have had that too.

However, at 8.10 the following morning, baby Lee appeared, 7 pounds 10 ounces of angel, all wrapped up in one tiny pink perfect package. He was stunningly beautiful.

Most of the other new mothers were out for the count catching up on missed sleep when I finally arrived back on the ward, but I was far too excited to sleep. I could not stop staring at this beautiful little being that we had created.

Mothers at that time did not discover the sex of an unborn child. You had to wait to see what God had given you. All expectant mums could always be heard saying that they didn't mind if it was a girl or a boy as long as it was healthy.

In my case, I had been desperately hoping for a son. I had my daughter and I wished for one of each. A perfect pair. So, when I heard his first cry, and when those magic little words uttered the words 'it's a boy, I could have leapt from the birthing table and kissed the midwife full on the lips. I was thrilled beyond belief.

Other mums seemed to enjoy the rest when their babies were wheeled back to the nursery, but I was having none of it; he was staying with me. It was all they could do to prize him off me for his nap after a feed. I just wanted to hold him close and gaze down at the little milk dots that had now formed on his little nose.

It was customary back then to remain in hospital for up to ten days after giving birth. In my case, this was a good thing as I was still in a lot of pain. Several nurses had teased me daily that I was acting like a drama queen as I hobbled along the corridor clinging to anything I could for support, as I made my way each day to the bathroom.

However, a very astute ward sister who was starting a new shift quickly identified that I had, in fact, dislocated both hips bearing down too hard in labour. I was then given anesthesia to pop them back in.

Those nurses learnt a valuable lesson that day and had a good deal of egg on their faces to boot.

I was treated with kid gloves following what could be regarded as a complete dereliction of adequate care.

But hey-ho, I didn't care. I had my boy.

I anxiously waited each day for a visit from my parents and Lucy, expecting them to be as excited about our new arrival as I was, but they didn't come which was disappointing.

The day finally arrived when I could take Lee home. There was a lot of discussion on the small ward about the speed at which my body had returned to normal. One lady, a farmer's wife, who had delivered her fifth girl, commented on the unfairness of it. Having given up on her figure after her third daughter, she could not help but show her envy not only because I had been given the gift of a son that she had so desperately wanted, but also that as I had changed that morning to go home, she had noted the complete absence of any stretch marks.

I was completely horrified when she lifted her nightgown and showed me a concertina of purple and red tram lines that criss-crossed her entire stomach and the tops of her legs.

My God, I thought, thank heavens I did not get afflicted with those. I could not see how that would have ever fitted into my new sexy image.

I remained confident that it would still be some time before I would be expected to come up with the goods in that direction.

My milk was now not just flowing but flooding in. Boobs the size of watermelons, and just as hard.

We went to collect Lucy and passed our new son around to everyone who showed an interest in holding him, and bit by bit, life began shaping back into a daily routine.

The house had sold, and we now had the money to go in search of our new home.

There was not a great deal available in the area in our price range, so it was not an easy task.

We found a little detached cottage opposite a church in the centre of town. It had three good-sized bedrooms and a large kitchen diner but had no back entrance or garden. It only had a yard with the ground level behind it at roof level.

Not ideal by any means, it was only good for storing the bins, which then had to be wheeled through the house on bin day.

I was desperate to get out of the caravan as it was impossible to cope with a tiny baby, and I was spending most of my time down the launderette. So, we agreed to go ahead and buy it.

It was not long after we moved in that Mother and Dad decided to put our family home on the market and move closer to us. I was not in favour of this at all as I felt I did not want them to part with the much-loved home which Dad had single-handedly and lovingly built for the family.

I wanted to be able to revisit with the children in years to come to show them where I had grown up, and just how clever their grandad had been in creating such a masterpiece. I could not bear the thought of someone else living there.

This was a very selfish attitude, I know, but I guess many people felt this way when saying goodbye to memories, even if, at times, some of them had been less than happy. It was still our family home.

But their decision had been made.

Dad had retired. Edward was now settled in the States, and they wanted to be closer to us and the grandchildren.

They found a lovely little bungalow on a small estate in the next town. The rooms were not nearly as big as where they were, but it had two guest bedrooms which |Mother had said were big enough for the children to stay over some weekends.

The town itself had a nice selection of shops, all located on one long flat high street. There was also a beautiful park that supported a large lake, and a good-sized play area for children, which also included a large paddling pool that was filled during the summer months.

All in all, I felt that they had considered everything carefully and chosen well.

Edward was now married, and they were expecting their first child. He had excelled in his job and had risen through the company ranks. He had now reached the lofty height of being a member on the board of directors of a company that designed helicopters for the American army.

Mother and Dad were naturally excited to go to visit them, to meet his new wife and see their recently purchased palatial home. So, a trip to the States was planned.

They were gone for a full month and returned home brimming over with praise.

They said that Edward's new home was huge, set in beautiful grounds.

Dad had built two large pillars at the beginning of their long driveway and hung two big, impressive gates. The photos were evidence of an excellent job done.

They had been invited to Edward's place of work and were taken into the boardroom and witnessed for themselves the large highly polished table that accommodated fifteen chairs, one of which displayed Edward's full name emblazoned on a brass plate. Some accolade indeed.

The pride that they both rightly showed in his achievements was obvious, which only magnified my failures.

Still, I was pleased that Edward had been so successful in what he had achieved.

Chapter 8

Lucy began sleepover visits to her grandparents' which she loved. She was older now and was more manageable.

Despite having decided to place Lee on the bottle, I still felt uncomfortable about him staying over for a whole weekend. My parents had, on a couple of occasions, offered to have him for the evening if we wanted to go out, but that was as far as I was prepared to go.

Mark had begun making more demands on me. We had already got into the realms of the sexy underwear and stockings. I had even agreed to some unconventional positions that I would not say that I had particularly enjoyed.

He soon tired of what was on offer and began making the kind of suggestions that quite frankly scared me to death. He was expressing a desire to have a three-way experience with someone. This I flatly refused to allow. But over the coming months, the pressure continued.

Every time we had sex; his pleadings intensified. He told me that this was the only sure way to fulfil his sexual fantasies; to deny him was breaking my promise of a more sexually fulfilling love life. I was informed that I was falling short of what was expected of me, giving rise to intense feelings of inadequacy added to which was the fear of losing him. I finally buckled.

I had recalled how I had felt a strange sense of arousal when seeing the woman on the stage naked on my honeymoon with Kevin, and when seeing the women in the windows in Düsseldorf.

I had decided that if I had to do this, I could only pull it off with a woman.

I agreed to go ahead but on my terms. It was to be a woman, not a man, and that he was not to take an active part but only watch.

I desperately hoped that this one-off event would sufficiently satisfy his lust, and he could continue with me happily with just the memory of it. I was either naïve or just plain stupid.

I was not sure how all this would be achieved but it was obvious that Mark had already given it some thought and already had a plan in place.

The next evening, he came home armed with a carrier bag full of sex magazines, in the back of which were advertisements for all deviant practices. With some, I had no knowledge or understanding that such things even existed until Mark explained them to me.

In fact, it was a complete revelation to me that people did some of these things. Some were altogether too shocking for words, making what we were about to embark upon mild in comparison.

There was a girl listed as an attractive bisexual blonde, aged twenty-five, looking for a sexual relationship with another woman of similar age. There was a box number for a reply.

A mixture of excitement, but mostly fear went through me as we sat down that evening to compose the reply to the advertisement which was posted off the following morning.

Her reply was swift and included a picture of a girl with brassy blonde hair, and a lot of makeup. Although she appeared average to look at, I would not have described her as attractive. A phone number and an address in Portsmouth were also included.

It crossed my mind as to how on earth I was supposed to have a sexual experience with this absolute stranger, but Mark seemed intent on pursuing it. I just wanted to get it over with.

We dropped the children off at my parents at the weekend and set off on this nerve-racking journey into the unknown.

By the time we arrived at the foot of a skyscraper block of flats, I was in a state of sheer terror, and ready to call the whole thing off.

We sat in the car for what seemed ages, with Mark cajoling and pleading with me to go in.

"We have come all this way, Rita. I won't come in with you the first time. I will wait out here and you can tell me about it later. Please, Rita, she is in there waiting for you. Just give it a go," he begged.

As I went up the seven floors in the lift, I pondered why it was that I was allowing myself to be manipulated in this way. If Mark was not happy with me sexually then maybe, he should find someone who could fulfil him.

The lift came to a shuddering stop, then the doors opened onto a long dark corridor. I paused outside the door of number 72, while I summoned up the courage to ring the bell. I took a deep breath and pressed it.

When the door opened, the blonde girl in the photo stood in front of me and smiled weakly. She said her name was Gloria and she stepped to the side to let me pass.

The flat was really dark. All the walls had been painted dark purple, there were beaded curtains where the doors should have been, and there were lit candles in saucers placed on the bare linoleum floors. She pulled a beaded curtain to the side to reveal a room with a bed in it, and a large spotlight pointed towards it.

I took a step back finding it hard to breathe; panic had taken hold of me.

"I'm very sorry," I blurted out. "I have made a terrible mistake; I can't do this." I dashed past her out through the front door into the corridor. By the time I had reached the car, I was in floods of tears.

"What's happened?" Mark asked as I leapt into the passenger seat.

"I can't do it; I think that she might have had someone in there filming. There is no telling what might have happened to me," I gasped.

"Don't cry," Mark soothed, putting his arm around me. "It was just not the right person; we will try something else.

I was just relieved to get out of there alive. In my mind, there was not going to be a 'something else.'

However, the following weekend found us on the road again, heading for London. Mark had been in contact with someone he thought sounded perfect, based only on the description in the magazine.

We had no photo which rang alarm bells for me, but Mark insisted that I was worrying unnecessarily.

We arrived at the address provided. It was a small mid-terraced property with metal railings that fronted a small garden full of weeds and a chipped concrete gnome standing on its doorstep. I phoned the number in the advertisement. A man answered and said that his sister had just popped out to get some wine and invited me to go inside to wait as he said that she would be back any minute.

"It's a bloke," he says his sister has gone for wine and will be back shortly. I'm not going in if she's not there," I told him defiantly.

"It's OK, Rita, don't be so dramatic. We can wait."

"Well, I'm not going in there until she comes back, and only then if he leaves."

There we sat watching the minutes turn into an hour. Mark was getting cross as we continued to wait outside for her return.

Relief flooded over me when, after an hour and a half had passed, Mark started the car to make the return journey home finally admitting that we had been duped.

I don't know what the outcome would have been if I had gone in. It does not bear thinking about.

Mark was in a terrible mood when we got home.

I made myself scarce until he had calmed down, quietly confident that this would now be the end of what I believed to be a crazy idea.

Several days had passed when Mark arrived home with bruises on his face.

"What the hell happened to you?" I asked.

"I've been down to London. That guy will think twice before he does that to someone else, and, if you think I'm bruised, you should see him. He deserved all he got," he said, triumphant.

Oh, my God, this was never worth it.

Why can't you just be normal, I thought. Surely other marriages did not have to endure these trials.

Mark continued to search the magazines for a suitable connection. He came across a girl who wanted a genuine loving friendship. After much discussion and searching for any pitfalls that could be associated with her, I responded to the advertisement.

Her name was Clare, and she was 7 years younger than me. She looked a kindly soul in the photos that she sent me and had the largest breasts I had ever seen. Mark's eyes lit up when I showed him her photo. He simply said, "WOW."

I began a somewhat lengthy dialogue with her by mail and on the telephone.

Mark was getting increasingly impatient for what he considered a far too cautious approach, but I felt safer getting to know her better before inviting her to our home. So much bad stuff had happened in the past that I was taking no chances.

I had been honest and upfront with her from the beginning about what was expected from the relationship, and on that understanding, a date was arranged for a visit from Friday until Sunday when the children were at their grandparents.

The visit went well as she was warm, kind, and loving. She was perfect for my first initiation into the world of deviation and, although it began somewhat awkwardly, I liked her. Her body was soft and voluptuous and exciting to explore.

Mark kept his part of the bargain and watched quietly from a chair strategically positioned.

It was very difficult at the beginning, as I was very aware that he was in the room, but I enjoyed the intimacy. Mark made love to me afterwards with renewed vigour.

If it meant keeping my husband happy, it was all worthwhile. I had convinced myself that we weren't hurting anybody after all was said and done, and it was kept well away from the children.

Oddly, I was eager to repeat the experience, and Mark was certainly in favour of it.

Clare spent a couple more weekends with us before the conversation turned to her staying for longer periods. We decided that she should stay in the spare room through the week and would only come into our room at the weekends when the children were at Mother and Dad's.

She arrived the very next Friday with what looked like most of her belongings. I had redecorated her room and bought new bedding and curtains and had made it look very welcoming.

I had explained to the children that a friend was coming to stay with us for a while.

She thoughtfully brought gifts with her for the children which helped to break the ice when they arrived home on the Sunday.

They took to her instantly and responded to her warm and loving personality. It was a huge relief as that had been my biggest worry. It very soon became apparent that Clare wanted to live with us permanently.

As a result, it was necessary to provide a plausible reason as to why a perfect stranger had moved into our home, a reason which would placate my parents. We decided to tell them that we had employed a nanny, as I had intended to return to regular employment.

Fortunately, they accepted this without question. When they met her, they said how lovely she was. I hated lying to them and was initially stricken with guilt regarding this most irregular lifestyle that we had embarked upon.

As I came to trust Clare more with the children, I began to like the idea of returning to the working world and began actively searching for work, giving some credence to my original lie, and making me feel better about the deceit.

Surprisingly quickly, I managed to obtain a job at a children's and baby's boutique called Popsicle in the mall in the centre of town. I absolutely loved the job and initially only worked part-time.

This very soon developed into a full-time post when the owner discovered just how capable I was of selling. I had increased sales remarkably since I arrived, which reminded me very much of my very first job when leaving school, in the little corner shop, where

I had successfully convinced customers that they needed to add cooked meats to their list of shopping lists.

I had finally found my niche in the world, something that I was good at, albeit a very small accreditation. Well, who would have guessed it?

Life had become so synchronised that it was hard to believe that 18 months had flashed by.

We had all got into a very workable routine. Clare clearly adored the children, and they were equally fond of her. She was able to devote so much more time to them than I could with her being home most of the time.

I must admit to feelings of jealousy given the fact that she was proving to be their go-to person of choice as opposed to me.

But I also accepted that she was indeed a little gem who I valued deeply, more as a friend really, but with bedroom privileges.

She only came into our room when the children were at my parents, but she never complained.

Over time, Mark had managed to sneak himself into the bed with us, but never crossed the agreed line except for the odd occasion when I felt a hand creep over for a grope of those beautiful large breasts. But by and large, he kept to his side of the agreement.

He, like the children, had bonded closely to Clare, but this became the accepted normal as we knitted together as a family unit.

It became obvious just how deep Mark's feelings were for Clare when his younger brother Derek came to visit for the weekend.

Derek, who was completely unaware of our situation, began blatantly flirting with Clare.

Clare seemed embarrassed by his approaches but seemed unsure of how to stop it.

Mark was becoming more and more concerned with these developments. He tried his level best to tactfully intervene but was failing miserably.

On the first evening of Derek's stay, it was getting late, and nobody seemed to be making a move to retire to bed. I started making up a bed for Derek on the settee in the hope that he would take the hint and call it a night.

Mark was trying diplomatically to make Clare aware that it was time to make her excuses and come to bed.

Derek, on the other hand, had no intention of retiring for the night and tried his level best to convince Clare that she should stay up a little longer to chat. He just assumed that Clare was on the market for a relationship and was clearly making a play for her.

Mark's approach to a difficult situation won the day, and Clare made her apologies and came up to bed.

The next day Derek stepped up the ante further by asking Clare to go out for a walk with him. She looked directly at us for our approval and was uncertain as to what to do when none was forthcoming. She appeared to have no other choice but to agree to go with him.

Mark fretted the whole time they were out, which seemed like hours.

By the time they returned, his mood had deteriorated further, and he was not speaking much to anyone, creating an extremely uncomfortable atmosphere.

Exacerbating the situation further, Clare was annoyingly laughing at everything Derek was saying, even things that were not remotely funny.

The day wore on and I was beginning to worry about how we would manage the bedtime routine.

To make matters worse, Derek had taken Mark's seat when he got up to use the toilet and had positioned himself next to Clare on the sofa. Tensions increasing further when he took hold of her hand.

I was shocked to see Mark turn on his heel and announce that he was going to bed.

I went on up a short time later leaving Clare to come up when she was ready, feeling sure that common sense would prevail, and that she had picked up on the fact that Mark was unsettled by her reactions to Derek.

I was awakened later in the night by a lot of shouting, crashing, and banging. It sounded as if someone was being murdered downstairs. I ran out onto the landing and leant over the balustrade to see if I could see what was going on. Two minutes later, the children were out of their beds frightened by all the noise.

The shouting had ceased, and a loud bang confirmed that the front door had slammed. I made the decision to stay upstairs to settle the children and get them back into their beds.

Shortly after, Mark came back up. His pyjama jacket was open with buttons missing, he was sweating profusely, and his hair was dishevelled.

"What's happened?" I asked, almost too frightened to hear the answer.

"She was in bed with that bastard is what's happened," he shouted.

"What did you do?"

"I threw him out on his ear," he replied as if to say what would you have expected me to do.

"Mark, Derek was not to know the situation. How could you do that to your own brother?" I asked surprised.

There was no further response; he simply turned on his side and went to sleep.

The next morning illustrated just how possessive Mark had become over Clare, as I assessed the damage in the front room.

Two legs on the settee were broken, bedding lay in a heap on the floor and the coffee table lay on its side with a broken fruit bowl, along with last evening's mugs, in pieces on the floor. My lovely potted plant lay completely unearthed from its pot and lay in two separate pieces on the carpet which was now covered in soil.

The thing that hurt the most was my broken standard lamp that had been a wedding gift from Mother and Dad, the shade of which was completely bent out of shape as if someone had thrown their full weight at it.

"OH, MY GOD!" were the only words I could utter as I surveyed the destruction.

"Where is Clare?" asked Mark as he came into the room with a concerned look on his face.

I ran upstairs into her room. The wardrobe doors lay open to reveal a line of empty hangers.

I slowly made my way back downstairs. I turned to face Mark as he waited for my response.

"She's gone," I said slowly "I hope you are happy with what you have done." With that, I turned and left the room.

Clare's sudden departure had a profound effect on us all, creating huge repercussions.

Mark, of course, had been quite rightly left with a lot of guilt.

It had all been so avoidable. If he had been straight with his brother from the start, there would have been no misunderstanding. I'm sure he would have understood.

I was instantly forced to leave the job I had come to love, thus having an impact on the home finances.

The owner of Popsicle was also not at all pleased with my sudden departure with no notice given. I was told I had turned out to be a complete disappointment to her and had placed her in an impossible situation.

I felt a huge sense of disloyalty, which I found very upsetting.

The biggest impact was felt by the children, far worse than I had first anticipated. Lee, only being 2 years old, did not really understand why it was that Clare was there when he went to bed and gone when he got up. I could tell that he missed her as he repeatedly asked where she was.

I was totally unprepared for Lucy's reaction, as she burst into tears when she was told and ran to her room. This would require much more sensitive handling.

Lucy kept up her mourning over the loss of Clare for many days to come. It was even proving difficult to get her to eat which was very worrying. I was relieved when, at last, we had turned the corner with the whole saga. Slowly, things started getting easier.

I could not have been more wrong. Future events proved otherwise.

It all started when I noticed money going missing out of my purse. It was only small amounts, but enough for me to start asking questions.

Lucy, now turned eight, was allowed to go to the corner shop just along the road to pick up a pint of milk, or a loaf of bread. I always allowed her to keep the change from what I gave her to buy some sweets for doing this little errand for me. But I was noticing that the quantity of sweets she was buying was growing exponentially.

I had noticed that the bag she was holding when she arrived home looked even larger than normal, so I asked Lucy to tip the contents of the bag out onto the table.

I knew roughly the cost of each packet and was fully aware that this pile of sweets far exceeded what Lucy had been given.

Questioning her in my most serious of tones, I asked her where she had got the money from to purchase such a large quantity of sweets. She was adamant that she only spent the remaining change from what I had given her.

So now she was telling bare-faced lies. I asked her point-blank if she had taken money from my purse, which she emphatically denied.

Using my mother's old technique, I told her to go to her room and reflect on what she had just said.

I informed her that when she realised that she had made a mistake, she was to come back down and give me the revised account of the facts.

I knew Lucy had a stubborn streak, but this was when I became aware of the full extent of it.

I waited, and I waited and still there was no sign of her coming down as the afternoon turned into evening.

It was now her bedtime and she had not had any tea. I was starting to waver. I went to her room and there she was, lying on her bed, staring up at her ceiling.

"Well?" I asked determinedly. "Are you ready to tell me the truth?"

She just stared at me.

"I already have," she answered defiantly.

"Lucy, I know you are telling lies. Just tell Mum the truth and we will say no more about it," I said, becoming more desperate to resolve the matter. Still nothing. "Are you hungry? It is your favourite for tea." I tried the tempting tactic. Still, silence prevailed. So, Lucy went to bed with no tea.

This situation was unprecedented. I would have to be the one to break this impasse. It was turning into a battle of wills, to say the least, and I was the one losing. I could not bear to see her go hungry.

The next morning, I called her down for breakfast. In a desperate attempt to regain an element of control, I told her,

"If I find out that you have taken money from my purse again, Lucy, I will have no alternative but to smack your bottom hard." With that threat issued, she just looked up from her cereal bowl, gave me a hard stare and shoved in another spoonful.

This incident was swiftly followed by another even more serious than the last.

Lucy had formed a friendship with a schoolmate who she called James. He lived with his parents down the hill in the pub called The Spotted Cow.

We had been in there a few times for Sunday lunch. It was a bit dark inside as there was a great many dark oak beams and furniture, but it was OK as far as pubs go.

It was a Sunday afternoon. Lucy had asked if she could go down to play with James. Apparently, they had a large rubber tyre on a rope in a large tree in their back garden. Huge fun, I was told.

I thought it over and decided that as it was a Sunday and well past the pub's closing time, it should be safe enough for her to go as everyone would have already made their way home.

I knew the owners and I had the phone number, so I agreed to let her go, with the proviso that she would be home for tea at 5 pm. This would give her two and a half hours which seemed more than adequate.

I was sitting quietly knitting when I heard the front door go. I looked at my watch and could see that Lucy had only been gone just over an hour. I waited for her to come into the front room to tell me why she had come home early.

When she did not come, I put my knitting down and plodded upstairs. She was not in her bedroom, so I made my way to the bathroom. There she was, on her knees, with her head down the toilet, heaving up the contents of her stomach.

Firstly, I thought she was ill, but very quickly recognised the strong odour of alcohol.

"Good God, Lucy, what the hell is going on?" I exclaimed in horror.

As she pulled away from the toilet, I could see vomit down the front of her clothes.

I got her undressed and into the bath to clean her up. I could not believe she had been drinking.

I got her into a clean nightgown and was just getting her into bed when, yet another projectile amount shot across the room, soaking her nightdress and her bedding, and to some degree, even me.

"Lucy, what have you been drinking and who gave it to you?"

She looked at me with tears rolling down her cheeks.

"James said it was called Scrumpy. He found it in big glass bottles in the woodshed. Please don't tell on him, Mum; he will get into terrible trouble," she begged.

"Then so he should just look at the state you're in," I replied with disgust. "At least it looks like you have brought it all up. Come on, let's get you and your bed changed and get you back in. Let's hope this will be a lesson to you. Now come on, get into bed; you will feel better after a sleep."

Having settled her down in a clean bed, I returned to my knitting now no longer able to concentrate.

I pondered how it was that things were going so badly wrong, when my eight-and-a-half-year-old daughter could go out to play on a Sunday afternoon and return home as drunk as a skunk.

Jesus, whatever next, I thought.

Come back, Clare, all is forgiven. My daughter misses you and so do I, I reflected.

I had hoped that this would be the final thing to go wrong and that things would settle down and return to normal, but I was again mistaken, when, a few weeks later, Mark announced that he was losing his job.

Sales had dried up in the area. His boss had left his wife and children for his long-time secretarial girlfriend and had put his house on the market, and his business into liquidation.

So, here we were yet again with no means of paying the mortgage.

After weeks of trying to acquire another job without success, Mark came up with the idea of starting a business.

He had been to look at a very large empty shop with an even bigger basement in the high street that had a three-bedroom flat above.

This idea, born out of a mixture of desperation and sheer insanity, was to sell the house, rent the

property, and fit it out as a hairdressing and beauty salon, gym, and sauna.

I thought this was a completely insane idea.

My previous attempts at hairdressing had been a complete failure. I could not see how this could possibly work.

However, over the next few weeks, and after a lot of convincing, I finally gave in to the idea, especially as Mark said we would employ qualified staff for the hair and beauty side of the business.

He would take care of the gym and sauna side, and my job would be to do the cleaning. Well, there's a surprise, I thought.

I would also keep the books, do the wages, and oversee the day to day running. Plus, of course, I had two children to care for.

But Mark reminded me that we would then both be there all day for the children through the school holidays. How could it possibly fail, he added excitedly?

So, the papers were signed for the shop lease. The house was put on the market, and we began buying the equipment that we were going to need. Every day was filled with excitement.

There was so much to do that thankfully, our sex life was put on the back burner as most nights we collapsed into bed exhausted.

Advertisements were put in the local newspapers for qualified hairdressers and beauticians.

The premises needed a great deal doing to it to get it ready.

Washbasins, hairdryers, and mirrors were fitted. On the upper floor, we had planned for the hair and beauty salon. Towels, gowns, and stock were ordered, and this was where my previous experience came in useful as I knew exactly what was needed.

Two beauty rooms were constructed and were kitted out with massage tables, treatment equipment and a vast range of cosmetics, lotions, and creams.

Our largest purchase was the sauna. It had to be a commercial size and did not come cheap. Mark spent a whole week tiling out the shower rooms and cubicles.

He worked so hard. It looked very swish when it was finished. The smell was amazing when we fired it up for its trial run.

The excitement was mounting now. We couldn't wait to be up and running.

The house had finally sold, and we were now able to move into the flat above the premises. The children had the two largest bedrooms on the top floor so they would not be disturbed by the evening business.

We had the bedroom on the next floor down where there was also a large kitchen and lounge area. It was a much larger space than we were used to, and our furniture looked kind of lost in it.

The floors were just hardwood, our small rugs covering very little, which did not do much to make the place look homely, but we had to focus everything on the business. There was no money spare for fitted carpet, so we would have to live with it for the time being.

It soon became apparent just how noisy it could be with two small children charging around on bare floors. Slippers had become a priority.

It was a huge relief to be able to pay off the huge mountain of eye-watering bills that had mounted up over the last few months.

Mark had applied for an alcohol license which he told me was imperative if we wanted people to enjoy a social evening after their workout and sauna, and this had been successfully granted.

We managed to buy a secondhand bar which Mark had great fun stocking and he installed five optics on the wall behind it.

I had never known him to drink before but understood that he wanted to try out his latest acquisition, as we enjoyed a glass or two in our new lounging area. We had purchased 12 White Nordic relaxers that folded up into cubes when not in use. They were very luxurious and gave the place an air of class. We sat looking around at what we had achieved and clinked glasses as we toasted our new venture.

Chapter 9

Our big opening day was fast approaching. All the exercising equipment had arrived and been positioned with a designated area for the weightlifting. Staff had been recruited, had been for their initial briefing and were fitted for their uniforms, proudly sporting the company logo of Spa. Tasia.

We were ready to rumble. Thankfully, the extensive full-page advertising with professional photographers had been effective. The phone had been going all week and appointments were flooding in with people anxiously wanting to try out the new facility. There was nothing else around remotely like it, and we had caused quite a stir.

The town crier had been booked, and the local mayor had agreed to come and cut the ribbons.

We were all buzzing with excitement as we unlocked the door on the big day and welcomed our first appointments across the threshold, treating them to a glass of bubbly. There was a lot of chatter as people were shown around.

The press was there and took notes and photos and interviewed several of our first customers as to their first responses to the facilities that were available, and to our relief, all sounded hugely positive.

We then got into the business of making money.

It was a very long day as when the hair and beauty salons closed, the gym and sauna trade began arriving and this side of the business did not close until 11 pm due to the fact we were a licensed business. Even then, people were in no hurry to leave and seemed to be enjoying the whole social side of things.

I could not believe how much money was in the till when we finally got to lock up for the night. I had to agree that if things continued like this, we stood a very good chance of soon becoming millionaires.

I had been so reluctant to take such a huge risk that Mark had practically dragged me along kicking and screaming to get me on board with the idea, but the walk to the bank the next day with the takings was clear evidence that he had indeed made the right decision and I greatly admired his bravery.

The next few months were a huge learning curve for me. I had to go to the tax office to be walked through every step of how to record the income from the business, and how to work out the staff salaries and the national insurance contributions.

Initially, I was a regular visitor at this office having never excelled at maths, or any other subject, come to that. Despite making sheaves of notes, it took a considerable time to get my head around all the complexities involved.

I got to know the staff who worked there very well and was grateful for their unwavering patience. Only by a process of repetition did it finally sink in, and I was able to achieve it unassisted. This achievement did wonders for my confidence. I now felt like an authentic businesswoman.

The business continued to thrive as word of mouth trickled around the local community and beyond, and we were getting a reputation for quality treatments.

We even had a visit from a doctor one day to ask what it was we were doing to help one of his patients who had suffered for years from terrible acne. Apparently, none of the usual treatments he had prescribed had improved her condition. However, he had seen significant improvement since we had been treating her, and he was intrigued to know how this had been achieved.

This was not only most flattering but also very good for business.

Our social evenings were also attracting people from the business community. This was to change our social standing in the community as invitations started flooding in for events and parties.

We were now mixing with society's elite. This warranted a posh car to keep up with the Jones's, and Mark went out and purchased a Marcus sports car, a real showstopper. I felt like a real fraud when I travelled in it, as people were expecting to see a film star getting out of it and were hugely disappointed when I emerged.

Mother had given me the real fur coat that Dad had bought her years ago. She said that she no longer went anywhere to wear it. This helped considerably with creating the new image that I felt I needed to portray.

Sad how you feel you need to conform to such superficiality. However, at the time, it seemed important to be accepted into this new world.

The months rolled by, and the business was going from strength to strength. Mark had taken to joining in with the socialising every evening and had started drinking heavily. It was not long before he started vocalising again about our depleted sex life.

He was not happy and had no qualms about telling me he wanted changes made. In fact, he was becoming quite angry about it, or the lack of it. We had regular conversations that took place after too many glasses of whisky, which I got to loathe the very smell of, as it always signified trouble in some form or other.

Walking on eggshells is not too strong a way of describing how difficult life had become regarding our marital issues. I tried explaining that I did not want to go down that same path again, but this was met with complete disdain. He would not let the subject lie and told me that he had found out about a female gay club and suggested that we go and check it out.

It was only to go for a drink to see what it's about, he prompted.

This did not sound too terrifying. At least it would be kept impersonal which would not impact on the children. I agreed to go just to see what it was like. I thought I could just stand and observe.

The following weekend, the children were dropped off at my parents. Relief staff were in place to cover the gym/sauna and we set off again into the unknown.

It did not open until 10 pm, so we had time to go for a drink first to calm the nerves. By the time we arrived, I was suitably chilled. It was a funny little place up a side street in the city. Loud thumping music emanated through an open door at the top of steep steps leading down into a dimly lit room, at the bottom of which could be seen a group of females leaning against a bar.

As we got to the bottom of the stairs, the room opened into a much larger space where people could be seen dancing as the lights flickered around them.

I followed Mark to the bar where he ordered two drinks. We were already being observed with a degree of suspicion.

I soon discovered the reason for this as I sipped my drink and glanced around the room; Mark was the only guy in the place.

Strangely, I had not been prepared for this and wondered how this would be explained in the event that we were asked.

It was not many minutes before the answer would become apparent when a stocky, masculine-looking woman in her thirties walked straight up to Mark and asked him straight out.

"What's this set-up then, mate?" she asked with a straight face.

I looked at Mark not knowing how he would respond to this direct line of questioning. He simply took another sip of his scotch and without even blinking, replied,

"I don't know what you mean by set-up; there is no set-up. I'm simply here enjoying a drink while my wife eyes up the local talent with a view to forming an attachment."

I looked at him in horror. I felt myself blushing to the roots of my hair. How could he put it so brazenly? I looked at the woman awaiting her reaction.

"Oh, is that so?" she replied, "And what will happen if your wife finds someone that takes her fancy – are you part of the package?" she asked decisively.

"Good heavens, no, what do you take me for? I am purely a bystander." He grinned.

"How very reassuring," turning towards me. She asked. "Do you want to dance, Hon?"

"Um, OK," I stuttered, allowing myself to be led onto the dance floor.

The mode of dancing was suggestive, to say the least. The person leading had to put one knee between the partner's two legs and grind the hips together to the beat. I have never danced like that before, especially with a woman, and found it strangely arousing.

I had several dances as the evening wore on and, surprisingly, quite enjoyed myself.

Mark seemed pleased with the outcome, which culminated in some aggressive lovemaking when we finally climbed into bed.

Our visits to the club soon became a regular event. The regular clientele came to accept Mark, and no longer considered him a threat. I had become quite attached to an attractive girl called Wendy who was much younger than me.

Over the last few visits, we had spent most of the evenings together, so it was no surprise when she asked if she could come back with me. Mark's face lit up when I told him. He told me to make it clear that he would be observing from a distance, which, surprisingly, she seemed OK with.

We sat together in the back seat of the car on the journey home and kissed. By now, it had come to feel very natural. I must add at this point that the experience did not disappoint. In fact, I was again completely oblivious to Mark even being in the room.

Over the next few months, Wendy became a regular visitor. Mark had again taken to joining us in the bed but was not involved in the sexual act. A couple of times I felt his hand creep across to try and grope. I was not happy with that, as selfish as it sounds; I had become quite fixated on Wendy and was not about to start sharing her. Therefore, it was a huge shock to arrive at the club one evening to see her cuddled up in the corner with someone else. I could not believe it! What had happened?

I waited all evening for the opportunity to speak with her which only came when she passed me on the way to the toilet.

"Wendy, what have I done wrong?" I asked.

"Nothing, why?" she replied, unfazed.

"Don't you want to be with me anymore?" This was a stupid thing to ask as she had obviously turned her attention elsewhere.

"I could not resist her besides, what else am I supposed to do all week?" She laughed as she walked away from me. I was stunned by the shallowness of her reply and took it very hard that I had been replaced so brutally and abruptly.

This appeared to be the normal pattern of events as over the coming months, I witnessed people changing partners with unusual regularity.

I had several more flings as time moved on but did not take them with any degree of seriousness. I had been very hurt initially and had learnt not to invest too much of myself in any of them.

It proved to be a very superficial type of lifestyle.

What I did ascertain, however, was how to spot like-minded people. So, when a group of women arrived for a gym session one evening, I knew instantly that one woman in particular was showing a great deal of interest in me in a way that had become very familiar. In fact, she could not take her eyes off me.

She was quite stocky, and not pretty in any way, but there was something mesmerising about her that I was instantly drawn to. Every time she came to the bar, she would tell me how beautiful she thought I was.

This was a revelation as I was not used to being told such flattering things.

When all the other ladies left, she stayed behind. She told me that her name was Cassy.

We sat and talked for hours, well after Mark had locked up and gone on to bed in his usual state of alcoholic overindulgence.

She told me that she was living with someone but said that they were tiring of each other. This, I discovered, proved to be one-sided when the phone rang and the woman on the other end asked if Cassy was still there and could she speak to her.

The conversation that followed confirmed that her partner was worried about her and wanted her home. It was then clear to me that Cassy was the one who was getting fed up, not the other way around.

I knew I should have stopped it developing further at this point but for some reason, I did not want to. To avoid a guilt trip, I purposely put the other woman out of my mind.

When Cassy finally kissed me, my tummy filled with butterflies and the urge to have sex with her intensified. I could not have stopped myself if I had tried.

We made love then and there on the floor; sex the like of which I had never experienced. It had been OK with Wendy, and the others, with anything being an improvement on my past experiences with the men in my life, but this, this was on a whole new level.

This is how it should feel, I thought. All those years of faking it and not knowing what it was really like to experience a real orgasm. I wondered how I had gone all those years thinking that was how all wives felt.

This was mind-blowing. Her whole focus was to pleasure me. I was well and truly hooked.

She arrived daily. She could not get enough of me. We used every opportunity to be alone together. I would even sneak her upstairs via the side entrance while Mark was running the evening sessions.

I knew that she would never have accepted him joining us in the bed. She referred to him as the pervert.

It did not take long for Mark to catch on that Cassy, now broken up with her partner, was paying me a great deal of attention and was becoming a regular visitor.

I started visiting her at her home while her mother was at work.

I'm sure that Mark was beginning to feel that he was losing control of the situation. He was feeling pushed out, and he was not at all happy about it.

Jealousy mixed with excessive alcohol was a dangerous combination. I was becoming quite scared of him; I was constantly watching for trigger points that would set him off, added to which I was now refusing to go to the club, putting paid to his pleasures.

He had started name-calling, swearing, pushing, and slapping. On one of these occasions, I was busy ironing when an argument erupted over my refusal to give in about not going to the club. As I put the iron down to adjust the shirt sleeve, he made a grab for it and tried to burn me with it, but I jumped backwards, and he returned it to its stand.

Then, over the same issue, he lifted the television and threatened to throw it out of the open window.

Things began to intensify further when the slapping turned to punching.

I told him that I was not prepared to put up with his violent behaviour and that if it continued, I would leave him and take the children with me.

It was then he threatened that if I did that he would come after me and kill me, which I fully believed him capable of.

I now had a little insight into the reason why his first wife may have left so suddenly leaving behind all her clothes and personal belongings.

He had walked away from that relationship with everything – the family home, the furniture, the car; everything except his daughter, whom he did not seem to value. He had shown no interest in having her in his life whatsoever. The fact that his ex-wife did not pursue him for child maintenance of any kind spoke volumes. She wanted him out of their lives completely.

However, I was not brave enough to take that step.

The time came when this sentiment was put to the test after a particularly heavy night on the scotch found me with a broken nose, cut lip, and a blackened eye.

He was engulfed with guilt the next day when he looked at the damage he had caused and swore that he would never lay a hand on me again.

I blindly believed him, telling the children that Mummy had fallen down the stairs. The only upside to this incident, if I had to find one, was that I got out of doing the school run.

Cassy could not believe it when she saw what he had done to me and threatened to kill the bastard, as she put it. I think she would have too if I had agreed to it, but I reassured her he had been very drunk at the time, and he had promised faithfully it would never happen again.

I also had to lie to my parents about why I was unable to take the children over for several weekends as I dared not let Dad see what Mark had done to me, or why.

I knew trouble was brewing again a short time later when having been drinking heavily all evening, Mark turned on Cassy, saying,

"Piss off, you fucking butch cow."

Fear instantly kicked in. Oh, my Lord, I thought, here we go.

Cassy did not want to leave as she could see where this might be heading. She could plainly see his anger bubbling, and sure enough, as soon as he had locked the door behind her, he leapt toward me knocking me off my feet.

"You bloody bitch," he hissed, grabbing a handful of hair with one hand, and ripping my top off me with the other.

"Please, Mark, don't do this," I cried, trying to grab his hand to take the strain off the pulling.

"You are more than bloody happy to pleasure yourself, you cow. Don't think I don't know what you're up to behind my back. You don't give a damn about me, do you?" he accused.

He had let go of my hair and I was able to get out of his reach. This empowered me to have my say. This was not the best idea I'd ever had considering the level of alcohol he had consumed, but throwing caution to the wind, out it all flooded.

"That's not true, Mark. I have bent over backwards to try to make you happy. I have never been enough for you. You started all of this, now you don't like it as it's not happening the way you want it. You hit me again and it will be the very last time," I threatened.

This was like pouring petrol on a fire. He made a dash toward me, grabbed me by the throat and threw me to the floor. I was badly winded. He leapt on top of me ripping the rest of my clothing off me.

He dragged me to my feet, unlocked the front door and threw me out on the street.

"Get out there where you belong, you fucking whore!" he screamed as he pushed me outside into the road and relocked the door. I staggered to my feet, hands trying to cover my bits, feeling very vulnerable.

I could see him through the window grabbing glasses from behind the bar and smashing them against the wall.

As I stood there, shivering, wondering what to do next, a police car pulled up beside me.

"What's going on here, love?" The concerned officer asked.

"It's my husband; he is drunk, and he is going berserk in there. I'm locked out."

The officer got a jacket from the back seat of the car and put it around my shoulders.

He then hammered on the door.

"Open up. Police!" he shouted.

The smashing stopped and a drunken Mark staggered to the door and unlocked it. I dashed by him and ran for the cubicles where I knew there would be robes hanging. I returned to reception where Mark was drunkenly informing the police officer that he had reacted that way as he had just found out that I was having an affair.

The police officer looked at me but did not comment on the accusation. He did not appear to want to get involved but asked me if I wanted to press charges against Mark for having assaulted me.

I looked down at the floor and said quietly,

"No, thank you, Officer." I handed him back the borrowed jacket.

I knew that this was the end. I had to get away from him, or my parents would be organising a funeral.

I remained in the salon that night. Mark came in early to sweep up the glass and clean up the mess from the night before. This task was undertaken in complete silence. He didn't even look in my direction.

I waited for him to go to the bank, and presumably, to go shopping to replace all the glasses he had smashed.

I reflected how blessed I was that being a Saturday, the children were already at Mother's for the weekend.

I flew upstairs as fast as my legs would carry me. I grabbed a suitcase from on top of the wardrobe and began stuffing in as many clothes and personal things as I could. I knew that time was of the essence. He would not be out for long. I threw on some jogging bottoms and a t-shirt, and I dragged the suitcase down the stairs.

I ran to reception and phoned for a taxi. I was told it would be ten minutes. This had to be the longest ten minutes of my life. The fear rising with every second that passed, I could see the taxi heading up the hill. He pulled up as if he had all the time in the world.

He went to get out to put the case in the boot, but I quickly rammed it onto the back seat and leapt in beside it, giving him the address of my parent's house.

"Please hurry," I urged.

I repeatedly looked out of the back window, terrified that I was being followed. As the taxi pulled into the road where my parents lived, I spotted our car in the distance. I was engulfed in fear.

I leapt out and hammered on the door. I was too scared to even retrieve my case or pay the driver. I was just desperate to get inside.

Dad opened the door and quickly assessed the situation as I pushed past him to safety. With only minutes to spare, Mark's car screeched into the drive and came to an abrupt stop. Dad took control and told me,

"Leave this to me, Rita." He left the house, closing the door behind him. I was terrified that Dad would get hurt.

I had no idea what was said, I only know that Mark left very quickly.

Here we all were, yet again, at Mother and Dad's and having to adhere to their routines and way of life, but I was grateful for the sanctuary. The relief I felt from being away from the stress of life with Mark was immeasurable.

I slept soundly for the first time in a very long time that first night. I explained to the children that Mummy and Daddy had decided not to live together anymore but that they would still see Daddy as often as they wanted.

I phoned Cassy to tell her what had happened. She was so relieved that I had finally gained the courage to get out.

The next day, Cassy came to my parents' house to discuss what we should do next. It was decided that I would consult a solicitor to put the wheels in motion to obtain a divorce. There was to be no reconciliation as I had put up with enough for far too long; my mind was made up.

I did not want to allow him access to the children due to his heavy drinking, but Mother insisted that it was his legal right and that

I really had no leg to stand on if he chose to contest it. He, as expected, was making life extremely difficult.

I tried to do what his first wife had done and say that I wanted nothing from him financially, hoping upon hope that he would walk away from the responsibility, but he was having none of it.

The desperately sad thing was that despite Lucy only ever knowing Mark as her dad, he made it clear he only wanted access to his son. I thought that was the ultimate act of cruelty.

This rejection was deeply felt. Lucy was absolutely heartbroken, and I felt her pain.

After sticking to my guns for well over a month, I finally gave in and agreed to let him have Lee for the weekend. He promised me that he would not drink, as this had been my biggest worry, yet it was a case of having to trust him to keep to his word.

Lucy watched them from the sitting room window as her little 4-year-old brother was hugged and kissed and lifted into the back seat of the car.

It was desperately sad. I tried to console her but could not find the right words. I just held her close and wiped away her tears.

My nerves were in shreds when the time passed that Mark had agreed to bring Lee back. I kept saying aloud,

"He's not coming, he is not going to bring him back."

"Don't be ridiculous, Rita, he is just running late," Mother replied.

However, I was well aware of what Mark was capable of. He would keep that child just to spite me.

As time went on, I was proven right. I got straight on the phone and demanded,

"Bring him back, Mark! You can't do this."

"Oh, but I can, and I have," he chortled slamming down the phone.

I turned on Mother, who got the full force of all my pent-up emotions.

"This is all your fault; I didn't want him to have him. I knew he could not be trusted. *Now* what the hell am I supposed to do?" I finished in floods of tears, collapsing in a heap.

Mother looked worried that her advice had had such devastating consequences.

"Bide your time, Rita," he won't be able to look after the child. He has the salon to run, plus the rest of the business, and now that you have left, he will have to get his head around the bookkeeping. Just bide your time; the child will be returned in no time."

This was of little consolation. I'm not sure I believed a word of it, but I had no other option, if I got solicitors involved, it would be a long and drawn-out process, which would make Mark even more determined to undermine me. As hard as it would be, I had to just simply wait it out.

Life had to go on. Dad took Lucy to school each day. Lucy would walk to Cassy's workplace after school and Cassy would drive her back to Mother's when she finished work.

Lucy had taken to calling into the salon on the way to Cassy's to check that Lee was OK and to stop me worrying.

This did little to reassure me as the reports that came back painted a bleak picture,

describing how dirty and dishevelled Lee looked, and on two occasions, she had found that he was still in his pyjamas. I phoned on several occasions to take Mark to task about all of this but as soon as he heard my voice, he would put the phone down.

Although I was grateful to my parents for yet again bailing me out of another bad situation, I was beginning to feel the need to be back in my own space.

Cassy had a well-paid job at the local printers. If I got a job too, we would be able to afford the rent for a place together.

We found a tiny furnished cottage in the back of beyond in a little village. It was an old-fashioned place on a quiet country lane, set in an overgrown garden. The furniture looked like what I remembered my grandmother had in her home. Still, it was a way of gaining back my independence.

We managed to move straight in with just our clothes as everything else was provided in the rent. This should be interesting, I thought, as I discovered the only means of washing clothes was a twin tub and a mangle, but Cassy offered to take me to the launderette once a week. Problem solved.

We had only been in the cottage a few days when the first signs appeared that Mark was out to instil terror back into my life.

It was around 1o'clock in the morning when we were awoken by the sound of a car screeching into the drive, horn blowing and headlights flashing on and off, lighting up the whole bedroom.

He had obviously followed Cassy back here and discovered our safe place.

The next few nights were spent living on my nerves, getting out of bed with every little sound to peer out into the blackness.

The days were spent at the Jobcentre scanning the boards for anything that I might be able to do that would generate an income. I was determined I was not going to rely on the government for financial assistance. I was young and healthy and could take care of my own affairs.

One card in the slot on the board captured my interest. It was at the local paint factory; they wanted someone to put the labels on the cans on a production line.

I removed the card and took it to the girl sitting behind a desk.

"Could you please phone this one for me to ask if I can have an interview today?" I asked politely.

"Are you sure? You did see that it's only for a six-week period," she said hesitantly.

"Yes, I read that on the card, but there is nothing else so it's better than nothing."

I would have swept the street if there had been a wage at the end of it. The appointment was made for that afternoon.

I was greeted by a middle-aged man in a white coat, which had splashes of paint on it, who told me his name was Mr Shaw.

He went on to explain that he was the manager of the paint shop and reiterated that it was only six weeks' work. When I nodded my agreement, he asked me how soon I could start. My reply rather startled him.

"I'm available right now if you wish," I announced confidently.

He laughed. "Tomorrow morning, 8.00 am sharp; come and find me and I will get you fixed up with a set of overalls."

"Thank you very much," I was overjoyed at my success.

I went to meet Cassy from work and could not wait to tell her my news.

"Well done you!" she praised.

"What are your hours, and rate of pay?" she asked as we made our way home.

I did not have a clue! I was so pleased to get offered the job; I had forgotten to ask about any of the details.

No matter, anything would be an improvement on nothing. I would find out all those things in due course.

The next day, I was up bright and early to hitch a lift in with Cassy. We dropped Lucy off at the breakfast club at school and I was in the factory fifteen minutes early.

Mr Shaw was fiddling with some machines. He looked up as I approached.

"That's impressive - you're early, just don't expect to be paid overtime," he announced as he pulled a card from his overall pocket.

"Here this is your clocking-in card, you will have to get it stamped when you come and go. Make sure you give the office all your details and they will explain about your pay.

One of the ladies will allocate you a locker and get you an overall. Ask her to show you where the canteen is."

So it was that I threw myself into the job with so much gusto that on my third day, I was approached by someone who announced his title as the shop steward.

"You have to slow down, miss," he said solemnly.

"Why is that?" I asked, surprised.

"There's been a complaint. You are working far too fast, and it is making everyone else look lazy; it's getting people's backs up," he announced grim-faced.

Having just left a lifestyle that overpowered and controlled me, I was not about to be bullied again by anyone, especially a man. I fully intended to start how I meant to go on.

"Well, that is just tough, as this is the speed I work at. If people don't like it, they will just have to pick up the pace themselves then, won't they?" I finished, turning my back on him, and continuing with my job, satisfied that I had made myself sufficiently clear but not realising that I had not heard the last of this.

I was relating the day's events to Cassy as we arrived home that afternoon when, on entering the front door, I quickly noticed that things were amiss. Items in the hall had been moved. The umbrella stand had moved from inside the door to the bottom of the stairs. The two pairs of slippers were now sitting on the fourth stair up.

That's weird, I thought. How has that happened? Then I could hear the radio on in the kitchen which I knew very well I had turned off when leaving that morning. I was beginning to get prickles on the back of my neck.

Oh no, surely not! I dashed into the front room and could see that things in there had also been moved. The sofa cushions were all lined up along the window ledge and the coffee table was upside down. I quickly followed Cassy upstairs to the main bedroom to find all the bedding piled up in a heap in the middle of the room. On the bare mattress, there was a note with the words YOU CAN RUN BUT YOU CAN'T HIDE printed in bold capitals sending a shiver down my spine.

He had got into the house. We had left the kitchen fanlight window open slightly. An old coat hanger lay on the floor which he had obviously used to lift the latch.

"Oh God, Cassy, won't he ever give up?!" I said with a mixture of despair and dread.

"He doesn't scare me; we will be fine," she told me putting a reassuring arm around my shoulders.

He appeared again that night just to drive his message home, horn blaring, lights flashing and this time, revving up the engine adding to the fear factor.

"Let him play these childish games; he will soon tire of it," Cassy said, turning onto her side and going back to sleep.

But he had put the fear of God into me. He had threatened to kill me in the past. Cassy might not take him seriously, but I certainly did. Now he had got into the house, it was even more terrifying. I was a bag of nerves from there on in and sleep was beyond me.

The next morning started badly as we both overslept due to lack of sleep. Neither of us had heard the alarm. We dragged on some clothes, bundled Lucy into the car and sped off, remarkably arriving at work only ten minutes late to find everyone standing in the road outside the factory. Cassy pulled the car to a stop to let me out.

"What's going on?" I asked one woman who was standing with her hands in the pockets of her overalls.

"The trade union guy has called a strike."

"Why?" I asked confused.

"Because of you that's why. You have single-handedly sabotaged the time and motion study, done to establish the volume of work expected of any employee in a working day. In short, you get the job done too quickly."

"That's complete rubbish; I do a good day's work for a good day's pay. I am not deliberately going to slow my pace of working to suit you lazy lot. If that is what is expected, then they have another think coming," I shouted back as I stormed past the crowd and made my way inside to clock in.

I was confronted by Mr Shaw who glared in my direction.

"Get out of here!" he demanded. "See what trouble you have caused? You haven't been here five minutes and you have hijacked my productivity quota for today with all my machines sitting here idle. You and your high and mighty attitude."

I could not understand it. I was only doing what had been asked of me. How could I have caused all this disruption by just working hard?

I went to the canteen. Why do I get everything so badly wrong? I pondered as I sat peering out at the assembled crowd outside as they glared back at me.

Work finally resumed at a much slower pace. I had been forced into adapting to this revised pace of working just to fit in. I had taken the full wrath of a whole shop floor and it had proved an uncomfortable experience.

There had been no further night-time disturbances, which was a huge relief. I discovered the reason for this one afternoon when Lucy returned from school and handed me a handwritten note in red crayon. It was from Lee.

"Oh, my God!" I exclaimed, jumping up and down. "He's letting me have him back," I screamed excitedly.

"He's got a girlfriend, Mum, that's why," Lucy Informed me.

Well, I'll be blessed! Mother was right after all; as soon as the child became an inconvenience to him, he would want to hand him back.

That weekend I was so excited as we went to pick up Lee and all his toys. Mark had refused me access to him for what had seemed like an age, my son being the only weapon he had left in his arsenal to use against me to get me to conform to his demands. That control would, at last, come to an end.

I could not believe how Lee had grown. He was at school now. I was so over the moon to have him home and hold him in my arms again.

I was totally absorbed in the elation of having him returned to me that I did not foresee the trouble I was creating for myself in the future with Lucy.

To her, it must have felt like I had abandoned her, as I showered affection on Lee. I was blind to the hidden hurt that I was inflicting upon her. It was unforgivable of me.

Even though there was no longer a need for her to go into the salon to report back on how Lee was, she continued to go there after school.

I was not happy about this and told her so, which seemed to only strengthen her resolve to go against my wishes. She was becoming defiant.

After giving the matter a lot of thought, I had come to terms with the mistake I was making with my two children and set about rectifying the situation by reducing the level of affection I had been showing Lee and trying to equal things out more with Lucy. However, the more I tried to include her, the more she pulled in the opposite direction.

I tried not to worry too much about this latest development, as I attempted to convince myself that it was just a phase and that she would grow out of it.

The contract for six weeks' work had come and gone, and I had managed to settle myself into the fabric of the work's requirements. I had shown that I was an industrious and conscientious worker that they could not afford to lose.

I was offered a permanent position, which also included a pay rise. It was now necessary to join the union, which meant that I had to make sure that I conformed to all union rules.

Now I would have to really slow my working pace down.

Chapter 10

The six months' rental on the cottage was coming to an end. I had hoped to extend the lease for a further six months, but the owner had made the decision to sell the property, so I just had to find somewhere else to live.

Ideally, I needed to be back in town for work and the schools. Having searched unsuccessfully for weeks for something suitable, I decided, out of sheer desperation, to contact the local council, which turned out to be a complete waste of time as it appeared that you had to be homeless before they would even consider helping, and even then, things were uncertain.

I grew more and more anxious the nearer the time came for my eviction day. I was searching the classified advertisements daily but with no luck. I was forced to contact the council again.

I tried to relate to the hard-faced woman behind the desk just how desperate was the situation we would be facing in just a matter of only days, but her expression showed me that she had heard it all before as she uttered the well-practised words.

"I'm sorry, there is nothing we can do unless you are actually homeless." Just to add to the fear factor, she added for good measure,

"Then you will probably only be put in a bed and breakfast in a different town."

I left with my heart in my boots. There was no way on the planet that I was going back to Mother and Dad again. I would rather pitch a tent in the local park.

It was my responsibility to put a roof over my children's heads. I knew that Mark would never agree to sell the business. I had run out of options. I had to find another way out.

The day finally arrived, and I had made my decision - a decision that would take all the courage that I could muster. I knew that things could go against me, and it could all go badly wrong, but I had been backed into a corner and just simply had to hold my nerve if I was going to pull off the impossible.

We were all up early, having packed two suitcases the night before. I picked up the packed lunch boxes and three cartons of juice from the kitchen table, closed the front door and posted the key through the letterbox as requested. I bundled the children into the car and set off.

Twenty minutes later, Cassy was unloading us and the suitcases outside the council office.

"Good luck," she uttered and crossed the fingers on both hands as she got back into the car.

I took a deep breath and pushed open the door, holding it there with one leg as I ushered the children in dragging the suitcases behind them. I positioned the cases in front of the main desk and sat two children down on one case, while I made myself comfortable on the other.

"Well, here we are then!" I announced in a firm voice.

"Excuse me?" the same stern-faced girl asked, staring down at us with an alarmed expression on her face.

"I said, here we are then!" I repeated. "Officially homeless."

"Now look here, you can't just come and park yourselves in here like this. I have told you, we have nowhere for you at this moment in time. You will have to go on a waiting list like everyone else," she glared back at me over the top of her spectacles.

"I have nowhere else to go except here. So, I'm afraid you're stuck with me," I replied, crossing my arms to illustrate the finality of the predicament.

"Don't you have any family members that can put you up short-term?" she asked with a strong emphasis on the word short, to try and gain control of the situation she now found herself in.

"Nope; like I said, I have nowhere else to go but here," I told he smiling broadly at her to reinforce my determination.

"Well, you can't stay sitting there!" she added, looking back at her work as if this would resolve the matter and I would get up and leave.

I didn't move a muscle. I simply sat there on those cases with the children. I had packed colouring books and crayons to occupy the time in case it was necessary to sit it out. I had read them several stories, and we had devoured everything in our lunchboxes and drunk our juice.

The woman had stated several times throughout the morning that we were wasting our time, and that this silliness would achieve nothing.

We remained steadfast and continued our vigil.

She ate her lunch in silence, looking up at us briefly. She went out and made herself cups of coffee but never offered me one, or the children a drink, come to that.

The afternoon wore on and I could tell that the situation was beginning to get to her. She began making phone calls in a whispered voice. She then announced,

"It's no use; I have done my best to get something sorted out for you but there is nothing available. You are going to have to leave now as I will be locking up soon."

I was beginning to think that I had blown it. I had played the game of poker with the system, and it looked as if the system had beaten me. However, I took a deep breath and made my last final attempt at holding my nerve.

"Well, I said to the children it looks as if we are here for the night so make yourselves comfortable. Perhaps we will have better luck tomorrow," I said, squeezing them tightly.

"You can't sleep in here with two children!" the woman declared in an alarmed tone.

"When needs must, one has to do what one has to do, it's this or the street."

"Oh, good heavens," she said, picking up the phone one final time.

I phoned Cassy with a sense of achievement.

"Come and get us; I have a set of keys," I said, elated.

We took the children straight to Mother and Dad's where they stayed for the whole weekend.

We went out and bought pots of paint and brushes and decorated the tiny little two up, two down cottage at the top of town.

It was a unique little place with very low ceilings and a tiny front door that you had to duck your head to walk through. It looked amazing after we had worked our magic on it, and I absolutely loved it.

We picked up some basic furniture at the local thrift shop and bought cooking utensils from Woolworths. They were cheap and cheerful, but everything was ours. I could not wait to pick the children up and show them our new home.

We had been advised that it was only a temporary solution and that I needed to get my name on the council house list as soon as possible, which is exactly what I did.

Things were getting back to normal. We had a nice little home, and I had a well-paid permanent job. Mark seemed happy with the new lady in his life; in fact, he had moved himself into her home with her children from a previous marriage.

If he was leaving me in peace, I did not care what he did.

The future was looking lovely. Well, this is what should have happened; however, life never turns in the direction you expect of it.

Lucy was becoming increasingly difficult to handle. She was still going into the salon after school, despite all my attempts to stop her. She lied to me as to her whereabouts, but I had it on good authority that she was in there every day.

What I failed to understand was that despite Mark having rejected her as not being his biological child regarding access, Lucy had only ever known him as her dad and naturally wanted a continued relationship with him, and to do this, she had little alternative but to lie about it.

One evening, she had asked to go to the cinema with a friend. I had asked all the right questions to verify this to be the case and was sufficiently satisfied it was OK to allow her to go.

She was now hitting her teens, so I was trying to instil a degree of trust between us.

I knew that the film would have finished by a certain time, and I allowed sufficient time for her to walk home.

As time passed and still no Lucy, I knew that something was wrong. I was beginning to feel that I had made a mistake in giving her my trust. I sat there wondering where on earth she could be when the thought struck me like a hammer blow. I picked up the phone and dialled the number for the salon.

A woman answered, her voice barely audible over the sound of laughter and thudding music. I had to shout to make myself heard.

"Is Lucy there?" I bellowed into the mouthpiece.

"Yes," came the simple reply.

"Well, this is her mother speaking. You had better tell her to get her backside home this minute or I am calling the police," I boomed before slamming the receiver down.

Twenty minutes later, Lucy staggered in through the front door smelling of alcohol and cigarette smoke.

"What the hell do you think you are playing at?" You have been told not to go in there, especially not at night."

"Dad was having a party; he said I could go."

"You deliberately lied to me, Lucy. I'm very disappointed in you. Have you been drinking?" I demanded as I drew closer to her.

"No," she lied. Because I could smell it. With that, she bolted for the stairs, disappearing up them as fast as her legs could carry her.

"Don't do anything you might regret," said Cassy, as I grabbed my coat, put on my boots, and flew out the front door.

I headed down the hill into town getting angrier by the minute.

By the time I reached the salon, I was geared up for a fight. I hammered on the door with all my might. I could see people inside dancing to the loud music.

I hammered again on the door until I raised the attention of a girl standing at the bar. She disappeared and a few seconds later,

Mark came into the reception area and stared at me through the glass looking back at me with a satisfying smirk on his face.

He made no attempt to unlock the door, he simply stood on the other side of the glass with that smirking expression on his face.

The anger inside of me broke like a dam bursting.

"You bastard!" I screamed as loud as I could muster.

"Blah Blah bloody Blah," he shouted back at me laughing and pulling grotesque faces through the window.

"She is only thirteen, Mark, and you have allowed her to come here and drink and smoke and get up to God knows what. Have you got no sense of decency at all? You are using her to get back at me." I accused now almost at the point of hysteria.

By this time others had joined in the exchange which only exacerbated the tension.

"Oh fuck off you stupid cow." He bellowed back at me.as the laughter from within grew louder.

"You stay away from my daughter; do you hear me?! I screamed, pummelling on the door with both fists to reinforce what I was saying. "Don't you dare allow her in here again, do you hear me, or I will call the police! That is no threat, Mark, that's a fucking promise," emphasized with one last thump on the glass to drive home the point. He simply put two fingers up at me.

I turned on my heel and headed back home.

"What happened?" asked Cassy, as I arrived home slamming the door behind me, still angry from my confrontation.

"If I catch her within an inch of that place again, she will never see the light of day again." I declared.

It had not dawned on me that I was being extremely selfish. It had completely escaped me that Lucy had not grasped that Mark did not have the paternal connection to her as he did for his son.

She was quite simply desperate for him to continue to be the dad that she had come to love since she was a tiny tot. I should have known just how devastating this had all been for her, but regrettably, I didn't.

All I could see was that Mark clearly had no respect for her which was putting her in danger.

The fact that she was now proving so difficult to handle was largely due to my total lack of understanding for her feelings. I selfishly expected her to unreservedly support what I was doing, simply because I felt it was the best thing for all of us. These errors of judgment would continue to have grave repercussions on our lives and our relationship.

Cassy looked at me with sadness in her eyes as she imparted the final issue of the day.

"Well, you may not have noticed in the heat of the moment, but she had borrowed your brand-new blouse which now has a nice big cigarette burn on the sleeve." She sighed sympathetically.

"Oh, my Lord," I said with a sigh as I sank down onto the chair. "I had not even worn that blouse. Teenagers - who would have them"?

Having read the riot act to Lucy, things again settled into a routine, or so it seemed.

I was enjoying the job and had made several friends, who we occasionally met up with on the odd evening out at the local social club.

I tried to stay out of the politics at work as someone was always grumbling about some injustice or another, but it was all rhetoric; nothing ever came of it. I just ignored it all and got on with the work.

It was a monotonous but simple system. At intermittent intervals on a conveyor belt, the paint nozzles came down and inserted a designated amount of paint into a line of moving tins.

My job was to slam the lids on at the end of the belt. The tins would then proceed down the line to be labelled, packed, and then shrink-wrapped onto pallets.

Mr Shaw had thought fit to award his own son Luke the lofty responsibility of maintaining the machines. He should be always on call in the event of any malfunction, to rectify the problem speedily so as not to affect production.

This tended to be the main cause of the majority of the dissent within the paint shop since Mr Shaw's son liked to bet on the horses and spent a great deal of time each day hiding himself in order to study the form of those running in the next race. So, when a problem did occur, invariably, Luke was nowhere to be found.

This particular morning, there had been more than the usual breakdowns, and in the absence of Luke, Mr Shaw had found himself repeatedly summoned to sort out numerous different problems that his son should be undertaking.

This was not conducive to his overall mood, but instead of taking his son to task about his increased workload, he would invariably take out his frustrations on the shop floor workers.

When a machine operative needed to use the toilet, the procedure to follow was to raise your arm to attract Luke's attention and ask for a bathroom break.

He would then come and take over your task to maintain the continuous running of the machines.

This system normally worked adequately well. However, in the absence of Luke, the responsibility fell to Mr Shaw, which inevitably annoyed him as it took him away from his own work.

On this day, I needed to use the toilet. I could not see any sign of Luke, so I tried to wait as I could see that Mr Shaw had yet again been summoned to deal with quite a major spill. The nozzles had come down and caught the side of the tins, depositing their contents directly onto the floor.

I looked around again - still no sign of Luke. I waited and waited. Mr Shaw, having now turned off the faulty machine completely, had returned to his office where I could see him clearly through the glass on his telephone.

I waved again. He looked straight at me and then turned his back. He obviously did not want to deal with me as he was trying to sort out his own problem. I looked around again for Luke, who was still absent.

Mr Shaw had come out of his office and was now heading at breakneck speed out of the paint shop.

I knew that I could wait no longer, or someone would be clearing up another spill of my making. I had no other choice but to press the off button on my machine and make a run for it. With a bit of luck, I could make it to the toilet and back and restart my machine before Mr Shaw returned, then he would know nothing about it.

Well, at least until the production figures for the day showed a drop. He would still be unaware of the reason for it.

There I was, sitting on the loo with knickers down around my ankles, when I heard someone enter the lady's toilet and start kicking the toilet door.

"Get out of there at once."

I recognised the voice of Mr Shaw. I was so taken aback that the only thing I could think of to say was,

"I haven't finished." I remarked stupidly. The kicking resumed.

"Get back to your bloody machine NOW!" bellowed the voice again, with more kicks to the door. As I came out of the toilet, he grabbed the lapel of my overalls and yanked me out into the corridor.

By this time, the shock of what had just happened subsided as I struggled to gather my senses. I pulled myself free from his grasp and turned on him.

"Excuse me, how dare you man handle me you have no right,"

"Who gave you bloody permission to turn your machine off? Get out of my paint shop," he seethed, his face purple with rage.

"What do you mean," I stuttered faced now with this new and unexpected dilemma.

"Clock yourself off and get off the premises and don't come back," he shouted, waving his arm at me.

I was in complete shock. How in the wide world did he think he could get away with treating me like that? It was a person's human right to be allowed to use the toilet, even I knew that.

One thing I had learned over the years was that I was no longer prepared to be bullied by anyone.

I had witnessed Mr Shaw, on several occasions, treating several women in the paint shop with less respect than could be considered acceptable, especially the younger ones.

He was not going to get away with that with me, I decided.

I clocked off on the machine and headed down the hill to the other department where I knew the trade union guy was based. I was informed that he was on his tea break, so I headed for the canteen where I found him enjoying a cup of coffee and a cigarette.

I plopped myself down opposite him at the table and proceeded to tell him what had just transpired.

"That's out of order, that is. Come with me," he said, putting out his cigarette and getting up from the table.

I followed him to a set of lockers where he produced a thick plastic-covered folder. He pointed to the phone number printed on the front and stated,

"This is the union headquarters. Ring this number and ask for Reg Harding. He will advise you the best way forward with this."

I thanked him for his help and made my way home. On arriving home, I got straight on it. I got through to Reg, a gravelly-voiced man who seemed very sympathetic to what I had experienced. He pointed me to the relevant pages in the union manual and told me to read through everything appertaining to the issue and went on to advise that I should fight the issue, not with Mr Shaw but with the head honcho, as he put it.

I spent the whole evening, and into the early hours, reading up on everything I needed and making notes as I went until I was confident in how I was going to proceed to take this forward.

The next day, I went about my mission with a determination that quite surprised me.

I arrived at work, clocked myself in, got into my overalls and went into the paint shop.

I started up the machine that I had been working on the previous day and waited for the expected reaction.

It did not take long for Mr Shaw to spot me; he came charging across and made a grab for the off button of the machine.

"What the hell are you doing in here? You were told yesterday to leave the premises," he barked.

"Mr Shaw, I have come to work this morning to inform you that I am taking the relevant action against you, with the full backing of my union, regarding your reaction towards me for switching off my machine yesterday as no one was available to relieve me to permit me to use the bathroom when I desperately needed to. And, for physically removing me from the ladies' lavatory, then subsequently removing me from my job, then finally from the premises," I said straight-faced and very calmly.

His jaw clenched and his mouth dropped open in absolute astonishment. He stared at me and then bellowed,

"Who the bloody hell do you think you are? Get out of here," he shouted into my face.

Obviously, no one had ever been brave enough in the past to question his behaviour. I think he thought that I might buckle under this latest threat.

But he had another think coming - this was the new me. I was no longer that eager-to-please timid little mouse who was frightened of upsetting people, going along with things I knew to be wrong. He had picked a fight with me, and I was going to take him on with the full backing of the law. I turned to face him. He took a step back.

"Mr Shaw, I'm going to switch this machine back on and continue my work as I have done nothing to warrant doing otherwise. I will expect an appointment to speak with Mr Harrison, the Director of this company, at some time convenient to him today, in order that I may make a formal complaint about your behaviour toward me."

With that, I reached across and pressed the on button on the machine and started work.

Mr Shaw did not quite know how to respond. He had clearly never faced the consequences of his actions before, and I could see that I had him rattled.

Thirty minutes later, Luke came to me and said that I was wanted in the offices. I was to go to the room marked 'Boardroom' on the second floor where Mr Harrison would see me.

I had had the opportunity to meet Mr Harrison on one previous occasion, when he had paid a visit to the paint shop. He had come over to my machine and we had got into conversation about Sussex where he had also originated. I had found him very interesting to talk to.

However, this was a different matter entirely, so I was not at all sure of his reaction to me causing disruption in his company.

I knocked gently on the door and entered when I heard the invitation.

"Please take a seat," he said politely.

He listened intently as I related in detail what had transpired the previous day. He sat quietly for a few moments looking at the ink dots on his blotter, then said,

"Rita, I understand you are upset; however, Mr Shaw has been with us for many years. He is a well-respected employee who has never so much as had the slightest blemish on either his standard of work, or indeed, his character. He has overseen the supervision of simply hundreds of workers in his department over the time he has been with us and has never had an allegation made against the fairness of his treatment," he said calmly.

"I don't doubt that; however, I put it to you that perhaps people find him intimidating and they have not been brave enough to challenge him before about his managerial style which, in this case, was simply unacceptable. We are now in the 20th century, Mr Harrison; employers are not permitted to either deny a person the use of a toilet or to physically manhandle them. He was clearly in the wrong in both instances, which is why I feel it necessary to draw this incident to your attention."

I continued to stare straight at him, my hands resting in my lap.

"Now, Rita, Mr Shaw is only two years away from his retirement date. Surely you would not wish to blot his exemplary record. It would be devastating for him to have to face disciplinary action at this stage of his career. He could well lose his job." He added trying to emphasize the severity of my accusation.

"Oh, I quite agree; perhaps that should have been more of a consideration to him before he chose to act in such an unprofessional manner," I concluded.

Mr Harrison smiled wryly at me.

"What are you proposing then, Rita, that you feel could resolve this situation in an amicable way for both parties?"

"Oh, that is very simple, Mr Harrison," I continued. "I want a full apology from Mr Shaw, and I will also require assurances that in the future, I will be permitted to turn off my machine in the absence of a relief operator, in order that I may use the toilet without the fear of reprisals, condemnation or physical manhandling, I believe that to be a perfectly reasonable request," I added.

The smile returned to his face.

"Please wait outside," he instructed.

I sat on a chair just outside the door not really knowing what to expect next, but I had made my case and felt it to be a strong one. I did not have to wait long as Mr Shaw marched past me without even as much as a sideways glance and entered the boardroom.

A few minutes later, I was summoned back in. I took the same seat as before and looked directly at Mr Harrison.

"Rita, Mr Shaw has something he wishes to say to you," he said now directing his full attention toward the man standing meekly before him.

I waited expectantly for him to say something. He had his head bowed looking at his hands in his lap. Without looking up at me, he said,

"I am very sorry that I reacted like I did; it was just that I was having to deal with a mechanical breakdown. It was just an inconvenient time. If I had known that you were so desperate to use the ladies, I would not have done what I did," he muttered, his gaze still focused on his lap.

I looked back at Mr Harrison.

"I'm sorry, Mr Harrison," I said, getting up from my chair as if to end the discussion there. "That is simply not good enough. The fact that my need to use the toilet was inconvenient timing for Mr Shaw should bear no relevance to why he behaved as he did. Maybe if his son had been on the shop floor at the time, doing the job that he is paid to do which is dealing with machine problems, there would have been no need for me to be made to wait at all" looking back at Mr Harrison awaiting a response.

"well, I feel sure that if Mr Shaw had realised your need was urgent he would have acted quite differently," he suggested smiling at me.

"No that is not the issue here," I replied "The fact that Mr Shaw felt compelled to cover for his son's absence by doing his job for him was no fault of mine, and certainly not a good reason for reacting the way he did. Neither was it acceptable to enter the ladies' toilets and proceed to kick down the door of the toilet that I was occupying. Neither was it acceptable to drag me out of the ladies toilet by my overalls, denying me the ability to wash my hands," By this time I was now in full flow but again Mr Harrison cut in to try to bring about a satisfactory conclusion

"Are you going to accept Mr Shaw's apology Rita, I believe he is being very gracious about the whole unfortunate incident," doing his level best to try to mediate. But I new my rights and this lack luster apology was not cutting it.

"No, I'm sorry, but there is nothing about this entire incident that is acceptable behaviour in any shape or form. It is very clear to me that Mr Shaw is refusing to accept any responsibility for what transpired yesterday, by attempting to shift the blame for his foul temper away from his son's negligence to do his job, to the fault being levelled at me for requesting a bathroom break, which, as I have previously stated, I am perfectly legally entitled to take.

I took a deep breath and continued on eager to make to make my case. It should not have to be necessary to have to convince someone that you are desperate to use the toilet, or to have to fit in with whatever the circumstances are at the time in the filling shop. One should be permitted to go when the need is evident. It is a basic human right." I said, directing my comments directly to Mr Shaw. I was determined that he was not going to get off the hook that easily.

"Now look Rita this is getting us nowhere," I sensed that Mr Harrison was becoming frustrated at his inability to resolve the matter. So, I stepped up the rhetoric further.

"I can see that it will be necessary for me to take this matter to the next level. I will prepare a full report of the incident that will be submitted to the local Union head office, who will, in due course, be in touch regarding the next stage of the proceedings. Thank you very much for your time, Mr Harrison." I said politely and turned to leave.

"Um, just a minute, Rita. Just be kind enough to wait outside for one more minute, please. I won't keep you long," he said, closing the door behind me. I sat again and waited. When asked to return to the boardroom, Mr Shaw was on his feet looking straight at me.

This time, the apology that came sounded sincere, fully accepting the blame for what had occurred. All the requested conditions had now been fully met, with the added assurance that should such a situation arise again in the future, I was to contact Mr Harrison directly on the number provided on his personal business card which he held out for me to take.

I returned to the filling shop elated that things had gone so well. I was quite proud of the way I had handled it.

Some of the ladies asked me when I was leaving and if I had been sacked. They seemed genuinely surprised that I was back on my machine. They had expected me to be out on my ear and could not understand that having picked a fight with Mr Shaw, I was still standing upright.

My euphoria was short-lived. I had stupidly failed to identify that the concessions I had cleverly gained applied to me, and only me. Therefore, as I started getting given the kind of privileges that the others weren't afforded, the backlash was strongly felt as it ricocheted back on me with full force.

Mr Shaw enjoying every minute of it. I assume he had seen it coming and had believed that its implications would place me in an untenable position which would ultimately force me into leaving.

But I had grown a backbone and I was determined to rise above such treatment.

It began with me being called all manner of names, and punishment by ostracism. When I entered the canteen, it would quickly empty out. If I spoke to someone, I would be ignored then backs were turned. I was being sent to Coventry. Those who had talked to me before were now intimidated by the others.

It was an uncomfortable situation that I was made to endure daily, but I had fought for my rights; they could have done the same, but they chose not to because they lacked the bottle. It was easier for them to take out their frustrations on me.

Mr Shaw also refused to have any dealings with me. If I needed instructions, it was Luke who delivered them. Whoever would have thought that I would pay such a high cost for my achievement to secure my rights? I would remain resolved.

Chapter 11

I managed to remain optimistic as I had received some brilliant news at home. I had been offered a three-bedroom house on the other side of town near Lucy's school and it was just perfect.

It seemed like heaven as we moved into what seemed an extraordinary amount of space.

However, we had enjoyed our time in our little cottage and would hold fond memories of our time there.

Life moved on; I had heard through the grapevine that Mark's relationship had broken down. I had been told that he had apparently been making Unacceptable demands on her I don't know hoe true it was, but it would not have surprised me. He had proved he was capable of anything when he had been drinking.

He had never requested a visitation with Lee, which I was pleased about, but sadly, birthday and Christmas presents stopped too. He had moved on again from another child.

Let sleeping dogs lie, I thought.

Lucy was now in secondary school. She had one very nice little friend who came from a very good family.

She had told me she was going to this friend's home straight from school and would be having tea there. She assured me that she would be home by 9 pm.

We had decided to take Lee to our social club. It was Bingo night. He always enjoyed going there as he would have his crisps and his coke and mark off the numbers on the card for me. We had not been home long when the phone rang. It was the hospital.

The person on the other end explained that Lucy had been brought in two hours ago, drunk as a sea lord.

She had been found, passed out, in the grounds of the local sports centre. Someone had phoned for an ambulance, and she had been taken to the local hospital where they had pumped out her stomach. She was now sufficiently recovered and ready for collection.

I could not believe what I was hearing. How could she have done such a thing? I grabbed my coat and we headed for the hospital.

What greeted us there was just shocking, to say the least. There sat Lucy, buckled over, looking an odd shaded of grey.

Her school uniform was wet with vomit, her make-up had run down her face, and her tights were ripped into holes.

The smell was almost unbearable and was easily identifiable as whisky. I stared at her in utter disbelief.

"I think you would be wise to instil in your daughter the gravity of what she has done to herself," the Sister declared sternly. "You need to be aware that she was bordering on alcoholic poisoning. If she had not been brought in when she was, she could well have died," the Sister told me in very stern terms.

"I am so sorry; I was told that she was going to a friend's house for tea. I had no idea." My voice tailed off as I looked again at the dishevelled mess in front of me.

"Umm, well, just make sure this never happens again. You are responsible for her, and her actions; you are her mother, are you not?" she said accusingly.

As I took Lucy's arm, I bent down close and whispered in her ear.

"You wait till I get you home."

Being in the confines of the car, the journey home was almost unbearable. I had to wind down all the windows in order to be able to breathe. The stench of stale whiskey was nauseating.

When we got back, I ran her a bath and bagged up the clothes for the bin. I did not get an opportunity to reprimand her as she went to her room where she slept off a mega hangover.

"It serves you right, young lady. You are grounded for the next month," I told her when she finally surfaced next morning looking very fragile.

After speaking to her friend's parents, I discovered that they had gone out for the evening, leaving the girls listening to music in the sitting room. Apparently, the pair had raided their drinks cabinet, then decided to go to the sports centre. They told me that their daughter was completely fine with no adverse side effects from this unfortunate episode.

Well, how the hell did my daughter get herself in such a state? I questioned myself.

Not long after this incident, I was faced yet again with the evidence that my daughter was sliding down a slippery slope of self-destruction. I was busy cooking tea when the doorbell went. As I walked through the hallway, I could see several people through the glass door; a woman, a teenage girl and someone who was in uniform, a police uniform. I opened the door.

"Can I help you?" I asked, concerned.

The woman was the first to respond.

"Your daughter ambushed my daughter on the way home from school, along with several of her friends, and has beaten the hell out of Gail. Just look at the state of her," she said, pushing the girl forward to emphasise her point.

I looked at the dishevelled girl who had dried blood below her nose. She had a swollen lip and a rip in the v of her jumper where the wool had unravelled.

"Oh, good Lord," I gasped, completely shocked and in total disbelief. "Are you saying that my daughter did this to you?" I asked, directing the question to the girl.

"Yes, it was Lucy; her and her friends were waiting for me in the fields on the way home. She just knocked me to the ground, then they were punching me and pulling my hair," she said, gulping back a sob.

The police officer then took over the conversation.

"This is a very serious matter; you do realise this is common assault."

"Yes, Officer, I do realise the severity of the situation," I replied in earnest. I could not understand what had possessed her to have instigated such an unprovoked attack.

"LUCY!" I screamed. She was standing at the top of the stairs looking terrified as she had overheard everything. "Get down here this minute," I bellowed. "What in God's name made you do such a terrible thing?" I asked accusingly.

"She was calling me names at break time," came the reply.

"And you think that entitled you to respond with this?" I said pointing to the battered blood-stained face of the girl.

"I'm sorry," she muttered with tears welling up in her eyes.

"Go to your room at once and stay there." Turning back to the mother, I said,

"I'm so very sorry. I can't imagine what possessed her to do such a thing. I can promise you it will never happen again."

"Are you happy with the outcome, Mrs Andrews, or do you wish to take the matter further?" The police officer asked the woman.

"Well," this kind of bullying has to stop. I mean, children should be aware there are consequences for their behaviour especially as serious as this, she continued. "But, as she has apologised, and I have her mother's assurance that her daughter will be punished, hopefully, she will learn a lesson from it. I think I can say that the matter has been suitably addressed." She finished looking at the police officer.

Breathing a sigh of relief that the matter would end there, I said sincerely,

"Oh, Lucy will most certainly learn a valuable lesson for what she has done, you can be assured of that," I told her.

With that, they were gone. I turned and leant my back against the front door. What on earth was I to do with this child? She seemed to be hell-bent on causing trouble. I went back into the kitchen where I pondered what a suitable punishment might look like.

Softening over the coming weeks, I found myself giving in to the constant pleas from both children for a kitten. I thought it might give Lucy something to focus on, so relented.

There was an ad in the local paper.

A litter had been born to a farm cat. There were six kittens ready to leave their mother, and they were going free to good homes.

I phoned up and arranged to go to see them that evening.

Both children and I got the bus with a cat box that our neighbour had lent us. When it said farm cat, I didn't know that the little critters would be completely wild.

They were in a barn and were in an old crate curled up with their mother.

They hissed, spat, arched their backs, and took off in all directions of the barn. It took nearly an hour to catch even one of them. There was no choice; we had to have the only one we could catch.

I did not know how we were going to cope with it when we got it home. I put the cat box down in the middle of the sitting room and tentatively opened the door of the box. In a flash of brown and black tortoiseshell, it flew past me and raced behind the sofa in the blink of an eye where it stayed for the next week and a half. I had put down a litter tray and food and milk on a special mat at the end of the sofa, and in the dead of night, it would creep out, eat the food, use the tray, and disappear again.

We were now the proud owners of an anti-social cat named Sage which Lucy had named because it was the colour of sage and onion stuffing! It took weeks, and weeks of patience to win the trust of this little wild creature, but we finally managed to, and she went on to become a lovable member of the family who we adored. She even had kittens herself and proved herself to be the most amazing mother, unlike me, who failed miserably.

The next trauma in my life was when I got up one morning and found a note on the kitchen table. It read:

MUM, I HAVE RUN AWAY DON'T TRY TO FIND ME I HAVE TAKEN SOME BREAD SOME MILK AND SOME BISCUITS I HAVE GOT MY SHEETH KNIFE I HAVE GOT MY UNIFORM AND WILL GO TO SCHOOL PLEASE DON'T WORRY ABOUT ME LOVE YOU LEE XXX

Oh, heaven help me, I thought. What did I do to deserve this?

I phoned work and explained the situation. Then, Cassy and I set about searching the area. Lee was finally found later that morning. He and a school friend had made a camp in a large tree in a wooded area not far from our house.

It transpired that Lee had concocted the plan to get his small friend away from his father who regularly beat the child.

I took them both back into school, where, following a meeting with the headmaster, the other boy's father was summoned and was given an extremely strongly worded ultimatum that social services would be involved should the matter come to his attention again.

I could not help being full of admiration for my son's motives on this occasion, and the matter was assigned to the history book. I still have that note to this day.

My six weeks of labelling had turned into three years. I had ridden out the storm of ostracism and things had settled down. I had reached the lofty height of quality control assistant. Mr Harrison had become a regular visitor to the shop floor and had even asked me out on a date.

Although it was very flattering, his invitation had been declined.

I was beginning to look to the horizon. I did not want to spend my whole working life in a factory. I began to search for a new challenge. I knew that I had an aptitude for selling so when an advertisement appeared for a shop manager in a unisex boutique in the next town,

I decided to apply.

I did not expect to get it, as I had no previous managerial experience, but I had an excellent reference from Popsicle and was sure Mr Harrison would give me a reference. I had nothing to lose. Anyway, I thought the experience of an interview would be beneficial.

I had bought a trendy outfit that I thought would be suitable. I arrived well before the time and hung about in the mall waiting for the time to pass, trying to anticipate the type of questions that might be asked.

I took a deep breath as I pushed open the door. It was bigger shop than Popsicle's and was one of a small chain of five.

A middle-aged man sat behind the counter. He introduced himself as Mr Aylesbury. He came across as quite stern which was a little unnerving, but I kept my cool as I followed him into the back room.

After a series of what seemed easy questions, he said,

"The store opens at nine o'clock. You would have to be in at eight-thirty to get things ready. I see that you live 4 miles away. How do you propose to get here for that time?" he asked.

"Oh, that is no problem," I lied, "I have my own transportation."

"Well then, that will be all. I require someone to start the week after next, so you will hear one way or the other in the next few days."

I thanked him and left. I thought it had gone reasonably well, but I had no knowledge of how many others may have replied who would be more qualified for the post than me, so I thought it best not to get my hopes up. I completely put it to the back of my mind.

The next day, Lucy and I went shopping and bought paint to redecorate Lucy's room. She and I were busy painting when the phone rang. The voice on the other end said,

"This is Mr Aylesbury. Am I speaking to Rita?"

"Yes, this is she," I answered, surprised.

"Rita, if you still want the position as retail manager, it is yours."

"Oh, yes please; thank you so much," I replied, genuinely shocked.

Immediately, I stopped what I was doing as it hit me that I had to now acquire a mode of transport.

By the afternoon, I had purchased a secondhand moped out of the newspaper. I went down into town and bought a crash helmet. All sorted, I thought, congratulating myself on my ingenuity.

I handed in my notice at the factory. Before I knew it, I was heading off to my new job.

I loved it! There was just me and one member of staff, but for once, I felt important.

It took me thirty minutes each day to get to work on my little pop-pop. I looked quite a spectacle dressed up in my wet weather gear, much to the children's amusement.

I managed to attach a small box on the back to accommodate my shopping.

Mother and Dad had downsized to a retirement apartment in the town where I worked. I made the mistake of popping in to see them in my lunch hour, which quickly became expected.

Mother would have lunch prepared, so I did not dare to arrive.

Yet again, I was placing myself in a position where I was living my life pleasing Mother.

On occasions, Dad would say to her,

"Perhaps Rita might like to do something different in her lunch break," this was quickly overruled.

"Nonsense, she has to eat something through the day so she might as well do it here as anywhere." Dad would look at me and raise his eyes as if to say 'sorry love, I tried'

It became the daily ritual which I castigated myself for starting but lacked the forcefulness to stop. As far as Mother was concerned, my newly acquired backbone had returned to mere cartilage, which had reverted me right back to my childhood, pleasing Mother instead of myself.

Mine and Cassy's relationship was suffering the test of time, as so often happens in the gay world. I did consider that maybe the constant family trauma played a part in the reason why things had become strained between us.

However, it was little surprise to me when she said she wanted to split. She had met someone else. I was rather relieved in a way. I wanted a quieter life and was fed up with being stared at whenever we went anywhere. I wished her well as we went our separate ways.

I was looking forward to time on my own, pleasing myself after so long. What joy.

I would miss the extra salary coming in, so it would be necessary to cut a few corners here and there, but I was on a higher salary myself now, so it was manageable.

True to form, nothing ever ran smoothly in our house. I was about to encounter the next nuclear event in the form of Lucy's foray into the world of boyfriends.

To say I was shocked was an understatement as I opened the door to the first love of Lucy's life.

There stood a grinning young man dressed in combat gear and laced hobnail boots that reached up to the calves of his legs. He had a completely shaven head, crooked crossed teeth, a Tattooed neck and hands, and a safety pin hung through his left nostril.

I think if someone had snapped a photo of my face at this point it would have clearly told the true extent of my first impressions of him even though I had made a monumental effort not to show it.

"Hi," he said as he brazenly strode past me into the front room and slumped himself down on my sofa, followed by Lucy who coiled herself around him as close as was physically possible.

I was not entirely sure how to react to this perfect example of a thug that was now snogging my daughter.

I tried to engage in conversation to find out a bit more about his background; maybe it was not as bad as it appeared on the surface.

If that had been my initial hope, then I was to be bitterly disappointed.

This young man, with the innocent name of Terry, was the son of a police officer; his mother was a cleaner in the police headquarters where his father worked.

It was explained very carefully that poor Terry had been evicted from home by his wicked parents who did not understand him.

They had cruelly thrown him out on his ear to fend for himself in a hard world. He had been forced to live rough and had been into drugs because of his depression but was clean now, Lucy informed me, with an element of pride as she gazed at him adoringly.

I could tell that Lucy had bought into this fairytale big time.

I had adopted the theory of better to welcome him into my home than have her running around the streets getting up to heavens knows what, especially with Lucy not having the best track record in the world.

I invited him to Sunday lunch. He turned up in the same clothes he had on previously.

As I observed him shovelling his roast in as fast as he could, I questioned why Lucy couldn't have gone for a normal boy. As I continued to study him, I tried my best to see what it was that Lucy found so appealing about him. I failed.

Over the coming weeks, I noticed items of food going missing. Whole packets of stuff started disappearing. The natural conclusion was that it was him. I would have gladly given it to him, had he asked, but he was just helping himself to things which I assumed was with Lucy's full knowledge.

I continued to say nothing, hoping upon hope that the relationship would run its course. But as time went on, I could see that this was not going to happen. Lucy was totally infatuated with him. In her eyes, he was the best thing since Elvis.

It was not until I started noticing money going missing out of my purse that alarm bells really started ringing. I knew that something had to be done, but what exactly escaped me.

Lucy's feelings for him had deepened over time. She could not bear to be apart from him for a second.

She also seemed very volatile of late and tended to blow a fuse over the smallest of things. The mere mention of any criticism levelled against her man, as she called him, sent her into a fiery tirade of foul language that I was completely unaware was even a part of her vocabulary.

It became obvious that this situation needed very careful handling.

I was still racking my brains as to how I should deal with my latest problem when the opportunity presented itself to bring things to a natural head.

The day started badly. Terry arrived at the house, covered in blood, with yet another tooth knocked out. He told me that he had been attacked, but I did not believe that for one minute just by looking at his bruised knuckles, which told a tale to the contrary.

It was the perfect time to address the missing food and the missing money, all of which was, expectedly, vehemently denied.

I had heard enough - it was time to lay down the law. I told him he was no longer welcome in my home, and furthermore, I wanted him out of my daughter's life. I could see nothing but trouble ahead for her if I allowed this relationship to continue.

Lucy rebelled against this decision with all her might, but I stood my ground. I made it very clear that I meant what I said. She still lived in my house; therefore, changes would be made.

That night, I phoned Edward in the States who now had two growing children of his own and was very sympathetic to my problems as I explained the dilemma I was facing, emphasising that I was at my wit's end.

He advised that as she was about to finish school, the best thing would be to send her out to him. He felt that he could show her other opportunities available to her. Show her an alternative path. He even said if she settled, she could stay, and he would make sure she got a good job.

He told me to get her a passport sorted, and that he would pay for her ticket. This was an amazing offer. I was so excited for her. I firmly believed that she would soon see things differently and that Ian would become a distant memory.

I went to bed that night overwhelmed by Edward's incredibly generous offer, which I was convinced would be the perfect solution to all the problems that I had encountered with Lucy.

This was an amazing opportunity for her that would open doors to an exciting new life.

I could not wait to share this news with Lucy the following morning.

However, the news was not met with the reaction I had expected; just a sullen resignation that this was not the golden opportunity that I described, but merely a punishment that had to be

endured. She was being denied access to the love of her life, which she considered to be spiteful and cruel.

In her eyes, I was the worst mother in the world. To say that she hated me with a vengeance was an understatement.

All the plans were in place for her departure. The day finally arrived, and we were heading for the airport. Despite being just fifteen, she was travelling as an unaccompanied minor and was, therefore, supervised.

Edward would be there to meet her at the other end.

I thought by now just a little bit of excitement would have crept in but, as I tried to kiss her goodbye at the departure gate, she turned her head away from me and walked on through without as much as a backwards glance.

"Oh well, I sighed. "It's for her own good." I was trying to convince myself that, in time, she would come to realise what an incredible opportunity this was for her.

My work in the boutique was proving a success as sales increased. Mr Aylesbury was a very strict boss who was obsessed with theft.

He had us counting all the units on the rails in each department daily. I had to subtract what had been sold from the previous day's count, and the remaining figure should correspond with what had to be on the rails that day.

It was a monotonous chore but had to be done. It made me acutely aware of what customers were up to as any theft at all would show up immediately in the day's count. I became as obsessed with theft as he was.

Still, he had taken on board my idea about taking on a young man to oversee the men's department of the boutique. I felt that it would be a great asset.

I interviewed several young guys and was happy with my final choice. His name was Cody, a nice lad with trendy appearance and lovely to the eye which might also bring in more ladies.

He was proving very successful as the guys found it easier to be served by him, as opposed to me and sales were showing signs of improvement already.

It was good that the boutique was doing so well, as I now found I had to refocus my attention back on Lucy. Despite all my hopes that things would work out well for her in the States, it was not meant to be.

Edward had telephoned me to say that he had done his level best to show Lucy the many benefits that life in America had to offer, but all his attempts had failed. She was coming home.

I just hoped that the six weeks away would have been sufficient time to get Terry out of her system.

I collected her from the airport and greeted her warmly, determined not to show the disappointment that I was feeling that she had thrown away the chance of a lifetime.

I threw my arms around her and told her that I had missed her terribly. I was much encouraged by her warm response as she hugged me back.

We had not been in the house more than ten minutes when she dashed upstairs and came back down a few minutes later in jeans that looked as if they had been sprayed onto her legs and a low-cut T-shirt.

"See you later," she said as I watch her disappear out of the front door.

"Where are you going?" I called out. But she was gone. Of course, I knew exactly where she was going - she was going to see him. Not back in the country for two hours and she was already seeking him out.

I just sat down completely dismayed. All that effort and it had all been in vain. I could have wept.

Having now left school, she had joined Terry on welfare, and they hung about the streets with all the other town reprobates. Frustratingly, I seemed completely unable to get through to her.

She was worth so much more. How she could throw herself away on such a waster was beyond me. I got myself in such a lather about it all.

Things finally came to a head one teatime when, having served her up a cooked meal, Lucy took one look at the food on her plate and said in disgust,

"I'm not eating that crap. I'll eat out."

"Eat out, will you?" I screeched, the red mist already descending.

I picked up the plate and threw it at the door, watching spaghetti drip over the door handle and onto the mat.

"You ungrateful girl, how dare you talk to me like that?!" Now at the level of complete hysteria, I made a dash toward her.

"Mum don't!" cried Lee, jumping in front of me as he could see the situation was already out of control.

I pushed him out of my way as I chased behind her up the stairs. She tried in vain to hold her bedroom door shut, but I was in such a rage that my strength overpowered her.

She leapt over her bed to try and escape me as I burst through the door, but all sanity had now completely deserted me. I had reached a point of no return. She held her arms over her head as my slaps rained down on her.

"I'm not taking any more from you!" I yelled. "I'm sick to death of you! Don't think for one minute that I'm going to put up with any more of your antics. You're making me ill with worry, do you hear me? You're making me ill. I'm not having it. It stops here; do you hear me?!" I shouted at her, almost cracking my voice.

With the red haze beginning to subside, I backed away from her, breathing heavily from the sheer emotion that I had summoned up from some unknown place within me. I knew instantly that I had crossed a line.

I went back down the stairs knowing that my relationship with my only daughter was now so badly fractured, possibly irreparably.

"Mum," said Lee, concern written all over his face at what had just occurred.

"It's alright, Lee," I told him, as I put two reassuring arms around him and held him close.

Where had I gone so badly wrong? my inner voice asked. But deep down, I knew the answer to that.

I had tried to prevent her from making the wrong choices in life like I had, but all I had achieved was to drive a wedge between us. Now I feared I had lost her love forever. Two minutes later, I heard the front door slam, and she was gone, into the arms of that moron, and there was not a damned thing I could do about it.

She did not come home. I didn't know which way to turn. I was on the verge of phoning the police when the phone rang.

A woman's voice said she was phoning to tell me that my daughter was safe and was with her on her farm. She went on to accuse me of beating my child. She said Lucy and Terry were going to stay with her and were now in her care.

She told me that Lucy didn't want to see me ever again and warned me not to contact social services or she would tell them how badly I had treated her, and not to try to contact her as she was never coming home. The phone went dead.

I phoned Mother and explained what had happened. I did not know where else to turn.

Mother sighed deeply and said,

"That child has been a worry from the start." Then, she added her usual gem of wisdom that was always trawled out in these types of situations: "Bide your time, Rita, bide your time."

Is that it? Is that the best advice you can come up with, I thought as my world was yet again unravelling? I was consumed with the worry of it all. I couldn't sleep; I couldn't eat.

Biding my time was easy to say although extremely hard to implement when one was having a nervous breakdown. There was nothing more I could do; I just had to wait.

Mother's wise words had yet again paid off as several weeks later, I had a phone call from Lucy. I was elated to hear that she had split with Terry. But then came the bombshell.

"There is something you need to know, Mum; I think I'm pregnant. I'm sorry, Mum," she added miserably.

"Oh, Lucy. Oh, my sweet Jesus."

I don't know why, but the mental image popped straight into my head of a bald baby with tattooed arms and neck, sporting a safety pin in its navel. A mini-Terry.

I fought to rid myself of this grotesque image and told her,

"You had better come home; we have a lot to discuss."

We sat and talked through all of the options available. Trying not to think about that mental image, I told her that if she wanted to keep it, I would stand by her; we would manage somehow. The relief I felt when she told me that she wanted to abort was unprecedented.

However, the very next day she had changed her mind. The day after she had flipped back the other way and the day after that different again.

"Now look, Lucy, you will have to decide one way or the other. We can't keep on flip-flopping like this. Time is getting on; if you're going to do it, you need to get on and do it. Arrangements must be made before it's too late. Whatever your decision, you need to be sure of it as there will be no going back on it once it's made." We talked it all through yet again, and the final decision was to abort.

"Now, you're sure?" I asked one final time.

"Yes," she was sure.

Two days later the problem had resolved itself when Lucy announced her period had arrived. She now had the chance to start afresh.

Things began to return to normal as Lucy's mood lifted. Apart from the odd altercation over something trivial, she was almost a joy to be around. She came home one day and told me she was going to flat-share with a friend in the city. She had managed to secure a job in a famous boutique in the City where her friend also worked, and yes, they could afford the rent between them, and yes, they would have enough to live on the answers to my many questions. She went on to explain that they would do all their laundry at the launderette, and whilst her friend's parents were providing some of the furniture, was there anything I could offer to throw into the mix to help them out?

The list of items still needed was endless, but I was so elated to be back in favour. I agreed to almost all of it. What I couldn't provide out of my own cupboards, I picked up in charity shops. Mother donated some bedding and curtains, and with a car filled to the gunnels, Dad and I set off to find the address provided.

It was the scariest journey I had ever made as Dad's knowledge of road signs seemed to have diminished over the years. I gripped the seat on several occasions as he drove straight through traffic lights, whatever the colour.

He shouted and waved his fist at people who honked him at give way signs as he ploughed on through regardless.

How we got there unscathed was beyond me. The sad thing was, I made a mental note to privately tell Mother of the danger he was, not only to himself but also other road-users. He should really consider giving up the car before he killed himself or others, or both.

Anyway, we unloaded our gifts to two very excited, grateful girls who squealed as every box came through the door.

After inspecting her larder to satisfy myself that they were not going to starve, I gave her some money just so they could top up their food supplies, knowing full well that it would probably pay for takeaways for the next week.

With that mercy mission completed, we made the even more perilous journey home with Dad trying to negotiate the rush-hour traffic.

Now safely back home with my nerves completely shattered, but with the full knowledge that my only daughter was, at last, starting to live a productive life, I let out a satisfied sigh of relief as I sank down below the bubbles of a luxurious hot bath. Life looked good again, I thought, as I stared up at the tiny spider in the corner of the ceiling. Well, for now, anyway.

Chapter 12

I had to find a way to bring in more money. I was sending money to Lucy every week as they were struggling to afford food. It was possible that her wages were being spent on going out clubbing, as opposed to filling the food cupboard, but I could not bear the thought of her being hungry.

No longer having Cassy's salary to help out financially, it was becoming harder and harder to cope.

Lee was complaining that everything he had for his birthday had been secondhand. He grumbled that his bike had been secondhand, and his skateboard had been secondhand.

Even the woman who worked in the corner shop at the bottom of the road told me that Lee had told her that he had never, ever had a lollipop. Showing me up like that, I could have brained him, the little bugger.

I did my best but having adopted |Mother's principles, I categorically refused to borrow.

If I could not afford to buy things outright, then we went without.

To boost my income, I had made the decision that as Lucy had now left home, I would rent out her bedroom to a lodger.

No sooner had the ad gone in the paper than the phone rang. I agreed a time to come to view the room. I was a bit concerned that it was a gentleman coming as the room had been painted pink for Lucy.

He was a grey-haired middle-aged gentleman called Denis Andrews. He told me that he worked in the dairy factory on the edge of town.

He had lost his driving license for a year for a drink driving offence and needed a room close to his work. He went on to explain that he would return to his own home at the weekends which sounded a perfect arrangement for me. He reassured me that he was a non-smoker as specified in the advertisement. So, what was not to like?

He agreed that he would have it and handed me the deposit and a month's rent in advance.

With everything settled, I was now able to focus on my work.

Cody and I had started to share bits and pieces about our lives. I learned that he had just finished a long-term relationship which had been painful for him, and he had discovered that I was currently unattached.

Somewhat embarrassingly, he started showing an interest in me. At first, I thought it was amusing, especially when he asked me to go with him to a nightclub where he worked weekends as a DJ. Of course, I told him not to be ridiculous; he was sixteen years my junior.

He kept telling me it was only a number and it meant nothing to him. It was the person that he was interested in, not the age gap, he told me constantly. He became most insistent.

The constant pestering eventually wore me down and I convinced myself it might be fun. After all, nothing could come of it, so I agreed to go.

This first night very soon escalated into many nights, which inevitably led to him coming back to my house, one bad decision made after a nice meal and one and a half bottles of wine. It worked; I was well and truly hooked.

He was so pretty; he had long hair which he wore tied back at the nape of his neck and had a continental look about him with an olive-coloured skin and the largest almond-shaped eyes and a physique of a, well, a young man. He was very eager to please and did all the things I enjoyed.

As the months rolled on, he began pleading with me to let him move in permanently. Although Lee thought he was wonderful, when I told Lucy on the phone what I was considering, she told me,

"What are you thinking, Mother? He is far too young for you! He is a DJ and girls always flirt with the DJ, so it will only be a matter of time before you're traded in for a younger model. You mark my words."

I did not want to hear this, although, I knew it to be true; girls did flock around him like bees around a honey pot. One night at the club, I had overheard one girl say to another,

"What the hell is he doing with her? She is old enough to be his mother."

I must admit that stung, but he continued to assure me that it was me and only me he wanted.

Well, as sad as it sounds, I was desperate to believe him.

I tried desperately to tell myself that the whole thing was insane and that no earthly good would come of it, but my heart had a stranglehold on my head as I ploughed in deeper.

I had now met his mother, who had readily accepted me despite us being roughly the same age. His father, who was separated from his mother, was also OK with us as a couple. So, the pressure was increasing; he was determined to win me over.

Mother had finally talked Dad into parting with his car.

I offered to buy it off them, paid back monthly, being easily achievable now that I had the rent money coming in.

I now needed to start taking driving lessons, although I had no idea how I would get around the problem of my shortsightedness. I knew I would be expected to read a number plate at a distance before starting the test. It seemed very possible that I would not even get to start the car.

It became a constant worry as I continued to shell out money for lessons that I could ill afford, but my new instructor assured me he had a plan.

On the morning of the test, I was a bag of nerves. This was going to be a complete waste of time and money, I decided. I'm bound to fail. My confidence was now completely eroded.

While I was waiting for the instructor to arrive, the doorbell rang. I opened it to see a young guy standing there with a concerned look on his face.

"Are you the owner of a tortoiseshell cat?" he asked.

"Yes," I replied. "Why?"

"Well, I'm sorry to tell you this Mrs, but I have just seen a van run it over. The bloke got out and flung it over that hedge," he said, pointing to the house opposite.

"Oh no!" I screamed, pushing past him, and dashing over the road into the garden of the house with the hedge.

There, lying completely still, was Sage her glazed eyes staring at nothing, and her little pink tongue hanging limply outside of her mouth. She was gone. I let out a sob as I scooped her up and carried her broken, lifeless little body back indoors. Preoccupied with how on earth I was going to tell the children, I had not noticed my driving instructor sitting patiently in his car.

"Come on, Rita, "he called. "We can't be late, or we will miss our slot."

I placed the little lifeless body on the mat inside the front door and got into the driver's seat, completely numb. I did not give a damn if I passed the stupid test or failed it. Nothing seemed important in the scheme of things.

It now became apparent how my instructor was going to deal with the issue of my eyesight. He told me to memorise the number plate of the car parked up the road in both directions, getting me to repeat them several times until he was satisfied. That was, of course, providing that neither car was moved before the examiner came out of the office.

Fortunately for me, it worked perfectly, as did the whole test, largely because the only thing that was occupying my mind was the death of my beloved cat. I had undertaken the whole thing completely on autopilot.

When we pulled up outside the office, the examiner said,

"Congratulations, I'm pleased to inform you that you have passed your driving test." He beamed, holding out his hand to shake mine.

But my thoughts were still preoccupied with the pain of how that van driver could have thrown Sage's little body over that garden hedge, and her little dead body still lying on my front door mat at home.

"Thanks," I said, no longer able to suppress my sorrow, bursting into heart-rending sobs, I took the certificate from him and hurried away. I bet he had never experienced a response to a test pass like that before.

The next day, Lee and I stood solemnly together with tear-streaked faces, as we held a little funeral service in our garden where Sage was laid to rest, with a china ornament of a cat to mark the spot. Life could be so cruel. All that remained was to phone Lucy and tell her the sad news.

I had finally given in to Cody's insistence that we were made for each other. He had now moved himself into our home.

Lee was thrilled. He really liked him as they did loads of things together. They both seemed more like brothers, always sparring like a couple of kids. Their favourite pastime was fishing.

They would both disappear for hours together, which was rather lovely to see, as Lee's father had not shown the slightest interest in him.

I assumed he had sold the business as he had now moved to Devon with his latest girlfriend.

I had written to him to ask him not to exclude Lee from his life as he had done with his daughter, but I received a very threatening reply from his new girlfriend, so I thought it best not to pursue it further.

It was his loss. Cody seemed to be filling the void beautifully.

It was decided that as we were now in a relationship, it was best for Cody to look for another job. I did not want to be accused of favouritism with other members of staff.

He was fine with this decision and was very soon back working. He still did his weekend DJ job, so with both our incomes plus the rent money from the room, we were reasonably comfortable financially.

Cody bought himself a camper van, and we would all go off to the coast for the weekends straight after work.

Life, at last, was stress-free.

Lucy was struggling to cope financially and had decided to leave her job in the city to come back home. I had to tell her that having her old room back was not an option as it was now rented out. I would have to find her a flat. She decided she was going to stay with a friend.

It was not long before I found out the friend's name was Tim. Tim's parents owned a well-known pub in the town.

He seemed like a nice lad. I was not surprised to hear that they wanted to set up home together, especially when I discovered they were expecting a baby. Lucy had left the entire contents of her previous flat behind, so we had to start again afresh.

With the help of Tim's parents, we set about scraping together all the things that they would need to make their new home comfortable for them and the new arrival.

Things had started to deteriorate at work as Mr Aylesbury's obsession with theft had taken an unacceptable turn.

There was a system in place where the staff were permitted a discount on all their purchases. This obviously benefitted the overall shop sales as it advertised the stock to its maximum potential. There was a book where all staff purchases were recorded with the date, description of the item purchased, its product code, its value, and the till receipt stapled to the page, thus, leaving absolutely no room for error.

One day, a staff member, who was supposed to be working with me, had phoned in sick and I was therefore left to cope on my own.

Mr Aylesbury arrived unexpectedly mid-morning and had insisted that I do a spot count. I tried to explain that it was not possible to count and serve customers as I was working alone. Mr Aylesbury did not accept this as a reason for not complying with this demand. I was told to do what I was told.

I made a start on the count, trying to ignore the girl who was looking through the jeans.

A minute or so later, I was summoned to the counter where the staff discount book was thrust in my face.

"Where is it?" he demanded, now attracting the attention of the girl looking through the jeans.

"Where's what?" I asked puzzled.

"The discount entry for what you are wearing; it's not in here. You clearly haven't paid for it, have you?" he accused.

My blood began to bubble. I snatched the book out of his hand, flashing the pages over and over until I came to the entry for the items I was wearing. I held the opened page in front of his face and said in a loud, angry voice,

"How bloody dare you accuse me of stealing from you, MrAylesbury. You should have looked more carefully before you make public allegations like that," I said, stabbing my finger at the page in question, once again glancing at the girl who was now witnessing this attack on my honesty. But I no longer cared that I was being overheard; I was now in full swing.

"I have been working today with no support staff, unable to use the toilet or even take a tea break, as I am not permitted to lock the shop. You dare to come in here and accuse me of theft in front of customers? You don't deserve honest, loyal, hard-working staff if this is the way you treat them. Now, Mr Aylesbury, as it's nearly lunchtime, you can manage your own damned shop while I take my break for the hour that I'm legally entitled to. When I return, Mr Aylesbury, you had better be ready with a full apology for the false accusation you just made, or I will consult a solicitor."

With that, I grabbed my coat and marched out of the shop to a round of applause from the girl still looking at the jeans.

Normally, I just bought a sandwich and returned to the shop to eat it. It was unheard of to take a full hour, but I was determined I would not return until the very last minute.

The shop was empty when I did return. Mr Aylesbury came straight to me and apologised profusely for his 'error of judgment, 'as he put it. But the damage had been done.

The search would now begin to find a new job.

With the new baby expected at any time, Lucy and Tim had been offered a three-bedroom council house. It needed redecorating but, apart from that, it was ideal. Five weeks after moving in, baby Sofia arrived. My very first granddaughter. She was absolutely perfect. I could not believe I was now officially a grandmother.

I wondered how Cody felt now being in a relationship with a grandmother, something I tried not to dwell on.

I had seen a lot of activity going on further up the mall and learnt that a national clothing chain store was taking over a double unit and were looking for a manager. It would be a lot more responsibility being a much larger store, so this was an exciting opportunity.

I did not think I would be lucky enough to get it, as my previous experience fell far short of what would be expected with this company. However, I had nothing to lose by applying. I would give it my best shot.

The day of the interview arrived. The store was a hive of activity when I arrived, as the shopfitters were in fitting shelves and rails.

The Area Manager was conducting the interviews. There were seven others applying for the post, which gave me a feeling of unease as I had convinced myself that the others must surely be more qualified than me. I decided my best approach was to just be myself.

It seemed to go very well; I even had him laughing at one point as he enquired what I would do if faced with the situation of a member of staff who was persistently late.

I told him that I had already dealt with that in my previous job. I explained that I had sent the other staff members home early, and the offender had to then stay late to undertake ALL the clearing up for the day, making up for the time they had lost in the morning.

I went on to add that it meant that I also had to stay late that day, but that it had only happened on the one occasion, so the lesson had been quickly learned.

I watched the post daily, waiting for the refusal letter to drop onto the mat. As the days ticked by, I was convinced that they were not even going to let me know that I had been unsuccessful. I had now given up looking out for the postman.

Then, one morning, I noticed a solitary Manila envelope lying on the mat. I picked it up and opened it. The company's name was in bold capitals at the very top.

Oh, here we go then, I thought. Preparing myself for the inevitable disappointment, I continued to read on.

Thank you for applying for the position of Store Manager of the latest store acquisition of our national chain.

We are pleased to inform you that you have been successful in your application and will be required to attend an in-store briefing on the above-specified date to make the necessary preparations for the recruitment of your staff.

It will be necessary to achieve this before the end of this month in order that you have your team in situ on receipt of your stock.

Please confirm your acceptance of this post at your earliest convenience.

Kind regards

Tim Reynolds Area Manager

No way: this can't be true. I foolishly re-checked the name on the envelope to make sure it had not come to the wrong person. No, it was my name on the envelope, and at the top of the letter.

Oh, my God. I read it through several more times before I believed it. I danced around the room clutching it to my breast. "I'm going to be responsible for selecting my own team of staff!" I squealed to an empty room.

Cody now appearing around the living room door, bleary-eyed.

"What's up?" he asked, running his hand through his dishevelled hair.

"I got it!" I cried, waving the letter at him. "I got the manager's job," I said, dancing about the room again. Running back to him, I flung my arms around his neck in the sheer euphoria of the moment. "It's almost double the salary," I added excitedly.

"Good for you! I told you not to doubt yourself, didn't I?" he said, planting a kiss on my lips.

Doubting myself had indeed always been my biggest hurdle in life to overcome. One thing I was really looking forward to was telling Mr Aylesbury where to stick his job.

It went down like a lead balloon. He accused me of being most inconsiderate by only giving two weeks' notice. He told me just how disgusted he was by my lack of loyalty and put the phone down.

I did not take it personally, as having had conversations with the managers of his other shops, I was aware that he treated everyone in the same way. He was just basically a miserable individual. Besides, I didn't care a jot about his opinion of me. Let the next manager put up with his meanness; I was moving on.

I worked my two weeks' notice without further contact from him and posted the shop keys through the letterbox in a plain brown envelope, ending yet another chapter.

I was so excited to be starting my new role. I hit the ground running and set about recruiting my new team.

Mr Reynolds was very nice and said he preferred to be called Tim. He gave me the freedom to organise the store as I wanted but gave helpful advice when he thought it necessary. I welcomed his help as it was always delivered in an advisory way. Between us, we set up the different departments.

I made sure that everything was labelled and sized.

I had meetings with the staff to advise them of the high standards expected of us all, the importance of good timekeeping and personal presentation. We covered the format for colour coordination, the need for the constant monitoring of the neatness of hanging garments, the proper way of folding and the art of window-dressing.

We had a whole session on how to legally deal with shoplifters, both the suspected ones and the caught ones.

Tim advised on the operation of the till, which was an absolute beast; it did its own daily stocktake. I had never seen anything quite so complicated. We all needed to have it explained several times over until we were all happy with it. There seemed an awful lot to remember.

Then I was advised on how to take the daily reading and the final stock adjustment level.

Everyone was working very hard and enjoying every minute of it. It was now starting to take shape and the excitement in the air was palpable.

We all arrived on opening day in our brand-new company uniforms, with me proudly sporting my gold badge with my name and 'Store Manager' printed on it.

There was a huge queue lined up right down the mall. We took the brown paper off the windows that had been hiding all the activities of the preparations. The team took up their places. The float was put into the till. I unlocked the double front doors and let the crowd pour in.

Very soon, the till started ringing. I was constantly filling up the carrier bag holder, always a good sign that things were flying off the rails.

Tim came across and put an arm around my shoulders and said rewardingly,

"Well done, Rita, you and the team have done an amazing job. I knew I had chosen well." He gave me a squeeze. "Now it's over to you. My job here is done. Give me a call after closing and let me have the final figure if you would be so kind," he said. With that, he was gone.

It was a fantastic opening day. I just couldn't believe how much money we had taken. I couldn't wait to phone Tim with the figures.

"Wow! That's amazing - much more than we had calculated. Well, done, little star, you should all feel proud of yourselves. Please pass my comments on to your team."

"I certainly will," I assured him. I was well aware just how far a little praise went. I had always found that people responded better to praise, especially when well-earned.

I reflected that it would indeed have been a valuable lesson for Mr Aylesbury.

The weeks that followed were hectic. Stock levels were depleting rapidly. Repeat orders were crucial so that sales were not lost. The delivery lorry was constantly at the back door unloading. We were continuously unpacking boxes.

I was learning all the time. I was now having to show percentage sales for each department against square footage allocated for each department, requiring constant adjustment as sales fluctuated, especially through the seasonal changes.

I was really enjoying the job, and my life in general. In fact, I had never been happier.

But again, this was about to change dramatically.

It was a Saturday. It had been a very busy day, and I was not looking forward to the evening as I knew Cody would be out on his DJ job.

I got home to find him in a very sombre mood. I took one look at his worried expression.

"OK, what's happened?" I asked, trying to be jovial.

"I don't know how to tell you this, Rita," he replied, concern written all over his face.

Now I was really worried, though still feeling that he was being overly dramatic. It can't be anything that bad, I decided.

"Well," he said, slowly dragging out the word. "As I was not working until this evening, I thought I would have a lie-in. I was woken when the doorbell rang. It was Lucy."

"Lucy! Why was Lucy here on a Saturday morning? She knows that I work all day on Saturdays!" I said, puzzled. "What did she want?"

Cody continued hesitantly.

"Rita, you need to know that she followed me upstairs when I went up to get dressed. She pushed me onto the bed and tried to kiss me. She was laying it on a plate." Now he was looking at me with fearful eyes, not knowing how I was going to react.

"What?!" I cried in utter disbelief.

"I'm so sorry, Rita. I thought it best that I told you. I was as shocked as you are. Of course, I pushed her off and told her to leave," he told me, injecting a note of sincerity to his voice.

I slumped down into the chair.

It had not gone unnoticed, Lucy's initial reaction when she had first met Cody, him being much nearer her age than he was mine, he certainly was eye-candy.

But if true, this was the ultimate betrayal. My own daughter making a play for my man; how could she do such a thing? I could not register what I was feeling, I could not take it in, it was so shocking.

I then remembered the view she had expressed when I first told her about him. She had said that it would be just a matter of time before Cody would tire of me and trade me in for a younger model, or words to that effect.

My breathing now erratic, I thought I was going to have a heart attack.

I picked up the phone and called her number. She answered straight away as if she had been sitting there waiting for the call. I told her to get here by 8 o'clock that evening, knowing Cody would have gone to work. l told her that I had something to say to her.

She did not seem the least surprised by the request and did not even attempt to ask the reason behind it.

When she arrived, she tried to kiss my cheek as she passed me in the hall, but I pulled away. She sat herself down on the settee. I sat down opposite her. Before I could even open my mouth, she said,

"I know exactly what this is about, Mum. I'm surprised he had the guts to tell you. I'm so sorry, I had no idea he was going to do what he did."

"Are you telling me that it was him who tried it on with you?" I asked, even more shocked.

"Yes," why what did he tell you happened?" she asked, and without waiting for a reply, she continued, "I had come to cut the grass. I thought it would be a nice surprise for you, as you have done so much for me. "Cody opened the door in a pair of boxer shorts, followed me into the lounge, pushed me onto the sofa and tried to get on top of me. I pushed him off me, told him what

I thought of him, then I left. I might have guessed that he would try and tell you a different version of events, but that is the truth, I swear it. You know I would never do anything to hurt you, don't you?" she added, now getting up to come over to embrace me.

I got up and walked away from her, my head spinning. I headed for the hallway to climb the stairs.

I think it best if you go now, Lucy. I'm not feeling well, and I need to go and lie down."

"OK, Mum, I fully understand, it must be a dreadful shock for you," she said, opening the front door to leave. I headed for the bedroom passing Lee on the stairs.

"You OK, Mum?" he asked as he looked at the tears now rolling down my face, no longer able to hold them back.

"I'm fine, sweetheart, I'm just tired," I told him as I hurried by him.

I closed the bedroom door and lay on the bed. What in God's name was I to do? Whose version of events was I to believe, who was telling me the truth and who had lied?

Do I believe Cody, who I was completely besotted with? If I believed him, it would be saying my daughter was the liar. I knew that would mean losing her, and my new little granddaughter Sofia, for good.

If, on the other hand, I believed my daughter's version of events, then it would be saying that Cody was the one who lied. How could I continue a relationship with him if he had tried to have sex with my own daughter? Then our relationship would be at an end, and it would be him who I would lose out of my life. My God, what an impossible position to be put in.

Why the hell did Lucy have to come to the house when I was not there? She did not need to cut the grass. I don't think she would even know how to start the bloody lawnmower.

Oh, my God. Why, why, why? It was all too much.

Now my life was about to fall to pieces yet again and I just could not bear it. I buried my face in the pillow and sobbed and sobbed.

I must have cried myself to sleep as the next thing I knew, Cody was home and was getting in bed beside me.

He tried to wrap his arms around me, but I instinctively pulled away from him.

"Well?" he said, propping himself up on one elbow. "What did she have to say for herself?" he asked, knowing by my reaction to him that her version of events must have differed from his.

"Cody, she says it was you who tried it on with her," I said coldly.

"Well, she would say that, wouldn't she and whose account do you believe then?" he asked, staring down at me.

"I don't know what the hell to believe, do I?"

"I'll tell you what you believe, you believe what I told you happened, because that is the bloody truth; you either believe me or you don't," he said, almost shouting it at me.

"Oh, Cody, if only it was that easy, I would be calling my own daughter a liar," I told him.

"It is that easy if you want it to be. The fact you cannot say that she is the one who lied says it all. You believe her, don't you? If you do, then it's over between us, you do know that don't you?" he replied, now getting out of bed.

"I don't know who to believe," I called after him as he left the bedroom. "Cody, please don't go. I need time to think," but he was already heading back downstairs.

That night, he had slept on the sofa. He was up well before me, and I found him unplugging all his stereo equipment in the living room. The front door was wide open, and, at the end of the path, I could see his van with boxes of his things in the back.

"Cody, please," I begged, trying to grab hold of his sweatshirt as he passed by me with another box, but he shrugged me off.

I started crying again but he took no notice, continuing to pile all his belongings into the back of his van.

Finally, he grabbed his jacket off the hook in the hall and was gone. Gone out of my life forever.

As hard as it had been to do, I knew deep down where my loyalties lie and of course it was with my daughter who I loved unconditionally.

Chapter 13

I could not believe that my life had changed so devastatingly in just twenty-four hours. This time yesterday, I had everything to look forward to. Now, my life was in ruins, and I was in the depths of despair. My eyes were so swollen with crying. It was a blessing it was a Sunday.

Lucy turned up again that afternoon.

"Are you OK?" she asked, as I opened the front door. Not replying to her question, I turned on my heel and went back into the living room. She followed me, looking concerned at my swollen eyes and tear-stained face.

"Where is he?" she asked, looking around the room.

"He's gone," I replied.

She came over to me and put an arm around my shoulder as I stood looking out of the window and said carefully,

"It's alright, Mum, it's for the best you know. He was much too young for you. I did warn you, didn't I? I said that he would tire of you, and it was just a matter of time before you would be traded in for a younger model," she declared as she hugged me to her.

I looked at her for a long while, unable to find the words. I had made my decision. Now alone again, I had to somehow find some inner strength to pull myself together.

Lee stuck his head around the living room door and asked,

"Mum, can we get a dog? Laurence's dog has just had puppies. Can I have one? Oh, PLEASE can we, Mum?"

I just looked at him and my heart melted. He was such a good lad, not a bit of bother.

"Yes, my son, we can have a dog," I told him fondly.

"Yeah," came the jubilant reply

I was in a terrible state as the days moved on. I found it hard to put on a brave face. I suspected that Cody would have gone back to his mother's. I also knew he would still be going to work.

There was nothing to be gained from looking out for him each day on my journey to work just to catch a glimpse of him, and to wave to him as we passed each other. It was a childish and stupid thing to do, but I just could not stop myself. He finally put a stop to it by continuously changing his route.

It was unbearable but I simply had to come to terms with the fact that it was over, reinforced by the fact that when I came face to face with him in the town one day, he was walking hand in hand with his ex-girlfriend.

He walked straight past me as if he had never known me. It was a truly painful moment, but nonetheless, a moment that forced me to move on.

Work was helping, as I had been given the responsibility of getting involved in several of the company's new shop openings. This was great fun as it took me up to Oxford and other far-flung places.

As my stocktake had proved to be so successful, I was sent to other stores to show the manager how it should be done.

This was an eye-opener for me, as I witnessed some quite shocking practices of poor management, a total disregard for accuracy.

I now understood just how valuable my training had been with Mr Aylesbury. His strictness, and obsession with theft and attention to accuracy, had given me an excellent grounding.

Perhaps I had much to thank him for after all.

I take back all I said, Mr Aylesbury.

I very rarely saw Lucy. She and Tim had now married, and her life was as busy as mine. Tim was a mummy's boy, who seemed to rely on his mother to give him whatever his heart desired. If they wanted a new double bed, his mother would get one delivered before the week was out.

She had managed to replace all the secondhand things I had given them with expensive new ones It seemed money was no object.

Tim was completely antisocial and did not seem to want anything to do with our side of the family. When I did visit, Tim would get his coat on and go out.

I asked Lucy on numerous occasions why she never visited me with Sofia, who was now growing so fast that I seemed to be completely missing out on her. I was just told that it was because I was always working, which was true, I guess.

The very next time I called by to see her, she told me that their second child was on the way and that it was a boy.

"Oh, wow, that's wonderful," I said, giving her a big hug, hoping that she might need me a bit more with two of them on her hands. I was desperate to build a better relationship with her *and* my grandchildren.

The next arrival, having only just set up home in the womb, already had most of its requirements catered for, but I asked the question anyway.

"What can I get for the new baby?" As expected, everything I suggested, Tim's mother already had it covered, having already shelled out for a new wicker and white -embroidered crib.

"Don't worry, Mum," I know you can't afford to buy new, now you're on your own."

That seemed hardly the point in my view.

"Best I leave it to Tim's mother then," I said resentfully, feeling quite jealous that I was not included in this closely-knit family unit.

The routine of work, with lunch hours at Mother's became so monotonous. I began to wonder if this was going to be it until retirement. I had been in this job for two and a half years and was getting ready for a change of scenery. I had achieved all that there was to achieve. It was time to move on.

A job was being advertised for a manager of a factory outlet shop coming to town. Most towns up north had one, the head office being based in Lancashire. They were now expanding into other counties.

I felt confident in applying. I had garnered everything I needed to pull off a shop opening single-handed, so to speak. I submitted my CV and waited.

Mother had to put her fly in my ointment, saying,

"I don't know why you keep chopping and changing, Rita. I thought you liked your job. What's the matter with you, why don't you stay where you are?"

"Because I feel like a change of scene," I replied. "This company is another step up; it not only sells ladies,' men's and children's clothing, it also sells footwear, luggage, bedding, and furniture," I told her. "It's an opportunity to further widen my skills."

"Well, I think you're being silly!" she added.

"Well, no surprise there then, Mother," I replied.

I wasn't surprised when I received the notification that I had been offered an interview. But I was under no illusion; it was still a long way to go before I had it in the bag. After all was said and done, I didn't know what qualifications the other applicants had.

However, I intended to apply the same principle as I had always done, to just simply be myself. It had worked so far. Each time I changed job; I had learned the necessary skills to take the next step.

The following week, I was sitting in front of two people, one calling herself Christine Goodman, who was apparently the company's buyer. The other was a guy called Adrian Fairfax, who introduced himself as one of the directors of the company.

It was he who did most of the talking. He had told me that he was impressed with my CV and asked all the questions I had now become familiar with. I felt I had handled the whole interview with confident professionalism, but you can never tell. If I did not get the job, well, that was OK too.

So, when the letter finally arrived to tell me that I had been successful, the start date told me that I needed to hand my notice in as soon as possible. I was needed on the job to get things moving as this time, I was expected to instruct the shopfitters on the layout.

I was also expected to handle all the advertising and promotions, and of course, the staff recruitment of a much larger team. I was excited by the new challenge.

Christine and Adrian turned up on stock delivery day. This did not go as well as first hoped. We had already got off to a flying start on the unpacking. The luggage, the ladies' underwear, the nightwear and all the footwear was already out on display with the surplus taken to the stock rooms behind the scenes.

There was a side to Adrian that I found unprofessional, telling one of my staff dirty jokes which she found hilarious and laughed at raucously. There was much to be done and he was purposely encouraging her to waste time. I needed her to get on with the work, not lark about.

Things intensified further later that morning following an incident that I found impossible to ignore, an incident that set me at odds with Adrian due to my strongly held principles on honesty.

The delivery drivers, having unloaded all their stock, were grouped together drinking coffee and chatting, when I happened to overhear Adrian say to them all,

"Go on, lads, pick yourselves a pair of trainers before you go."

I turned to see the four drivers walk down the shoe aisle, where, after some discussion on style, they all brazenly picked a pair of trainers each off the shelf and proceeded to walk out of the shop, get into their lorries with their free perks and drive away.

I could not believe what I had just witnessed. This was something quite unprecedented and I could just imagine what Mr Aylesbury would have said about that. I was upset and worried about it.

I felt I had to relay what I had just witnessed to Christine.

I asked If I could have a private word with her. It was a delicate subject to broach, so I was naturally careful how I worded it. Having heard me out, she simply smiled and said,

"Adrian always lets the drivers have a gift as a thank you for driving down from the North. It is a very long way to come, "she informed me.

"But it's their job, isn't it? They get paid for that, don't they?"

"Well, yes, of course, but it's something Adrian likes to do. It's simply a little thank you gesture," she replied.

"But what about my stock levels? How will I account for four pairs of trainers missing?"

"Adrian is a director, remember; I'm sure he will make the necessary adjustments." Christine said, clearly not wishing to discuss the issue further and now walking away chuckling.

Well then, he should know better, I thought. I did not believe for one moment he would adjust my stock levels at his end. He would simply forget it happened.

My store would therefore show a deficit of four which would ultimately reflect on me. I took great pride in the accuracy of my stock and found his attitude extremely unprofessional. What kind of example was he setting my staff? That it was acceptable to help yourself to things off the shelf?

No, this was not acceptable in any shape or form.

I went back to the store and saw Christine laughing with Adrian. They were both now looking directly at me, Adrian with an expression on his face that probably belied his true feelings on what he had just been told.

This did not bode well for me; I had questioned Adrian's actions and shown him to be unprofessional which he would not take lightly. I knew that I had made an enemy of him on the very first day.

This proved to be the case when it had been necessary for me to take to task a member of staff had been making a great many errors.

It just so happened it had been the giggling girl who had been laughing at Adrian's dirty jokes on the first day. Even though this girl was becoming well known for offloading her jobs onto others while taking too many smoking breaks, I had, for the fourth time that day, discovered that she had wrongly priced items of stock.

When bringing this to her attention, she explained that she was having problems seeing the print on the invoices. She then went on to tell me that she normally wore glasses but preferred not to wear them to work as she didn't feel attractive in them.

I explained the importance of getting the prices of the goods correct, or any inaccuracies would clearly show up in the overall figures.

Following this discussion with her, she took the liberty of phoning Adrian to complain about me. She had apparently told him that I had accused her of making too many mistakes, which she denied, and told him that I had demanded that she got herself some glasses.

I was subsequently called to the phone and was told in no uncertain terms to stop picking on the girl. The implication was that I had it in for her. He told me if there were any more complaints. I would not be working for the company for very much longer.

The word soon got around. Inevitably, certain staff members now began taking advantage of my weakened position, making it impossible to maintain any form of authority. I had been compromised as to how I managed my staff making it extremely difficult for me to do my job.

One young man called Pip, short for Philip, decided he would only come to work if he felt in the mood, not even having the decency to ring in with an explanation for his absence. He was bosom buddies with the giggly girl with the bad eyesight. Between them, they thought they had acquired the perfect recipe on how to undermine me.

I had given Pip several verbal warnings, telling him his constant absences were unacceptable, and made him aware he was skating on very thin ice.

One day, when he finally decided to honour us with his presence, I was waiting for him. I issued him with his first written warning, which he instantly tore up in front of me, and marched back out the door with the comment.

"You'll be sorry! "As a passing shot.

Thirty minutes later, Adrian was on the phone to me. "What the hell is going on down there, Rita? I've just had Philip on the phone who has informed me that you have just thrown him out of the shop."

"Is that so?!" I replied. "Well, may I advise you, that young man has not put in as much as one full week of work since starting, and after three verbal warnings issued with no effect whatsoever, I have found it necessary to issue a written, which he has just torn up and thrown in my face before walking out. Might I also point out that the fact that senior management has thought fit to undermine the authority of the shop manager over that of the staff, it's not surprising that it leads to this type of conduct."

With that, he put the phone down on me.

Oh well, that's put the cat amongst the pigeons, I decided. A few minutes later, the phone rang again; it was Adrian.

"I have just spoken again to Philip and told him that I am now aware of your version of events, and I can't begin to tell you the tirade of abuse and foul language that I have been subjected to. I'm not going to be spoken to like that. I have sacked him," he said sternly.

Well, I'm damned, I thought. He expected me to put up with unacceptable behaviour, but when it came to his authority being questioned, he was having none of it.

"I will get the advert out for his replacement at once," I responded.

Two minutes later, the giggly girl with the bad eyesight came into the office and explained that

Pip had phoned her and told her he had been sacked.

"You can't do that," she exclaimed defiantly.

"To begin with, it was Adrian who sacked him, not me, but he had it coming," I replied.

"Well, if that's your game, you can stick your job. You haven't heard the last of this. We will take you to the unfair dismissal tribunal," she exclaimed as she too walked out the door.

I phoned Adrian back and told him.

"Just thought I would let you know that there will be two advertisements going in for new members of staff, as his best friend has just threatened the company with unfair dismissal and has also walked out in protest."

"OK, so be it. Thank you, Rita," he said, putting the phone down.

When Lucy's new baby arrived, they called him Curtis. Only six months later, I was told that child number three was on its way.

Good Lord, I thought, are they trying to break some kind of record?

The store continued to thrive. My new team had gelled nicely; we were like family, all working together and supporting each other.

I had been on my own for some time now and some of the girls in the shop were trying to get me to go out socially with them. I always declined, not wanting any repeats of my past disasters. I had been badly scarred by the pain of it all.

Lee was now a teenager and would be leaving school in a year. Even he began asking why I did not find a 'friend,' as he put it.

"No, I'm too old for that kind of thing now," I told him.

"Nonsense, Mum, you're not old, you're still attractive; any guy would be pleased to go out with you."

"That's very flattering, Lee. I will think about it, OK?" I said, trying to end the conversation at that. But I had underestimated just how intent Lee was for me to start living life again.

Several months earlier, I had bought Lee a secondhand CB (citizen's band) device as I thought it would be fun for him. He loved the thing! He set it up in his bedroom and spent hours in conversation with others. He made many friends on it and spoke to them most evenings. He also managed to pick up police messages on it which he also found interesting. Although I was not sure of the legality of that, it seemed harmless enough and it kept Lee happy.

However, one evening, I was heading up the stairs to use the toilet when I heard his dulcet tones emanating from his room.

"Are there any rich farmers out there? Please copy, are there any rich farmers out there for my mum? She is very beautiful, copy," he repeated.

I did not wait to hear any replies. I just screamed.

"LEE! WHATEVER THE HELL, YOU THINK YOU ARE DOING ON THAT THING, STOP IT RIGHT NOW!"

The machine went quiet.

Whatever next, that boy of mine, I thought. But it did make me chuckle. The odd thing was it got me thinking.

Maybe it was time to start thinking about socialising again.

I had noticed an advertisement in the newspaper under the heading Lonely Hearts; it read,

The Tender Love and Care Dating Agency.

Are you ready to begin a new life full of fun and adventure, try out new hobbies, share holidays, and possible romance? Then come and join our friendly group. We meet up every Friday. Don't hesitate to ring this number and ask for Angela.

Over several days, I think I must have picked up the phone and put it back down again well over thirty times and bottled out, while an internal argument ensued within me.

Don't be ridiculous; you sound positively desperate. And then-What have you got to lose? You don't have to commit to anyone!

And then - You're only going to get yourself in over your head again and land up getting hurt. And then - You could always come home if you feel it's not for you. And then - Your history should tell you that this is a disaster waiting to happen. And then - Oh, for God's sake, Rita, grow up! You're acting like a child. Pick up the bloody phone!

"Hello, this is Angela speaking," a quiet motherly voice said.

"Oh, hello, my name is Rita," I said, not wanting to give my surname.

"Hi, how are you, Rita? Have you phoned in connection with Tender Love and Care?"

"Yes, I just wanted to know a bit more about it first, though," I replied hesitantly.

"Of course; well, like the ad says, we all tend to meet up once a week for drinks at my house where we plan what we will do over the coming weeks regarding hobbies and interests.

We have skittle nights, cinema nights, meals out, dances, horse riding, um, oh and day trips away, and loads of other things. Some want to stay within the group, others choose to arrange personal activities like theatre dates, or meals out and such. It's totally down to what you feel is comfortable for you. But we do have a lot of fun. Do you think that you would like to join us this Friday?" she asked finally.

"Oh well, alright," I replied hesitantly.

"That's great! We meet up at 7 pm. I live at 14 Newbury Crescent opposite the park; you can't miss it - it's the one with the caravan parked in the drive."

"Thank you, see you Friday then," I said, putting the phone down.

Rita, what have you let yourself in for now? I asked myself. Well, in for a penny, in for a pound.

I must have learnt something from all the mistakes I've made so far in my many attempts at this stupid thing called love.

Maybe this time, if there is to be a this time, I might have finally got the hang of it.

Over the next six months, I had become a regular participant in the group's activities. Angela had told me that she thought that I would not remain single for very long. However, I treated the invitations to go out very cautiously, preferring to remain within the safety of the group.

They were a very mixed bag, with very different backgrounds and personalities, but, by and large, a friendly bunch.

On the rare occasion when I did accept an evening out, I made it clear it would be strictly on a 'friend' basis, and it always remained a once-only event.

Therefore, over time, I had gained the reputation of being a bit of an ice maiden, which I was perfectly happy with as I thought that it was a fitting description of me.

After many failed attempts at getting me hooked up with someone, Angela made it clear that I was beginning to ruin her reputation as a matchmaker. I believe, for this, she plotted to rectify the situation.

It was a Saturday afternoon and I had just got home from work after a particularly busy day. We had just started our sale and it had been full-on. I was looking forward to a hot bath and an early night. The phone rang; it was Angela.

"Get your glad rags on. We are going to a dance with the group."

"No, Angela, thank you but no thank you. I have had one hell of a day and I'm looking forward to a date with my bathtub," I told her.

"Now, Rita, don't be ridiculous. It's Saturday night; no respectable singleton stays in on a Saturday night."

"No, seriously, Angela, I'm not in the mood. Count me out on this one, but thanks anyway," I told her decisively, expecting that to put an end to it, but she was not letting it go so easily.

"I will be round to pick you up at seven o'clock on the dot; be ready," she finished, putting down the phone and denying me any prospect of further refusal.

Who the hell did she think she was, I thought stubbornly, telling me what to do? The damned cheek of it. If I didn't want to go, I wasn't going to go; it was as simple as that. I was quite cross about it.

However, as the time grew closer, the usual side of my personality stepped in, and the little inner voice began chipping away at my defences, saying things like, 'What is wrong with you Rita? Have you really lost the ability to enjoy yourself? It's coming to something when all you want is to go to bed early. You will probably enjoy it once you're there. Don't be lazy, Rita; buck yourself up. Put the effort in; you're growing old before your time. What is happening to you?'

When the doorbell rang at seven o'clock, I was ready to rumble with the best of them.

"Good. I'm glad you saw sense," said Angela, smiling broadly. "I thought I might have to drag you out of bed," she said as she opened the car door for me to get in.

"By the way, can I introduce you to Tom?" she said, looking back at me from the passenger seat. "He has just joined the club; I've told him that we are a friendly bunch," she said, laughing.

I have well and truly been set up here, I thought, as I looked into the pair of eyes looking back at me from the driver's rear-view mirror.

Mmmm, I thought, very nice. I'd always been taken with a person's eyes. These eyes were kind of, well, kind; that's the only way to describe them.

The evening was as expected. All the gang were there. I had a few dances but mostly chatted with everyone. Mr Kind Eyes offered me a drink, but I declined the offer. It turned out to be a nice evening. Angela deliberately drove past my house on the way back, saying,

"Everyone back to mine for coffee." This left me with no alternative.

Having finished an unwanted cup of coffee, I stood up and asked Angela to phone for a taxi to take me home.

"You will give her a lift back, won't you, Tom?" she said, looking directly at him.

"No, it's OK," I jumped in. "I'm happy to get a taxi. Angela, can you please phone for one?"

"Rita, it's no problem really. I'm leaving now too, and I'm going right by your place," Tom said.

I had been shoved into a corner and had no other option but to agree if I did not want to appear rude, I sat next to him making small talk as we made the short journey home. He pulled up outside my gate and looked at me and asked,

"Do you fancy going out sometime?"

"I don't know. I'm actually away on business next week, so things are a bit uncertain at present."

This was, in fact, true. I had been summoned to my first managers' meeting up in Lancashire. The company was putting all their managers up in a hotel for four days. I was really looking forward to it.

"No problem, here take my phone number, and if you fancy an evening out when you get back, give me a call," he said casually.

I took the piece of paper from him, thanked him for the lift and waved him on his way.

The trip to Lancashire was brilliant. The hotel was lovely - very luxurious. There were around thirty managers staying there. It was a good opportunity to get to know them all and to exchange views and opinions on many shared issues.

We were given a tour of the factory that made the cosmetics that we sold in our shops which was interesting. We were all given free samples of the new lines and posters that we could utilise in our stores. We were shown around the clothing ranges being introduced over the next six months so that we knew what to expect for display purposes.

Adrian chaired the meetings. He came across a different person on his own territory.

Each of us was given an opportunity to bring to the table new ideas on how best to improve sales, and the possibility of further diversification into other areas to increase profit.

Each manager in turn was asked to provide their figures to date, compared to the previous year, which was not relevant in my case as it was my first year of trading.

It was fascinating to hear how the different regions varied, and the reasons given in the case of stores that had underperformed, and how best to try to improve sales in the coming year. It was an extremely useful exercise which provided me with a great many ideas that I could take away with me to implement in my own store.

I discovered that only a few of the larger stores sold furniture. Unfortunately, mine was not one of them.

Chapter 14

On my return, I had been so preoccupied implementing all my newly acquired ideas that I had quite forgotten about Tom's invitation to go out, but, over the last couple of days, I had started toying with the idea. I got the piece of paper out and looked at the number written on it; it felt a bit forward to be the one to ring him. The piece of paper sat by the phone for a further three days before I plucked up the courage to act on it.

When I did, Tom sounded delighted to hear from me. We chatted briefly and arranged to go out the following Saturday evening. I could not believe how nervous I was; I felt like a teenager getting ready for a first date. He arrived right on time.

"Have a good time!" Lee called out with a smirk all over his face as I was heading out the door. I pulled a face at him and closed the door behind me. I slid into the passenger seat of his car and smiled.

"Hello, Tom," I said, glancing at his profile.

"Well, hello there," he replied warmly.

The first thing that jumped right out at me was that he had a clothes peg attached to the right corner of his shirt collar.

Oh my God, I thought. Do I tell him? Maybe he had taken it off the washing line and had not realised it was there. I decided not to embarrass him. I kept quiet.

Then he noticed me looking at the foghorn sitting in the centre of his dashboard.

"I see you've noticed the foghorn, that is for either of us to use if either of us mentions our exes at any time during the evening," he said with a wry smile, honking it loudly to prove the point of it.

"Oh!" I laughed, covering my ears from the din it made. "What a novel idea."

We went to a country pub first and had a lovely meal and a bottle of wine. I must confess I was quite attracted to him. He was very nice looking in a mature kind of way, and so easy to talk to. He had a lovely sense of humour too, which I liked very much about him.

He confessed that his son had told him that he could not possibly go out in his old corduroy trousers with the faded knees and had taken him on a shopping trip to bring his fashion sense up to date.

I was starting to relax in his company. Laughter was a great lightener, especially when he asked me why I had not mentioned the clothes peg on his collar, purposely put there as an ice-breaker.

We talked endlessly for hours. He told me that he worked offshore on an oil rig in Abu Dhabi.

He spent one month away and one month home. Gosh, that must be a tough regime, I thought, but he told me he had been doing it for many years and was used to it, although he said it played havoc with any form of social life. I could quite understand why.

We then went to a nightclub where he took me onto the dance floor and took me in his arms for a classic waltz.

It was a lovely evening. The time just flew by and before I knew it, we had once again pulled up outside my house.

"That was a very enjoyable evening. I haven't laughed so much in ages," I told him, and I meant it. There was something very easy going about him.

He leant across and kissed me gently on the cheek saying, "Yes, I enjoyed it very much too. *And* I would love to repeat it."

"Me too," I said, getting out of the car.

I was surprised to find Lee waiting up for me when I got inside.

"Well, how did it go?" he asked.

"Yes, very nice, thank you, and don't ask any more questions because that's all your getting," I told him, heading up the stairs.

Angela phoned the next day.

"How did you get on with Tom last night?" she wanted to know.

"How do you know I was out with him last night?" I asked, puzzled.

"Ah, you'd be surprised what I know," she laughingly informed me.

"I will tell you what I told my son. Yes, very nice, and that's all you're going to know."

"That's great news! Now that I know that my reputation is still intact, I'm satisfied with that," she told me with a final peal of laughter before putting down the phone.

Over the next two weeks, I saw Tom several times. He had been to the house, and he had briefly met Lee, who had breezed through, said 'Hi' and out again.

The time had come round far too quickly for him to go back offshore. Reluctantly, we said our goodbyes.

It was a long month to wait before seeing him again, but I found myself getting excited about his return and the prospect of picking up where we had left off.

The first night he was back, we spent a lovely evening getting to know each other better and sharing more personal details of our pasts. I wanted to get mine all out there so I could start with a clean sheet. I did not want him to find things out about me at a later date that perhaps he may not approve of.

So, out came all the dirty washing; I hung it all out on the line for him to see. It was down to him to pass judgment on my somewhat colourful past if he chose to do so, but he didn't.

He listened to the whole sorry saga and simply said,

"Wow, you're going to find my past very dull in comparison. I hope you won't find me too boring, he laughed.

His life was indeed far less vivid, although, I'm sure, equally as painful for him. Apparently, his wife had tired of the years of job-dependent separation. His constant comings and goings had played havoc on their marriage, with his wife having to bring up their three sons largely on her own. So, in Tom's absence, she had met someone else who had provided the things that she felt her life lacked.

Having moved most of her belongings out of the family home, she had simply placed a note on the kitchen table containing a brief explanation and left.

A hell of a bombshell to have to return home to. It must have been extremely hard for him, and I felt for him.

He explained that he had come to terms with it and had blamed most of what had happened on himself. This said a hell of a lot about the man, in my opinion.

I had only been to his house on the one occasion, as he was in the process of selling it as part of his divorce settlement.

As the months came and went, And the closer we became, so Tom became a more integral part of my life.

The months he was away were terrible. I missed him terribly despite receiving regular mail from him. I was like a teenager bubbling with excitement when he was due home again.

His house had finally sold, and he was going to have to move in with his mother, which he was not looking forward to.

It felt like a natural progression to start having a conversation about him moving in with us. I had met all his relatives, and he had met mine, so things were progressing.

Of course, this needed very careful consideration, as my past indicated, since decisions made based on the heart and not the head had not fared well for me, to say the least.

But this time, things felt completely different. Tom had all the qualities that had been lacking in previous relationships.

This time I was looking for kindness, understanding, thoughtfulness, patience, honesty, and a caring, loving, and nurturing nature. He possessed all of these qualities in shedloads.

But above all, I trusted him. When he told me that he cherished me, promised me that he would never hurt me and that he would do everything in his power to look after me, I believed him wholeheartedly. The time had come to put my trust in him; it was now or never.

The following month, on his return home from his job, he moved in with Lee and me.

Lee was delighted. He now had his own relationship with a girl at the bottom of the road and was pleased to see me settled with someone who he considered a genuinely nice guy.

I had been offered the opportunity of taking over a new store which my company was opening in the next town. It was three times larger than mine and would accommodate furniture.

This was an opportunity that I just could not miss so I accepted.

Mother was not best pleased as it meant that I would no longer be calling in during my lunch break. She naturally tried to talk me out of it, but my mind was made up. I was taking the next step up on a constantly rising career ladder. It was what I was good at, and I was loving it. Eight weeks later, I was in and trading.

Life was good.

We continued on the treadmill of Tom away for a month then home for a month. We had decided to buy my council house, taking advantage of the generous discount on offer; we were very lucky.

Tom bought Lee his first little motorcycle. For the next few months, we had to endure the sound of its engine as he rode around the block, hour after hour, every evening, flashing past the house on full throttle, the sound disappearing, then picking up again as he flashed by again on endless circuits. He drove the neighbours insane, but he absolutely loved it.

Then one day, he stood in the kitchen and announced,

"Mum, I would like you to meet Sally."

I looked around him to where a shy timid little thing was half-hiding behind him and who practically whispered a hello.

The fact that he wanted to introduce her to us meant that this was going to be a meaningful relationship. Lee was not the type of lad to have lots of girlfriends. He was a hugely loyal lad.

Over the coming months, they became more besotted with each other and were inseparable, almost joined at the hip. I got it, though, as I remembered how I had been with Kevin at the beginning.

Lee had now left school and had taken a temporary job where I had previously worked, at the paint factory.

He got on very well there and liked the job. He came home one day and told us that they had offered him a full-time position, which he was thrilled about as it was good money.

Tom was not sure that he was doing the right thing. He advised him against it as he saw very little prospect in it for Lee over the long term, and asked Lee to consider an apprenticeship.

It would be a lot less money, but Tom told him that if he stuck it out, it would pay dividends in the end.

I could not help remembering that same advice being given to me once. But I knew Tom only wanted the best for him. Perhaps mother had thought the same for me, I pondered.

But unlike me, Lee was under no pressure.

I was surprised and glad that Lee had agreed that it made good sense and had decided to take Tom's advice. They went through the advertisements and came across a local company looking for an apprentice car mechanic. Now that would be a good thing to get into, Tom advised. He knew that Lee loved engines as he was always tinkering with his motorcycle.

The very next morning, Lee phoned up and got himself an interview, which he attended, and was offered the position. Thankfully, he seemed set for a good future.

Life seemed settled for everyone; Tim and Lucy now had three lovely children and had decided to buy their own home, with the help of Tim's mother, of course.

Lee and Sally had decided to get a flat together, which found me yet again scraping things together to help them out. It was their first little home together and they were so proud of it. Now we were all settled - such a relief.

The months rolled on and before we knew it, we found we had been living together for over a year. Tom was ready for a change of pace.

He was tired of the perpetual drudgery of the journey abroad every month and then having to face the month of separation.

He had made the decision to apply for an offshore job in Scotland. It would be two weeks away and two weeks at home, which would be much better for both of us. There was, apparently, also the option of a company bungalow. Tom asked me if I would consider giving up my job and moving with him so that we could spend more time together.

I loved my job, but I had discovered that I loved Tom more. The thought of not having to endure that awful punishing regime of separation was positively appealing for both of us.

No further discussion was necessary. I handed in my notice at work and surprised myself that I felt no sadness about leaving. It was more about the excitement of what the future held for us both. Tom accepted the new position.

Lee and Sally moved out of their cramped little flat and moved into our house, which we were leaving furnished, and we were off.

Mother, as expected, was not amused with this latest development.

It was a lovely fully furnished three-bed bungalow with quite a decent-sized garden. It was unclear to me why the company would provide an employee with this standard of accommodation but who was I to complain.

I got up early the first morning to see Tom off to work. I had just sat down with a cup of coffee when the doorbell went.

Who on earth could that be? I asked myself as I looked through the glass front door at the outline of a woman in a red coat.

"Hello, I'm May, your cleaner," she said in a broad Scottish accent. Picking out the only bits that I could understand.

"I didn't know, I mean, I haven't asked for a cleaner," I replied, uncertain of quite what to do.

"No, no, I work for the company. I clean for whoever is living here. I come in every day from 9 o'clock until 11 o'clock, except at the weekends; then it's down to you," she said, smiling broadly.

I was genuinely shocked. Me having someone to clean my house every day. Oh, I didn't know how I was going to get my head around that!

"I'm very sorry I didn't know you were coming; I have not had a chance to make the bed or wash up the breakfast things yet," I said, sounding dumb.

She laughed out loud.

"Och, yer no needin' ter do that. That's what I'm here fer," in her wonderful Scottish accent as she passed by me and went into the kitchen.

She was a lovely kindly soul who I took to instantly. So much so that over time, I made sure that I was up early each day, bed made, washing-up done and the kettle on, so that when she arrived, we could sit and have a cuppa together and a good old chin wag.

On several occasions, she told me that I should not be doing half her work so that we could sit and drink tea, but I didn't care. I looked forward to her coming; I loved her company.

Tom was out from early morning for a twelve-hour shift and generally came home exhausted, ready for a meal and a bath, then crashed out.

I had been so used to working full time that it was a big adjustment to make. I had never had to spend so much time on my own. If the truth be told, I was finding it somewhat lonely, and a tad boring.

I passed a lot of my time walking around the town window shopping.

I found the Scottish people very friendly. Perfect strangers would come up to you in the supermarket and say things like, "I see you have avocados in your basket; they have them on special offer next door at half the price."

That wouldn't happen where I was from. People would think you were off your trolley if you were to do that, probably telling you to mind your own bloody business.

I actually loved it, and soon found that I was adapting much the same principles to how I interacted with people. It was a much more pleasant and cordial way of life.

After a year, Tom's contract was coming to an end. He had decided to go self-employed. He secured another job, still offshore, two weeks on and two off.

Lee and Sally had bought their first house and had already moved in, leaving our house empty, so we had made the decision to return.

It seemed strange coming back; absolutely nothing had changed in our absence. Still the same neighbours, same shops, same friends, same everything.

The only things different were Mother and Dad. They were beginning to look frailer, especially Dad, who seemed to have lost weight.

I spoke to Mother, voicing my concerns, but she just brushed it off and told me he was fine and explained that they were both just getting old. She remarked that she was pleased I had returned as I could help them out more.

I decided it was time to get back into the working world. I missed the cut and thrust of things. I began searching the jobs ads and spotted one that sparked my interest.

A charity was looking for a Retail General Manager to take over the running of their retail division, responsible for the profitable operations of their chain of shops covering three counties.

I considered this with an element of caution; this was a huge step up. Was I aiming too high? Perhaps this was a bit out of my league? Self-doubt again reared its head. I sat on it for several days before deciding to give it a shot, after all, what did I have to lose?

It took several days and a lot of updating before I was finally satisfied with the presentation of my CV, making sure it was an accurate and honest reflection of my capabilities to date.

I carried it about in my handbag for a further two days, still unsure if I was doing the right thing.

That weekend, I happened to mention to Mother what I was considering. Her response made the decision for me.

"What on earth are you thinking, Rita? That's not something you would be up to doing. It is going to be far too much for you to take on. I think you would be making a big mistake applying for it. You won't get it and then you will only be disappointed. Why don't you go for something small, something local, something simple?"

I listened quietly, got up from my chair and announced, "Well, I best be off then." I kissed Dad on the top of his head as I passed his chair.

I left their flat, walked to the bottom of the road, took out the envelope with my CV from my handbag and popped it into the letterbox.

Three weeks later, the reply came. I could not believe my luck. I had been offered an interview!

This was something on a completely different level.

I approached the day with huge trepidation. I sat in a large office on the second floor of a large building along with eight other applicants. My nerves almost got the better of me.

When it was my turn to enter the boardroom, I came face to face with five serious faces staring back at me from the other side of a highly polished table.

I took a seat in the solitary chair facing them, took a deep breath and went into my well-rehearsed account of my previous work history.

It wasn't as bad as I had feared, in fact, quite the opposite. I found that I had enjoyed the whole process. But no one was more surprised than me to find a week later that I had been shortlisted to the final three and had been invited to the next stage of the process.

This was a far worse experience to go through, as I had got myself in such a state about it that the night before attending this crucial meeting, I had made the grave mistake of having a glass of wine to settle the nerves and help me sleep. One glass led to two, by which time a 'don't care' attitude had taken hold. Consequently, the day of the interview arrived with me sporting the mother of all hangovers.

I spent the first hour of the morning arguing with myself back and forth on whether I should telephone to remove myself from the process. However, ridiculously, something forced me through the pain barrier, and I took myself and my bloodshot eyes back to that solitary chair and subjected myself to a further grilling in somewhat of a blur.

I could not wait for it to be over. I drove home and went straight to bed. Accepting that I had well and truly blown it, through the stupidity of self-doubt, I thought it best to put the whole sorry event out of my mind and set my sights on less lofty aspirations more locally, as Mother had suggested.

When the phone rang, I very nearly started hyperventilating. I had to grope for a seat to sit on. I also had to ask the person on the other end of the phone to repeat the whole conversation again.

I was told that despite it being an extremely close call, I had, in fact, been the successful applicant, and that they were delighted to inform me that I was being offered the position of General Manager of their retail chain.

They were looking forward to the exciting changes that I planned on implementing to take the organisation forward to higher profitability that I had mentioned in my second interview. They understood that I was available immediately so could I please make myself available to undertake the required handover period from the outgoing Manager who was retiring from the role in two weeks?

I put the phone down and sat staring out of the front room window, still numb from the shock of it.

Now, who would have thought it? Little ole Rita, who left school without a single qualification to her name, never good at anything and expected to fail at whatever she attempted. Well, I had shown them all, hadn't I? I had done it. Something to take away from this experience after a lifetime of mistakes.

Every day you get up, you have another chance to be a better version of yourself. You just have to be brave enough to take it.

Without a doubt, I would accept this position. I would implement those exciting changes to take the organisation to bigger and better profitability, which I had apparently talked about at that second interview, changes I had no recollection whatsoever of discussing, and I would damned well make a monumental success of them, whatever they were.

I could not wait to tell Mother my exciting news. The only thing she could think of to say was,

"You've only just got back from Scotland, Rita. What about me and your father? You were supposed to be spending more time helping us. You won't be much of a help if you're running around the country, will you?" she complained.

"I'm delighted that you're pleased for me, Mother," was my response to that.

Dad followed me to the door to see me out. He put his arms around me in a bear hug and said reassuringly,

"Your mother and I are really proud of you, Rita. You have done so well."

"Thank you, Dad," I replied, returning the hug, and kissing his cheek.

I started my new job with a mixture of apprehension and excitement. I was given a large office on the top floor of the head office building.

It was very grand, kitted out with a computer, filing cabinets, and, on the wall behind the desk, a massive map of the area that the charity covered. It felt a slightly daunting and formidable task.

I also had my own secretary who was in an office next to mine. Now, I really felt I had made it to the big time. I was responsible only to the Chief Executive, who trustingly gave me a free hand to make the changes I felt were needed.

I hit the ground running. I requested an itinerary of all the stores, and for the managers to be notified that I would be visiting. I needed to familiarise myself with all aspects of how things were currently set up to establish how things could be improved upon.

It soon became apparent that things had been allowed to slide over time, as my predecessor had grown weary of the task in hand. The light had gone out, so to speak, and the way of working had become antiquated. I was still working in the handover period, so I naturally had to go carefully so as not to tread on old toes, although making mental notes on what areas needed more immediate action than others.

Each store had one paid manager and one paid assistant manager. Then there were the volunteers. Overall, there were nearly five hundred of them across the whole area, who made up most of the workforce. They were all unpaid and dedicated their time freely for the good and the love of the cause that they supported.

I learned very quickly that this part of our team had to be treated very differently from the paid staff, as they were the backbone of the organisation and without their support, the organisation would collapse.

Where you could give store managers instructions, with the volunteers, one could only request and do so with the greatest of care. I had to develop a whole new technique of making a volunteer believe that any changes made to how things used to be done, had, in fact, been their suggestion. Invariably it worked, but on the odd occasion, I did encounter a negative reaction. The average age being well over retirement sometimes leant itself to stubbornness.

It was crucial to get each one of them onside before I could even begin to make changes, however, by and large, they made a wonderful and supportive team.

It was a steep learning curve, but a very interesting one. Once I had formulated my strategy, I set about the implementation of it.

Firstly, I had meetings with the financial director to discuss investment possibilities. Things had never been applied as a business model before and had been treated very much on an ad hoc basis. In basic terms, it had remained very archaic and had never moved with the times.

I had to feel confident that I had an annual budget in place, plus, a long-term strategy approved by the directors. I also requested that I liaised with the directors on a six-monthly basis to ensure that things were still financially on track, and to report back as to what had been achieved thus far. With this agreed upon, I set about the task in hand.

Phase one: It was very clear to me from the onset that some of the stores which had originally been chosen for their peppercorn rents, were far too small and not placed well in the town. It would, therefore, be necessary to relocate them to more prominent sites in order to maximise customer footfall.

This entailed negotiations with landlords, the setting up of new leases, meetings with solicitors, purchasing new fixtures and fittings and project-managing builders and shopfitters with attention to layout and design. Then there was advertising and promotions, keeping to set deadlines and the acquisition of public liability and buildings insurance.

I found it especially frightening that there were no procedures currently in place in any of the stores that adhered to any health and safety regulations. This was something that required immediate attention.

Phase two: There were towns within the area where there were no stores at all. This had to be rectified. It was crucial to have a presence in each town. This I deemed crucial, not only from the fundraising perspective within the parameters of the retail decision but would also have a beneficial effect on raising the profile of the work of the charity within the community it served.

Having tackled these important issues, it was time to look at bought-in merchandise. I began with the basics; calendars, diaries, and Christmas cards which had to include a strong message of the organisation's ethos.

Regarding the calendar, I managed to make it personal to our area. The first year that I produced it, I managed to get a local artist on board. He provided watercolours of local scenes through the seasons which would go on sale in all of our stores. We achieved three reprints in the first year.

The diaries were also very saleable as they looked like leather and contained our corporate message in gold letters on the front, and a giving page inside if people wished to donate further.

These corporate products increased in sales, year in, year out, and were highly successful in increasing the revenue for the charity.

Another success was the bridal wear store that I opened in the city centre, which also had a section on the second floor that accommodated art, and music. I took full advantage of empty shops in the city centre, on a rent-free basis, by creating pop-up stores, where we would sometimes get six months' free trading before the landlord managed to re-let the premises. It was a rapid process of get in, fit it out, make as much money as possible, remove fittings and leave. It sounds like a lot of hassle, but it proved very lucrative and well worth all the effort.

The more stores that came on stream, the more our message circulated, and the higher the volume of donations that came through the door.

It then became necessary to find a sizable warehouse to accommodate it, then extra staff were needed to process it, and extra delivery vans to distribute it.

I then began opening two shops in several of the larger towns, one of which would accommodate the sale of secondhand furniture and electrical goods. Retired qualified electricians were recruited to certificate the items before being sold.

Larger vans were then required to accommodate furniture deliveries, leading then into house clearance, which inevitably meant the opening of yet more furniture stores.

On and on it went. Each day was a challenge, which was both rewarding and fulfilling.

My six-monthly progress meetings were met with continued praise and congratulations.

This rapid expansion brought about its own difficulties as I singlehandedly struggled to keep abreast of a constantly increasing workload. I found myself getting up in the night to try and get a heads up on my mail to save myself time when I got to work each day.

Everything was starting to suffer, my job being the only thing I could focus on. It occupied all of my time. Everything else had to take a back seat.

I had failed to realise the damage I was causing myself, and the detrimental effect it was having on my mental health. I was beginning to suffer a cross between complete exhaustion and total burn-out. I had taken on the work of three people. Why nobody could foresee this pending collapse is truly remarkable.

The problem was finally identified one morning when I was driving into work and found myself parked up in a lay-by, shaking from head to toe, unable to go any further.

Enough was enough, I had hit a brick wall mentally. I was signed off work for six weeks, providing a much-needed reality check.

It had hit me like a mallet that I had damned near driven myself into the ground. The organisation was then forced to accept their responsibility for the state I was in and had acted swiftly by recruiting a deputy for me to ease the workload.

Better late than never, I guess.

Life moved on. Lee and Sally were making plans for their wedding.

I got used to Tom's comings and goings. I had the best of all worlds: The excitement of his return, the first week home being all loved up, the second week getting all outstanding jobs done, then seeing him off on the train at the end of the fortnight.

I would rush home, clean the house from top to bottom putting everything back in its rightful place, and enjoy the feeling of once again having ownership of the television remote.

The whole process was to be repeated in two weeks' time.

Tom had decided to buy a smallholding with a semi-detached cottage. He explained that the cottage needed a little work done on it, which he planned to undertake himself in the two weeks that he was home on leave.

I agreed with this plan because, despite the fact we were both on good salaries, it would be more cost-effective to do things ourselves.

I naturally asked if he thought he had the expertise required to achieve this plan. He simply said that what he didn't know, he would read up on.

I must confess this did make me slightly apprehensive, but I thought well, how hard could it be to fit a new kitchen and bathroom. I was heading for a rude awakening.

We had decided to put a caravan on-site to enable Tom to work on the improvements to the cottage. He had purchased two static caravans, placed them side by side, knocked a hole between the two and made them into one larger accommodation.

We were now able to rent our house to generate more income. The work began.

A few months on, the full meaning of the words, "It will need a little work done on it," became very clear as I stood inside an empty shell gazing up into the eaves. The only things remaining of the original cottage were the four walls and a roof. There were no internal walls and no upper floors; it had been completely gutted.

Tom had even dug down under the original floors to put in underfloor heating.

When he hit the water table, the water getting deeper by the minute, I suggested to him that perhaps the time had come to stop digging.

The months rolled on with only a certain limited amount achieved on the cottage, as work had to come to a grinding halt every two weeks. But we were happy.

We got twenty chickens for fresh eggs, and we were also the proud owners of thirteen sheep, and two beautiful Jersey cows. We also had three beautiful Persian cats. I loved all the animals.

However, the reality of owning them kicked in when the sheep heartbreakingly made their final journey to the slaughterhouse and came back in plastic bags for the freezer.

I had made the grave mistake of naming them, so, in the freezer they remained, as the thought of seeing Freckles on a dinner plate was inconceivable.

We were heading into our first winter. The weather had turned bitterly cold. It became harder and harder to work inside the cottage. All the old plaster had to be painstakingly chipped from all the walls, a task which had fallen to me. Every weekend saw me perched precariously up a ladder with hammer and chisel and with blue fingers, while Tom was tucked up nice and warm in an office on his oil rig.

Getting up every morning proved exceptionally tough as ice formed on the inside of the windows of the caravan. It was not unusual to wake to find the duvet frozen to the bedroom wall. I manage to tear several duvet covers by trying to disconnect them.

Another summer arrived and was just as uncomfortable, as the heat in the tin box was equally unbearable.

We decided to try and inject a bit of pleasure into our lives. We got married, then went to the Canary Islands on honeymoon. This was all a lovely distraction from the task in hand.

That summer, in a moment of sheer madness, I offered to take all the grandchildren to Butlins holiday camp. I can say categorically that I counted down every minute till it came to an end, but I know the children loved it.

Lucy and Tim had decided to divorce. Lucy had discovered that Tim had committed a one-off misdemeanour. She then instantly marched into the arms of another in retaliation. There was to be no reconciliation, as, in her eyes, a cardinal sin had been committed. The marriage was at an end.

Lee and Sally had themselves entered marital bliss. I knew it would not be long before our fourth grandchild would make an appearance.

Chapter 15

I continued to pay my weekly visits to see Mother and Dad. I was getting increasingly worried about Dad's health. He seemed to be wasting away before my eyes. He was drinking a lot of fluids and eating far too many sweets.

I was very aware from past events that he hated the doctors and would normally refuse to go.

I, therefore, took it out of his hands and made the appointment for him to have a thorough checkup.

On my next visit, I was told that the results showed nothing untoward which was a huge relief. Perhaps it was, after all, just old age as Mother had kept telling me.

But one afternoon, I received a phone call from Mother to say that Dad had been rushed into hospital with a suspected heart attack.

I was out of work, into the car and at the hospital in record time. Seeing his frail little body in that bed broke my heart. I sat holding his hand with tears streaming down my face. He turned his head and looked at me with colourless eyes and said in a weak voice,

"Aww don't cry, my duckling. Don't you worry, it's going to be alright. I'm not in any pain."

I could not bear to see him like that. I sat with him until visiting ended and reassured him I would come back that evening.

I went to be with Mother as I knew she would be in a heap; after all, they had never spent any time apart.

I arrived to find her in the kitchen making tea.

"What's happening?" she asked as I took a cup from her.

"I couldn't bear to see him like that. It was heartbreaking. He looked so frail lying in that bed," I told her. "What happened?"

"Well, we had just finished breakfast and he just threw up; he was as sick as a dog. It went everywhere. I have only just finished cleaning it up. I'm convinced I can still smell it. Or it could be just in my nostrils. Can you smell it?" she asked and continued, "I said to him, oh good God, that vest was clean on this morning; couldn't you have made it to the toilet?"

She took a sip of tea before continuing. "The paramedics said that they were pretty sure it was his heart," she declared, cutting two slices of cake, and placing them on plates.

I was shocked to my core by her reaction to this truly dreadful event. She was more concerned about him messing up his clean vest than him having a heart attack.

"Mother, he could have died," I told her accusingly.

This comment obviously did not register, or just simply didn't warrant a reply.

I stayed with her until the time came for evening visiting.

"Are you coming with me, Mother, to see Dad?" I asked, hoping that she would say of course she was, but she replied to the contrary.

"No, no, I will leave it up to you this evening; perhaps tomorrow."

I entered the hospital and made my way towards the ward where I had found Dad earlier that day. I went through the double doors and was just passing the nurses' station when a staff nurse stepped in front of me and asked,

"Excuse me, but can I have a word?"

She took me into a side room and bent down and got a brown paper envelope out of a desk drawer. As she handed it to me, she said,

"I'm sorry to have to tell you but your father had another coronary this afternoon. There was nothing more that could be done, I'm afraid." She was still holding out the brown envelope for me to take.

I just stood there staring at her, speechless. I was totally unable to process what she had just said.

She pushed the brown envelope closer to me and told me solemnly, "His personal effects."

I took the envelope from her and looked down at it. Is this it? Is she telling me he has died and that this is all that remains of my beloved dad?

"That's impossible," I said in utter disbelief. "I was talking with him this afternoon; he told me not to worry that he wasn't in any pain."

"I'm sorry," she repeated, before leaving the room.

I found the way this devastating news had been imparted very cruel and downright heartless. It had magnified my pain one hundred-fold. It had been a body blow, the pain of which would never be forgotten.

I opened the envelope. There inside was his watch, his wedding ring, and his wallet.

Inside his wallet was a single ten-pound note that Mother had insisted he always carried, in case of emergencies. There was also a card with an angel holding the hand of a little girl on the front.

The bishop had gifted it to me on the day of my christening, I had no idea that he carried it around with him in his wallet.

I made my way back to Mother's, determined to try to deliver this terrible news gently, and with the utmost care. She listened in silence and then said,

"You will need to phone Edward, he will need to organise his flights. Arrangements will have to be made for the funeral. He will, of course, be better at organising that than you would, Rita, so the sooner he gets here the better."

"Do you want to give Edward the news?" I asked her.

"No, you do it. It would be better coming from you."

The phone calls were made. It was harder breaking the news to Edward than it had been imparting it to Mother.

Edward was angry that Dad had not been connected to a heart monitor. He said it was well known that people could suffer a second attack shortly after having had the first. He was on his way, and he was going to expect answers as to why things had not been done correctly.

I stayed with Mother that night so that she would not be left alone. There was only the one bedroom, so I had to sleep on Dad's side of the bed. It was a terrible thing to endure. I could smell him on the sheets and pillow.

It was a long and painful night, finally sobbing myself to sleep next to a quietly snoring mother.

The next morning, I awoke exhausted, with red and swollen eyes, still unable to comprehend what had happened, and still not wanting to believe it. I looked across the bedroom at Mother who was on her hands and knees piling Dad's clothes into black bin bags.

"What the hell are you doing, Mother? You can't possibly be clearing out Dad's things," I said in utter disbelief.

"Stop being so sentimental, Rita; it's only clothes. They're no good to him now, are they?"

I managed to salvage from the bag a cable knit cardigan with leather buttons that I had knitted for him several years ago and which he had worn constantly. I had to have something of his to hold dear. Clutching it to my heart, I told her.

"I'm going home. You are clearly coping with all this just fine."

Edward managed to get across from the States in record time and proceeded to take over the reins of making the necessary arrangements for the funeral. He had been into the hospital and had attempted to exert his authority regarding Dad's care, or lack of it.

However, he got short shrift. He was told that Dad had died of a massive coronary due to advanced diabetes, causing such extensive damage to his heart that when the second attack had occurred, the heart was unable to withstand it.

How was this possible? He had recently been examined by his doctor and had been told that there was nothing wrong. Why hadn't his doctor discovered that Dad was suffering from diabetes?

Edward went on to tell me that when the hospital had tried to obtain Dad's medical records, they discovered that no medical records existed for him. Not only had he not attended the appointment I had made for him, but he had no previous medical records whatsoever.

When I put this to Mother, she told me that he had left the house that day to go to the appointment. She had no reason to believe that he had not attended.

Maybe if he had, he would be here today, I thought sadly. That was typical of Dad, never wanting to worry anyone. How terribly sad. I would miss him so much.

Mother got through the funeral without shedding a tear. All the attending relatives said how brave she was.

Me, well, I was in an awful state from start to finish. I felt the pain of never being able to see him or hear his voice again almost unendurable. Edward stood up to the day like a man, but I could tell he was struggling to keep it together. A few days later, he was back on the plane heading home.

I continued to visit Mother every week. For the first few months, she appeared to have adjusted to life on her own extremely well. But, as the weeks went by, she began phoning me daily. It had all caught up with her.

As it finally sunk in that she was facing the future alone, she headed into a deep depression. She began self-medicating with alcohol. On occasions, when I arrived on a Saturday afternoon, I witnessed her hiding her glass as I came through the front door.

I did my best to include her in everything we were doing as a family. She would come to Sunday lunch once a month, along with Tom's mum, who was also on her own. Tom's dad had died in very similar circumstances of a sudden heart attack some years ago.

I wrongly thought that my mother and Tom's mother would have this tragedy in common, a kind of shared grief, but my mother made no attempt to get on with her.

Tom's mother was a lovely, kind, quietly spoken lady. She was extremely gifted and made all her own jams and chutneys, and homemade wine. She was well recognised for her most amazing wedding cakes.

She was a clay artist and played the organ in the local church. She never felt the need to talk about her achievements. She was what you call the salt of the earth, just a genuinely lovely lady.

Mother had spotted very early on that I had formed a close bond with Tom's mother and, try as she might, she could not hide her jealousy of her. She did her level best to try and cause friction at some point throughout the day. She would begin by making snide remarks, which bordered on the unkind. She took every opportunity to disagree with things Tom's mother was saying.

It got to the point on one occasion where I had to step in to stop Mother in her tracks.

This resulted in her, in floods of tears, demanding to be taken home. I did not understand why she chose to be so beastly. Tom's mother had done nothing to deserve it.

In the end, it became necessary to have them separately, with Christmas being the only exception, which I came to dread as we walked on eggshells throughout the day.

The work on the cottage was progressing at a painstaking pace.

Summer came and went. The third winter was now upon us, and boy, oh boy, was it a bad one.

One night, my neighbours phoned me at two in the morning, worried as they watched the caravan rocking dangerously from side to side in gale force winds, fearing it was about to blow out of the field completely.

"I'm fine," I reassured them, climbing back into bed, and hanging on for grim death.

We had reached the point in the cottage renovations where we were putting down floor coverings.

I tried to be clever and arranged for a tiler to come and lay the kitchen floor tiles while Tom was away at work. On his return, he took one look at the floor, decided that they weren't running straight, and spent the next two weeks painstakingly taking them all up.

Wow, another lesson learnt. I was becoming a real pro at learning lessons.

Over several months, Mother had become increasingly difficult, especially regarding my work.

I kept receiving calls from the hospital asking me to come and collect her. She had, for the umpteenth time, summoned an ambulance, which had, yet again, resulted in a hospital visit. Following a full examination, they had, yet again, found nothing wrong.

She had us dragged back from holiday on two occasions feigning serious illness. Again, nothing wrong.

We could not go anywhere for fear of being called back home, let alone the fact that she was wasting valuable hospital time.

This prompted the intervention of a social worker whose report indicated that Mother, who was now 82 years of age, was struggling to come to terms with her husband's death and was quite simply lonely. It went on to say that this behaviour was a form of attention-seeking.

She arranged for Mother to go into respite care for two weeks where she would have company and a more structured day-to-day existence.

Mother absolutely loved it there, where she certainly got all the attention she craved.

The guy running the place, whose name was Colin, was amazing. He treated all the residents like members of his own family.

For some unknown reason, Mother had convinced herself that the treatment she received from Colin was, in some way, different.

This was completely untrue. Colin was simply very good at his job, but he suggested to me that it might be simpler to leave her with this illusion.

She took part in all the daily activities and had even made a male friend. It appeared to have filled the empty void for her.

In the coming months, Mother completed two of these fortnightly stays before making the decision to move into the residential home permanently.

I was not at all sure. I felt she was being too hasty -a decision that she may well come to regret.

I begged her to give it a bit longer, but she was adamant. She had made up her mind.

She contacted the estate agent, put her home on the market, gave away all her unwanted belongings and never looked back.

Visits now were made to her new care facility where I found her happy and contented.

We had finally reached the stage that everyone looks forward to when renovating their home.

the choosing of carpets and curtains and buying all the new furniture. This was an exciting time. I was in my element.

Almost five years had passed since that monumental speech; "It will need a bit of work done on it."

We were now ready to move out of the caravan and into our beautiful new home. I was so proud of what Tom had singlehandedly achieved. We could now focus all our efforts on the landscaping, and creating a water feature, something I had always wanted.

This completed, we sat back to admire our efforts.

It was two days before Tom was due back offshore. We were sitting in our new conservatory enjoying a glass of wine. looking out across the fields at the evening sun as it disappeared over the horizon.

I sighed deeply in appreciation of all we had achieved, just happy and content to be enjoying the fruits of our labour.

I looked across at Tom as he sat, deep in thought, gazing beyond our water lily pond.

He turned his head to look at me and said nonchalantly,

"Oh, by the way, there is a guy coming tomorrow morning at ten-thirty to measure up.

"Measure up?" I stupidly repeated.

"Yep," he responded, looking back out across the fields.

"We are putting the house on the market and moving to Spain."

I stared back at him in utter disbelief, unable to get even a gasp out in response to what he had just said.

I knew him well enough to be aware of exactly what had prompted this monumental decision. I knew it was based entirely on his concern for me.

He had hinted as much when he was home on his last month's leave. He had sat me down and said that I had given my heart and soul to a job that had hammered me into the ground and damned near pushed me over the edge. He told me he appreciated just how much I had sacrificed over the last five years living in the caravan, helping him with renovating the house while holding down a full-time and demanding job. He appreciated the strain I had been under with the loss of my dad, and the worry over Mother.

All the signs were there of what was going through his mind; I just hadn't connected the dots.

He had obviously given a lot of thought to how he was going to sell this radical idea to me and had decided on the direct approach.

"You and I are going to give up our jobs. We are going to sell up. We are going to finally be together. No more living half the year away from each other. I know. The next time I'm home, we are going out to Spain to check it out. So, you had better hand in your notice.

Now, it's our turn; we are going to live the dream. Please say you agree," he said, drawing me closer into his arms.

I had waited so long to have the home of my dreams. Why didn't I just say, "No, I don't want to give up my home or move to another country away from my children and grandchildren"?

But what came out of my mouth was,

"OK."

It was completely insane; I couldn't help but wonder what the hell I had just agreed to. As expected, the children thought we had completely taken leave of our senses.

"Why would you ever agree to do that? Sell the cottage and move abroad - you must be crazy," Lucy said when I told her.

The only thing I could think of to placate them all was the offer of free holidays.

Mother, however, took the news well as she was enjoying her new-found status as the special one.

I gave the expected month's notice and began the preparations for the trip into our new future. Flights were booked and we were going for our first foray into a new life.

We needed to establish just where in this huge country we wanted to relocate to. This was no small task.

We began our search in the South, which turned out to be bad planning as it was the hottest season of the year, and it quickly became apparent just how unbearably hot it could get.

Over the course of a week, and accompanied by pressurising estate agents, we viewed several villas with sea views in and around Madrid which is famous for the bullfighting. The Spanish are passionate about this age-old custom, but it did not appeal to us at all.

We decided to move our search further North.

We were on our guard from the get-go, as we had heard some real horror stories of people buying properties only to find the property lacked the necessary planning permission.

These illegal homes had to be demolished with the new owners invariably losing their life savings.

One couple had come badly unstuck when they bought and paid for an old farmhouse, only to find that when they got the keys, the previous owner's elderly relative was still occupying one of the rooms, and by Spanish law, was legally quite within their rights to do so.

The couple had to accept their situation and learn how to get on with their new lodger. This was a serious lesson to be learned for anyone buying in Spain. Get yourselves a Spanish-speaking English lawyer and read every single word of the small print. If at all unsure, don't buy.

Of course, this was not about to happen to us - we were far too savvy to fall into these types of traps.

Yeah Right.

Week three, and the search continued as we moved further up the country, this area having a much more comfortable climate. We stayed in a quaint little Spanish town near Tarragona, about half an hour south of Barcelona.

We were especially impressed with the friendliness of the locals despite not having a scooby about what they were saying.

I made a mental note to myself to take some Spanish lessons when I returned to the UK.

There appeared to be a great many bars on the main street which we noticed were filled with English ex-pats downing copious amounts of alcohol at 10 o'clock in the morning. This did not bode well for our new life in the sun. We would have to avoid these habits if we were to live here.

We were looking forward to the next day. We had an appointment to view a property that we were quite excited about as the details said it had sea views from every veranda.

We had arranged to meet the agent, whose name was Ian, at midday. We had come to know him quite well, as we had been viewing various properties with him over a three-day period and had become quite friendly. I was beginning to trust what he told us which, for an estate agent, was a rather rare quality.

When we arrived at the villa, we were greeted by a middle-aged couple whom we judged to be in their early sixties. They may well have been younger, but a common mistake that a lot of retirees make is they give in to the desire to sit out in the sun all day. This had likely taken its toll on this pair, giving that their skin resembled the texture of leather.

We were invited into the main living area where there was a television blaring out on an English channel.

The couple made no attempt to turn it down, making it difficult to hear what was being said.

We could not fail to notice that the couple were still in their pyjamas. We discovered, as the conversation progressed, that they had decided to sell to move back to England.

They apparently hated everything about their chosen lifestyle. There was nothing to do, they declared, except to watch the television, drink alcohol, and sit in the sun. It was not even worth getting dressed in the morning, they added, which explained the PJs.

This was a real eye-opener. We were beginning to question our decision to move out to Spain. Perhaps it was not such a good idea after all. We may well have had a narrow escape.

We felt relieved that we had only the one day left before returning home to rethink our future once again.

Oh dear! I then remembered I had already handed in my notice. Oh boy!

Our new friend Ian had offered to take us out for lunch on our last day. Show us the local sights, he said.

He picked us up at midday in his old Jeep, which had seen better days. On the way to the restaurant, Ian explained that he was taking us to see Miravet Castle.

To reach it, we had to cross the river De Ebro on a hand-operated ferry, which, amazingly, managed to squeeze eight to ten cars at a time onto its little wooden platform. This was no mean feat in a fast-flowing river.

Health and Safety seemed nonexistent as a small flimsy chain was all that prevented its heavy cargo from being emptied into the river. It felt as if we had travelled back a hundred years.

Miravet Castle was steeped in history, with the most amazing views as far as the eye could see, north and south of the river and the surrounding land. It had been founded by the Moors, but after the conquest of 1153, it was then handed over to the Master of the Knights Templar.

It underwent massive reconstruction, transforming it into one of the centres of Christian power in the Iberian Peninsula.

For me, it felt hugely atmospheric. As I stood gazing down through a heavy metal grid into the dungeons below, I was able to picture what it must have been like to be imprisoned in that dark underground space.

I saw all the metal rings set deep within the walls where the Knights Templar tethered their horses. It was most awe-inspiring.

Lunch was in a local restaurant at the foot of the castle; the food was excellent. The proprietor obviously knew Ian well, returning frequently to the table with another carafe of wine. It became clear that Ian preferred the wine to the food, as he poured yet another glass of it.

It seemed rather rude not to join him.

Three hours later, we all staggered out of the restaurant. So much for our vow not to join the boozy brigade. We made our way back toward the ferry to make the return trip across the river.

Due to his much-diminished sense of distance, undoubtedly due to the copious amount of wine consumed, Ian made several unsuccessful attempts to position his Jeep onto the bobbing platform.

Why we found the situation so hilarious is uncertain as it could have led to dire consequences.

With the perils of alcohol now firmly established, Ian then said that he had one last property he wanted to show us. Probably not the best time to view it as our judgment was now seriously impaired, but we were in his vehicle, so options were limited.

Besides, he did not wait for a reply; he simply swerved off the road and headed at breakneck speed along what could only be described as a dried-up riverbed.

"Only two other couples have viewed this, but the track was too long, and it put them off," he remarked, looking back at us. "It only takes 30 minutes which is nothing really, is it? I can guarantee it's well worth the journey."

I was beginning to wonder what the waiting list was for spinal surgery back in the UK, trying to stop my teeth from rattling as we bumped across tree roots whilst swerving to avoid boulders.

What if you run out of milk? I thought. Funny how men don't think of the practicalities.

Well, we were almost there now, and the alcohol was helping, to some degree, to anaesthetise the painful parts.

Suddenly, we had reached a clearing, and, just up ahead, we could see this stunning house nestled into the hillside surrounded by olive and almond trees. It was quite a shock finding this amazing edifice in the middle of nowhere.

We had one more dice with death to endure before reaching this outstanding prize. Ian needed to negotiate a track that was only the width of his Jeep and had a four-terrace drop on one side.

I wondered if Ian's alcohol level had sufficiently depleted in order to successfully undertake such a risky manoeuvre, but, unfazed, he ploughed on still at breakneck speed.

I screwed my eyes tightly shut, clenched my buttocks like they had never been clenched before, and held my breath until I could feel my face run out of colour.

But he pulled off what I perceived to be the impossible.

"There you go, that was not so bad, was it?" he said, bringing the vehicle to a shuddering stop at the bottom of a set of natural stone steps.

Despite being in the middle of nowhere, the house was indeed worth every single bump and shake of that journey. It was a uniquely beautiful newly built house set in 13 hectares of stunning and immaculately kept land, covered in olive and almond trees, with the most breathtaking views of the mountains.

Everything inside had been built to a very high spec with no expense spared. There was something quite outstanding about it. It was on a whole different level to everything we had viewed to date, and at a fraction of the cost, possibly due to the track. But, as Ian had rightly said, it was well worth the journey.

There, at the top of the steps, stood a middle-aged couple who introduced themselves as Mr and Mrs Kingston, a lovely English couple who owned a huge fruit farm across the valley. They told us that they had built the house especially for their son, who had planned to move over from the UK to farm goats.

After spending time at his parents' while the house was being built for him, he made the decision that it was too quiet for him and had moved himself back to London,

leaving his mother and father to dispose of a property into which they had invested both time and money.

Typical of kids, I thought.

Of course, we asked what we thought were the right questions to establish both the honesty and integrity of the transaction, which we felt was expected of us, but it was all largely irrelevant.

We were having this house.

What track? What drive? I could easily adapt to dried milk, if I had to, couldn't I?!

We spent another hour discussing the finer points with the Kingstons,

The best asset for a property in such a remote location was that the house had its own water supply, which was stored in a tank underneath the house, which was pumped from the Kingstons bore hole and was included in the contract for water to be supplied as requested for a small annual fee. This was a huge saving as most remote dwellings had the added expense of drilling their own wells.

We were told we would be the proud owners of eight hundred fine and ancient olives trees which produced roughly 11 tons of A-grade oil a year, sold to the local cooperative.

It also had 242 beautiful almond trees and two fig trees. Must not forget the figs; they were for personal use only due to there being only two of them. I adored figs so it was worth a mention.

We could do this. Spanish Labourers had been working this land for centuries, hadn't they? We were modern man with modern technology. It would be a breeze and a blast. Bring it on.

Business concluded, we said our goodbyes and made our way back down the track, which strangely did not seem as bad on the return journey. We ended up at Ian's office in the village of Tivisa where we paid the deposit, signed the paperwork, and sealed the deal.

Before we knew it, we were back on the plane heading for home. Had we really done this crazy thing?

Yes, we had. Now I had to knuckle down and enrol myself in the local college to take a crash course on learning the language.

We needed to get the house on the market. I needed to get the cats vaccinated against rabies. So much to think about. Oh well, head down, press on.

Chapter 16

We were entering into a demonic phase; well, at least I was. Tom had gone back to work his notice. I began filling boxes with everything I could find medical-related:

Bandages, lint, eye drops, pain killers, finger splints, potions for muscle sprain, tablets for nausea, diarrhea, constipation, snake bite, flea bite, disinfectant, cotton wool, pills, and potions of every description. I even had toenail fungal infection covered.

Any observer would conclude that I was preparing for a journey to a far-flung galaxy. It did occur to me through this process that they did have chemists in Spain, however, I was acutely aware that not being proficient in the language, it would be almost impossible to explain with just hand signals that I needed something for diarrhea.

Now satisfied that I had covered all medical emergencies, I set about packing up the house.

The house sold very quickly which did not surprise me. Preparations had reached fever pitch. Tom was home and was making the necessary arrangements to move all our belongings out to Spain. I assumed this to be a man's task, so I left him to it.

With everything now in place, the day had finally arrived. This was actually happening, I thought as we sat amongst a sheer mountain of cardboard boxes waiting for the removal van to arrive.

The sound of an engine could be heard in the distance.

"This is him!" Tom called out as he looked up the road at the approaching lorry. It was the largest pantechnicon I had ever seen as the cab sailed on by the gate and came to a halt five or more minutes later.

A rough-looking guy hopped out and walked back to the gate. He introduced himself as Carl and explained that he was able to move ex-pats out to Spain, otherwise his lorry would be empty going out. He imported car parts back from Europe. All cash in hand, of course.

We proceeded to load the entire contents of our four-bedroom house, the garage, our barn, and the garden shed. Even our car was prized on.

It took the three of us the best part of a day to load it up to its gunnels. I don't believe we could have got another thing on if we had tried. The only thing that remained was the picnic table. I decided I would gift it to our neighbours.

"See you in three days," Carl called out from his open window as we waved him goodbye.

It had been a hell of a day and we were exhausted.

We sat on the bottom step of the stairs looking around the empty room with a tinge of sadness.

It had been a truly monumental journey to transform this house into a home, and we'd had such little opportunity to enjoy the fruits of our labour. But we must look forward to a brand-new chapter in our lives together.

"He looked a bit of a rough diamond, the driver, didn't he? But he was actually very nice, and helpful too," I said as I reflected on the day.

"What's his surname?" I enquired casually.

"I don't know his surname, only his first name," he told me casually.

"What? But you have his contact details, his address and stuff, don't you?" I asked.

"Nope. I answered an advertisement in the Exchange and Mart magazine. It said if you want the contents of your house moving out to Spain, call this number," he said, handing me a scrap of paper.

"Oh, my God, Tom, mean to tell me we have just loaded the entire contents of our house, and everything we own, onto a lorry belonging to someone for who we only have the name of Carl and a mobile phone number?"

The expletives used on this occasion are simply unrepeatable. My very chilled, and utterly laidback husband uttered only a short response.

"Stop worrying, it will be fine."

"But he will deliver it, won't he? He will want to be paid, won't he?" I asked, hoping for reassurance.

"I had to pay him up-front, Rita, or he would not have agreed to do it," came the shocking reply.

Oh, good Lord, I thought, as I held my head in my hands. We had fallen at the very first hurdle. We had lost everything, and we hadn't even got on the plane yet.

We are now part of a statistic of all those who have gone before us who have come badly unstuck due to their own complete and utter stupidity. We were now officially one of the horror stories that are frequently seen on the TV.

Nothing else for it, I locked the front door, climbed into Lee's car with two cats in cat boxes on our laps and had one final look back through the rear window at my beautiful house as it disappeared into the distance.

We were staying with Lee and Sally overnight, as Lee was going to drive us to the airport the next morning.

We were up early, excitement building; we made our way to Heathrow.

We said our goodbyes, with the promise that as soon as we were sorted, they could come out to visit.

I watched anxiously from the airport departure lounge as the Animal Centre staff carried our two precious cats into the hold of the aeroplane, taking great care not to spill the water containers attached to the inside of their carriers. Much reassured by the care in which this task was carried out, we settled down to eat the customary fried breakfast that one must have at an airport.

In next to no time, we were on the plane. It is a relatively short flight in which you are encouraged to fit in a meal. It would make a lot of sense to avoid the fried breakfast, but we, like most people, can never resist the temptation.

The meal had only just been cleared away when the wheels were bumping down on the runway. We had arrived.

We waited patiently at the end of the carousel for our cases. I was intrigued to see what was attracting people's attention at the far end where the luggage enters the carousel. It soon became evident as the carousel rumbled and creaked its way toward us.

In utter horror, I could see the two-cat carriers, upside-down under a pile of suitcases.

In the time it took for them to reach us, I had convinced myself that our beloved pets would have surely died from sheer fright.

As they got closer, I could see four paws gripping the sides of the carriers, staring back at me from their upside-down position. It was clear that some Spanish people were not animal lovers.

Having managed to bring my cats back from the brink of heart failure with soothing talk and many strokes, we left the airport to pick up our hired van.

We would have to stop to pick up some essentials. There was nothing at the house until the lorry arrived. If the lorry arrived. We stopped at a superstore just outside Tarragona to pick up food supplies, two sun loungers, two duvets, two pillows, two cat beds, two litter trays, and, of course, the all-important dried milk.

We were informed that we would need to go to the rear of the store to a loading bay to collect the sun loungers. At least, that's what we thought we were being told. We loaded up the hired van with all our other purchases and followed the arrows to the loading bay where there were two young men zooming around on forklifts trucks unloading a lorry.

We carefully avoided parking anywhere near the lorry and quickly loaded our two sun loungers into the back of the van.

Tom reversed out careful not to get near the lorry but had not checked the other side which, only minutes earlier, had been perfectly clear. In those two minutes, one of the young men had parked up his forklift to the left of us and had left the forks in an upright position.

What followed was a metal-on-metal screeching noise, which seemed to last for several seconds.

We jumped out of the van and stared open-mouthed at the two parallel grooves which now formed a new pattern down the side of our newly hired van.

"What's the chances of that happening? You could not make it up, could you?" I said to Tom in total disbelief.

The words ill-fated came to mind as we continued our journey in total silence. We had only been in the country for two hours and we had already trashed a vehicle.

It was, therefore, not surprising that our arrival at our new home one hour later did not generate the same euphoria as we had hoped for.

Trying to put the day's events behind us, we packed away the provisions into the spanking new kitchen cupboards, looking out of the window at the cats as they explored their new garden.

Poor little souls, they had certainly been through the mill, I thought as I watched them pee for a good five minutes or more.

I would make it up to them, I decided, as I reached for a can opener to get into a tin of red salmon.

The first night was magical. We took our sun loungers outside and slept under the stars with a cat curled up at the bottom of each lounger.

This was an act of sheer recklessness, as the Kingstons informed us the next day when they called around to welcome us to our new home. Apparently, bobcats and wild boars roam the land at night. That's not to mention snakes and rats.

Ignorance is bliss, so they say.

The day was spent exploring our land; it was stunning. The Kingstons had left it in immaculate condition. The trees were perfectly pruned, not a weed in sight.

We climbed the hill behind the house and looked out across the terraces to the mountains on the other side of the valley. I reflected on all those gone before us who had walked these terraces and had worked the land over centuries to make a meagre living.

It was then that I made a silent vow that as the new custodians of the land, we too would honour to the full our part in its history.

Day two came and went. Day three was approached with a sense of apprehension. We awoke on day four in the stark realisation that there was no lorry. Well, I did, anyway.

All day I unfairly harped on at Tom, I just could not help myself.

"It's not coming. I told you, didn't I? How could you have been so trusting of a stranger?" I nagged. "What should we do? Do we have a plan B? We should have heard something by now, shouldn't we?" I demanded.

All day, I kept doing ridiculous things like repeatedly checking the mobile was fully charged and standing outside looking across the valley where just a small area of the track was visible in the distance.

By the evening, my mood had plummeted into a dangerously dark place; a state of mind that I had never visited. Tom was doing everything humanly possible to make himself invisible.

I hardly slept a wink that night as I rolled the problem around and around in my head like a tape recorder on constant repeat.

The next morning, we were sitting in silence eating breakfast, worry etched on both our faces, when the long-awaited call came.

"Hi!" said the voice on the other end. "It's Carl! I'm sorry I'm late getting to you. I have been snowed in, in the Pyrenees, due to the excess weight I'm carrying. Couldn't even get a phone signal until now. But it's clearer today, so I think I will be able to get going. I should get to you by late morning tomorrow."

I took this news in as dignified a way as I could muster under the circumstances. I wanted to shout and scream but managed to contain the urge. Now feeling the enormity of my guilt, I turned to Tom saying,

"I'm so sorry, darling. I've been a real cow, haven't I?" He just smiled and went to put the kettle on. I don't know how he puts up with me, I thought.

The next day, we watched the horizon for that familiar shape that would blot out the sun with its presence.

"It's here!" I shouted excitedly, I had just seen it turn off the main road. We followed it with binoculars for around fifteen minutes as it slowly edged along the narrow track, then came to a standstill. We continued to watch for a further ten minutes but there was no further progress.

We leapt into our damaged hire van and roared down the track to establish what the problem was.

There stood Carl, leaning against the side of the lorry, smoking a cigarette.

I could no longer contain my relief. My fear of him having absconded with all our worldly goods now abated, I jumped from the van, running towards him, flinging myself at him.

"Carl!" I gushed, flinging my arms around his neck. "You made it!"

"Ha, ha, I bet you thought I had done a bunk with all your stuff," he laughed.

"That never once entered my mind," I said indignantly, stepping back with feigned surprise, looking at Tom, hoping he would back me up in this downright lie. Bless his heart, he kept his silence.

Carl had been forced to stop due to the narrowness of the track. We did not know how we would overcome this latest dilemma. So, we summoned our new friends, the Kingstons, for advice.

Fifteen minutes later, they arrived with a Spanish guy on a tractor-trailer. With their help, our two vans, and the tractor-trailer, and many more journeys later, we had dragged the entire contents of the lorry through the dried-up riverbed, depositing it all on the drive outside the house.

Carl, being the absolute star of the show, had done all the unloading. What a stalwart, I thought to my shame; how could I have doubted him? Yet another lesson to be learned.

It was far too late to start unpacking so we sat amongst the entire contents of an English country cottage, poured ourselves a large glass of wine, and watched the sun disappear over the mountains.

Tomorrow, we had to get everything from outside to inside. Another busy day on the farm.

With the help of Anthony Kingston, we managed to purchase our own van, register it for tax and insurance, which now meant we could return the hired van, something I was dreading but it had to be faced.

So many more exciting things lay in store for us in our new life in sunny Spain. Just as well we don't know what's ahead of us sometimes.

The next few weeks were spent setting up the new systems which were imperative to function in the back of beyond.

Tom had spent several days ensuring we had power. We had brought with us from the UK a large generator, and the thirty massive batteries. Tom also erected a windmill, which, after he attached it to the batteries in the stone log shed, whirled away rhythmically. We then purchased two gas bottles to fuel our cooking.

All set up now, we were able to focus on putting in place the paperwork side of our farm.

I don't know how we would have coped without the assistance of the Kingstons as they held our hands through the process of registering our olive production at the local cooperative.

We were also required to notify the local ayuntamiento, (the town hall) for the purpose of payment of rates.

All these things seemed to be conducted in different towns, so the help from the Kingstons was invaluable.

I had managed a crash course in Castilian Spanish in a UK college whilst waiting for the completion of the legalities of the house purchase, but that in no way equipped me for what would be required. My understanding was still only proficient in the absolute basics of 'hello,' 'goodbye' and 'can I have a cold beer, please?'

This was complicated further by the realisation that we were now living in Catalonia, which is a completely different language to Castilian Spanish, with Catalan leaning more to French, making my earlier efforts completely futile.

I decided to enrol myself with a local Spanish teacher. Her name was Andriana, and she lived in an apartment on the coast over a Spanish restaurant. She was very pleasant and advised me to continue with Castilian as it was a more widely used language around the world, whereas Catalan was specific only to Catalonia. This made sense to me at the time, but what I failed to recognise was that I would still be unable to understand the locals.

Still, I soldiered on.

The work on the farm was split into seasons. We had arrived just before harvesting so we were flung in at the deep end. Winter was now upon us, and it was a shock to find that Spanish winters in the north were colder than parts of the UK. The season for harvesting olives was between November and the end of January.

We set about buying a small tractor and trailer, large nets to be placed around the foot of each tree and an assortment of plastic scrapers, which resembled giant forks, designed to scrape the olives off the branches into the nets below.

We were up early every day, and, kitted out in our winter clothing, we headed out in our van with our packed lunch and flask of tea for a full day of harvesting. We worked from eight until four in the afternoon. We ate our packed lunch in the van with the engine running, trying to thaw out to face the afternoon ahead.

We had never worked so hard. Hats off to the ancestors who had to earn a living from it. But we loved every minute and found it therapeutic. I was extremely fastidious about capturing every olive, even those that had already fallen to the ground before the nets were put in place.

The best part about the process was the trip to the cooperative.

We always had an audience of other farmers who gathered around us as they enviously watched our premium A-grade olives being emptied into the hopper.

It became a great source of pride to us watching as our olives continued their journey along the conveyor belt into the big presses which squeezed out every last little drop of the precious oil.

Finally, with the harvesting complete, we were now heading into the pruning stage. This proved to be no mean feat with so many trees but at least the weather was improving making it a much more pleasurable experience.

We set ourselves a daily target which we tried desperately hard to meet. It was crucial we had all the trees pruned by the onset of the burning season, as there was such a limited time frame allocated to the process.

You were required to obtain a burning certificate from the local council giving the necessary permission to burn between certain dates and times of the day. This was to avoid any risk of fires, as the temperatures began to rise. Once the certificate expired, the burning had to cease, finished or not. This increased the pressure to get the job done.

This part of the process could be extremely dangerous, as I found out to my cost when one moment of lack of concentration cost me the loss of the front of my hair and my eyelashes as one fire got out of control. It was a terrifying moment.

With this part of the process safely behind us, it was time to fertilise the land. The whole cycle of upkeep kept us continuously busy. There was always something to be done.

Somewhere in the routine, I had to make time to phone Mother, for if I missed a call, she would be on the phone to ask the reason why.

We managed to eke out some time to look around the area. We found that the best restaurants to eat out in were where the locals ate, the food being authentic Spanish dishes as opposed to the coastal areas where all that was on the menu appeared to be burgers, or fish and chips.

Anyway, we much preferred to be amongst the Spanish as they certainly knew how to better handle their alcohol.

Most evenings, we hiked up the terraces to the top of the hill, with our little followers, the cats, trailing behind, something they enjoyed doing as much as we did. As we sat looking out across the valley, we decided to get a dog.

We wanted to give a home to a needy animal, so, the very next day found us heading toward an animal shelter.

Having visited an animal shelter in the UK, I was totally unprepared for the standards I was about to witness in this country.

Beyond the wooden entry gates, there were exotics as well as domestic animals housed in massive concrete compounds with deep gullies down either side.

Dogs, predominantly of the mongrel varieties, were packed into these compounds like sardines. It was a truly pitiful sight.

Pussy-eyed, bony creatures stared back at me lifelessly, some not even having the strength to hold up their heads. Several extremely distressing-looking animals looked as if they would not see the day out.

A worker came with a hose pipe and directed its water jet directly into the compound, soaking every occupant to its skin. The faeces on the concrete floors was now forced outwards into the side gullies and down the drains at the end. I could see newborn puppies in amongst the chaos. It was truly horrendous. Clearly, none of these animals looked well enough for adoption.

I'm sure the shelter staff were doing their best, but the sheer volume of occupants made it an impossible task.

We were advised that the puppies running loose around the perimeter paths were ready for adoption. Apparently, these animals were given one month to find a family, then, if unsuccessful, they would join the others in the concrete compounds.

Initially, we had only planned on having one dog, but because of the conditions, I wanted to take them all to save them from this truly shocking fate. After much discussion, we left with two sweet but totally different little individuals. We collected everything required from the superstore to make our new additions to the family comfortable and made our way home with them.

Within forty-eight hours, these two little puppies had fallen sick. We rushed them to the local English-speaking veterinarian who confirmed that they were both suffering from distemper.

After three weeks of daily visits to the vet for treatment, one had passed away. Two days later, the other one had succumbed.

The vet told us that these clearance centres were rife with this terrible disease. The whole sorry business had been heartbreaking and extremely costly, one we decided never to repeat.

The vet had done his best to save these puppies and, although he had failed through no fault of his own, he took it upon himself to find us a replacement.

He called to tell us he had just had a female puppy brought in who had been found on the roadside, believed to have been thrown out of a car.

I was immediately apprehensive; the loss of those puppies had badly affected us. But the vet assured us that he had fully examined this one and found her to be healthy. He had given her all the necessary vaccinations and she was good to go. Despite Tom's reservations, I managed to convince him that it would do no harm to look. Knowing me, he was well aware what that could mean.

We jumped into the van and made our way to the vet's surgery and were shown into the rear of the premises where we saw, sitting alone in a cage, the strangest-looking dog I had ever clapped eyes on. Her ears were nearly as big as her body. I knelt down for a closer look at her. She came close and put her paw through the bars and touched my arm. That was basically all that was needed.

We were on the way home with her on my lap. We had to stop at traffic lights where a bunch of kids were waiting patiently to cross. One child pointed at her and they all started laughing. I knew they were laughing at her ears. I became instantly defensive, sure evidence that this little scrap had already crept inside my heart.

The decision was made there and then that a fitting name for her would be Bella, ears, or no ears.

In the months that followed, Bella grew into those ears. She had a lovely nature and got on extremely well with the cats. She was full of fun and extremely loyal.

One day, some wild boar crossed our path on a walk through the woods. She flew at them as if her life depended on it. This provided us with a sense of security when out in the woods as these animals could be especially dangerous when they had young in tow.

The days came and went. We had a swimming pool built in front of the house in time for the children to come to visit. Lee and Sally had not long had their second child who we had yet to meet, so it was an exciting time. We took them around all the sights, and they enjoyed our new home after they got over the shock of the track. We found this to be the case with all our visitors.

Life was never ever dull and there was always something I managed to fall foul of.

Like the time I was outside pulling up weeds when my attention was caught by the sound of bells clanging. I looked up to see the goat herder standing on the very top terrace with his herd of goats.

Not having previously seen this sight, I was naturally thrilled by his presence and began waving frantically at him. He responded likewise, sitting down on the top stone wall while his goats ambled down the terraces munching the many herbs growing in abundance, rosemary being one of their favourites. Oh, that's why goat meat tasted so wonderfully herby, I thought. Tom came out of the house and was horrified to see the reason I was waving.

"Get inside, Rita!" he exclaimed. "Those damned goats are breaking down the stone walls holding up the terraces. Unless you want the job of rebuilding them, stop waving, and let the guy move on."

Well, how was I supposed to know that? I was only trying to be neighbourly.

There was also the time he caught me waving at a low-flying aircraft. I was again subjected to the same treatment and was told in no uncertain terms to get indoors. It was explained to me that the aircraft was spraying insecticide, to eradicate the olive fruit fly, and unless I had an innate desire to take a shower in the stuff, I needed to stop waving at it.

Friends had also warned me about the Processionary Caterpillar, so-called as they moved along their paths in a long chain of individuals, nose to tail. They held an incredibly powerful toxic protein in the tiny little hairs on their bodies which is released if touched.

These nasty little critters are extremely dangerous to adults and children alike, and almost always fatal to dogs and cats. This information imparted to me on an evening out, having consumed copious amounts of the red stuff, terrified the living daylights out of me and set me on an unnerving path of constantly looking out for them, convinced that I would, at some point, fall foul of them. It was six months later that I discovered that they were only prevalent in Southern Spain.

There were more terrifying moments, one of which was when I witnessed two rats the size of hares running out of the woodshed in my direction. This could be a hostile place at times.

Tom also had his moments; one day, he bolted indoors, screaming,

"There are enormous snakes on the patio."

I went out to investigate, and sure enough, there were two massive Montpellier snakes. These are considered one of the five most venomous snakes in Spain and can grow up to two metres in length. Well, here were two of them on our patio, entwined in rapturous abandon in the gruesome art of snake-mating.

I simply got a broom and skillfully directed the handle of it under what I deemed to be the middle of the writhing mass, trying to equalise the weight to the opposite ends of the broom. The mating continued as I managed to manoeuvre the heavy, moving bulk over the wall.

This interrupted the act of intimacy as the two of them slithered off in opposite directions.

"All sorted," I announced, putting the broom back in the cupboard, completely unaware they were so venomous.

"Phew! That was scary," Tom said, taking one final glance out of the window to double-check that the situation had indeed been resolved.

I had a similar situation with a scorpion, only this time, poor Bella was the subject of the attack.

I had just got into bed when I heard Bella kicking up a storm in the kitchen. I was out of bed in a flash and dashed downstairs to the kitchen where I witnessed our little dog facing up to an adult scorpion. Again, reacting without thinking, out came the broom once more. I opened the kitchen door and brushed it out onto the patio in one fell swoop. It had the rest of the night to change locations, so it was with the hope that it would be gone by the morning that I went back to bed.

Our endless encounters with wild boar also added extra interest to the day, almost to the point where we were becoming quite blasé about our reactions to them when coming face to face with them on our daily walks.

This was our way of life over the next five years. I had changed Spanish teachers several times but was still unable to master the language.

The rigorous workload of the farm was taking its toll, and, after a great deal of soul searching, and as painful as it was to leave this amazing place, we made the decision to sell up.

We found a house with mountain views on a small housing complex just outside a little village. The accommodation was all on the first level, the ground floor comprising of garage and storage space.

Tom took one look at this and decided that there was sufficient ceiling height on the ground floor to easily create more living space which would double the size of the property and increase its value. Yet another good business opportunity. The farm was sold, and the old villa was purchased.

We had made a massive profit on the farm, so this time, Tom hired builders to undertake the work, and before we knew it, we were living in another dream home with a luxury pool. Tom purchased a one-hundred-year-old olive tree and had it lifted by crane and placed into the centre focal point in the garden. He built a beautiful stone wall around it and inserted lighting inside, so at night, it became a wonderfully lit -up feature.

We purchased palm trees, ferns, cacti, and many more brightly coloured plants native to Spain.

We ran plastic pipes with holes in all around the garden which we covered with shingle so that when we needed to water the garden, we simply turned on the tap.

It was absolutely stunning and was, rather amazingly, featured in a regional magazine. A wonderful accolade.

We received terrible news. Edward had phoned to say that he and his wife Hazel had rented an apartment for the week whilst visiting Mother. He said Hazel had not felt well and had decided not to join him to visit Lee and Sally that first evening.

Edward had gone alone; he had a quick coffee with them and made his way back to the apartment. On arriving back, he had found her collapsed in the bathroom. He called an ambulance, but the paramedics established that she had passed away. It was the most terrible shock for him.

Because they were American citizens, the American Embassy had to be involved and they contacted the police as it was a sudden death that had to be investigated.

I got straight on the next flight home to be with him at this terrible time. Hazel, unbeknown to the rest of the family, had been battling cancer for some time and had already had a double mastectomy, and half her stomach removed. The cause of death, however, had been a blockage in the main artery in her neck. Poor Edward.

She was cremated at the local crematorium, and Edward flew back to the States with her in a casket. It was a terrible shock for both of their children.

Back in Spain, I made up my mind to learn the language if it was the last thing I did, which it probably would be. I had no idea it was going to be so hard.

It suddenly came to me one day, as I stood gazing into a ladies' dress shop window in the village, that if I was going to achieve this much sought-after goal, I needed to immerse myself in the language.

Without further thought, I opened the door to the dress shop and walked in.

"Hola, buenos días," I said to the woman behind the counter, and she responded with the same comment.

"Puedes ayudarme yo quero appender l'idioma de Español, però es muy difficili para me porque yo no puedo praticar mucho. Si es possibile a trabajar aqui en tu tienda con no dinero. Entonces yo puedo oir la gente cuando estaban hablando Expañol. Strangely, she understood what I had asked her which I believed interpreted literally as:

Hello, good day. Can you help me? I want to learn the Spanish language, but it is awfully difficult for me because I'm not able to practice much. Is it possible to work in your shop with no money then I can hear people when they are speaking?

She told me her name was Sofia, and she spoke five languages: Castilian Spanish, Catalan Spanish, English, French, and Italian. She fully understood my problem but said that the ladies who shopped in her shop were predominantly Catalan. However, she said that if I wanted to come in and work alongside her, she would speak to me in Castilian.

Wow! I could not believe my luck. Three mornings a week, I would turn up for work, and Sofia would chat away to me.

As the weeks went on, I discovered that it was her parents' shop. Sofia and her husband, who was called Enrique, lived in an apartment on the coast.

I learnt all the different names for the clothes, underwear, swimwear, and all the items on the haberdashery side of the shop. They sold a bit of everything.

I explained my past experiences at shop fitting, and Sofia asked me if I could make changes in her shop. She wanted to bring it up to today's standards.

I was naturally happy to help. We sourced new fixtures and fittings, racks, and shelving. She closed the shop for three days in order to complete the work.

It looked amazing when it was finished, and she was absolutely thrilled with it. However, her parents seemed stuck in the past and preferred it how it was. However, as time went on, they had to admit it had made a big difference to the takings.

I had become very friendly with Sofia and Enrique. Tom and I began to be invited to their family gatherings, birthdays wedding anniversaries, and any other family festivities. I was becoming more and more proficient at the language.

Sofia invited me to go with her to Barcelona when she went buying new stock for the shop. This soon became a regular occurrence. She came to trust me to choose things that I thought would sell well. Several times, she tried to pay me a wage, but that had not been the agreement. I would not hear of it. I was gaining so much from the experience and was learning all the time.

The children and grandchildren were regular visitors, and life was blissful. But both Tom and I had a couple of health scares. For me, it was a lump in the breast. For Tom, it was a bleed at the back of his eye. We could not fault the Spanish health care system; in many ways, it was superior to the UK, especially regarding the waiting lists, but it had set us thinking about the future.

We had enjoyed everything about Spain, the people, the climate, the food, the culture, but maybe the time had come to make plans to return.

We had also begun noticing a very worrying trend. Hundreds of new villas had been built all along the coastline but were standing empty. They were clearly not selling. Yet, the building continued at an unprecedented rate. The estate agent's windows were full of new properties for sale. It was evident to us that the bottom was falling out of the property market.

This inevitably forced our hand. We knew the time had come to return to the UK and it should be sooner rather than later.

It was sad it was coming to an end, but we could honestly say that we had made a real go of it, and not fallen foul of any disasters. Maybe we had just been lucky, but I like to think we had made the right decisions at the right time.

So, yet again, our lovely home was on the market. We knew it would sell quickly as it was so unique, and sure enough, the very first people who came to view it instantly fell in love with it and gave us the full asking price, which included all the furniture.

We had doubled the purchase price so had done well. The new owner even purchased our car from us.

Tom did a trip over to the UK with a trailer full of our belongings. He rented a self-contained cottage on the side of a farmhouse, left the trailer there and drove back out to Spain to pick up me and our tribe of pets. After an anxious journey on the ferry with all the animals in the middle of a storm, we finally made it back onto terra firma in the UK.

Chapter 17

The accommodation Tom had rented for us all was only to be a stopgap until the money came through from the sale of the house in Spain, but it was far from ideal. The spiral staircase to get to the only bedroom was downright dangerous, and it was far too small for us all. We had to find something else. It would mean we would lose the four months' rent remaining on it, but it was worth it to get something more comfortable.

We viewed a bungalow that was advertised in the local paper and could not believe its location.

We pulled into this tree-lined drive with two statues of lions sitting on huge ornate pillars on either side of the entrance. The bungalow was situated to the side of a country estate. It was gorgeous with panoramic views over the estate to the rear where deer wondered majestically.

Yes, this would do us nicely, I told the woman as she showed us around. Luckily, she had no problem with two cats and what was now a very large dog with smaller ears.

Our belongings were moved in the following day.

We spent six months living like Lord and Lady Whatsit but sadly, yet again, it was time to move on. The money was in the bank from the Spanish house so now, with cash in hand, we were able to begin looking for another home.

We had made such profits on the sale of each of our homes over the years that we were now in the very favourable position of being mortgage-free.

We had been to look at a property close to a national park. It had amazing views, equally as good as the rented bungalow.

Although it had been modernised, Tom, as always, could see the potential for increasing its value further by knocking down two internal walls. He knew that he could completely transform the look of the place. He had such a good eye for improvement. We put in an offer which was accepted.

Tom completed the planned renovations in six months and added an ex-showroom display office, that he purchased from a company that was shutting down. It was all bells and whistles, and it ran around three sides of the room and had lights illuminated the fitted shelving. It was the bees' knees. Up went the for-sale boards. By now, I didn't even bother unpacking.

The agent who had initially sold it to us came out to revalue it. Indignantly, she informed us that we couldn't possibly add eighty thousand to the price we paid for it six months previously, despite the changes we had made.

Tom, however, felt that the changes we had made warranted the revised figure and was adamant that it was achievable. In response, she told us,

"You can ask what you want, but that does not mean you're going to get it." And she promptly left.

Three days later, a couple with two teenage sons came to view. Once the teenagers saw the office, we believed it to be a done deal.

The phone call from the agent came later that afternoon. They had offered the full asking price.

So here we go again.

Time to move nearer to all the children, and dare I say, Mother, who had made it very clear she was expecting much more from me now that I was back in the country. We were in a kind of sticky situation, as our buyers had no chain and wanted to be in as quickly as possible.

This put a great deal of pressure on us to buy something else quickly. We frantically searched the internet with no success. We were fearful our buyers may see something they preferred more and pull out. It had to be considered that we may well not be lucky to achieve the asking price again.

So, on impulse, we decided to buy a four-bed detached house on a housing estate. I knew before the week was out that we had made a mistake. Not being used to close neighbours, we found this property's location claustrophobic.

The UK property market was also now beginning to tumble. We could see we needed to act quickly if we were not to get caught up in the property slump that was heading our way. Tom wanted to try and improve on it first to give it its best chance of a sale. He took down the wall between the kitchen and dining room, opening it up into a lovely big open space, which was a great improvement.

He also put in a new bathroom and a new en suite. Then up went the for-sale boards.

As the weeks rolled by, it was evident that this property was not going to be easy to sell. We had only received some crazy offers from speculators trying to grab a bargain.

Edward, on his annual visit to see Mother, introduced us to his new wife, Anne, who I took to instantly. She was very different from his first wife, who tended to be a little reserved. Anne had a much more outward going personality, and, with us both having the same sense of humour, I found I instantly gelled with her.

Edward had found a property online that had just come to the market which he thought would be just up our street. It was a detached bungalow sitting in the centre of an unusually large plot. To be honest, it did not look much at all from the pictures.

"It's worth checking it out, though," I told Edward, not wanting to seem ungrateful for his input.

We had had a heavy snowfall the night before the appointment to view it. The snow had turned the grounds of this very tired property into something rather magical, and without wishing to sound romantic, it felt that it was calling out to us.

The agent explained that two elderly sisters, who used to run the local post office, had owned it. One had passed away, and the other had been moved into a nursing home.

It was clear from the décor and the style of the place that this was another property that would need a total refurbishment.

This would need careful consideration, as we would have to somehow live in it whilst we were doing the work. However, due to the size of the plot and its huge potential, Tom and I looked at each other and said in unison to the agent,

"Yes, we love it."

When we arrived home, I phoned Edward and told him that he had, cleverly, found us our forever home.

We then phoned the agent dealing with the sale of our property and reduced the price. For the very first time, we had to withstand a loss. But hey, rough with the smooth, they say, don't they? A young couple with a child bought the house. We were pleased that it had finally sold.

We were on our way. We were just itching to get our teeth into our next and final project. Tom had made the promise that this would be our last renovation.

The look on the face of the guys that moved our furniture was priceless as they took in where we had moved from, to where we had moved to. I think they felt a bit sorry for us as one guy said, sympathetically, as they were leaving,

"Don't worry, love, it will probably look a bit better when you have got your own stuff in there."

I found this very amusing. I felt like saying, 'Come back this time next year and see the transformation.' I knew what my Tom was capable of achieving.

We wasted no time in getting the plans drawn up with the architect and submitting them to the local council. The worst bit was waiting for the approvals to come back so that we could make a start.

We focused on the land, taking down the old shed, cutting down all the firs that surrounded the land and erecting smart fence panels in their place. There was plenty to get on with. The approval was in, and work began with a gusto.

We lived, ate, and slept in what used to be the sisters' living room, and cooked our meals in a tiny little galley kitchen that could only accommodate one person at a time.

The building work continued around us.

The plan was to build two large extensions at opposite ends of the existing bungalow. This was a large project, and I was under no illusions as to just how long I would be washing off builder's dust.

Now, living closer to Mother, I found I was expected to visit at least three times a week and seemed to always get talked into staying for lunch, whether I wanted to or not. She had again me into doing her bidding. Colin had now retired, which had not helped the situation. Mother was no longer the special one.

When new a manager takes over, what often happens is that much of the original staff leave. There are always significant changes made to how things used to be done as the newly appointed manager makes her mark on the role.

Mother, having lost the use of her legs due to suffering from the dreadful disease osteoporosis, now required a lot more personal help. Tom and I purchased an electric wheelchair for her to give her some independence, which, for some time, seemed to give her a new lease of life.

She would go up to town in it and buy her snacks, and buzz around the park and feed the ducks. It gave us things to talk about on my visits.

Mother had taken a dislike to the new staff who had been assigned to her care and was determined she would not make life easy for them. She began kicking against the new rules.

I would sit and listen to the stream of complaints about this, that, and the next thing on my thrice-weekly visits, which were becoming a longer and longer drawn-out ordeal as Mother continued to complain that I was not giving her enough of my time. I came to dread saying the eight little words.

"Well, I suppose I had better get going." Which were always met with the same response. "No, no, you're not going already, surely." Making me then feel it necessary to add.

"Well maybe just another half hour, then I really must go," and kicking myself for yet again giving in to her.

Why was I so weak? I could not understand why it was I couldn't say no to her. It was beginning to wear me down. Tom tried his best to advise.

"Tell her no! Tell her that you need to get home because you have a life too and have things you have to do. You're beginning to spend more time with her than you are with me," he added jokingly, but I knew what he was saying was true.

For some reason, I was incapable of implementing it.

Edward had never offered to spend a Christmas with Mother so I thought I would ask him if he could take a turn to give me a break, knowing the strain I was under. But Edward did not relish the idea. However, he did pay for his daughter to come over from the States to be with Mother.

It did not sit right with me, however, to put that teenager through spending a Christmas on her own with her elderly grandmother and all the other seniors in a care home.

So, yet again, Tom and I found that we were once more sitting down to Christmas dinner surrounded by people being hand-fed, whilst others dropped most of the food on the floor or down the front of their cable-knitted cardigans.

I was beginning to resent Edwards's ability to put his mother's needs or, in fact, my needs, at the bottom of his priorities. Just one year free of this unbearable duty was not a big ask in my opinion. But it became apparent that this was never going to happen.

It was, however, evident that when he visited once a year, he was treated like the chosen one. He could do no wrong in her eyes.

I still did not get time off from the grinding routine, as I was expected to attend as usual. I was told it was the least I could do to spend time with Edward after he had come all this way to visit the family.

Mother had all year to talk to me, so mostly all conversations were directed toward him, making my presence a complete waste of time. Of course, Edward was well aware of his prodigal son status. It became the brunt of many a joke about his eyes being a more intense shade of blue than mine.

Things deteriorated further as the months turned into years.

Mother began phoning me three to four times a day, complaining that the staff were not coming when she rang for them.

I would phone the main office and would be told that the staff were summoned constantly throughout the day, and they always responded to her calls.

On another occasion, when she feigned illness and was yet again hospitalised, I received a phone call from a ward doctor who had fallen for the lie that I had not been in to visit her since she had been admitted. She had given him my phone number and asked him to ring me to ask me to come to see her.

I was absolutely flabbergasted. I could not believe that a doctor would entertain getting involved in people's personal arrangements.

But Mother could be very persuasive. I had, in fact, been in to visit her the previous evening and had stayed with her for the duration of the visiting time. It was staggering that she could have told such a bare-faced lie. This was control at its worst.

I did go in that evening, for the sole purpose of removing my phone number from her handbag.

On this occasion, Mother had refused all the tests that the hospital had tried to do to establish what was wrong with her, and she was discharged back to the care home the following day.

Each time I visited, there would be some issue or other. One day, I arrived to be told by the woman who worked in the laundry that Mother was a racist.

This naturally had caused the most appalling hullabaloo. When I got to the bottom of it, Mother had told the newly appointed black member of care staff that she had once owned a dog with the name beginning with the N-word which, of course, she had disgracefully used in its entirety, causing huge offence.

I had to explain the fact that Mother had not meant any harm, and that she had owned a dog which had been given this name and had not actually understood the connection to be wholly unacceptable.

On another occasion, she accused a member of staff of stealing her clothes, which had been sent to the laundry, and had not been returned, again causing great upset to the woman in the laundry who still had not recovered from the racist issue.

Then there was the issue of the cleaner who Mother liked to chat with while she cleaned her room. The poor woman had as much trouble getting away from Mother as I did.

The woman was accused by her manager of spending too much of her time in Room 101, which consequently resulted in her receiving a written warning and she was moved up to the second floor.

Mother was furious that, yet another pleasure had been denied her.

The home had also stopped Mother from going out in her electric wheelchair following an incident in the centre of town where she had nearly caused a serious accident and had stopped the traffic in the for 30 minutes while the local bobby investigated.

She was escorted back to her residence by the same bobby, with Mother declaring it was not her fault.

The home was obviously not happy to have the police at their door regarding one of their residents and felt they were no longer prepared to take the risk of another incident.

This latest restriction was met with the most horrendous tantrum that I had yet witnessed.

I was slapped around my face for allowing the home to confiscate her wheels which she deemed to be her only remaining pleasure.

I returned home that day in floods of tears. It was all I could do to stop Tom from going over to have it out with her.

But Mother was unaware of what was still to come.

She had, in the past, enjoyed the social activities that went on each day. Nevertheless, she was being spiteful to those who came in on dayshift, telling several of them that she should be given priority on everything, as she lived there, and they didn't.

She caused so much trouble over this that the manager decided to move her to another lounge before the daycare people arrived, thus, depriving her of all the activities.

She was now destined to sit with those who sleep through the entire day, only waking for mealtimes, when they could repeat the process of dropping food down their fronts.

This again being confirmation to Mother that she was being victimised.

Future visits were spent with her crying, and wailing, and begging me to take her to live with us.

The sheer thought of this filled me with complete dread. I tried to explain that it was not possible which intensified the wailing even further.

How could I be so cruel and heartless? She had never treated her mother so badly. She had done her duty by her mother; she had her to live with her. Cared for her until the end. I was a selfish, ungrateful, and uncaring daughter, I was told vehemently.

I thought I could resolve this issue by bringing Mother to the building site called home for a day out, thinking that she would then understand why it was she could not come to live in our home.

This required hiring a taxi that could take a wheelchair. We had hardly got to the bottom of her road before she started asking how much longer the journey was going to take.

Then, the taxi had hardly pulled out of our drive before Mother began asking to be taken back to the home. She didn't want to miss lunch, she declared.

I reminded her that she was going to stay for lunch with us, but she was adamant she wanted to go. So, the taxi had to be summoned back, making the day a complete disaster.

However, having witnessed for herself the chaos that we were living amongst, it did not put a stop to the crying and the wailing, as I was to discover on my very next visit

If I imagined that things could not get worse, then I was wrong. Mother had accused a member of staff of what sounded like common assault. She claimed that following an argument that had broken out between Mother and another resident in the dining room, a member of staff had taken Mother to her room, pushed her onto her bed and dragged her clothes off her and told her she had to remain in her bed for the rest of the day.

I had to admit this was extremely concerning as there was evidence of bruising, which, of course, had to be taken very seriously, and necessitated my reporting the incident to the home's manager. The Home rules required the suspension of the care worker involved until an investigation into the allegation could take place.

The issue then involved the owners of the care home, who subsequently involved the police, who then were required to alert social services.

It was at this point that Mother decided to backtrack on her allegation and say she had banged her arm on the commode.

Apparently, I had no right to have reported the incident, and it was I who was responsible for making matters worse.

She demanded the allegation be withdrawn, as she said she was very worried that there would be repercussions from other members of staff.

"You don't know what they're like here," she told me. "Please, Rita, just tell them I don't want to take it any further."

I wanted the investigation to take place as I believed that something untoward had taken place. In my mind, the bruising was far too severe to have been inflicted by a commode, as it began by the wrist and continued up to her neck.

It looked very much to me as if she had been extremely roughly manhandled and I wanted this matter dealt with but was informed that old people have a tendency to bruise easily.

They had conducted an internal investigation, and, due to Mother's past behaviour, had found in favour of the member of staff.

Someone then came to my home who claimed to be a retired police officer, to tell me that the care home, social services, and the police had formed the opinion that senility was setting in, and they had unanimously decided to treat it as such. The matter had been fully investigated, and there was no culpable evidence of wrongdoing, therefore, the matter had now been closed.

There appeared to be something decidedly suspicious regarding the handling of this entire episode that made me feel extremely uncomfortable.

In my view, the level of bruising could in no way be age-related, neither could it be connected to senility. I had been forced to leave it there, as Mother was very concerned about her level of care going forward. I made sure that the accused member of staff, who had now been reinstated, would no longer be responsible for Mother's personal care.

This rule lasted roughly six weeks when, due to staff shortages, the girl was officially permitted to again answer Mother's bell.

This being the case, I decided to closely monitor the situation and began visiting her at different times of the day. I purchased a camera to install in her room, but I was scared the home would spot it and consider it an infringement on personal liberty.

On one occasion, I arrived late morning and found her still in her nightclothes, still in bed with the curtains not drawn, and her breakfast dishes still on her tray.

She was lying in a soaking wet bed. She said she had rung the bell many times throughout the morning to request assistance to use the toilet, but, as no one had responded to her call, she had been unable to hold it.

This was inexcusable and I told the manager so in no uncertain terms. She admitted that because several staff members had phoned in sick, she was unable to cover all bases.

I was promised that this would not happen again.

Nevertheless, I found myself in her office the very next week. Mother had complained about a sore back. On investigation, I discovered a huge pressure sore the size of an orange at the base of her spine.

What in heaven's name was I going to do about this? I was so worried about her standard of care that it enveloped my every waking thought. Was Mother right, was this the repercussions that she spoke of for her speaking out, and my consequent involvement? I demanded a registered nurse come to daily dress the sore.

I was so worried I found I had no alternative but to get Edward involved. He just told me that there was not a great deal he could do living in the States. He did agree to make a phone call to the manager, but he got the same response as I was getting. To be honest, I don't think he wanted to get involved.

I tried to talk to Mother about getting her moved to another home, but the mere thought of a new home at her time of life frightened her out of her wits.

I lay awake at night worrying how I could help her, make things better for her, but everything I did seemed to make matters worse.

The whole thing was causing me severe mental anguish. Tom had told me for my own peace of mind that I should cut back on my visits. He could see the worry of it all was making me ill.

But I couldn't possibly back away from her when she needed me the most, despite the effect it was having on me.

I took to increasing my visits rather than reducing them, just to make sure she was receiving the level of care that was expected. I was forever in and out of that office complaining about something or other.

The Management were clearly sick to death of me.

I noticed Mother was losing a lot of weight. I could not understand why this had not been picked up by the staff. She was supposed to be weighed after her bath each week. I asked if I could see her care plan, which the home was reluctant to give me access to, but I insisted.

The reason became clear when I finally got my hands on it. Mother had not been weighed for the last seven months. There was a logical reason for this, I was informed. It was simply because the weighing scales were broken.

As soon as I had uncovered this, the care plans were conveniently rewritten and backdated with this omission now rectified. The more that came to light, the worse things became.

Mother had always kept a daily diary by means of which, unbeknown to her, I could follow her daily routines. She used to get a weekly bath which was also when her sheets were changed. I had noticed that this was happening less and less frequently.

This too was taken up with the manager, as the same caregiver who had been involved in the initial investigation was the very person who was now responsible for Mother's baths and bed changes.

Also reported were the pills that I found under her bed when I was looking for her slippers, the very pills that Mother was prescribed to be taken daily to control her pain.

It was one thing after another. It was intolerable, too much to bear. I was beside myself with worry for her safety.

Then the day came when I got a phone call from the home to say Mother had taken ill, and they thought it advisable that I come.

When I arrived, I found her alert but looking very frail. They allowed me to move one of the recliners from the main lounge into her room, which is where I stayed for the next five days and nights, only going home to shower.

The home was providing me with a meal once a day, which I paid for. Other supplies were brought in from home.

Each day that went by, Mother became weaker.

I telephoned Lee and Lucy as it had become clear to me that she was unlikely to survive this latest illness.

They both came that same day. In fact, Lucy was there when Mother opened her eyes briefly, clasped my hand, and said, in a moment of clarity,

"Rita, I want you to know you have been a wonderful daughter to me over the years. I could not have asked for better."

She had finally recognised my worth. This was a truly moving occurrence, as I believe that this was the only time, she had shown me gratitude for my dedication to her. I just burst into floods of tears.

"I don't bloody believe it; after all she has put you through! She certainly left it a bit late to tell you that," Lucy said, putting on her coat to leave.

"Shush," I whispered I did not want Mother hurt in what could possibly be her final hours.

Lucy had little concern for her grandmother, as, in the past, she had also been the victim of her spiteful ways.

She had stopped visiting her years ago, as Mother would always greet her sarcastically with the words,

"Who are you?"

I was sitting silently staring at that frail little body in the bed, when once more her eyes flickered open, she looked across at me and said in almost a whisper,

"What are you doing here, Rita? Go home!" she said remarkably forcefully.

"Ok, I will pop home for a quick shower. I will be back shortly," I told her tenderly, tucking the bedclothes in around her, which she promptly pushed back down.

I was just getting undressed to get in the shower when the phone call came. The voice on the other end said,

"Rita, we have just been in to check on your mother, and I'm so very sorry to have to tell you that she has passed away. Don't you think it very strange, that she almost waited for you to go? said the girl a little too lightheartedly.

I sat there holding the phone unable to take the news in.

"But I have only just left her. She had said, 'Go home, Rita'." I said stupidly. So yes, I did feel that there was an element of truth in what she said.

However the news she had just imparted finally sunk in and I am ashamed to say that I felt as if a double-decker bus had just been lifted off me. I make no apologies for that because I knew that I had done my very best for her over the years. Despite everything.

I now felt I could breathe again, I was free. My time was now my own. Life was good again. I could take a holiday without the fear of being called back. I could finally sleep through the night, no longer having to worry about the phone ringing, or what problems would face me the next day. I could laugh again, something I had not done for a long, long time.

Edward and Anne came over for the funeral. It was so lovely to see Anne again. It was quite a jolly affair, more of a family get-together, really. I wondered what she would have made of it.

The work on the bungalow was moving on at a gentle pace as Tom was determined to do it all himself. As each room was finished, I moved in to do the decorating.

Each time the family visited, they received the guided tour, showing them the latest achievements. I was so proud of Tom; he worked solidly, never doing anything by halves. Everything had to be just so to pass the critical eye of the building inspector.

We had lost one of our cats when we lived at the mansion. She had been 20 years old, so it had been expected.

But when we lost our Bella that was heartbreaking. She had been such a wonderfully loyal gentle soul who had made it to the grand age of fourteen. Never once in all those years did, she give us cause to regret having adopted her. She had been a valuable member of our family who would be sorely missed by all.

Not many months later, our second cat sadly passed away. They had all aged together, but it was extremely painful to have lost them all in such a short space of time.

For this reason, we vowed never to get another pet.

Despite losing Mother, Edward and Anne continue to visit every year. The house had reached the point of completion. We could finally accommodate visitors, which was lovely.

Edward kindly offered to pay for our tickets to go to America to visit them, which was a very generous offer. We could travel now, no longer having the responsibility of Mother to restrict us.

As promised, the tickets arrived, and we were getting very excited about going. Tom had visited the States before, but I had not. I had heard so much about it from Edward over the years that I couldn't wait to go and witness it all for myself.

Three weeks later, we received the devastating news that Anne had been diagnosed with a brain tumour. They were going to try to operate, but it was apparently embedded deep within her brain.

This was indeed shocking news. We also felt bitterly sorry for Edward who was facing this for a second time.

Of course, our trip was no longer possible. We would just hope and pray that things would go well for them both.

The great-grandchildren had started arriving making family gatherings larger and larger, and the birthdays and Christmas lists more and more expensive.

Tom had said we needed to start just giving to the little ones as it was becoming a big expense every year, but I continued to give to them all.

"Family is important, and money is not everything," I told him.

I loved all my grandchildren equally and tried to spend as much time as I could with all of them.

But I had formed an exceptionally close bond with my grand-daughter, Kelly, from a very young age. I think this was because they lived closer to us than all the others, so I tended to see more of her.

She spent all her school holidays with us. I undertook all doctor's, and dentist's appointments, then on to orthodontist's appointments, due to full-time working parents.

We spent holidays away together, just Kelly and me. As the years had gone on, Kelly and I had found other things we could share together. We went to the cinema, ate out at restaurants, and had spa days. We shared so many wonderful memories of happy times together.

On Kelly's 18th birthday, I gave her a card with money in with the words that read, 'You are, and you will always be my world'.

On the day of her school Prom graduation ball, she had insisted on coming to me first, determined that I would not miss out on her big day. a touching show of love.

I also formed an especially close bond with Lucy's second youngest Michelle and also Lucy's youngest, Lindon. When he was first born, his parents could not decide on a name for him. He was nearly a week old when I remarked,

"Lucy, you can't keep calling him baby; you need to find a name for him. He will need to be registered soon. What about the name Lindon?" I questioned.

Strangely, that name hit the spot, and that is the name they agreed upon.

Lindon was an absolute joy to be around. He loved all board and card games. Each day, when he visited, was spent on these activities only pausing for meal breaks. He also liked the park, the cinema and swimming. We laughed so much it made my face hurt.

Those grandchildren continued to grow like weeds.

I managed to fit into my life two operations for the removal of a malignant melanoma. Two years on, I'd had no further problems.

Also, one operation for a complete knee replacement, due to a severed tendon after having fallen down the steps of a country home whilst on a visit there with the WI.

I had to be carried back to the coach for the return journey home. I always managed to show myself up somehow or other.

All part of life's rich tapestry, I suppose.

We had backtracked on our vow not to get another dog, but Bella had left such a large hole in our lives that I nagged and nagged until Tom gave in. This time, we went for a pedigree Bichon Frise. I purchased a book to read up on the breed before getting her, as I had been reliably informed that they can be an extremely strong-willed breed. I needed to know what we were letting ourselves in for.

Strong-willed turned out to be a complete understatement. This dog, which we chose to name Daisy was something else.

A complete diva and no mistake, who demanded from the get-go to sleep on our bed.

A dog who does not tolerate Tom getting too close to me, thus, making carnal relations problematic. We were forced to use deception to get her out of the bedroom for these occasions.

A dog who will only eat freshly cooked meat, and never the same meal two days running.

A dog who is prepared to savage anyone or anything that sets foot inside the gate or any part of the garden, or indeed, the house. This covers a myriad of species, birds, squirrels, it even includes the common housefly. A dog who rules the roost and no mistake.

The timing of the dog's arrival could not have been worse, as Edward phoned to tell us the earth-shattering news that Anne was losing her battle with this deadly disease cancer.

I needed to go out if only to support my brother at such a terrible time. It was important to me to be able to say my goodbyes to her.

Tom fully understood my reasons for going and he remained at home dog-sitting.

I had never journeyed anywhere alone before, let alone somewhere as large as America. I was scared to death I was going to get on the wrong plane.

Tom took me to the airport and saw me through to the departure gate. He stood waving me goodbye and embarrassingly witnessed me being dragged back by an official-looking guy, who informed me that I had gone through the staff entrance.

Oh, good God, I thought, I couldn't even make it onto the plane without getting it wrong.

This did not bode well. I had visions of landing up in Singapore or some other far-flung foreign land.

To make things even more complicated, I had to change flights to complete the onward journey. I was required to collect my luggage from one plane, get across the concourse by an underground train, then rebook my luggage back onto my connecting flight.

A hugely complicated procedure to pull off, in my opinion. If I could not get to the departure gate without an error, what chance did I stand changing planes?

Because I was so terrified about getting it wrong, Tom had phoned Edward to ask him to meet me at the first landing location. Edward being Edward flatly refused.

I just had to suck it up, as they say.

Getting through immigration was another ordeal as an incredibly frightening man barked orders at everyone waiting in the queue.

"Get back behind the line!" he screamed at everyone. One guy chose to challenge him by saying,

"I am behind the line."

But he failed to notice that his toes were just over. This resulted in the official leaving his cubicle, marching towards the guy who had challenged him and giving him an almighty push, sending everyone standing behind him backwards like a load of skittles. Consequently, when it came to my turn to undertake the necessary checks, I was quaking in my shoes.

"Where are you going?" he barked.

"South Carolina," I replied timidly.

"No, you're not," he declared sternly, observing my tickets.

"Yes, I am," I replied, confused.

"And I said no you're not, you are going to Savanna, then on to South Carolina," he said, staring straight at me.

"Well, I know that, but South Carolina is my final destination," I responded, trying not to be intimidated by this person.

He stared at me for several seconds before barking,

"What is the purpose of your journey?"

"Why do you need to know that?" I asked defiantly.

"I repeat, what is the purpose of your journey? Failure to provide the required information will result in you being detained," he almost bellowed.

Wow, I decided I was up against a man with power issues.

"My sister-in-law is dying, and I am going to say my goodbyes before she passes, and support my brother at this terribly sad time, as this will be the second wife that he has lost to cancer."

I announced this in a matter-of-fact voice which I hoped would embarrass him. I thought that I might have given him cause to how he deals with people. I quite expected him to feel a little ashamed by his attitude, but I was wrong on both counts as he now barked,

"How long do you intend on staying on your visit to the United States of America?"

Whoa, this man lacked any sensitivity whatsoever! I could not believe that he failed to comprehend the gravity of the reasons for my trip that I had just carefully outlined to him.

"Well, I'm not entirely sure how long it takes for someone to die in the final stages of a cancerous brain tumour, but I had intended to stay until she finally succumbs," I said, giving him the full force of my disapproving stare.

Again, he stared back at me. I think, though, I had chipped a little through that tough exterior, as he clearly realised, I was not easily intimidated by him.

I went on to have my fingerprints taken, my eyes scanned, and my passport stamped in complete silence.

I could have done without that, I thought, as I set off on the next stage of my journey.

Edward had agreed to meet me at my destination and was waiting for me when I arrived which was good of him.

We went straight to the hospital. Edward had warned me that the disease had utterly ravaged his lovely wife's appearance, but I was completely unprepared by just how much.

Anne, once the beautiful redhead with the stunning smile, lay at an odd angle in the bed propped up on a mountain of pillows.

Her hair had gone, and she had two hard lumps which could be seen clearly protruding through her now-thinning skin. Edward had told me that these were stents inserted into her head to ease the pressure on her brain.

Her eyebrows and eyelashes had not escaped the toxic treatments that she had been subjected to either. Her bones were now very prominent under her translucent skin. Even the enamel on her teeth had been affected as they were now quite yellow.

She was being drip-fed as she could no longer swallow, and her once-vivid blue eyes had somehow been diluted to almost colourless.

I tried very hard not to let the shock of her appearance show on my face as I wrapped my arms around her frail form. She recognised me instantly and tried to squeeze my hand but didn't have the strength.

It was truly heartbreaking to see what this terrible disease had done to her, rendering her almost unrecognisable.

We stayed by her bedside from early morning until early evening every day for a further ten days, watching her deteriorate before our eyes. It was the most heart-rending thing I had ever experienced.

The drugs had been increased to such a high level they were causing hallucinations, and she was convinced she could see terrifying things in the room. Despite her frailty, it was all we could do to keep her in the bed at times.

Why, oh why must someone be made to suffer so? I thought it was not only unfair but downright cruel. It was truly unbearable to witness.

We just longed for the end to come and for her suffering to cease. Our prayers were finally answered.

We arrived one morning to be told that she had passed away quietly in her sleep. I cried bitter tears, not only for Anne but also for Edward. This was the second wife he had lost to this terrible disease. It was cruelty personified.

My brother did not even have his family around him to support him, as he, yet again, faced life alone.

His children lived at opposite ends of the country. They had not spoken to each other in years.

Edwards's son had always been antisocial. He lived alone with only his dog for company.

He had turned against his sister when he had discovered she was gay, a disclosure that Edward also found difficult to accept. I had had a conversation with him about it. I had advised that she was still the same person, still his daughter, whatever her persuasion.

I also reminded him that if he did not take a more liberal view of his daughter's preferences, he could very well lose her.

I did not disclose to him how I had come by these pearls of wisdom, and that I too had experienced an alternative life for some time, but with the change of direction, I had just simply outgrown it, if there was such a possibility.

I reflected on the time when I used to be jealous of Edward but looking at his life now and how it had panned out, I felt great sadness for him, with no possibility of grandchildren, and a life that had been filled with tragedy.

How fortunate am I? I thought.

It was time to head home. I made it back safely with Tom waiting for me to take me home.

I walked back through the front door fully expecting little Daisy to have forgotten who I was. We had only had her a week when I left.

But I needed not have worried as I was practically eaten alive. I guess that was the point when she crept through the little chink within my heart which was the beginning of her getting her own way on everything.

The next family drama was when Lucy told us that she was leaving her second husband, Andy. She had met and fallen head over heels in love with a much younger woman.

My God, I thought, such traits seemed well ensconced in the families' genes.

As you would have expected, I took this latest news without batting an eyelid. I was introduced to this latest union quite early on, whilst they were still at the loved-up stage and couldn't keep their hands off each other.

It would have been churlish of me to issue the same warning as Lucy had afforded me regarding the age difference all those years ago, so I kept my own counsel.

There was even talk of marriage. I could see no point to that, but they seemed set on it.

I couldn't help feeling sorry for Andy who I had always had a lot of respect for. He had been an extremely hard-working guy, and the most amazing father to his only son.

I made a point of letting him know that he would always be welcome in our home.

He had been a much-loved member of the family for a long time, and I refused to turn him off like a light bulb.

Chapter 18

Twelve years had passed since we walked across that virgin snow to look around a shabby little two-bed abode, and it is with great pride that I can say, with the renovation finally finished, we are now the proud owners of a five-bedroom luxurious home with a glorious wrap-around garden filled with an abundance of colourful blooms, and wildlife.

As I sit on the swing settee with a glass of wine in one hand and Tom by my side, I look out across the lawn at Daisy happily chasing a butterfly and watching the sun starting to disappear below the rooftops and I count my blessings.

I reflect upon the entire journey, and what a journey. 16 house moves, 10 jobs, 3 husbands, 2 children, 3 stepchildren, 10 grandchildren, 7 great-grandchildren, and the fortune to have traveled halfway around the globe.

It had indeed been a difficult journey, but a lot had been achieved despite humble beginnings. I had come so far. Who knows what more was still achievable? The world is my winkle; or is it my oyster?

Whoever would have guessed that this once quiet, timid, insecure, and painfully shy little child, who lacked the merest shred of confidence, and had chronic low self esteem would have gone on to cram so much life into one lifetime.

Overcoming all the trials and tribulations against all the odds. Achieving things once believed impossible. Finally finding my place in the scheme of things.

It had certainly been the most amazing life, full of twists and turns, ups and downs, rough and smooth, happiness and sorrow, all interspersed with a heady mix of exciting adventures along the way. Dare I even hope to dream that there would be still one more adventure yet to come?

As I sit here in this amazing place that we now call home, I reflect upon just how very blessed I am to be able to share all of this with someone so very special, who I love dearly. In Tom, I had finally found my soulmate who treated me with love and respect.

I couldn't help but wonder what my life might have been like had I not gone out on that very first evening, when all I had really wanted to do was to have an early night. Fate had been so kind in aligning our stars to enable our paths to cross.

My eyes filled with tears as I wondered what on earth, I would do without this wonderful man sitting beside me, this kind, caring, and loving man who had given me a life I could have only ever dreamed of. He had quite literally given me the very top brick of the chimney, as the saying goes.

"Hey, why so serious?" Tom said, putting his arm around my shoulders.

"Oh, nothing," I replied, smiling, "I was just thinking how lucky I am to have a wonderful husband like you and wondering what in the world I would do without you," I added.

"Without me?! You silly goose, and where do you imagine I'm going?"

he asked with laughter in his voice. "Now look at this; someone drank my wine," he said, holding out his empty glass for a refill.

He leaned over and kissed my cheek as I took the glass from him laughing.

He never could take a compliment without getting embarrassed. Yet another endearing thing about him.

"I love you," I told him, getting up to fill his glass.

"I love you too," he replied blowing a kiss into the air.

Just two weeks later, I was busy arranging some flowers from the garden into my favourite large blue-green vase, when I noticed our car pull into the drive. Oh good, I thought, he's back. Now I can start the lunch. Automatically, I went to open the front door to greet him.

"Where's the shopping?" I asked, realising that he was empty-handed.

"I didn't go shopping," he replied, his face noticeably ashen. "I went to pick up my tests results from the hospital. Rita, they told me I have stage 4 cancer."

I felt my legs buckle beneath me, and as I hit the floor darkness swallowed me whole.

9 781802 272369